D0392365

Other Dell Books by Nan Ryan:

NAN RYAN

A LIFETIME OF HEAVEN

A DELL BOOK

Published by
Dell Publishing
a division of
Bantam Doubleday Dell Publishing Group, Inc.
1540 Broadway
New York, New York 10036

The trademark Dell® is registered in the U.S. Patent and Trademark Office.

ISBN: 0-440-21075-5

Printed in the United States of America

ACKNOWLEDGMENT

Mrs. Louise Gregg, Wichita Falls, Texas, for her early and continued encouragement

For
Kathe Robin

Chapter 1

"Who's ringing that goddamned bell!"

Nick McCabe, awakened from a deep, drunken slumber by the incessant clanging of a bell, muttered again, "Who the hell's ringing that bell!"

Nick's bloodshot silver-gray eyes cracked cautiously open. For a long moment he didn't move an eyelash. Couldn't. Just lay there listening to the irritating toll, wondering if there actually was a bell ringing or if it was only a ringing in his head.

With slow, deliberate effort Nick lifted his dark aching head a scant couple of inches off the pillow. And cursed the excruciating pain made immediately so much worse by the slight movement.

"Ohhhh, Jesuuusss," he moaned miserably, and his head fell back to the pillow.

Beads of perspiration broke out on his forehead and upper lip. His stomach churned violently. His temples throbbed.

The bell continued ringing.

Not the least bit confident that his arms would work—much less his legs—the suffering Barbary Coast saloon keeper first attempted to wiggle one finger. Just a pinky finger. In seconds he was fairly sure he had the finger going. He couldn't be totally positive because he didn't dare lift his banging head to have a look.

Hell, maybe the damned finger hadn't moved at all. Maybe it was just the eternal clanging of the bell pulsing through it, the same way it was reverberating through his hurting head.

Nick stayed at it. He experienced a fleeting flash of relief when he managed to get his weak arms working well enough to laboriously raise himself up onto his elbows. Darkly whiskered chin sagging onto his bare heaving chest, Nick licked his dry lips with a thick tongue and let his slitted eyes move slowly around the dim, cool interior of his spacious upstairs apartment.

He saw nothing out of the ordinary. Only the familiar, comfortable living quarters he called home, with the heavy masculine furniture and the window shades all drawn against the sun. No sign of a bell. Or bells.

In no mood for any playful nonsense, the badly hung over Nick McCabe carefully turned his dark aching head around to glare down at the woman in bed beside him. The beautiful young woman seemed to be sound asleep. Stretched out on her stomach, her long mane of glossy dark hair half swirled over her bare back and falling over her face, she was obviously innocent of any bell-ringing mischief.

Still, Nick reached over and suspiciously peeled the covering sheet off the slumbering brunette, halfway expecting to find the bell concealed somewhere on her person.

The naked beauty sighed softly in her sleep, rolled her bare ivory shoulders slightly, and snuggled deeper into the softness of the mattress, squeezing the feather pillow in pale slender arms.

And slept peacefully on.

Scowling, Nick McCabe muttered oaths as he stumbled out of bed. His bare legs were so weak and wobbly he stood flat-footed for a long moment beside the bed, tottering, weaving unsteadily, uncertain if he could stand for any length of time, much less walk.

Nick felt the room around him spin and sway crazily. Felt the floor beneath his bare feet pitch and roll. Cursing like a waterfront sailor, he lifted his hands to clutch his aching temples.

The mysterious bell continued to ring.

Its persistent banging was in perfect tempo with the fierce pounding in Nick's head.

Naked, nauseated, and nasty-tempered, Nick McCabe stalked around the large room, foolishly searching for the loudly ringing bell. Finally it dawned on him. There was no bell in his quarters. The disturbance was coming from the street below. Some drunken reveler was still on a binge and bent on waking the entire neighborhood.

Well, by God, the inconsiderate bastard would answer to Nick McCabe!

Swearing and sweating, Nick clumsily tried to hunch into his discarded trousers. Dizzily hopping across the floor on one foot while vainly attempting to get the other into a trouser leg, he stumbled and crashed—face first—to the floor. More angry than hurt, he flopped over onto his back and lay there panting and moaning, a vein pulsing on his damp forehead.

And still the bell continued to ring.

Nick stayed on the floor until he could maneuver the dark trouser legs up and over both feet and then down the long, muscular legs he held weakly raised into the air. His feet fell back to the floor with a loud thud.

"Oh, Jesus," Nick muttered, again resting. "I can't do it. I can't get up. I can't get my damn pants on."

Then, hands firmly gripping the waistband of the trousers, teeth gritted in concentration, Nick lifted his brown buttocks up off the floor, keeping feet and shoulders pressed firmly to the deep carpet, and wrestled the trousers up over his bare bottom.

He rested again, rolled up into a sitting position, and finally stood up. Buttoning the pants as he went, Nick McCabe crossed the big bedroom to the heavily draped and shaded windows fronting onto Pacific Street.

Pants only half buttoned over his flat belly, black hair tumbling carelessly over his perspiring forehead, Nick McCabe snatched the velvet drapes open wide, jerked up a fringed window shade, and thrust his head out.

Keeping his red, stinging eyes tightly shut against the harsh pervasive sunlight, Nick shouted loudly to the annoying bell ringer, "All right, Mac, meet me down front with your fists raised!"

On the sidewalk below a young woman stood in the very center of a small group of men. Startled by the loud threat, Kay Montgomery's head snapped around and her wide blue eyes lifted. She caught only a fleeting glimpse of a big, dark, bare-chested man.

The oddly assorted gathering of panhandlers and beggars and drunks and pickpockets that Kay Montgomery had attracted with her bell ringing began to murmur excitedly, talking among themselves, their eyes growing bright with excitement, waiting for the coming fireworks.

Slowly lowering her brass bell, Kay Montgomery waited too.

Upstairs Nick McCabe yanked open the interior door leading from his private quarters and stepped out onto the wide upstairs landing. He headed for the marble staircase and descended the gleaming steps two at a time.

Downstairs he hurriedly crossed the silent, cavernous saloon. In the big room's shadowy light, Nick bumped into a poker table. Howling with outrage, he picked up a chair and slammed it down on the green baize, scattering stacks of carefully counted colored chips all over the table and onto the floor.

Furious, he pressed on, doggedly weaving his way toward the raised marble entrance of the profitable Pacific Street saloon he had owned and operated for more than a decade. The pride of the Barbary Coast, Nick often boasted.

The Golden Carousel Club.

Kay Montgomery winced when the Golden Carousel Club's heavy black leather double doors burst open and a blinking, obviously enraged man stepped out onto the sidewalk. Her presence concealed in the close press of men, Kay experienced a twinge of unease as she cautiously peeked through a small opening over someone's bent elbow.

She saw, standing in the bright California sunlight, a tall, unshaven, half-naked, barefooted man. Wavy black hair was falling onto the man's furrowed forehead directly above a pair of the meanest-looking silver-gray eyes she'd ever seen. Broad-shouldered, dark-whiskered, the angry man stalked purposely forward.

The muscles in his long bare arms bunching and flexing, his cold-eyed gaze sweeping the assembled gathering, Nick McCabe lifted his tight fists, spoiling for a fight.

"Okay, put up your dukes," he ordered, his dazzling white teeth gleaming in his darkly whiskered face. "Which one of you apes was ringing that damned bell?" Narrowed silver eyes scanned and touched each male face. "Step on out here and fight me like a man."

A buzz of excitement and nervousness rippled through the huddled knot of waterfront regulars.

And through Kay Montgomery.

Nobody moved.

Nobody said a word.

Until, swallowing hard, Kay Montgomery defiantly lifted her proud chin, determinedly pushed her way through the crowd, and stepped up to face the dark, dangerous stranger.

Standing before Nick McCabe, Kay Montgomery tipped her head back to look fearlessly into his narrowed silver eyes. She calmly lifted her right hand directly up in front of Nick's dark, scowling face. Clutched firmly in her slender fingers was a shiny silver bell.

While Nick McCabe glowered at her, Kay gave the bell a decisive shake. Its small clapper banged loudly against the bell's hard metal wall.

"Dammit to hell," Nick swore as his bloodshot eyes momentarily closed and his unshaven face screwed up with pain as the bell's loud ring vibrated through his throbbing head.

Kay Montgomery slowly lowered the bell and waited.

Waited until those mean silver-gray eyes again opened to focus on her upturned face.

In a clear, calm voice she said to the angry, evil-looking man, "It was me. I was ringing the bell."

Nick's raised fists slowly lowered to his sides. He glared at the brash young woman. Cheated out of his opportunity to throw some well-placed punches, Nick ground his teeth in frustration. Hot-blooded, trigger-tempered, Nick rarely found himself at a loss on how to handle a situation. Had she been a man, he'd have fed her the damned bell. But she wasn't, and he couldn't touch her. Although he felt like shaking her until her teeth rattled.

Nick stared at the woman. She looked quite young. Her pale face was smooth and unlined. Her eyes were a deep sparkling blue, and they were fixed on him as if he were the one behaving offensively. Her nose was small and well shaped with a hint of tilt to its delicate tip. Her mouth was set in a determined line, which didn't hide the fact that her lips were poutily pretty, the top one curving into a perfect cupid's bow.

Nick couldn't determine the color of her hair. Covering her head was a black straw polk bonnet with streamers tied snugly beneath her chin. She wore a long-sleeved blue jacket with a stand-up collar that buttoned down the front. Pinned to the collar was a silver S, shining in the bright San Francisco sunlight. Her long plain skirt was of the same blue as her jacket. On her feet were black leather shoes.

Nick squinted as his eyes slowly returned to her face. Then to her hat. Across the black bonnet's brim was a broad band of scarlet ribbon on which was inscribed in gilt THE SALVATION ARMY.

Nick McCabe smelled trouble.

He'd read a bit about the Salvation Army and its founder, a British hellfire-and-brimstone street preacher bent on rescuing the perishing from the slums of London. Nick knew that the dedicated Salvationists hadn't been content to stay on their side of the ocean. In the last decade the zealots had invaded the streets of New York, Philadelphia, and St. Louis, pestering the honest working, drinking man. So now they had arrived on the West Coast.

Kay Montgomery stared unblinking at the tall, threatening man with the harshly planed, satanic-looking face, mean, mesmeric silver eyes, and broad, naked chest. Foolishly she wondered if Lucifer himself had come down to earth and taken on the flesh-and-blood form of mortal man.

Kay inwardly cringed but silently vowed she wouldn't show her fear of this tall, dark emissary of evil.

Switching the shiny silver bell to her left hand, Kay put out her right and said, "Allow me to introduce myself. I'm Captain Kay Montgomery. I've traveled a great distance to bring the message of the Salvation Army to San Francisco."

"Allow me to introduce myself," Nick replied coldly, taking Kay's upper arm and maneuvering her away from the crowd of curious onlookers. Gently but firmly slamming her up against the exterior wall of his saloon, he said, "I'm Nick McCabe, owner of the Golden Carousel. What can I do for you, Captain?"

"You can get out of my way," replied Kay, clawing at his imprisoning fingers. "You've disrupted my meeting and—"

"So you're captain in this army of meddling Bible spouters?" Nick rudely cut in.

"A warrior for Christ, Mr. McCabe," Kay calmly corrected him.

"I see." Nick nodded his dark head. "Well, honey, if you're captain to a handful of the righteous, I'm a four-star general to a massive legion of sinners." He finally favored her with a slow, devilish grin and lowered his voice almost to a whisper. "Now, as one officer to another, I'll grant you the professional courtesy of allowing you to peacefully withdraw from *my* theater of operations."

"I can't do that," Captain Kay Montgomery coolly informed him.

Still smiling, Nick wrestled Kay's brass bell away from her and ordered, "Beat it, baby! You're on my battleground and I want you out of here. You got that, Captain?"

"Sorry, General," Captain Kay evenly replied, "I take my orders from a higher command."

With that Kay laid a hand flat against Nick's naked chest, pushed with all her might, quickly brushed past him, and walked away.

The bell gripped firmly in his tanned hand, Nick shook his dark, aching head.

He called after her, "I'm warning you, Captain, stay the hell away from me and the Golden Carousel Club!"

Chapter 2

 Captain Kay Montgomery had no intention of heeding the vile saloon owner's warnings. The Army was here to stay, whether Mr. Nick McCabe liked it or not. Right here on San Francisco's wicked waterfront, she fully intended to wage an all-out war on sin and corruption.

Kay Montgomery was a sensible, straitlaced, and very determined young woman. Just past her twenty-fifth birthday, Kay was tall, slender, and attractive. An abundance of fiery red hair was concealed beneath the black bonnet she wore. Her wide-set eyes were a remarkable shade of vivid blue and ringed by a double row of long, luxuriant black lashes. A handful of girlish freckles were scattered across the narrow bridge of a proud, turned-up nose. Her full-lipped mouth hinted at an innate fiery sensuality.

That suggested sensuality was as yet untapped, and Kay Montgomery was totally innocent of its presence. If hers was a strong passionate nature, that burning passion was focused fully on the Christian duties before her. Kay Montgomery was filled to overflowing with a fiercely burning determination to redeem the sinners and care for life's unfortunates.

Industrious, compassionate, and zealous, Captain Kay was admittedly—to her despair—possessed of the redhead's mercurial temperament, a dangerous shortcoming she struggled valiantly to overcome. She was not always successful.

Nick McCabe, the arrogant, unkempt saloon owner, had angered Kay, though she did her best to conceal it. Suspecting this would not be her last run-in with the sinful, Satanic-looking Nick, Kay purposely softened her expression, paused, and turned back to look at the half-naked man who had taken her silver bell.

While she felt like shouting angrily at Nick McCabe that he couldn't tell *her* where she could wage her battles against sin—that nobody could—Kay wisely held her tongue. Sweetly she smiled at the tall, threatening man, raised her right hand, and snapped off a crisp, military salute.

"Till we meet again, General McCabe."

"Aw, dammit to hell." Nick groaned.

Captain Kay spun around and strode away, walking at a heads-up pace, the black bonnet with its scarlet piping set squarely atop her proud head, black shoes with high-top laces digging in, the long strides steady and purposeful. A brisk professional image.

Sin didn't stand a chance.

The summer sun was sinking into the Pacific that hot August evening when Captain Kay Montgomery wearily climbed the stairs to her spartan, closet-small room. Located on the fourth floor of a tumbledown rooming house in an alley off Kearney, the gloomy room had been Kay's home since arriving in the Bay City exactly one week ago. A week that had seemed more like a year to Captain Kay Montgomery.

As soon as Kay was safely inside her close, stuffy room, she bolted the door and placed a chair against it, hooking the chair's tall back snugly under the brass doorknob. She sighed, untied her bonnet's long streamers, and lifted the black straw from her head. She dropped it onto the tilted chair.

Kay reached up, removed a few well-placed pins from her hair, and allowed the thick, flaming tresses to spill down around her tired, aching shoulders. Wishing she could take a long, hot bath, knowing it was out of the question, Kay lit the lone lamp atop the scarred bureau, pulled the musty curtains shut over the room's one window, and began to slowly strip away her hot blue uniform.

Naked in the lamplight, Kay poured her precious ration of fresh water from a cracked porcelain pitcher into its matching bowl, saving only enough water to drink with her evening meal. She then stood before the bureau with its cracked clouded mirror, sponging off her pale, slender body. As she bathed, she cast nervous glances at the locked door.

Already the nightly noise had begun.

Loud shouts and laughter coming from the other rooms and from the darkened stairwells. The cacophony would continue until morning, robbing Kay of much-needed rest. The paper-thin walls concealed nothing of what went on behind the closed doors of her fellow tenants.

Raucous laughter and loud singing. Snarling curses and blood-curdling screams. Breaking glass and dreadful retching. Nasty threats and vicious fights. Squeaking bedsprings and guttural groans. Such were her neighbors.

Kay had heard it all each night since her arrival in San Francisco.

And, while she was often disgusted, sometimes mildly frightened, she was neither surprised nor shocked.

Kay had served for the past two years in the worst slums of Atlanta, Georgia. She'd seen life at it vilest, rawest. She'd been so caught up in the battle against poverty and sickness and crime, there'd been no thought of anything else.

She was a pretty young woman and she'd had many opportunities for romance. But Kay strongly felt that there could be no preoccupation or intrusion with her life's work. Her mission for the Lord so totally absorbed her, she had no time to consider love and marriage.

Kay finished her cooling sponge bath and pulled a clean white cotton nightgown quickly over her head. She opened the top bureau drawer, took out a dwindling block of hardening rat-trap cheese and a crust of slightly stale bread. The cheese, bread, and a full glass of water were Captain Kay Montgomery's complete supper. She didn't eat all that was there, despite the fact that she was so hungry she felt weak. Kay ate sparingly. She had to save a portion for tomorrow's sustenance.

After her meager meal, Kay read by lamplight from her well-worn Bible until her eyes grew so heavy she was sure she'd be able to sleep no matter what went on around her. Yawning, she laid the Bible aside and gently lifted a small photograph from the bureau.

A photograph of a boyishly handsome man. Light, expressive eyes shining with merriment. Thick curly hair tumbling carelessly over his forehead. Wide mouth stretched in a warm, familiar grin.

Kay affectionately smiled back at him, then returned the photo to the bureau. Cupping her hand around the lamp's globe, she blew out the light, said her prayers, and climbed into bed.

Kay stretched, sighed, and closed her tired eyes.

But she didn't go to sleep.

Kay was worried.

More worried than she'd ever been in her life. Her deep concern was not for herself. It was for the smiling man in the photograph. Her younger brother, Curly Montgomery.

He and the money were missing.

What had gone wrong? Why had she been unable to locate her brother upon arriving San Francisco? Why was Curly keeping his whereabouts a mystery? Was he hurt? Was he missing? Was Curly lying helpless someplace, hoping she'd find him? Had he been shanghaied—taken from the waterfront and forced to sail the high seas with

some nefarious captain? Or was he—could her dear, sweet brother be
. . . be . . . ?

No, no!

She wouldn't let herself think such.

Kay's eyes came open in the darkness as she thought about her dear
red-haired baby brother. Tall, freckle-faced, sunny-dispositioned, Walter "Curly" Montgomery was and always had been Kay's best friend in
all the world. As soon as she was back with her brother, everything
would be fine.

Ignoring the revolting sounds all around her, Kay smiled and assured herself that she *would* find Curly. She'd find him soon and then
the two of them would carry out all their well-laid plans. Together they
would accomplish the enormous tasks that lay before them.

They would establish a Salvation Army station in the city of San
Francisco. They'd recruit soldiers on the streets, make saviors of the
sinners, bring the lost into the fold.

Captain Kay Montgomery was willing and ready for her challenging
assignment, and she knew that the diligent, devout Major Curly Montgomery was ready as well.

She and her only brother were so fortunate. They had been raised
by two gentle God-fearing people. Theirs had been a Christian home
filled with love and laughter and understanding.

How proud she and Curly had been that summer day two years ago
when their dedicated parents were called on by the Corps' illustrious
founder, Britain's General William Booth, to carry the Salvation
Army banner into Atlanta, Georgia. Their mission: to organize the
Corps in the big southern city.

She and Curly had left their St. Louis home and gone with their
parents, had worked alongside the tireless pair through Georgia's
sweltering summers and cold, rainy winters, bringing hope to the
hopeless, food to the hungry, shelter to the homeless.

And then, after less than two short years of service in Atlanta, Kay
and Curly could hardly believe their good fortune when they—just the
two of them, brother and sister—were chosen to carry the Army's
never-ending war on human misery to California's northern coast!

Kay vividly recalled that warm April day when she and Curly received their marching orders. The official missive was addressed to
them both. To Captain Kay Montgomery and Major Walter Montgomery.

The two of you are jointly appointed as officers in charge of San Francisco #1 Corps. . . .

The marching orders went on to explain that they were to be given a year to prove themselves. Exactly one full year in which to get the Army's West Coast station established, operating, and self-sufficient. Toward that goal, they would be sent to San Francisco with $20,000 of the Army's money. Along with money they would carry a deed to a piece of valuable city property. There on the Corps-owned property, they were to build a rescue mission.

It was made clear that Curly was to go alone to San Francisco. With the money and the deed entrusted to him, he would, upon his arrival in the Bay City, immediately begin construction of the rescue mission. When the building had begun and he had found suitable quarters for himself and his sister, Curly would promptly send for Kay.

Kay had hidden her mild disappointment that she was not to go with Curly. She realized, she diplomatically conceded, that a great deal of reasoning and thought had gone into the decision.

So Kay and her soldier parents had bid the beaming Curly an affectionate good-bye and he had left for the West Coast the last week of April, 1893. The Montgomery family had received glowing letters from Curly telling of the construction of the Rescue Mission, of the remarkable progress he'd had in recruiting soldiers, and of the sweet, angelic girl he had met.

The summer had passed and still Curly had not sent for Kay. Kay grew impatient. Curly's letters stopped coming. Kay grew concerned. Eager to help the hardworking Curly with his difficult endeavor, Kay waited no longer. She boarded a train for the West Coast to join her baby brother.

But in the week she'd been in San Francisco, Kay had been unable to locate Curly, the mission, or the girl.

Kay felt her chest constrict with worry for the big lovable brother of whom she'd always been protective. She was so afraid something terrible might have happened to the happy-go-lucky Curly. Curly was so completely trusting of everyone, so ready and willing to see only the good in others. He possessed a childlike openness and innocence that was incredibly appealing, but dangerous.

Kay shivered in the hot darkness. Something was very wrong. Something had happened to Curly. Since his letters had come as regularly as clockwork—and then had stopped abruptly—she could only assume that her brother was being held against his will. In this city where they'd kill you for a dime, what might have happened to a young man carrying thousands?

Curly was alone somewhere out there in the city, needing her help, hoping she'd find him. She would find him. She'd rescue him from the wicked streets of San Francisco.

And they *were* wicked.

Into Kay's troubled thoughts flashed the disturbing image of a dark, menacing man, naked to the waist, towering over her. Snaring her with hot silver eyes. Holding her with strong brown fingers wrapped bitingly around her upper arm. Threatening her in a commandingly cold voice. Stealing her well-worn silver bell. Ordering her to stay away from him and his Golden Carousel Club. An unshaven man who'd been fast asleep at the noon hour.

No telling what he'd been doing all night.

Kay shuddered involuntarily. She was not fooled. Instinctively she knew.

Knew all about the tall, dark saloon owner she'd met but once. Kay sensed it. Felt it. Knew it.

Nick McCabe was a rogue.

A wicked rogue.

Chapter 3

"Come, join our army, to battle we go,
Jesus will help us to conquer the foe,
Fighting for right and opposing the wrong,
The Salvation Army is marching along . . ."

 Captain Kay Montgomery's clear soprano singing voice carried above the din of snorting horses, shouting men, laughing women, and hawking vendors crowding the busy Barbary Coast thoroughfare.

Determined she'd sing loud enough to wake the devil himself, Captain Kay led her small army of two—a sunken-eyed, cadaverously thin little man she'd found sleeping in an alley and a painfully shy young lad who stuttered badly—down Kearney Street.

It was Monday. Early afternoon.

Captain Kay's pair of green inductees were eager to emulate their slightly built but stalwart lady leader. Both men earnestly yearned to lend their supportive voices in the rousing fight song sung by their fearless, feisty captain.

Unfortunately, the thin middle-age former wino who possessed an amazingly beautiful baritone could not remember the song's lyrics. The bashful young man had quickly memorized every uplifting word, but couldn't quite get them out of his mouth.

Undaunted, Captain Kay Montgomery marched proudly down the eastern side of Kearney on that sunny Monday afternoon, past the line of deplorable dens known as Battle Row, singing and holding high the Army's red, yellow, and blue banner of Blood and Fire. Sublimely ignoring the catcalls and curses directed at her, Captain Kay was dedicated to storming the very strongholds of the iniquitous.

And if ever there was a spot on God's own earth that was filled with the iniquitous, it was San Francisco's Barbary Coast. Bounded on the east by the waterfront, on the south by Clay and Commercial streets, on the west by Grant Avenue and Chinatown, and on the north by Broadway, it was a sprawling, teeming domicile of depravity. Its very name—the Barbary Coast—was synonymous with lusty immorality.

Captain Kay Montgomery meant to acquaint this wicked region's immoral with the Immortal. Clearly it was up to her to introduce the disreputable to the Divine. The criminals to the Celestial!

So with traditional Salvation Army gusto, Captain Kay was again leading one of her evangelistic forays, just as she had each and every day since her arrival in the Bay City just ten days ago.

Nick McCabe, owner of the Golden Carousel Club, had been only one of a growing number of dangerous-looking gentlemen annoyed by Kay's presence on the Coast. Several Barbary bar and brothel owners had threatened Kay with bodily harm—or worse—if she didn't get on a train or ship and "get the hell out of San Francisco."

Dismissing all threats as idle, Kay brazenly marched down the sidewalks outside the sleazy pleasure palaces, followed by the two recruits. Kay's converts did not wear the distinctive blue of the Corps. But it was only because she'd not yet raised enough money to outfit them properly. Soon she'd see to it that both were smartly uniformed as befitted a Salvation Army soldier. And when the meager collections began to grow, she'd look into purchasing band instruments and teaching the two to play.

Her fair face aglow with excitement, her head full of plans for the future, Captain Kay continued to march and to sing. On such a clear, beautiful day she was filled with optimism and a strong sense of well-being. She had the warm, wonderful feeling that everything was going to be all right. Better than all right.

She'd find the missing Curly, and soon, perhaps even today. And once she and her brother were reunited, they'd get on with their life-long work. In the months and years that lay ahead, they'd see their San Francisco Corps #1 grow into hundreds of dedicated men and women soldiers.

"Fighting for right and opposing the wrong,
The Salvation Army is—"

"Excuse me, Miss."

Interrupting Kay's spirited singing, a beefy gray-haired man stepped directly into Kay's path. "I'm Constable Norman Busey and I have a—"

"Good morning to you, Constable Busey." Kay smiled warmly. "I'm Captain Kay Montgomery, Salvation Army Corps. Will you join my soldiers and me in our march on—"

"Miss, I won't be marching, and I'm afraid you won't either."

Kay continued to smile at the fleshy-faced man with the gray bushy eyebrows, drooping gray mustache, large, misshapen nose, and brown puppy-dog eyes.

"But why ever not, Constable? It's a perfect day and I must spread the—"

"Miss, I'm ordering you to stop your marching and singing! Now are you going to obey, or must I take drastic action?"

Kay's smile slipped slightly. She lowered her colorful banner. "Constable Busey, is there a law against my marching down a street? Is it a punishable offense to sing in San Francisco?"

"A fistful of complaints have been registered against you by—"

"Nick McCabe?" Kay's well-arched brows shot up.

"Not just McCabe, Miss. At least a dozen of the saloon owners are squawking."

"I see. Do these gentlemen run this city, Constable Busey?"

"They ain't gentlemen, Miss. And they sure run the Barbary Coast."

"And you as well, I take it?"

The constable's face flushed with color. His lips pursed beneath the drooping mustache. He shook his gray head wearily.

"Why cause me trouble, Miss? You don't belong down here. You're not safe on these mean streets. You're going to get hurt if you don't leave. Be a good girl and go peacefully, won't you? Find someplace else to save souls."

"Look around you, Constable." Kay waved her banner meaningfully at the dives, bagnios, and barrooms lining both sides of Kearney. "*These* are the souls that need saving." She smiled again and boldly stepped around him. "So it is here we will march forward into battle." Signaling her army of two to follow, Kay started to walk away.

"You're not marching anywhere but jail," said the constable, reaching out to take Kay's arm.

Kay's recruits, who had been silent throughout the exchange, immediately came to their leader's defense.

"Unhand her, Busey," ordered the skinny middle-aged Giles Lawton, his sunken eyes flashing with anger.

"T-t-t-take y-y-your ha-ha-hands off Ca-Ca-Captain Kay!" Bobby Newman's boyish face grew beet red with frustration as he protectively stepped between Kay and the armed constable.

"Now, son, get out of my way if you don't want to get hurt," Constable Busey said, not unkindly. "This is between me and the little lady."

Kay laid a gentle hand on Bobby's shoulder. "It's okay, Bobby. The constable's only doing his job." Reluctantly the young man moved aside. Kay stepped forward. She told the constable, "You have no right to do this and I will not come peacefully."

"Suit yourself," the constable said, finally out of patience.

The first thing Kay knew she was being hauled away to jail for marching without a permit, disturbing the peace, and a whole host of other trumped-up charges filed by the Barbary Coast's powerful purveyors of perverse pleasure.

More angry than frightened, Kay's temper blazed as the constable literally dragged her down Kearney by her left arm, his big hand clutching her elbow so firmly she felt as if her arm was being jerked from its socket.

Poor Bobby Newman and Giles Lawton did their best to save her, but they were no match for the long-barreled revolver Constable Busey had quickly drawn to enforce the law. The pair followed closely on the heels of the armed constable and his preacher prisoner, each graciously offering to be locked up in place of the remarkable young woman who'd been the first person to show them any kindness for as long as either could remember.

Giles Lawton cursed the bullying constable. Bobby Newman stuttered excitedly. Kay calmly reassured her worried recruits. The constable bellowed for them all to shut up.

The strange quartet quickly drew an audience. Sharpies and hustlers spilled from doorways of card parlors and pool halls. Drinkers wandered out of saloons. Gaudily painted women poked sleepy heads from upstairs windows of brothels, curious about the commotion. And slick-haired, pin-striped owners of the card parlors, pool halls, saloons, and bordellos quietly smiled to themselves, confident that after a couple of nights in the cooler, the pesky Salvation Army captain would catch the first train back east.

The grim-faced constable and the struggling Salvation Army captain reached the corner and turned down Pacific Street. Whistles and hoots followed Captain Kay as she was dragged off to jail. Bets were taken on how long she'd keep that stiff upper lip once she was thrown into a flea-infested jail cell among the coast's worst riffraff. The locals taunted and poked fun at her. Drunken sailors shouted obscene proposals. Derisive laughter filled the air.

One of the low-lifes who sauntered out to take part in all the fun was Three Fingers Jackson. A slightly built, sallow-complected man with beady black eyes and an irritating habit of constantly licking his thin upper lip, Jackson had earned his nickname at an early age. Caught cheating in a high-stakes card game when he'd been in San

Francisco for less than three months, his severed index finger had been left lying atop the green baize table along with his extra ace and the money he'd attempted to steal.

Three Fingers Jackson stood now on the sidewalk just outside his highly profitable Pacific Street Top Hat Club.

A leering grin on his face, Three Fingers shouted to Kay, "Salvation lady, I'll post bail if you'll come to work for me at my club." His suggestion immediately met with loud approving applause and wild cheers from the mostly male crowd. Licking his thin upper lip, Jackson added, "I bet you'd look right pretty wearing what my girls wear: silk top hat, white lapels, black satin trousers. What do you say?" He withdrew a fat roll of bills from his inside suit pocket and waved it about.

A hush fell over the crowd. Everyone strained to hear what Captain Kay's answer would be. The blue uniformed-and-bonneted young woman turned flashing blue eyes on Three Fingers Jackson. She smiled sweetly at the sneering saloon owner.

And in a firm, clear voice she confidently informed him, "All your girls will be trading in those silk hats and satin trousers for Salvation Army blue before I leave the Barbary Coast, Mr. Jackson."

The statement brought howls of laughter. Everyone knew that Three Fingers Jackson's girls were some of the most notoriously naughty creatures ever to work the Barbary Coast. And that was very naughty indeed. Jackson proudly advertised the fact that his girls had never heard of an act too depraved to perform. For a generous fee there was nothing the talented ladies would not do to ensure a customer's enjoyment. No perverted pleasure they refused to supply.

Three Fingers's laugh was loudest of all. But his voice was deadly cold when he warned, "Come nosing around my place, bothering my girls, and I'll own you, just like I own them. You'll find yourself upstairs in my joint, on your back beneath a dirty, drunken sailor who's been at sea for months. You hear me, preacher lady?"

"God bless you too, Mr. Jackson," Kay replied calmly, saying no more, responding to his lewd threats in exactly the way she had been trained to handle such ticklish situations.

Silently Kay prayed for Three Fingers Jackson. She prayed for herself as well. Prayed that she would learn to better control her temper. She shouldn't be angry with Three Fingers Jackson. But she was. Her face was burning with her white-hot anger, and it was all she could do to keep from shouting at the foul-mouthed man.

Kay was almost relieved when she and the constable reached Front

Street and the Barbary Coast's aging brick jailhouse. She was hastily escorted around a counter, through a door at the back of the squad room, and down a narrow corridor separating a number of barred cells. After being handed into one, the door clanged shut behind her instantly.

Kay winced and whirled around when a wild-eyed creature in the cell next to hers grabbed at her through the widely spaced bars. Shaking badly from delirium tremens, the stench of his soiled clothing and filthy hair taking Kay's breath away, the pitiful soul held his trembling hand out to her.

"Please." His voice was no more than a hoarse croak and his bleary eyes were swimming in tears. "Help me, I'm sick. I need a drink of whiskey. Do you have a drink?"

Captain Kay Montgomery took a long, spine-stiffening breath and carefully laid her blue, red, and yellow banner on the cell's narrow cot. She stepped up to the bars separating them, smiled compassionately at the poor wretch, and took his chilled quivering hand in her warm firm grasp.

"We'll drink of something much better than any whiskey," she assured the lost soul.

Nick McCabe didn't hear of Captain Kay Montgomery's incarceration until late that Monday evening. Sequestered in his office, Nick had spent the long afternoon playing poker with a trio of San Francisco businessmen.

It was after six when the game broke up. The gentlemen hurried outside and into a carriage waiting behind the Golden Carousel. They were swiftly, discreetly whisked away from the Coast and up the hill to their mansions where their blue-blooded families would soon start dressing for dinner.

Immediately after their departure, Ling Tan came into the smoke-filled office, an empty serving tray tucked under his arm, a feather duster in one hand, a box of air-freshening incense in the other. Nick circled his big mahogany desk, dropped down into the swivel chair behind the desk as the silent Chinese servant began collecting dirty liquor glasses.

Ling Tan had been with Nick for the past eight years. The widowed Chinese man had brought his tiny eight-year-old daughter along when he answered the advertisement Nick had placed in the *San Francisco Chronicle*.

"I'm sorry, Ling Tan," Nick had apologized, "it would never work."

Nick's silver-gray eyes lowered to the small, pretty child clinging shyly to her father's hand. "I need a full-time houseboy. Someone to live right here on the premises." His gaze returned to Ling Tan. "The Barbary Coast is no place for a woman or a child."

"Excuse please, Mr. McCabe." Ling Tan had pleaded his case. "Ever walk through Devil's Kitchen or Rag Picker's Alley? Ever have occasion to go down in big dark underground chamber called Dog Kennel?"

Nick had. He'd seen firsthand the pestholes and horrid squalor where the city's Chinese population was forced to live.

"Well." Nick's brow furrowed. He paused, thinking. Then said, "Dammit, the job is yours, Ling Tan. Where's your wife, the girl's mother?"

"She die last winter in cellar where we live. Too cold there. Damp all the time."

Nick frowned, then nodded. His eyes went again to the tiny little girl with the solemn too-old face and the shiny jet-black hair. "The two of you will live here above the club. But the child is *never* to be downstairs. Or anywhere except your own private quarters down the hallway from mine. Is that clear?"

Smiling and bowing, Ling Tan couldn't hide his gratitude and relief. "Ming Ho very well behaved girl. Never see her if not want to."

So Ling Tan and Ming Ho had moved into the largest, most opulent living quarters they'd ever had: three light, airy rooms connected by a long, carpeted hallway to Nick's spacious apartments.

Ming Ho *was* a well-behaved girl and a bright, pretty one as well. On her sixteenth birthday just past, Nick had presented the grateful young woman with a bank note to cover the cost of her upcoming college education. Ming Ho dreamed of being the first Chinese female physician in the city of San Francisco. Her proud father and Nick saw no reason why her dream could not become reality.

Now as Ling Tan tidied up Nick's office, Nick could tell the silent man had his nose out of joint over something. Figuring it had nothing to do with him, Nick soon rose from his chair, stretched, and asked casually, "Anything going on this afternoon? Did the *Ella Mae* finally make it into port?"

"No *Ella Mae*. Ship delay another twelve hours." Ling Tan turned snapping dark eyes on his boss. "Constable pick up soul saver off street. Frow her in jail!"

"Who? Oh, you mean the Salvation Army gal?" Nick threw back his dark head and laughed. "That's what you're mad about?"

"Not right! Frow little girl in stinking, dirty jail. Don't like. How you like if frow Ming Ho in jail? You like?"

Continuing to laugh, Nick walked around the desk, thrust his hands into his pants pockets, and stood smiling down at the bristling Chinese servant.

"No," Nick finally admitted. "I wouldn't like it if Ming Ho was thrown in jail. But Ming Ho is a sweet young lady who knows how to behave and mind her own damn business. Captain Kay Montgomery is not."

Unconvinced, Ling Tan again said, "Not right. Don't like!"

"Ah, calm down, Ling Tan. It serves the meddling Southern do-gooder right," Nick said callously. "Let her cool her heels in jail for a night or two, maybe then she'll get her skinny butt off the Barbary Coast and back to Atlanta, Georgia, where she belongs."

Ling Tan glared at Nick and turned quickly away, muttering under his breath. Laughing again, Nick walked out of the office, leaving Ling Tan to stew.

But it was not an hour later that Nick summoned Ling Tan to his apartments. Thrusting some bills into Ling Tan's hand, Nick said, "Go by the Union Pacific and pick up a one-way ticket to Atlanta. Then run on down to the jail, and if the foolish little Bible spouter gives her word she'll take the ticket and use it, blow her bail." Nick paused, thinking, and threw more greenbacks down on the gleaming mahogany table. "Make that first-class accommodations. And do it the Chinese way. Don't let anyone see you."

"You're a good man, boss."

"Get out of here."

Ling Tan stole silently, swiftly through shadowy alleys to the brick jailhouse on Front Street. Looking all around, seeing no one, he slipped inside, hurried forward, and announced his mission, placing the money on the counter.

"Sorry. Too late," the bailiff announced.

"What mean, too late?" Ling Tan's face tightened with worry. "Something happen to Missy Montgomery?"

"Gone."

"Gone? Bailed out?"

"That's right."

"Who bail out?"

"A woman whose face I couldn't see. It was covered with a black veil. Stood the bail, spot cash. Didn't leave a name." The jailor shrugged muscular shoulders. "But I've seen her up on the hill once or twice. The mysterious Lady in Black."

"Lady in Black?" Ling Tan's face suddenly broke into a wide smile. "Ahhh so. Ahhhh so."

Chapter 4

The Salvation Army captain hadn't been seen all week on the busy streets of the Barbary Coast.

Club owners congratulated themselves.

Likely as not the little lady had been so chastened and so terrified by her brief incarceration in their famous jail, she'd eagerly fled the coast the minute her cell door was sprung open. Had simply disappeared like so many other pious do-gooders who'd wisely given up on changing this pagan playground. Just another in a long line of self-righteous scaredy cats, frightened of life and of living.

Frightened of the way life was lived on the free-wheeling Barbary Coast. And never was life more free-wheeling than on Saturday nights.

On this particular Saturday night—the first of September—one of those relieved club owners was in his usual high spirits. Nobody enjoyed Saturday night on the Barbary Coast more than the owner of the prosperous Golden Carousel Club, Mr. Nicholas Daniel McCabe.

At his best—freshly showered, cleanly shaven, and elegantly attired in black custom-cut tuxedo—Nick McCabe was an irresistible romantic hero to a host of breathless females. Wicked enough to be interesting; strong enough to keep any woman from dominating him.

There was a smoldering, challenging look about Nick McCabe that suggested to the woman bold enough to be searching for thrills and adventure that he could and would show her an extraordinary time. Yet Nick was no soft matinee idol ladies' man. To any man looking for trouble, the lean, dark saloon owner had that don't-trifle-with-me appearance. A rough-and-ready kind of guy, Nick was more than willing to take on any and all comers.

He was, through and through, a fearless fellow with an abundance of cockiness and an ever-ready smirk. A man with the power to win women's hearts and smash men's jaws.

Nick stood exactly six foot two in stocking feet and weighed 182 pounds. His hair was as black as the darkest midnight, his complexion a smooth clear olive. His eyes were a remarkable silver-gray and could effortlessly telegraph a myriad of silent messages. His nose was Roman straight, his well-shaped mouth wide and decidedly sensual.

In excellent health and in his prime at thirty-three, the good-looking Nick stayed in tiptop shape by sparring daily with his massively built bouncer, ex-heavyweight British bare-knuckles champion, Alfred Duke.

Quick-witted, forceful, and impossible to dislike, the tall, dark, sinfully handsome Nick was never one to spend much time in vain worry or regretful reflection. Nick's entire life had been spent on San Francisco's racy waterfront. The dives, dance halls, and depravity of the infamous Barbary Coast were as much a part of Nick as his air of supreme self-command and the frequent flash of dazzling white teeth as he blandly smiled his sins away.

Nick knew who he was and what he was and was perfectly pleased with himself, thank you very much.

Nicholas Daniel McCabe was quite simply a handsome heart-stopper and a worldly scamp who had little purpose in life and saw no sin in anything that brought pleasure or profit or both. He lived for the moment. Yesterday was gone and forgotten. Tomorrow might never come.

Women couldn't resist the wicked Nick McCabe, and the frustrating fact that the tall, dark charmer refused to take anything seriously only added to his masculine appeal.

Nick's wide easy grin could melt the hardest of hearts, and he had yet to meet the female who could resist him when he turned on the full, potent blast of his animal appeal. Keenly intelligent, restless by nature, easily bored, Nick often suspicioned that he might have enjoyed the unique challenge of a woman who refused to fall into his arms. Had there been such a woman.

Which there hadn't.

And wasn't.

Still Nick hummed a catchy tune as he soaked in his porcelain bathtub on this warm Saturday evening. He looked forward to the pleasant nighttime hours stretching before him.

Nick knew his Golden Carousel Club was sure to be jammed with merrymakers on this lovely Indian summer night. And a number of those making merry were sure to be San Francisco's elegantly attired, big-monied, blue-blooded smart set.

For the past six months—since the early spring—it had become quite fashionable for the Bay City's wealthy aristocrats to come "slumming" down to the Barbary Coast. Restless, bored, jaded, the vast majority had far too much money and too much time on their hands. They were forever seeking new diversions. The pampered patricians thought it great sport to spill out of their opulent mansions along Silk Stocking Row, climb into their magnificent carriages, and order their liveried drivers to take them down the hill. To drive them to the Barbary Coast about which it had oft been said no gentle breezes ever blew.

But where there constantly raged a seductive sirocco of sin.

Smiling, Nick McCabe abruptly lunged up out of his bathtub. He reached for a large white towel, swirled it around his glistening, tanned body, and stepped out onto the carpeted floor. Knotting the towel atop his left hipbone, Nick sauntered into the bedroom and poured himself a drink. He dropped down into his favorite easy chair, lifted his long muscled legs atop the worn leather ottoman, and crossed his ankles.

Nick flipped open a silver box at his elbow, withdrew a fragrant long, thin cigar, and sniffed it. He put the cheroot between his lips, lit it, and puffed it to life.

Black wavy hair still damp and falling over his forehead, silver eyes narrowed against the drifting cigar smoke, Nick's tanned face suddenly changed. The last traces of his smile vanished. He took the cigar from his mouth, slowly blew out the smoke, and sighed.

Never once in all the Saturday evenings he'd played host the well-heeled upper-class crowd who visited his Golden Carousel had he met a pretty woman in their number. He idly wondered if among the idle rich there *were* any really good-looking ladies. He'd met dozens who were elegantly gowned and perfectly coiffured and dripping with diamonds, but none could actually be called beautiful.

Not honest-to-God, peaches-and-cream-complexioned, lusciously long-limbed, angel-faced beautiful.

Maybe tonight his luck would change.

There was music and the tinkle of dealer's bells calling for drinks and cigars. The rattle of the chuck-a-luck cage, the clink of Mexican dollars, and the quieter click of ivory chips and markers.

Laughter and squeals of delight from lucky faro players. Cheers and whistles for long-limbed entertainers in glittering sequins. Oohs and aahs over tempting foods served by efficient white-jacketed waiters.

Nighttime at the Golden Carousel.

The hour was swiftly approaching ten o'clock.

The Carousel Club was filled to capacity with a diverse and lively crowd. Drinking, laughing, thrill-seeking highbrows freely rubbed elbows with sleazy, dangerous, thrill-seeking lowbrows.

At the very back of the crowded club, beside the double doors leading into the saloon's kitchen, a gigantic man stood with his feet slightly apart, his big hands locked behind him. His keen hazel eyes swept back and forth over the crowded house.

His great height—six foot five—made it easy for him to see everything and everybody. His massive muscular body made it equally easy to handle any trouble that might break out.

Alfred Duke, a ruddy-faced, good-natured Englishman, towered head and shoulders above any crowd. And if need be, he could take out any half-dozen men by himself using only his lightning-swift fists. The big Englishman was an ex-heavyweight pugilist who'd once been the bare-knuckled champion of all the British Isles. Never beaten in the ring, Alfred Duke was lured to the colonies by the promise of big money and bigger fame.

And for a time both were his. Then one day the fame ran out and Alfred Duke found he was penniless.

Still, he liked to laugh and say he had enough memories from those glory days to warm him sufficiently in his old age.

Alfred Duke had something else as well.

He had a friend.

Nick McCabe gave the big guy a job as his chief bouncer, and the grateful Englishman had been a fixture at the Golden Carousel Club for the past seven years. Fiercely loyal to Nick, serving as personal bodyguard as well as club bouncer, Alfred Duke was known as Big Alfred along the Barbary Coast.

Nobody wanted any trouble with Big Alfred. If a fight broke out in the Carousel Club, Big Alfred ended it in the blinking of an eye. If a gambler became disgruntled over a loss, Big Alfred was there to quietly escort the loser to the door. If a patron became verbally or physically abusive with one of the female entertainers, the foolish clown found himself swiftly tossed out on his ear.

If a jealous lover or vengeful competitor or dangerous hoodlum came gunning for Nick, they first had to get through Big Alfred.

Only a fool would try.

Big Alfred manned his station there by the back kitchen door, knowing exactly where his boss was at any given minute. He knew as his searching hazel eyes continued to keep careful watch on the boisterous crowd that Nick McCabe was walking down the dim hallway toward the entertainers' dressing room.

Nick knocked loudly on the dressing room door and waited. Dressed for the evening, Nick wore one of several custom-cut black tuxedos with shiny satin lapels, satin cummerbund, and narrow black satin stripe going down the outside seam of each trouser leg. His snowy white shirt had a stiff, pleated front and high starched collar set off with a black silk bow tie.

Nick's shoes were of shiny black patent. While he waited for the girls to open the door, Nick idly lifted his left foot, hooked it around his right calf, and buffed the already gleaming shoe on his trouser leg. He repeated the action with the right foot.

"Boss, it's you!" An incredibly happy-looking, small woman with glossy chestnut hair opened the door and smiled warmly up at Nick.

Her name was Rose Reilly. She was billed as the Wild Irish Rose. Eternally joyful and smiling, Rose's almond-shaped emerald eyes had sparkled brighter than ever for the past several weeks. Rose had fallen in love. With a patron.

"Rosie, honey," Nick teased, "promise you'll try and cheer up before showtime."

Rose giggled gleefully, drew the tall man inside, and said, "Girls, it's the boss."

"Nick. It's Nick," several women murmured breathlessly. Feminine laughter and excited chattering softened and died. A dozen entertainers in skimpy sequined costumes and glittering headdresses eagerly gathered around the tall, dark Nick.

With lips painted bloodred, cheeks heavily rouged, eyes outlined with charcoal, the women smiled warmly at Nick. Each openly adored their strikingly handsome boss.

All, that is, but Rose.

"You look absolutely beautiful, girls," Nick said, smiling at each one in turn. A collective "thank you" rose from the pleased women. "You'll be happy to know that the house is packed tonight. You're the reason they've chosen the Golden Carousel," Nick told them, diplomatically adding, "I'm a lucky guy. The Carousel has the loveliest ladies on the Barbary Coast or any other coast."

Applause and pleased laughter from the girls. Nick raised his hands for silence.

"I pride myself on running a high-toned, classy joint. Now, we got a number of important patrons in the cabaret tonight. Many of these men have brought their wives, so let's do our best to show them a ritzy kind of fun and excitement."

"Count on us, Boss." A black-haired woman stepped forward and did an impromptu bump and grind, throwing her pelvis out toward Nick.

Nick laughed good-naturedly.

Then said, "It's almost ten, so . . ." Smiling, he backed away, stopped, and pointedly addressed a couple of girls who were brand new to the Carousel. "I'm not a hard taskmaster, kids. No visible tattoos. No drinking from the bottle." He paused and added, "Remember, if you act like ladies, the customers will tip you like ladies. Got it?"

"Yes, sir," they said in unison.

Nick grinned appealingly, lifted a tanned hand, kissed the tip of his long index finger, and tossed the kiss to them. "I'll be watching the show from my box," he said, and left.

Outside Nick hurried back down the hall and into the club, weaving his way through the crowd toward Big Alfred. He checked with the huge bouncer to see if everything was going smoothly. Leaning down close to Nick's ear, Big Alfred assured his boss all was well. So far. Nick nodded, turned to look leisurely out over the crowded club.

He blinked and did a double take.

A couple was just arriving. They crossed the marble entrance, stopped, and stood on the steps above the cavernous room. Nick had eyes only for the woman.

An honest-to-God, peaches-and-cream-complexioned, lusciously long-limbed, angel-faced beautiful woman.

Nick felt his legs weaken, his belly tighten.

This beauty was dressed in a form-fitting evening gown of shimmery white satin. Her ivory shoulders and arms were seductively bare. Diamonds winked on her swanlike throat and at her small perfect ears. Her hair was an incredible shade of white-blond and dressed sleekly atop her head.

As Nick watched, the blond beauty took the arm of her companion. She smiled up at tall slim man with dark blond hair who was dressed in elegant dark evening clothes.

Acting purely on instinct, Nick plunged eagerly through the crowd. He reached the striking pair before they had completely descended the marble steps leading down onto the Golden Carousel's main floor.

Pretending to take no notice of the willowy blond beauty in alluring white satin, Nick flashed her tall escort his warmest smile, thrust out his hand, and said, "Nick McCabe. I own the place. Welcome to the Golden Carousel."

"Why, thank you, McCabe." The blond man firmly shook Nick's hand. "This is our first visit so maybe you could show us around."

"Be my pleasure," said Nick, forcing himself to keep his eyes off the woman.

"Good. Thanks," the gentlemen said. Then, finally: "Pat and Adele Packard, Nick."

"Pat," Nick smoothly acknowledged, but his racing heart sank with disappointment. The vision in white satin was married! And to the man standing before him. Slowly Nick turned to the beautiful blond woman. Nodding, he murmured, "Adele. May I call you Adele?"

"Certainly," she replied, flashing him a smile. "Nick." The way she said his name made the tips of his fingers tingle.

Her gaze immediately left him. She looked out at the crowd. "My goodness, so many people. Will there be a table available?"

"Adele's right, McCabe." Pat possessively took her bare arm. "Perhaps we should we come back another time."

Tempted to say yes, dreading the prospect of spending an evening with this exotic creature when he couldn't lay a hand on her, Nick graciously invited the couple to join him in his private box.

"Why, Nick, we'd love to," the beautiful Adele Packard said. "Wouldn't we, Pat, dear?"

Chapter 5

Ever the genial host, Nick smilingly ushered the handsome pair across the crowded floor to the very back of the enormous club. At the club's far right, he guided them up the mezzanine stairs to a secluded table set alone and apart on a small protruding balcony.

Nick's specially constructed private box was in fact a high-backed semicircular banquette upholstered in lush black velvet. The banquette's table, draped in snowy white damask reaching to the carpeted floor, was quickly pulled aside by a helpful waiter so the trio could slip into the cozy nook with ease.

The lady, naturally, was seated between the two gentlemen, and so a tortured Nick found himself next to the dazzling blonde. So close he was vitally aware of the gentle rise and fall of her soft, unhampered breasts against the evening gown's low-cut white satin bodice. A whiff of her expensive perfume further intoxicated him. Surely the incredibly seductive scent clung to every luscious curve and hollow of her pale, sensuous body. Or so Nick imagined.

The lady's blond hair, in the box's dim, subdued light, was an extraordinary shade. How delectable Adele Packard would look if she took the diamond restraints from that marvelous hair and let the heavy tresses spill down around her bare shoulders. Nick itched to run his fingers through that silky, silvery hair of such a striking shade it couldn't possibly be natural.

Or could it?

Nick assumed a pose of easy relaxed control, ordering chilled champagne and engaging Pat Packard in polite table conversation. Too smooth and too smart to allow his fierce attraction for Packard's wife to show in any form or manner, Nick was relieved when the champagne arrived and was poured into sparkling glasses. His throat was unusually dry.

Nick started to take a sip of the bubbly, but Adele Packard stopped him.

"Wait! Wait, both of you. I must propose a toast," the velvet-voiced Adele announced.

Nick inwardly cringed. Good God, was it the couple's wedding anniversary? Did the sentimental wife want to drink to their years of wedded bliss? Jesus, he'd have to sit there and grin like a fool while the beautiful Adele gave her husband a big mushy kiss.

Nick mentally steeled himself.

The blond Adele Packard said in a low, pleasing voice, "To dear friends and new friends." She paused, then added, with a touch of smoky seduction in her voice, "May the new become the dear . . . before this lovely night ends."

She held out her glass.

"Hear, hear," said Pat Packard, nodding, and touched his glass to hers.

"Friends," Nick said, feeling decidedly uncomfortable as he dutifully clinked his glass against Adele Packard's.

His discomfort grew when Adele turned flirtatious dark eyes on him. Looking directly at his mouth, she raised her stemmed glass to her parted lips, dipped the tip of her pink tongue into the champagne, then licked her full soft lips until they glistened wetly with the wine.

Nick wanted to kiss her so badly he hurt.

He quickly turned up his own glass and thirstily drank down its contents in one long swallow. The waiter appeared to pour him another. Nick nodded his dark head gratefully and was relieved when the already dim lights lowered even further, casting him and his guests into shadowy darkness.

And signaling the start of the show.

All eyes, including Adele Packard's, were directed to a large semicircular stage where footlights illuminated closed heavy curtains of black velvet. From somewhere back stage the band began playing "My Wild Irish Rose."

Patrons burst into applause and men began chanting, "Rose! Rose! Bring out the Wild Irish Rose."

"If you'll excuse me," Nick said, leaning across the table to be heard above the din. "I'll be back momentarily."

Thankful for an excuse to get away for a few moments, Nick made his way backstage. In the wings he withdrew a clean monogrammed white handkerchief from his inside breast pocket and dotted the drops of nervous perspiration from his hot, tanned face. He straightened his bow tie, hitched up his trousers, and buttoned the open jacket of his black tuxedo. He shot both arms forward, making certain exactly the right amount of snowy white cuff showed below the tux's black sleeve.

Nick glanced over at the smiling, waiting Rose Reilly. He winked at her and then stepped out in front of the black velvet curtains.

"Ladies and gentleman, the Golden Carousel Club is proud present to you the most beautiful girl on the Barbary Coast."

The heavy black curtains slowly lifted. At center stage, a pretty young woman stood before a shoulder-high dressing screen fashioned entirely of a pale-rose gauzy see-through material. The small woman looked dainty and demure in a full flouncy long dress of rose-hued organdy trimmed in delicate ivory Belgian lace.

On the woman's small hands were pristine white gloves and on her head was a saucy straw bonnet, its rose taffeta streamers tied snugly beneath her firm chin. Atop her right shoulder rested an open parasol of shimmering rose silk, which she twirled coyly. A narrow pink satin ribbon snugly hugging her slender neck was adorned with a freshly cut pale-pink rose, the delicate petals brushing Rose Reilly's curving throat. Rose smiled brilliantly at the adoring crowd.

Nick finally lifted his hands for silence.

Waiting until the shouts had died down, he said, "And now, right here on our stage . . . our own Miss Rose Reilly." He extended his hand to the smiling girl in rose organdy. Whistles and shouts from the crowd. "Let's all put our hands together for the Wild Irish Rose!"

More thunderous applause as Nick, leading the applause, backed away and the pretty Rose Reilly, accompanied by the hidden orchestra, begin to sing in a innocent, almost childish voice.

> "My Wild Irish Rose,
> The sweetest flower that grows . . ."

Back at his box, Nick quietly slipped into the black velvet banquette only to find that Adele Packard had, in his absence, scooted farther toward his side of the cozy, shadowy cubicle.

"Excuse me, Adele," he whispered, and slid in beside her.

"Of course, Nick," she replied, favoring him with a wide, friendly smile. And stayed right where she was. Her eyes returned to the stage.

Nick glanced helplessly at Pat Packard. Pat's undivided attention was directed to the gorgeously gowned girl singing "My Wild Irish Rose." Eyes as round as saucers and mouth slightly ajar, the polished aristocrat was either appalled or delighted. Or both.

Adele Packard had—unknowingly or purposely—left Nick so little room in the banquette, he was in danger of falling off the upholstered, curving velvet seat. He had no choice. He was forced to lift his long

right arm, place it along the banquette's high back behind Adele, and
grip the top tufted edge tightly.

Rose's song ended.

She took her bows and then went into the *real* crowd-pleasing portion of her act. It was not her voice alone that made Rose the biggest
draw of the Carousel Club—the most celebrated star on the entire the
Barbary Coast. The sweet-faced favorite of the coast's paying customers, the Wild Irish Rose had a unique act. One that never failed to
thrill and please the eager panting crowds.

Nick was accustomed to Rose's nightly performance. He generally
paid no attention when she was on stage. As a rule he was on the door
greeting latecomers, handling some last-minute problem, or in his office relaxing for a few minutes.

Even when he was out front hosting important customers in his box,
he was too preoccupied with seeing to it that his guests were enjoying
themselves to take notice of Rose. Laughing, drinking, talking, he
never paid attention to Rose's routine.

Tonight was different.

He couldn't very well converse with Pat Packard. The Nob Hill
patrician was totally engrossed in watching Rose. At the same time
Packard's beautiful wife was sitting so disturbingly close to Nick, Nick
was afraid if he turned his head to look at her, they'd practically bump
noses.

So he watched the show.

Collapsing her saucy silk parasol, Rose gave the audience an impudent toss of her head and an ankle-showing flounce of her frilly skirts.
Then coyly she went around behind the gauzy dressing screen. Only
her smiling face and rose-clad shoulders were visible above the gossa-
mer screen.

Rose reached up, leisurely untied the taffeta streamers of her straw
bonnet, and took the hat off. She waited a long, teasing moment, then
dropped the discarded bonnet over the screen amid shouts of encouragement. Rose then began to slowly, seductively undress while the
unseen orchestra played a ballad. Each article of clothing that came
off was tossed carelessly over the gauzy pink screen to the rousing
delight of the audience. Watching the lovely young woman silhouetted
behind the thin screen sensuously disrobing was eerily suggestive of
peeping through a stranger's window.

Nick, along with the whistling, leering crowd, sat there in his darkened black velvet banquette watching a lovely young woman strip off
her hat, her gloves, her frilly rose gown. To his extreme displeasure, he

became mildly stimulated. That sensual excitement escalated with each feminine garment that was tossed over the screen.

Nick knew the reason.

It had little to do with Rose Reilly.

The rising excitement came from being seated in such close proximity to a dazzling blonde he found incredibly desirable while another dazzling woman shed her clothes.

It was strangely, wildly erotic. It was as if there were only the three of them in the noisy, smoke-filled room. Just he, Adele Packard, and Rose. And Rose's seductive stripping was but a persuasive prelude, a lovely symbolic exercise for the sole benefit of Adele and him.

Nick felt as if he and the beautiful Adele were sharing an intense secret sexual experience, despite the fact that they neither touched or even looked at each other. It wasn't necessary. While they stared mesmerized at the disrobing Rose, Nick could *feel* Adele beside him, her willowy body as taut and as hot as his own. It was sweet agony. Shared intimacy. Thrillingly clandestine.

A uniquely carnal experience made all the more exciting because it was shared with a blond beautiful lady whom he would never be allowed to touch.

On stage the Wild Irish Rose had shed every single article of clothing. Straw hat, white gloves, pink parasol, rose dress, and a provocative array of lacy pink satin underthings and stockings lay discarded on the stage in front of the sheer screen.

Rose's long chestnut hair was loose and falling around her smiling face. Her small perfect body was as bare as the day she came into the world, shielded from the electrified crowd by nothing more than the thin gauzy pink dressing screen. The effect was stunning. Rose looked nakeder than naked.

Nick's hot silver eyes clung to the beautiful woman behind the screen. But it was the beautiful woman seated beside him he was seeing. His arm upraised and resting on the banquette behind her, Nick felt Adele's slender body tremble slightly against his ribs. The gentle motion vibrated throughout his tense, lean frame.

At last the Wild Irish Rose removed the fresh-cut rose from her throat. Seductively she rubbed the long-stemmed blossom over her pale silky body. Then she tossed the rose out into the crowd.

Men shouted and lunged for the rose, pushing and falling in their quest for the blossom.

At the exact moment that Rose's carefully thrown flower reached

her audience's grabbing hands, Nick McCabe felt Adele Packard's soft
hand touch his muscular thigh. And slide swiftly up to his groin.

Nick's heart hammered wildly in his chest. His breath caught in his
throat. His eyes slid helplessly closed.

And Nick McCabe heard bells.

Chapter 6

 She had a brand-new bell.

And a tambourine too.

Captain Kay Montgomery was still very much in the city of San Francisco. True, she hadn't been seen on the coast's busy streets for the past week. But it wasn't because she'd turned tail and ran.

Kay was not easily frightened. It would have taken a form of punishment a great deal more severe than being thrown into jail to get rid of her.

Nor did she give up easily. Kay hadn't given up on bringing God to the godless of the barbaric Barbary Coast. She'd not been seen on the streets because she'd been otherwise occupied.

Freed from jail Monday evening when a stranger posted her bail, Kay didn't get the opportunity to thank her unknown benefactor. She'd managed only a fleeting glance at a black-gowned, black-veiled woman getting into a gleaming black coach. The coach had quickly disappeared into the gathering dusk.

The Lady in Black had eluded her.

On leaving jail, Kay had taken with her the undernourished, badly shaking man from the next cell. She had herded the sick soul directly to Bay City Hospital and demanded that he be admitted. Asked who intended to pay for his care, Kay assured the staff she would be responsible.

So, reluctantly an orderly in a fresh white jacket and trousers led the babbling, trembling man upstairs. Kay stayed at the sick man's bedside for the next forty-eight hours, bathing his profusely sweating face, clinging to his frail, shaking hand, climbing up on the bed to bodily hold him down when the monsters of his alcohol-riddled mind came forth from the darkness to terrify him.

By sunset Wednesday the poor fellow was beginning to rest a bit easier. He couldn't recall his name, so Kay called him Matthew after the first book of the New Testament. The hollow-eyed Giles Lawton, one of Kay's two recruits, ordered her to leave the hospital, to get some sleep. He'd sit with Matthew. After all, who knew better than he what Matthew was going through.

Kay agreed.

But she up again bright and early Thursday morning. Armed with the well-worn photograph of Curly and with her youthful cadet Bobby Newman in tow, she went on another all-out search for her missing brother.

She had to find Curly.

And the army's missing money.

Kay decided that Curly was no longer on the Barbary Coast. If he ever had been. Convinced she'd been looking in the wrong part of the city, Kay and Bobby climbed the hill to the heart of San Francisco. Kay went first to the police department. No one had seen or heard of a Curly Montgomery.

She next tried rooming houses, tenements, and economy hotels. No luck.

On Friday the pair went to the city hospitals. No such patient had been admitted. The churches. Sorry, no young man fitting his description was among their flock.

Saturday came.

The first day of September. With the changing of the calendar came the startling realization that the year of trial granted to Curly and her was no longer a year. Only eight months remained!

Kay and Bobby again spent the better part of the day searching for Curly, with the same disheartening results. Sensitive to his leader's deep disappointment, Bobby made a suggestion as they tiredly walked back down the hill toward the Barbary Coast.

Bobby reminded Captain Kay that while she had been keeping watch over Matthew at the hospital, he and Giles had collected some much-needed money for the Army.

"L-l-let's b-b-uy a new b-b-ell and ma-ma-march on th-th-th—" He couldn't quite get it out. So he started over. "L-l-let's b-b-b—"

"Yes!" Kay enthusiastically agreed. "We'll purchase a brand-new bell!" She affectionately squeezed the young man's arm. "Oh, Bobby, that's a wonderful idea. We'll buy a bell and . . . we'll get a tambourine too! You'll bang the tambourine to the glory of God."

Nodding eagerly, his eyes shining, Bobby said, "B-B-bang the ta-ta-tamb-b-b—"

"Absolutely! You'll bang the tambourine. I'll ring the bell. And Giles will carry the Blood and Fire banner!" Excited, she rushed on. "We'll go right this minute and buy the bell and tambourine. Then on to the hospital, look in on Matthew, and collect Giles. And tonight when every joint is jumping with sin, the three of us will invade one of the wicked establishments."

"I-I we-we'll—we'll—"

"Yes, we certainly will, Bobby! We'll storm the ramparts of the busiest, the worst, the most ungodly saloon on the Barbary Coast." Kay defiantly lifted her chin. Her blue eyes flashed with excitement and determination. "And I know just the one we'll attack!"

At eleven that night, Captain Kay Montgomery stood before the massive black double doors of Nick McCabe's Pacific Street Golden Carousel Club. The saloon's plain white stucco front had no windows at ground level. It was impossible to have a peep inside.

Kay's eyes lifted to the row of windows above. Her gaze automatically went to the one on the far left. The window at which she'd first seen Nick McCabe.

Kay felt a tingle of apprehension skip up her spine.

She lowered her eyes, drew a deep breath, and turned to smile confidently at her waiting recruits.

"Fellow soldiers, we are the shock troops of God. Here to storm the forts of darkness. To topple the citadels of sin." Kay looked from young Bobby with his tambourine to Giles holding the banner of Blood and Fire. "The sinners' place of worship is the saloon! Their God their unbridled appetites. They are slaves of intemperance who must be told about the healing of Divine Love."

Smiling, Kay boldly led Bobby Newman and Giles Lawton through the padded double doors of Nick McCabe's Golden Carousel Club.

Kay's smile froze on her face when she was inside and standing on the gleaming marble threshold. Clutching her new silver-plated bell, Captain Kay stared with round, astonished eyes.

Much larger and plusher than it appeared from the outside, the crowded Carousel Club looked amazingly like the man who owned it. Saloon and proprietor were a perfect match. Big and dark and dangerous.

And unquestionably handsome.

The spacious cabaret, spread out below, was rectangular shaped and extremely high-ceilinged. Off to Kay's left a wide marble staircase led up to an open second-floor landing where widely spaced mahogany doors were all closed.

Below the broad landing and to the left of a wide center walkway that divided the club equally in two were gaming tables manned by

dark-suited, slick-haired croupiers. Cigar-smoking gamblers were
crowded around faro and craps tables. Patrons trying the chuck-a-luck
shouted and squealed as the dice tumbled around topsy-turvy in the
cage. Hopeful bettors pressed up close to the spinning wheel-of-fortune.

To the right of the broad marble walkway, in a large area carpeted
in deep smoky gray, were rows of tables for dining and drinking, filled
on this warm September evening with laughing, happy people. At the
far back of the club, heavy black velvet curtains were swiftly being
lowered on a stage that covered the entire wall.

Below the large stage was a polished dance floor where couples
spun, turned, and swayed suggestively.

Liquor flowed. Laughter abounded. Lewdness prevailed.

Kay had seen all that before.

What she hadn't seen before—and was seeing now—held her there
on the white marble apron of the cavernous saloon unable to move or
to look away.

At the very center of the large crowded saloon, located squarely in
the middle of the wide open walkway, was a hexagonal mahogany bar
where a pair of bartenders in white shirts and black bow ties calmly
poured drinks.

Above their heads, directly over the hexagonal bar and suspended
from the two-story-high ceiling, was a steam-driven revolving golden
carousel. The carousel's gilded horses went slowly up and down as
they traversed the circle.

On those gold-gilt horses were real live women riding shamelessly
astride and waving to the appreciative crowd. Nearer naked than
clothed, the female riders wore indecently skimpy garbs of glittering
colored sequins. Their full bosoms practically spilled from the low-cut
tops of their sequined costumes and their long, shapely legs were bare
all the way past their thighs, save for sheer stockings and flirty garters.

Their slippered feet were stuck into white-and-gold stirrups that
dangled from the gilt horses' saddles. The brazen beauties pretended
to be riding real flesh-and-blood steeds. Hunkered down, knees hugging the lifeless beasts, hands clutching the golden reins. One rider, a
pretty, youthful-looking woman with chestnut hair and revealing rose-
sequined outfit, abruptly stood in the stirrups. She lifted her hand to
shade her eyes as if she were a tired cowhand out on the range,
searching for a place to pitch camp for the night.

"Right here, Rose!" shouted a big-bellied, bald-headed man from a
table below. Slamming his knee with the flat of his hand, he called,

"End of the trail, sugar! Come sit on my lap!" The lascivious fat man lifted outstretched arms to the turning carousel.

A laughing black-haired woman astride one of golden horses began to slap its shimmering hindquarters with a gold-and-white leather quirt. Whistling, laughing men took bets on whether the brunette would win the imaginary race.

Captain Kay Montgomery realized she'd been standing there staring far too long. She couldn't help herself. She was absolutely horrified. She was also helplessly fascinated.

Kay had seen plenty of sin in her day. Always it had sickened and saddened her. Never had there been anything remotely appealing about the dark world of vice.

But Captain Kay Montgomery, in her twenty-five years of life, had never witnessed a frivolous scene of sin like the one she looked on now. Much as she longed to convince herself that the panorama of evil spread out before her was totally disgusting, it simply was not so.

Shocking, of course. Wicked, yes. Sinful, undoubtedly.

But disgusting?

No. No, it wasn't.

Kay was strangely hypnotized by the daring drama unfolding before her wide blue eyes. Never one to try to fool herself, Kay was forced to admit that the near-naked women astride the gold gilt horses *were* stunningly beautiful. And, to Kay's amazement, many of the patrons seated at round, damask-draped tables were attractive, elegantly attired gentlemen. There was even a scattering of lushly gowned ladies in the crowd.

There was music. There was delicious-looking, wonderful-smelling food. There was fizzing champagne served in crystal long-stemmed glasses. There were open displays of affection. There was laughter, gaiety, and fun.

Seductive.

Tremendously seductive.

Kay's awed sweeping gaze moved slowly around the club until it came to rest on a private box where a handsome trio appeared to be reigning royalty. Kay caught only a glimpse of a fair, slender gentleman and a lovely blond lady.

Then she saw *him.*

Spotting Nick McCabe was the best thing that could have happened. The sight of him snapped Kay out of her dreamlike trance.

Teeth gritted, hackles rising, she whirled around. And caught Bobby and Giles openly ogling the scantily clad beauties riding the golden carousel.

"Attention!" she snapped, more irritated with herself than with them.

The recruits turned shamed faces on their leader.

"We are here for one purpose. To attack, capture, and hold this Kingdom of the Devil!" Kay turned back to face the glamorous battlefield, squared her slender shoulders, lifted her new silver bell, and gave the command.

"Forward, march!"

Chapter 7

 The trio proceeded down the marble steps and into the heart of the bustling saloon. Captain Kay exuberantly rang her silver-plated bell. Bobby banged the heel of his hand against the tambourine. And Giles waved the Army's colorful banner.

Kay had a spring to her step and a determined gleam in her clear blue eyes as she led her troops through the maze of tables filled with laughing, drinking revelers. Gently but firmly she admonished the carousing patrons to turn away from evil. To follow her and hear the Salvation Army's message. To come and learn of a more rewarding way of life.

Kay stopped at a table filled with leering, howling men. She brazenly tapped a silver-haired, distinguished-looking gentleman on the shoulder, diverting his attention from the shameful exhibition taking place up on the Golden Carousel.

"Excuse me, sir," Captain Kay said. "You seem to be enjoying yourself."

"Indeed I am." Sizing Kay up, the dapperly dressed, slightly tipsy man added, "You're probably cute when you're not wearing so many clothes." He laid a hand on her arm. "I'd like to see you up there astride one of those golden horses." He laughed heartily and so did his table companions.

Kay freed her arm. "How would you like to see your daughter up there on the Carousel?"

The man's wide smile slipped, then vanished. "Leave my daughter out of this!"

"Would you be proud of her?"

"Don't be absurd." His lips thinned. "I wouldn't want my daughter in a place like this."

"I'm sure your daughter wouldn't want her father in a place like this," Kay gently told him.

She hit a nerve. She could see it in the man's changed brown eyes. She'd spoiled the fun for him. Scowling, he reached for his shot glass, downed the fiery whiskey in one gulp, and abruptly rose from the table.

"It's late," he said to his friends. "I better get home."

"Good for you, Mister," Kay said, praising his decision. She noted his well-tailored suit, his immaculate appearance. "You don't belong here."

The silver-haired man eyed Kay's severe blue uniform, her black polk bonnet. "Neither do you, Miss."

"You're wrong," she firmly told him. "This is exactly where I belong."

He shook his head. "Then good luck. You'll need it."

"God bless you," Kay called after him as he hastily exited the saloon.

Exhilarated, Kay murmured heartfelt "thank yous" to customers generously dropping coins and bills into Bobby Newman's outstretched tambourine. With heightened determination, the trio continued to work the celebrating crowd, attracting attention and causing a general disturbance.

Jubilantly Kay rang her new silver bell.

At the same time—up in the dim privacy of a plush black velvet banquette—Adele Packard's soft tormenting fingers had just released Nick McCabe. Her bold, delicate hand once again appeared above the table. She reached for her stemmed champagne glass and smiled innocently at Pat Packard.

Nick's heavy-lidded silver-gray eyes opened fully. The muscles in his long legs stopped jumping and bunching. His breathing returned to normal. His heart rate slowed to a steady, even beat.

But still he heard bells.

Seconds passed.

Nick shook his head.

Minutes.

Jesus! He really *did* hear bells.

Nick's dark head snapped around. His narrowed silver gaze swept the press of people in the grand salon below.

"Son of a bitch!" he muttered under his breath.

"Something wrong, McCabe?" Pat Packard asked politely, his own inquisitive gaze following Nick's narrowed glance.

"No. No, nothing," Nick said evenly. He felt like shouting, "Hell, everything's wrong! Not one but two bothersome women are bent on ruining my evening. This misbehaving blond temptress here in the banquette and a flame-haired fanatic down on the floor."

"A minor disturbance," Nick casually added with an easy smile. "Nothing that can't be quickly handled."

Nick shot a hard glance to the back of the club and Big Alfred. The enormous bouncer had already spotted the captain and her cadets. He was waiting, looking to Nick for instruction. Nick had only to incline his dark head toward the front doors.

Big Alfred was immediately under way, heading toward the Salvationists. The massive, bull-necked Englishman caught up with the soliciting soldiers at a crowded craps table.

Captain Kay had disrupted the game.

She'd elbowed her way up to the table, reached down, and plucked the ivory dice up off the green felt layout.

"Gentlemen, this is not the only game in town," she loudly announced to the startled players. "Won't you follow me out of this gambling hell? Come and learn how to win a prize far more lasting and precious than mere money."

"Drop those dice, lady," warned the stern-faced dice dealer.

"She's holding up the game," grumbled an impatient gambler.

"Get her out of here," slurred another.

"I'll handle this," Big Alfred said, stepping up behind Kay. Taking her arm, the Englishman turned her from the craps table and said, "Lass, I'll have to ask you to leave now."

"We're not leaving." Kay tipped her bonneted head back to look up at the ruddy-faced giant. "So kindly let go of me."

"Now, lassie, don't make this hard on yourself or on me." Big Alfred tried reason. "Surely you can see that you don't belong here. A respectable, clean-living lady like yourself." His ruddy face had a kind, open expression as he wrestled the dice from her hand and added, "Now take your bell and boys and go peacefully, child."

"And if I refuse?" quizzed Kay.

Big Alfred's face drew up into a tortured frown. "Then I'll have to order you to leave."

"Order me? By whose authority? The owner's?"

"Aye, lass. I work for the gent who owns this saloon and—"

"So that's it," Kay interrupted. "Nick McCabe!" She immediately looked toward the proprietor's private box.

Nick McCabe was staring straight down at her. And he was angry. He shot a hand up in the air and jerked his thumb decisively toward the front doors. He glared at Kay. Kay glared right back at him.

Big Alfred exhaled wearily but wasted no more time. He didn't lay a hand on Kay, but he grabbed up her two troopers by the scruffs of their necks and dragged them away.

Gamblers cheered. The dice rolled again.

Taken aback, Kay blinked in disbelief. She paused briefly to regard Nick McCabe with acid distaste. Then she rushed after Big Alfred and her choking, struggling recruits.

"You let them go!" she demanded of the big Brit. "Do you hear me? Unhand my soldiers!"

Right on his heels Kay followed after Big Alfred, taking no notice of all the jeers and shouts of derision.

Kay tried valiantly to keep a lid on her famous temper.

She was not successful.

Angrily snatching her black polk bonnet off her head, Kay slapped impotently at the Englishman's broad back with her straw hat. A lock of flaming hair tumbled into her snapping blue eyes. She blew it aside with a huff, her temperature rapidly rising. Logic was lost in the heat.

Instinct guided Kay's actions.

Her face as red as her hair, she stormed wild-eyed after a man who was so huge and so powerful he was having no trouble holding her recruits aloft, one in each giant paw. Without breaking a sweat, Big Alfred carried the kicking, struggling pair through the cheering crowd, up the white marble entry steps, across the polished threshold, and out the black double doors.

Throughout Kay followed, beating on his back with her straw bonnet and hotly ordering him to unhand her soldiers or else.

Big Alfred swiftly tossed the pair of frightened recruits into Pacific Street.

But he wasn't quite swift enough.

He had barely cleared the club's doors and reached the sidewalk when a furious Captain Kay jumped up and banged the big bully on the head with her new silver bell. The well-placed blow knocked the Englishman out cold and the bell out of Kay's hand. Big Alfred immediately crumpled, falling atop the surprised troopers.

Captain Kay whirled around and marched right back inside the Golden Carousel. Smoke coming out of both ears, her tight fist clutching the streamers of her crushed polk bonnet, she purposely paused on the marble threshold in a defiant stance.

Hot pinpoints of white light glinting from her blue eyes, she looked straight at Nick's box. Kay watched as he rose and left the table. She knew he was coming after her. She tossed her head and fearlessly descended the entranceway.

Nick saw Kay the second she reentered the club. Surprise gave way to wrath. His eyes flashed with silver fire. Without a word to the Packards, he rose and started toward the red-faced, wild-eyed Captain Kay.

The angry adversaries met face to face directly before the wheel-of-fortune. Nick's hand shot out, his long tanned fingers encircled Kay's upper arm. He drew her close.

"I thought I was rid of you," he said in a voice dangerously low. His silver eyes blazed down at her from a mean, dark face.

"You'll never be rid of me, McCabe," Kay told him firmly, her heart beginning to beat faster. She twisted from Nick's grasp, turned and addressed a portly man standing before the spinning wheel. "Sir, are you prepared to meet your maker?"

Nick grabbed her away from the blinking, startled player. "You're going to meet yours right here and now if you don't clear out!"

"You don't frighten me, McCabe. Not one bit," Kay said in a too-loud voice. "Men who are all bluster and swagger never do."

"Pipe down!" Nick warned harshly, glancing about, longing to avoid making any further scenes. Lowering his voice, leaning close to her ear, he added half cajolingly, "Come on, Captain. You've had your fun. Go on home."

"Why, this *is* home," she told him, sweeping the hand that held her crushed bonnet around in a wide, encompassing arc. "These people are His children. My brothers and sisters, and I love them. It's my duty to tell them of the Master's kingdom."

"Listen, sister, the Golden Carousel is *my* kingdom. I'm the only master."

"You dare add blasphemy to all your other sins?" Kay shook her head piteously. "I shall pray for you, McCabe."

"Pray all you like, Captain, but not in here." He stood blocking her path, tall, arrogant, and challenging. "Now are you going?"

"And if I don't?" Kay remained rebellious. "Surely even a scoundrel like you wouldn't manhandle a woman."

"That does it," Nick said.

His dark face a mask of rage, he reached out, grabbed Kay, and forcefully swung her up into his arms.

"Put me down!" Kay shouted, incredulous, finally intimidated.

Caught off guard, she was stunned by his lightning-swift possession. Shocked that the powerful arms holding her tightly had the firm consistency of steel. She felt her soft breasts being crushed against the flat, hard muscles of his broad chest. Try as she might, she couldn't push him away. Through their closely pressing bodies Kay could feel the strong, regular beating of his heart. Somehow it was extremely unsettling.

"Let me go this minute, McCabe, or you'll regret it," she shouted at him. "Help! Help! Somebody help me."

Ignoring Kay's empty threats and the patrons' derisive laughter, Nick McCabe strode determinedly through the hurly-burly with Kay struggling in his arms. Resolutely he marched, Kay kicking and clawing, past gaping, applauding customers. Agilely he climbed the white marble steps and headed for the double doors.

Nick kicked one of the black leather doors open wide and strode through it. Deaf to Kay's screeches and blind to the wild red hair that had come undone and whipped about in his face, he set her on her feet on the sidewalk. But he continued to hold her with one long arm clamped tightly around her waist.

Bracing Kay's slender, squirming body against his own, Nick roughly jerked her uniform's high collar open. Kay's red face grew redder and she clawed at his hand. Still Nick managed to deftly undo several buttons. Outraged, fearful of what he might do next, Kay crossed her arms protectively over her breasts.

"Don't flatter yourself," said Nick.

He reached into his pocket, withdrew several greenbacks, and stuffed the bills down into the opened bodice of her blue jacket. Kay winced when his long fingers grazed naked flesh.

Unmoved, Nick said, "Here's your contribution." He shoved the money down inside Kay's white cotton chemise. "Now stay out of the Golden Carousel."

His hand immediately slid up to encircle Kay's throat, thumb and long fingers firmly gripping the sides of her slender neck so that she couldn't turn away.

Nick lowered his dark, chiseled face to within inches of Kay's. So close she could feel his warm breath on her cheeks. His narrowed silver eyes holding her startled blue gaze, he said in low, dangerous tones, "I've been patient this time, Captain Kay. I won't be again."

His tanned fingers lingered for a moment longer on her soft throat. He saw the firm set of her jaw, the snapping heat in her expressive blue eyes. His hard face softened slightly. His full lips turned up into a hint of a devilish grin.

"Sweetheart, you stick to your suckers and I'll stick to mine."

Nick released her then, dusted his hands together, and straightened his black silk tie. He motioned his bouncer, now rousing and rubbing his aching head, to follow him back inside.

Big Alfred obeyed.

But Nick wasn't looking and the Englishman grinned and winked at Kay. He admired her spirit.

In truth, so did Nick McCabe.

Grudgingly.

Chapter 8

 Nick's grin was easy and charming as he strolled back inside. He sauntered up to the box where the Packards awaited. Standing, he extended an open hand to Adele Packard. Her eyes questioning, she placed her pale fingers atop Nick's hard palm.

Nick bent from the waist, pressed his lips to the back of her hand, then straightened.

"If you'll both forgive me, I think I'll make an early evening of it." Nick released Adele's hand and turned to Pat Packard. "Truth is, I haven't been feeling too well lately."

"Sorry to hear that, McCabe." Pat Packard was gracious. "Nothing serious, we hope."

"No, no," Nick assured, tapping his chest with a lean index finger. "A little lingering congestion from a summer cold. Nothing more. Doc says I should get plenty of—"

"I know exactly what you need, Nick," Adele Packard interrupted. "A hot toddy. Pat fixes a hot toddy like no one else in San Francisco."

Nick decisively shook his dark head. "I'm sure that's true, but a good night's rest . . . that's what I need." He smiled and added, "You two stay as long as you like. Order anything you want. Compliments of the house. I've enjoyed this evening tremendously." Nick shook Pat's hand, anxious to get away.

To his dismay, the white-gowned Adele Packard reached out, caught his arm. "Our feelings are going to be terribly hurt if you don't join us for at least one nightcap." She clung tenaciously to Nick's tuxedo jacket sleeve. "Our carriage stands waiting outside. The coachman is on the box." Nick was vigorously shaking his head but Adele hurried on, "We can be up the hill in no time. William will drive you back down—once you've had your rejuvenating toddy."

"No." Nick was firm. Between this rich man's wayward wife and the stubborn Salvation Army captain, Nick had had enough of this evening. "No, I'm sorry."

"Pat, do something," Adele demanded.

Pat Patrick gave her an exasperated look. "Now, Adele, dear . . ."

"Pat, did you hear me!" She was adamant. "Tell Mr. McCabe that we simply refuse to take no for an answer."

Sheepishly Pat Packard looked up at Nick, shrugged, and asked hopefully, "Can't we persuade you to come uptown for a quick hour? My sister's a rather determined woman and she—"

"Your sister?" Nick interrupted, his dark eyebrows lifting inquisitively. "You're her brother?" He shot a hard glance at the cool, cunning Adele.

Smiling with self-satisfaction, she nodded her perfectly coiffured blond head and her eyes gleamed with naughty mischief.

"Dear me," Adele trilled. "Have we unwittingly misled you?" She laughed low in her throat. "Unforgivable! We apologize, don't we, Pat." Not giving her brother the opportunity to answer, she added, "Do you feel up to just one little nightcap, Nick?"

"What are we waiting for?" Nick's killer smile was back in place. Dramatically he laid a spread hand on his chest. "I have just made a remarkable recovery."

The Packards laughed.

So did Nick.

Outside the trio split up. Pat Packard graciously, at Adele's suggestion, agreed to take a hansom cab back to his Mason Street home atop Nob Hill.

They said their good nights and Nick and Adele climbed into the waiting midnight-blue carriage. Adele settled herself comfortably on the claret-colored leather seat, turned, and smiled invitingly at Nick. Nick sat there, his long legs crossed, leaning back, looking thoughtfully at the platinum-haired beauty.

He noted the rapid beating of the pulse in her ivory throat. And how her dark eyes flashed in the shadowy light. The white satin of her evening gown shimmered, and Nick knew she had begun to tremble with expectation.

His legs came uncrossed. He unbuttoned his tuxedo jacket. He smiled at the blond beauty, knowing she was dying for him to kiss her, determined he would make her wait.

Nick moved closer. He took her hand in his and found the slender fingers stiff and cold. He laughed, a low, teasing laugh. He placed her hand atop his hard thigh and released it, lifting his long arm around her. He gently squeezed her bare shoulders and drew her very close.

Head tipped back, her eyes on his firm sensual mouth, Adele Packard waited breathlessly for Nick to kiss her. Nick's lips parted, slowly descended, and then paused an inch from her quivering red-painted mouth. He left her lips unkissed, lowered his dark head, and pressed his hot open mouth to the delicate hollow of her throat.

He placed a long plucking kiss there and heard Adele Packard whisper his name. Lips never lifting, Nick's dark face began slowly moving downward. He continued kissing the warm ivory flesh exposed above Adele's daringly low-cut white evening gown. And when, fifteen minutes later, the gleaming midnight-blue carriage pulled to a stop, she was squirming and sighing, her hand clutching at the raven hair of Nick's head, her dark eyes closed in sheer ecstasy.

With the ease and grace of a man to the manner born, Nick stepped down to the pebbled drive before Adele Packard's baronial Nob Hill mansion on lofty Sacramento Street. He turned to help the shaken Adele alight from the carriage.

The blue carriage rolled away.

He and Adele Packard stood facing each other in the chilly San Francisco summer night. A gentle wind out of the east ruffled Nick's wavy black hair. And pressed the slithery fabric of Adele's white satin evening gown against her voluptuous curves. A foghorn sounded far out on the bay.

Nick stepped closer.

Without a word he reached up and plucked the diamond-studded restraints from Adele's fancy coiffure. He watched enraptured as her white-blond hair cascaded down around her ivory shoulders. A loose lock blew across her upturned face. With his little finger, Nick gently brushed it back.

"It's nearing midnight," he idly commented.

"The carriage doesn't turn into a pumpkin at the stroke of twelve, Nick," Adele said softly. "Nor do I."

"All evening long I've wondered," Nick continued, his intense gaze locked on the shiny white-blond tresses tossing about in the chill night winds, "is that the *real* color of her hair?" His eyes finally lowered, met and held hers. "Is it, my sweet?"

"Come inside," Adele murmured breathlessly. "Find out for yourself."

Midnight had come and gone.

Kay wearily climbed the wooden stairs to her rented fourth-floor room. Her feet ached. So did her back. She was tired and dirty and hungry. Selfish though it was, Kay couldn't help wishing for a clean, soft feather bed. And a deep porcelain tub filled with glistening bubbles. And a white-clothed table atop which an array of rich, tempting foods was laid out.

Mentally she scolded herself.

She should be ashamed of herself! Thousands of homeless would be grateful for any kind of shelter from the cold; the simplest of meals to stave off their constant hunger. She was a fortunate woman. There was no excuse for this uncharacteristic and unforgivable lapse into fruitless envy.

Kay knew what had caused it.

It was seeing all those well-dressed people, laughing, eating, drinking. Enjoying themselves in Nick McCabe's evil, elegant saloon. Kay ground her teeth. No doubt about it, the wicked certainly did flourish! The dark, sleek Nick McCabe surely dined on the finest of foods, wasted gallons of hot water for his daily bath, and slept on the softest of clean, snowy-white sheeted beds!

Stop it, Kay warned.

When she'd given herself a harsh talking-to, she retired for the night to her narrow, lumpy cot. Stretching and sighing with the physical pleasure of simply lying down, she felt herself begin to relax fully. The tension left her tired shoulders. Tight, aching tendons in her slender legs slackened.

Kay's habit was to make plans each night at bedtime for the following day. To carefully chart a schedule for her and the soldiers.

Kay sighed heavily. Then yawned.

She was *so* weary. Right now she really didn't feel up to charting tomorrow's strategy. She didn't feel like thinking, much less planning. She wanted to do nothing more than float in that peaceful never-never land somewhere between wakefulness and slumber.

She sighed again, more deeply. Heavy lashes closing over her burning blue eyes, Kay gave in to fatigue. Ungoverned thoughts took over, flitting through her brain. Unbidden images rose in the darkness.

From out of her subconscious came a vivid memory of Curly celebrating his sixth birthday. Clearly Kay could see the tousle-haired, awkward Curly; both knees skinned, his two front teeth missing, happily blowing out the candles on a big chocolate birthday cake.

As quickly as he had appeared, the six-year-old Curly was gone. Nudged aside by the disturbing vision of a fully grown, potently masculine Nick McCabe. Kay sleepily wondered what the handsome sinner with the silver eyes had been like when he was six years old.

Her lips twitched involuntarily. She pictured a beautiful child with a mass of jet-black curls and those strange, pale eyes so striking in a handsome little olive face.

Kay couldn't hold the image. It vanished swiftly and the grown-up Nick was back. Nick with his dangerous gaze resting fully on her. Nick with his incredibly powerful arms holding her crushed against his warm, solid chest. Nick with his long, tanned fingers thrust down inside her uniform jacket.

Kay flushed with heat and shame. She turned fretfully onto her left side and drew her knees up to her chest. She squenched her closed eyes more tightly together in an attempt to shut out the sight of the dark, devilish Nick.

She deliberately summoned Curly back into her thoughts. Not the child, but the man. Her compressed lips again stretched into a smile. Her brother, thank Heaven, was the exact opposite of Nick McCabe. And not only in looks.

Nick McCabe was an unprincipled, hedonistic infidel who drank, swore, gambled, and made love to an untold number of women.

Curly Montgomery—bless his sweet heart—was a moral, selfless young Christian Soldier who did not drink, swear, or gamble. And he would not know a woman in the biblical sense until he had taken the sacred vows of marriage.

Curly crowded out all thoughts of Nick McCabe as Kay exhaled slowly and sleep crept steadily closer. Where, oh where, was Curly? Now, this minute? What was her dear, missing brother doing in the middle of this dark, chilly San Francisco night?

A scant few blocks from Kay's shabby fourth-floor room, a beautiful young woman with glossy chestnut hair anxiously opened the door to a cheerful, attractively furnished dwelling on Vallejo Street. Smiling, she unlocked the door and rushed inside.

A tall young man awaited her. He came swiftly to his feet. A broad grin instantly appeared on his boyish face. It was matched by the happy smile of the young woman.

The pair met in the center of the lamp-lit room. At once they were in each other's arms. They kissed eagerly, anxiously, as if it had been days since last they'd been together. It had been but a few short hours.

"I thought the time would never pass," the man said hoarsely, burying his face in the woman's fragrant chestnut hair.

"I know." Her childlike voice was muffled against his white shirt front. "I missed you so."

"Guess what? I won thirty-five dollars playing faro down at Three Fingers Jackson's place."

"That's wonderful. I made a hundred dollars in tips."

He hugged her tight.

"We're rich."

"Mmmmm. You hungry? Wanna send out for steaks and a bottle of wine?"

"I have an appetite," he said, stroking her hair, "but not for a steak."

She laughed, then raised her head to look up into his eyes. Her slender fingers going to the buttons of his white shirt, she said, "Me too, darling. Me too."

They hurriedly began undressing each other. In seconds the woman's skimpy glittering pink costume and the man's clothes lay discarded on the carpeted floor. Naked, they stood in the mellow lamplight, clinging to each other, kissing hotly, murmuring endearments.

The tall, spare man held the small woman's pale, soft body possessively close to his own. The woman stood on bare tiptoe, her arms locked around his neck.

"Do you know," he said, looking into her sparkling eyes, "that it's been almost twelve hours since we last made love?"

She giggled girlishly. "Twelve hours and twenty-five minutes. But who's counting?"

"I love you," he said. "I love you so much I thought I couldn't stand it till you got home."

"I know, darling," she breathed, bending her head to sprinkle kisses over his bare chest. "But I'm here now. Back in your arms where I belong."

"Yes." He groaned, his eyes closing.

Trembling with pleasure, the man's large hands lifted to gently urge the woman's head back. Cupping her glowing face, he again looked into her eyes.

"Promise you'll make love to me the rest of the night, darlin'."

"I promise," she said, nodding. "All night. Every night."

He lowered his face to hers. She stretched up on tiptoe to kiss him. When at last their lips separated, the starry-eyed young man said, "Rose, sweetheart. My wild Irish Rose. I love you, Rose."

"And I love you," she replied in a soft whisper.

Her fingers tunneled eagerly into his thick healthy hair. Sighing with joy, she clutched double handfuls of the flaming red curls she loved to touch.

"Curly," she breathed. "My darling Curly."

Chapter 9

 An aged Chinese flower girl slowly pushed her cart along Pacific Street on a dark, cloudy September afternoon. The woman was small and pudgy and wore baggy black pants and a drab green silk jacket, faded and frayed at cuffs and collar.

Her shoulders were stooped and rounded. Her watery brown eyes blinked owlishly at passersby. Her cheeks sagged against the corners of her mouth, forming sad droopy creases.

The old woman moved at a snail's pace along Pacific, her veined and wrinkled hands pushing the creaking wooden flower cart before her.

Abruptly she stopped.

Her watery brown eyes blinked, widened, then shone with a new light. Her tired, stooped shoulders straightened minutely. The corners of her drooping mouth lifted into a smile.

All because a tall, lean man had just emerged from a white stucco-fronted building. He stood on the sidewalk squinting up at the gray leaden sky. He sniffed at the scent of rain in the heavy air.

The man's wavy black hair was neatly brushed back off his high forehead. He was immaculate in a freshly laundered ice-blue cotton shirt and a pair of carefully pressed buff-colored trousers. On his feet were English glove-leather brown shoes.

Nick McCabe felt someone's eyes on him. He turned his dark head, saw the old Chinese flower girl, and started toward her.

Smiling broadly.

"How's my best sweetheart?" he asked, reaching her. Nick gently touched the old woman's wrinkled cheek, and added, "You're looking mighty pretty this afternoon, Kou Jen."

The beaming flower girl automatically lifted a veined hand to push back wisps of coarse gray hair that had escaped the long plaited queue hanging down her back. Joyfully she watched the tall young man carefully choose colorful blossoms from her loaded cart. Kou Jen helpfully pointed out to him the freshest flowers.

She also filled Nick in on what she'd heard that morning down at the Mission Pier fish market.

Her brown eyes darting cautiously around, she leaned over the cart and spoke in low, conspiratorial tones. "Nichoras, very sad thing happen. Two more Chinese children disappear from streets yesterday."

Nick stopped choosing flowers. His warm smile vanished. Pinning the old Chinese woman with narrowed silver-gray eyes, he muttered, "God, no! Jesus Christ!" His dark, handsome face was as hard as granite.

Kou Jen nodded. "Grab up little children and sell them into—"

"I know," Nick cut her off, sickened at the thought. "It has to be stopped!" Nick bit out his words.

"What have to be stopped?" asked Ling Tan, Nick's slender houseboy. He approached with an empty straw basket over his arm. "Good afternoon, Kou Jen." Ling Tan politely bowed to the old flower girl.

"A pleasure to see you, Ling Tan." Kou Jen returned the bow and smiled.

Seeing Ling Tan made Nick think immediately of his servant's young daughter, Ming Ho. Nick said, frowning, "Two more Chinese children are missing off the streets."

The aged flower girl said, "Your daughter Ming Ho very pretty young girl. Not safe."

Nodding, Ling Tan replied, "Most dangerous. I caution Ming Ho many times. Tell her she not to go out alone."

"She must *never* forget," warned Nick.

Nick placed his gathered bunches of flowers into the straw basket Ling Tan held out. He didn't stop until the large basket was filled to overflowing with colorful blossoms.

Bowing and bidding the old woman good day, Ling Tan hurried back inside, carrying Nick's basket of flowers. Nick waited until his houseboy had gone. Then he pressed a shiny twenty-dollar gold piece in Kou Jen's hand. Her old eyes danced with delight at his generosity.

But Kou Jen shook her graying head and protested, "No, Nichoras Daniel McCabe!" She clutched the large heavy coin tightly in her hand. "No can take. Pay too much for flowers."

"Did I?" Nick asked, as if surprised. He shook his dark head. "Sorry, Kou Jen, I have nothing smaller." He shrugged wide shoulders.

Eagerly pocketing the gold piece, a smiling Kou Jen asked, "Business good, Nichoras?"

Nick grinned. "With Rose Reilly there's been standing room only on—on—"

Nick abruptly stopped speaking and listened.

Did he hear bells?

Before he could turn to look, he heard more than bells. The sound of a poorly played coronet and the throb of a booming bass drum carried on the rain-scented air.

Nick McCabe's thick eyebrows always grew darker whenever he got angry. They were almost black now.

He slowly turned as the first sprinkles of rain fell from the leaden sky. Nick never noticed. His undivided attention was directed to a slender, blue-uniformed woman a block away.

Captain Kay Montgomery, silver bell in hand, led her ragtag platoon of soldiers up Pacific Street. Heading right in his direction. Her army had grown in number. Nick counted an even dozen men following the fiery captain. Some wore uniforms, others were dressed in ragged street clothes.

For a long moment Nick watched the advancing Army with a mixture of resentment and admiration. He sighed and shook his head. The flame-haired Army captain was one stubborn female. A royal pain. Clearly there was no scaring her. She was here to stay and the devil take the hindmost.

She halfway reminded Nick of himself when he was a kid of twenty-one and had opened his first joint on the Barbary Coast. The big boys had tried their best to shut him down, to muscle him out, to scare him away. It hadn't worked. He'd hung in despite the threats and beatings and strong-arm tactics.

Nick sighed heavily and looked down at the old flower girl. He caught Kou Jen smiling, her watery eyes atwinkle.

"So," he said, "you've heard about the religious invaders, have you?"

The old woman smiled with merriment. Bobbing her gray head, she said, "I hear red-haired lady preacher march right inside the Carousel Club." Giggling like a young girl, she added, "She hit Big Alfred on head and knock him senseless!"

"That's a fact," Nick admitted. Finally he grinned. He looked again toward the advancing Salvation Army. His gaze rested solely on the slim, black-bonneted leader. "What say, Kou Jen? You agree that feisty red-haired captain's just askin' for trouble?"

Smiling up at him, old Kou Jen said, "Captain might hand out some trouble too, Nichoras."

Continuing to grin, Nick's dark head swung around. Nodding, he winked at the old Chinese woman, then rolled his eyes skyward and said, "Heaven help us."

*   *   *

Captain Kay spotted Nick McCabe standing on the sidewalk with the old Chinese flower girl. Her heart skipped a couple of beats and the wispy hair at the nape of her neck stood on end.

Kay told herself that Nick McCabe didn't make her the least bit nervous. She was totally unconcerned with his presence. Let him stand there on the sidewalk and watch to his heart's content. She couldn't—wouldn't—be bothered by anything the black-hearted saloon owner might choose to say or do.

But Kay was more than a little relieved when Nick abandoned his post, driven indoors by the lightly falling rain. With that annoying hindrance out of the way, Kay marched confidently forward. She was guardedly optimistic on this overcast rainy afternoon.

Captain Kay felt that she had made progress, had done *some* measure of good since arriving on the coast. Her Army was growing and so were the meager contributions. They'd collected enough money to purchase a shiny brass coronet, a big bass drum, and an accordion. And, in her opinion, the dedicated soldiers playing the new instruments didn't sound half bad.

Giles Lawton was a natural on the coronet. Bobby Newman's fervor as he beat on the bass drum overcame his lack of perfect rhythm. And Matthew—the dried-out drunk from the Front Street jail—had obviously played either the piano or the accordion his past years, even if he couldn't remember it. He was amazing. He could play perfectly any religious song she mentioned.

So with shining blue eyes and hopeful heart, Captain Kay Montgomery proudly led her Army down Pacific Street, attracting the curious, irritating the jaded, and offering hope to the lost.

The Army halted. They came to a parade rest directly in front of the closed and darkened Carousel Club. Lifting her well-worn Bible, Kay preached to the gathering crowd, her manner one of open friendliness, her message presented in simple, straightforward words.

The falling rain increased steadily. Sporadic sprinkles soon turned to large, wind-driven drops. Captain Kay and her troops were undeterred. They calmly abided, refusing to let a little rain dampen their spirit.

While water dripped off her wide hat brim and peppered her fair face, Captain Kay stood unmoving, unblinking in the middle of the street, bent on bringing the Divine word to all those who would listen.

As Kay spoke, her firm, clear voice lifting to be heard above the growing rainstorm, a trio of handsomely dressed people came out of

Three Fingers Jackson's Top Hat Club half a block up the street. A man and two women.

The man was of medium height, his head totally bald, and his left eye was covered with a black patch. He held a huge black umbrella over the heads of his two tall, expensively attired female companions. The trio was in high spirits, laughing gaily as they made their slow, unsteady way to their waiting carriage.

The bald gentleman with the black eye patch was the first of the three to spot the Salvationists. He pointed them out to his tipsy companions. The elegant ladies were amused and delighted by the strange performance taking place in the middle of the rainy street. Both insisted they move up closer. To watch the show.

Laughing and stumbling, the trio came closer. They stood on the sidewalk beneath the large umbrella and listened. Soon the three began shouting insults. They poked fun at the Salvation Army, especially at the lady leader. They found it great sport to ridicule Captain Kay Montgomery and her cause.

Kay ignored the drunken hecklers.

She continued with her message, again lifting her voice so she could be heard over the pounding rain and the jeering of the well-dressed hecklers. She let the shouted insults slide right off just like the rivulets of chill autumn rain that streaked down her face.

Warming to their newfound diversion, the rude snobs were enormously enjoying their japes. Cruelly they mocked and jeered. A gathering crowd took up their chant.

But their game came to a decisive and abrupt halt when Big Alfred Duke, Nick's massive bouncer, suddenly appeared from out of nowhere.

Laughter died on their lips when the huge Brit, his ruddy face bloodred with anger, stormed over to the trio.

He ripped the black umbrella from the surprised bald man's hand, then rushed out into the street to hold it protectively over Kay's head. His booming voice louder than the thunder crashing down over the bay, the Englishman ordered the gathered crowd to maintain a respectful silence or answer to him. Daring anybody to make a peep, he smiled kindly down at Kay and gallantly invited her to continue with her sermon.

Kay looked up at the large man and silently thanked him with her eyes.

Stunned into complete sobriety, the bald man with the black eyepatch silently backed away, keeping his one good eye trained on the angered giant. His two nervous lady friends swiftly followed suit. All were soaked to the skin and their finery ruined by the time they reached their carriage.

The rain stopped in half an hour.

But Big Alfred Duke stayed with Captain Kay and her Army throughout the long, cloudy afternoon. And on into the early autumn dusk.

He listened. He learned. He marched. He sang.

And when darkness descended over the coast, Nick McCabe paced restlessly in his office. The hour swiftly approached for the Carousel Club to open its doors. All afternoon and evening he'd been looking for his English bouncer.

Big Alfred wasn't in his room. No one had seen him.

Not the croupiers or the waiters or the musicians. None of the female entertainers had seen the big Brit. No, said the cooks, he hadn't been in the kitchen to eat his evening meal. It had grown cold on the table.

Ling Tan was summoned to Nick's quarters. "Do you know which joint is presently Big Alfred's favorite gambling spot?"

Ling Tan was quick to answer. "Alfred spend free time at English Jim's Royal Palace on Grant."

"That's it, then," said Nick. "He got to shooting dice and lost track of time. Will you go get him, please?"

"Sure thing, boss. Go now. Chop chop."

But later Ling Tan, out of breath and shaking his head, returned to inform Nick that no one at English Jim's or at any of Big Alfred's former favorite hangouts had seen the big Brit.

"Most apologetic, boss," Ling Tan said.

"He'll show up," Nick calmly assured the Chinese servant. "Go on. I know it's your evening to play *pai jow* with your friends."

"You sure?" Ling Tan reached up and pulled the long plaited queue over his left shoulder. "Not necessary I go."

Nick grinned. If Ling Tan had to miss his weekly Chinese dominoes-style game of *pai jow* he'd be fit to be tied. Nick pointed to the door. The smiling Ling Tan bowed and eagerly backed away.

Puzzled, half worried, Nick again took out his gold-cased pocket watch, checked the time, and shook his head. From a gleaming silver box atop his mahogany desk, he withdrew a dark, thin cigar and lit it.

Nick dropped into his swivel chair behind the desk, leaned way back, closed his eyes, and tried to think where Big Alfred might be.

A loud knock came on his office door.

Nick's eyes came open.

"Come in."

"Boss, I *am* sorry," the gigantic Englishman plunged into the room apologizing. "Awfully sorry. Really I am."

"Doesn't matter." Nick came to his feet, smiling with relief.

"I can explain, Nick."

"Not necessary," Nick assured him. "Go on. Get cleaned up and have your dinner."

Big Alfred made no move to leave. Just stayed where he was, standing across the desk from Nick, looking embarrassed or upset or both. Nick again became uneasy.

"What is it, Alfred? Something wrong? Something happen this afternoon?" Nick looked at his friend with questioning silver eyes. "Jesus, pal, you can tell me. Whatever it is, I'm with you. A heavy gambling loss? Need money? You got it! Some kind of trouble? Hell, we'll get you out of it and—"

"No, no, boss. Nothing like that," the brawny Englishman said.

Nick drew on his cigar, blew the smoke out slowly. "What's on your mind, my friend?"

"Nick, laddie, I have something to tell you and I do hope you'll not be angry."

Nick smiled easily. "Certainly not. I've never been mad at you, have I?" Big Alfred shook his head. "So? Spit it out."

"Well, laddie, you remember the red-haired Hallejulah lassie that—"

"Hit you on the head with her bell and knocked you cold? Yes, I remember her."

Big Alfred grinned. Lifting a big broad hand to touch his head, he said, "The lass does have a wee bit of a temper, but otherwise she's a mighty fine lady. She is."

Nick's dark left eyebrow lifted. "What's Captain Kay Montgomery got to do with your being late?"

"I've been with the Hallelujah lassie and her troops all afternoon." He paused, drew a big, deep breath. "Nick, it's a long shot, but you know I've always been a sucker for the underdog. That little red-haired Army captain's got a real struggle on her hands and a long hard road ahead of her. But, laddie, she's a real scrapper, and I'm casting my lot with her."

Nick stabbed his cigar out in a crystal ashtray. "What the hell are you saying?"

A wide, sheepish grin came over Big Alfred's face. "My boy, much as I hate doing it, I must leave you."

"Leave me?" Nick's eyebrows darkened dangerously and shot up. "You can't mean it. Why? Why, for God's sake?"

"Aye, that's the reason. . . . for God's sake!" The massive Brit said proudly, "Laddie, the Hallejulah lass converted me. I've joined the Salvation Army!"

"Holy smoke!"

Chapter 10

Nick McCabe's mood was foul, like the late-morning weather along the Barbary Coast. The sunless day, another in a long string of gloomy, depressing days, matched Nick's disposition perfectly.

Unshaven, wearing only a pair of tan gabardine trousers with the top button undone, Nick paced his spacious upstairs quarters above the shuttered saloon. Fidgety, agitated, he had turned his dark head and glared at Ling Tan when the Chinese servant brought in a breakfast tray. Ling Tan had made a hasty, silent retreat.

The tray still sat untouched on a table.

Those who knew him best had steered clear for the past three days, giving the bad-tempered Nick a wide berth. Ling Tan was fully aware of what was eating his boss. Nick's anger over losing Big Alfred had not yet cooled.

Born without one pinch of diplomacy, Nick burned when faced with disloyalty. Stung by the Brit's betrayal, Nick nonetheless chose to lay most of the blame where it actually belonged.

Squarely at the feet of the Scripture-quoting, red-haired Salvation Army captain.

Alfred Duke had only two weaknesses.

One was gambling. The big Englishman couldn't resist the turn of a card, the roll of the dice. A bet of any kind made his hazel eyes gleam, his big palms grow moist with excitement. He never allowed a day to pass without making at least one wager.

Alfred Duke's other frailty was women.

The keenly intelligent giant normally saw right through the cleverest of sharpies' schemes. He could smell trouble long before anyone else. He had no qualms about smashing faces and sending troublemakers to the hospital.

But when it came to the fair sex, Alfred Duke was the world's biggest pushover. An overgrown boy whose Mama had taught him to treat women—all women—with the highest degree of respect. Alfred Duke had learned the lesson well. He looked on women as fragile, rather helpless creatures to be protected and revered.

That there might be those among their number who were as wily and dangerous as the meanest of waterfront riffraff never occurred to Alfred Duke. A bad or manipulative woman? That couldn't be. He'd never met one.

Wantonly exposed in skimpy sequined costumes or modestly covered in prim, proper attire, there was something of the pure, blessed Madonna in every woman God had created. Just ask Alfred Duke.

Nick's eyes narrowed and his lips tightened.

Big Alfred, bless his guileless heart, hadn't stood a chance against the formidable Captain Kay Montgomery.

Damn the troublemaking little bitch!

Nick sat down and immediately bounced up again, prowling around his dim dreary apartment. Restless, edgy, he decided what he needed was a good stiff drink.

His narrowed gray glance touched the stoppered crystal decanters on the nearby drink trolley. Whiskey. Scotch. Gin. Brandy.

Nick snarled under his breath.

Goddammit, why was there no rum? Why was there never any rum? Who the hell wanted bourbon or brandy at ten in the morning? Rum mixed with chilled orange juice. That's what a man wanted for breakfast, for Christ sake!

Aggravated, Nick snatched a rumpled white shirt from a chair back, shoved his long arms down into the sleeves, pulled the shirt up on his broad shoulders, but didn't bother buttoning it down his naked chest. Wearing only house slippers on his tanned feet, Nick stormed across the room.

He jerked open the apartment's front door, stepped out onto the second-floor landing overlooking the silent saloon, and headed for the stairs. Squinting in the deep shadows, Nick immediately noticed that one of the club's black double doors stood open to the gray dismal day.

Warily he descended the marble steps, caught a movement at the hexagonal bar beneath the stilled carousel, and went forward to investigate. Nick's dark scowl turned to a smile when he saw who was there.

Stuffing the long tails of his wrinkled shirt down inside his trousers, Nick said, "What are you doing here by yourself? Couldn't sleep?"

"No. And I was tired of lying in bed. Thought if I dropped by the club I could scare up a drink." On the polished mahogany bar sat a bottle of rum and a crystal pitcher of chilled orange juice. "You don't mind, do you, Nick?"

"Hell, no. In fact I'll join you." Nick smiled for the first time that morning. "Long as you're back there, pour me a slug of that demon rum into some juice."

"Coming right up."

Preoccupied, Captain Kay Montgomery made her cautious way along Pacific Street in the thick morning fog. Up since daybreak, she had gotten a lot done. An early practice session with the Army band. Then she and Big Alfred, his gargantuan arms loaded with bags of food, called on half a dozen needy families. After that the brief daily stop by the Battery Street Orphanage.

She rushed now toward California Street to catch one of those terrifying cable cars for a ride up to the city's financial district. A good hour early, Kay couldn't wait to keep the appointment at an attorney's office. To pick up a key from him.

The key unlocked the door of an empty waterfront warehouse.

Captain Kay had no idea how Big Alfred had managed, but last evening the Englishman had disappeared for a couple hours. He'd returned with a huge grin on his florid face and the announcement that he'd located a place for the Army's temporary headquarters. An abandoned waterfront warehouse was theirs to occupy for the next six months! The building's owner had recently sold the property to the city for razing, but contract closing and possession wouldn't take place until April 1, 1884.

"Now, lassie, the place isn't much, you understand? It has been standing vacant for years," Big Alfred had pointed out.

"I couldn't be any happier if you'd delivered the Taj Mahal," Kay had exclaimed excitedly. "This is wonderful! Winter's coming on and we need a . . . who? Who is our benefactor, Alfred?"

"Ah, now, lassie, does it make any difference?"

"No, but I'd like to thank him. To at least write a letter of—"

"That won't be necessary, Captain. I told her how grateful you'd be."

"Her? Did you say her?"

"Now I've done it." The Big Englishman's face flushed. "I promised not to disclose her identity."

"And you haven't," Kay assured understandingly. She smiled at the big, kind-hearted man, lifted her slender shoulders, and said, "I have no idea who owns the warehouse, nor do I care."

"Aye, lassie, that's the spirit," said Big Alfred.

Kay strongly suspected she knew who the mystery angel was. The same woman who'd paid the bail for her release from the Front Street jail. And had disappeared before Kay could thank her.

The Lady in Black.

Now as Kay hurried up Pacific Street considering how grand it would be to hold her prayer meetings in a building since the San Francisco sun couldn't always be counted on, the sun suddenly broke through a dense blanket of fog.

Kay laughed aloud. She stopped for a minute, blinked in the brightness of the unexpected light, then set off again, picking up her pace.

Kay's wide smile soon vanished.

She made a sour face when she reached the Carousel Club. Automatically she tipped her bonneted head back and glanced at the upstairs window.

Lowering her eyes, Kay started to smile again. She needn't be worried about running into the sinister saloon owner at this early hour. Most likely he was passed out in a deep, drunken slumber.

Disgusting!

Kay noticed that one of the Golden Carousel's black entrance doors was open. She shrugged and continued her approach. If you asked her, the smelly gin palace could do with a good airing!

Just before Kay reached the saloon's open door—she was still a few steps away—she heard voices. Then one voice. A distinctly familiar male voice that made her stop short.

Kay's hand flew to her breast. Her heart began to thunder against her ribs. Her eyes closed and her lips fell open. She stood there on the sidewalk in the brilliant sunshine, shaking her head as if to clear it.

Kay opened her eyes, listened, and heard it again. That well-remembered voice. That warm, appealing baritone. Speaking rapidly, with the customary high degree of boyish excitement. Talking fast. About a woman. A beautiful woman.

At last a pause.

And a deep, low-pitched voice making an unhurried reply. Then rumbling male laughter.

Kay burst eagerly forward and poked her head in the Golden Carousel's open door. Squinting and blinking furiously to see, she peered into the club's dim interior.

And there, across the grand salon, framed in a shaft of sunshine, the King of the Barbary Coast stood enveloped in a blue haze of cigar smoke.

Nick McCabe, a black stubble of beard covering his lower face, his white shirt open indecently down his dark chest, lounged against a tall bar stool. He held a glass in one tanned hand, a thin cigar in the other.

He was laughing.

Kay grimaced with distaste.

Her gaze quickly dismissed Nick, went anxiously to the tall man who stood behind the bar. He held a liquor bottle in his right hand, a glass of juice in the left. He was grinning as he poured colorless liquid from the bottle into the juice. He drank of the liquor-laced juice, then placed glass and bottle on the bar.

Kay's eyes went from wide to wider.

Chapter 11

"Curly," she said soundlessly, her lips trembling. "Dear, dear Curly." Seconds passed before she found her voice. "Curly Montgomery!"

Startled, both men turned at once to look, but said nothing.

On seeing Kay, Curly Montgomery blinked and swallowed hard. Nick's silver eyes narrowed while a dark look flashed across his unshaven face.

Kay came charging toward them.

Unsure of what she might do or say, Curly hastily turned up the liquor bottle and took a long, spine-stiffening pull of straight rum. He set the bottle down and wiped his mouth.

He inhaled and put what he hoped was an irresistible grin on his boyish face. Then he placed his hands atop the polished bar and agilely leapt over it.

"Kay." He threw his long arms open wide. "Kay, my own dear sister, come here to me!"

"Curly, oh, Curly," Kay cried in undisguised joy, and happily threw herself into his outstretched arms.

Curly enfolded his slender sister in his close embrace.

"It's really you. Oh, thank God. You're alive, you're alive." Kay sniffed into his shirt front. "My baby brother. Are you all right? Curly, I've been so worried. I was so afraid you'd been badly hurt and—"

"There, there, Kay," Curly gently interrupted. Tenderly comforting her, he patted her back and murmured, "I'm fine. Just fine."

He winked at Nick over her head. Nick nodded almost imperceptibly and took a drink.

As if Curly hadn't spoken, Kay continued, her words muffled against his chest. ". . . and to every hospital and . . . the police station . . . possibility you had been shanghaied . . . knocked on the head . . ."

On and on she chattered, almost incoherent with relief, clutching tightly to Curly's shirt front as if she would never let him go while tears of happiness filled her eyes. Curly let her talk. His hands lifting, he thoughtfully untied the streamers of her black straw bonnet and drew the hat from her head, handing it to Nick. Nick dropped it atop his knee.

". . . and always the terrible nagging fear that you'd been robbed and killed for the mission money . . . wondered so many times if you'd been left lying in an alley somewhere and . . . and . . . oh, Curly, Curly, you're safe, you're all right . . . you . . ."

She was winding down, slowing her speech, regaining her composure. Kay finally stopped speaking. For a moment longer she stayed as she was, her forehead resting on her tall, lanky brother's chest, her hands gripping his shirt.

Her head lifted. She leaned back and looked up at Curly. Her tear-filled eyes began to change. To snap with anger.

"Curly Montgomery, what are you doing here in this vile place? Where on earth have you been all these weeks?" Kay released her grip on him.

She took a step backward, glaring at Curly, waiting for an explanation. Nick, seated on the bar stool at her elbow, had forgotten his own earlier anger. Mellowed by the rum, he thought idly that Kay's hair, caught in the shaft of sunlight, was the exact color of burning embers.

Unfortunately, that remarkable shade of hair was not the only thing about Captain Kay Montgomery that burned.

Her temper burned as well.

Kay's fair face turned bloodred. Her eyes shot off sparks of blue fire. Her balled fists went to her hips and her firm chin jutted pugnaciously.

Nick was both amazed and amused by the quick transformation. Gone was the tearful, relieved older sister crying and clinging desperately to the prodigal brother in happy reunion.

In her place stood a fiery, unforgiving woman whose exploding white-hot anger was so impressive in its ferocity, Nick was glad it wasn't directed at him.

"Answer me, Walter Curly Montgomery!" Kay was shouting. "Where have you been all this time I was worried sick?"

"Now, Kay, honey, it hasn't been that long." Curly tried to win her over with another of his best boyish grins. It didn't work. Curly grew nervous. "I got a little sidetracked is all and I—"

"Sidetracked?" she hissed. "You got a little sidetracked?"

"Well, yes, I did. I . . . look, as soon I got to town, Kay, I started thinking about building the mission. You know, just like I was supposed to do."

"And? Where is it? Where is this mission? I couldn't find it. Is there a mission, Curly? And why aren't you there?"

"Well, now, Kay, slow down. I'm coming to that part." Curly cleared his dry throat, wishing he could reach for the bottle, take a big drink of rum. He didn't dare. "Like I said, I was going to start building the mission on that lot the Army held a deed to and—"

"Held? Did you say held? Don't you mean holds? Doesn't the Army still have the deed and the property?"

At the mention of the deed, Nick McCabe squirmed a little. "If you two will excuse me, I'll—"

"We most certainly will not!" Kay snapped, already smelling a rat. She cut her eyes suspiciously at Nick, then back. "Curly Montgomery, you came to San Francisco entrusted with the deed to a piece of valuable property and twenty thousand dollars in cash. Do you have the deed? The money? I demand some straightforward, honest answers."

"I—I, ah . . . located the lot." Curly inclined his head. "It's close to the waterfront, not far from here." He tried one last adorable smile on his angry, older sister. No results. He stumbled on. "I . . . ah . . . figured it'd be a good spot for the Army's station . . . you know, since we needed . . . I mean, we need to . . . to be close to all the . . . the . . ."

"Sinners!" Kay supplied the word, glancing pointedly at Nick.

Nick quickly turned his head, looked around searchingly, then tapped his chest with a forefinger, his expression one of mock inquiry that asked, "Who? You mean me?" Then he smiled with deviltry when Kay's jaw tightened visibly.

"Yes. That's right." Curly was nodding eagerly. "I needed to be close to the sinners, so that's why I—I . . . spent so much time down here on the Barbary Coast and . . . and . . ."

"Just where is the Army's new mission, Curly? I've been all over the waterfront. I haven't found it."

"Well, that's just it, Kay, I'm trying to explain. The mission's not quite built . . . not yet. You see—"

"No, I don't see," Kay cut in. "Or do I?" She visibly bristled. "Tell me I'm wrong, Curly. Tell me you'd never be foolish and irresponsible. Say you'd not allow one penny of the Army's precious money to be spent on anything other than the saving of lost souls."

Curly hung his head in shame. "It's not like you're thinking, Kay."

"Then tell me how it is."

Nick plucked Kay's black bonnet off his knee and again started to rise. She turned on him, "Stay right where you are, Nick McCabe!"

Nick shrugged and eased back down.

Curly slowly lifted his head. "It's no use. I can't lie to you, Kay. I never could."

He looked at her with such misery in his blue eyes, Kay softened a little. She lifted a hand, touched his jaw, and said softly, "No, you can't. Tell me, Curly. The truth."

Curly inhaled deeply. He shook his head despairingly, ran long fingers through his flaming, tousled curls. Pitifully he said, "I came to do so much good, and did so bad."

Heartsick, knowing even before he told her that Curly had squandered the Army's money, Kay gently urged him to come clean, to talk about it, to tell her everything.

Curly said nothing. Looking totally miserable, his blue eyes pleading, he did his best to play on her sympathy.

Unmoved, Kay thoroughly, pitilessly interrogated him. She fired question after question at him, demanding explanations, ordering him to supply truthful answers, bristling with impatience if he took too long to reply.

The inquisition was conducted with single-minded purpose: to get the facts, whatever they might be. Kay was relentless. She bullied and badgered Curly until she finally got at the truth.

The more she learned about what had happened, the sicker she became. Feeling as if someone had doubled up a fist and hit her squarely in the stomach, Kay found it all too impossible to grasp.

Her only brother, the boyish-looking Curly, had joined the ranks of the sinners almost the minute he'd reached San Francisco. Now, quite by accident, she had found him in a saloon. Found the sweet, innocent boy who had never given her family one minute's worry drinking hard liquor in the middle of the morning, as if he were accustomed to such loathsome behavior.

And that had been only the beginning.

Her head throbbing, her stomach churning, Kay looked with disbelief at the tall, lanky red-haired man admitting he had gambled away the Army's money.

"How much money did you lose?" Kay asked. "You know how badly we need every cent. Why, hats with polished visors are ten dollars apiece and a full uniform costs—Curly, have you forgotten we were given only a year?"

"No. No, I haven't forgotten."

"One year to prove ourselves! And four months of that year have already passed! How much? How much of the Army's money did you lose?"

"All, Kay. I lost it all."

Kay felt she was going to be violently sick. "You lost it all? Dear God, Curly, how could you? Where? Where did you lose it?"

"I gambled it away, Kay. Does it matter where?" Curly said. "It's gone. Lost. I lost it! Who cares where it went?"

"I do," Kay shouted, glaring at him. "I care! I want to know where the Corps money went!" Nick McCabe cleared his throat. Kay immediately whirled on him. "It was you, wasn't it? Curly lost it here in the Golden Carousel, didn't he? All that money went right across those green baize tables and into your well-lined pockets! Am I right, Mc-Cabe?"

"Curly spent some time at the Carousel's tables." Nick was noncommittal.

"*Some* time? How long did it take, McCabe? How many hours did my brother spend here before you managed to take all his money?"

"Kay, stop it," Curly said. "I deserve your wrath. Nick doesn't."

"Oh, doesn't he?" Kay's red, angry face swung back to Curly. "The deed? He take that from you too?"

"Nick didn't take anything from me, Kay. You're totally out of line and if you—"

"*I'm* out of line!" She exploded, cutting him off. "*I'm* out of line?" she repeated, incredulous. "You're worried about this man's feelings? This . . . this greedy, grasping purveyor of sin who took the Army's money and . . . and . . . the deed? Did you let him have the deed too?"

"Well, not exactly," Curly said. A glimmer of hope lighting his vivid blue eyes, he said, "Nick's only holding it until I can raise enough money to . . . to . . . he's promised not to sell it to anyone else and . . ."

Kay's knees turned to water. Curly had not only lost all the Army's money. He had gambled away the title to the piece of valuable waterfront property meant for the mission. It too was now in the hands of Nicholas Daniel McCabe.

". . . and so all we have to do is pay Nick the weekly sum of a hundred dollars," Curly concluded hopefully.

Kay's bloodred face was now drained of color. She felt weak and dizzy, afraid she might faint.

"I believe," Nick said, genuinely concerned for Kay's welfare, "you'd better sit down for a minute, Captain. You look a little pale."

"How could you let this happen?" She wheeled angrily on him. "Why didn't you do something? Why didn't you stop him?"

"Why, Captain." Nick's expression was one of innocence. "Am I *your* brother's keeper?"

The paraphrase made Kay more furious. She blamed Nick for everything that had happened. And he wasn't the least bit sorry! It wasn't poor Curly's fault. It was Nick McCabe's! Nick had led him astray. Nick had fleeced Curly.

Kay glared at Nick, her fists again planted firmly on her hips. She spoke with the unbending assurance of someone who was solidly in the right.

"You are despicable," she said. "A no-good, two-bit hustler and card shark!"

"Kay!" Curly warned.

She went on. "A drunk and a womanizer! You liar, you thief, you—"

"You'll be insulting me in a minute," said Nick.

"You'd steal the pennies off a dead man's eyes. You'd sell your grandmother to buy yourself one more week in this fur-lined den of iniquity! You are the vilest, the lowest . . . and you call yourself a man?"

"Only as a term of reproach, I assure you." Nick's silver-gray eyes shone with a hint of amusement.

"Kay, stop it, Nick never—" Curly touched her arm.

"Shut up, Curly!" She shrugged his hand away, never taking her eyes off Nick. "You are wicked through and through, Nick McCabe. The devil's own spawn!"

Livid, out of control, Captain Kay Montgomery stood there in the shaft of morning sunlight and gave Nick McCabe the tongue-lashing of his life. Allowing her to vent steam, Nick now knew for certain what he'd only suspected before. Perfect as she might be otherwise, Captain Kay Montgomery had at least one very human shortcoming.

She couldn't control her temper.

Finally she was done. She waited for him to speak. He said nothing.

"Well? What have you got to say for yourself, McCabe?"

Unrepentant, Nick further infuriated Kay when—as if he had never missed one day of Sunday school—he quoted in a voice low and level, " 'A soft answer turneth away wrath; but grievous words stir up anger.' " He favored her with a wicked smile and coolly added, "Proverbs 1:15, I believe."

Chapter 12

 Kay saw red.

She wanted to sock Nick McCabe right in his smug smiling mouth so badly she could taste it.

Not trusting herself, she snatched her bonnet off his knee, whirled angrily away, reached up, grabbed Curly by the ear, and dragged him out of the saloon. A surprised Curly yelped loudly with pain and indignity. She never heard him. She heard nothing but the infuriating sound of Nick McCabe's low derisive laughter.

"Owwww!" Curly howled when they got outside. "Let go, Kay. That hurts!"

"Does it? I hope so!" Kay gave his ear a painful twist before releasing it.

"God almight—uh . . . ah . . . gee whiz," Curly muttered, rubbing his red, stinging ear.

"So? Taking the Lord's name in vain is now another of your sins? What else, Curly?" Kay grabbed his sleeve at the elbow and roughly jerked him along the sidewalk. "Drinking! Gambling! Swearing! You took to it very fast, little brother! Learn anything else from that satanic Nick McCabe?"

"Kay, for Pete's sake, people are staring," Curly protested.

"Mother, father—me, you, we've been stared at all our lives!" his sister hotly reminded him. "You were never so sensitive before!"

Kay dragged the brother who had fallen from grace straight to her Kearney Street rooming house. Forcefully she shoved him down into the room's one chair, then paced back and forth in the small space before him, trying to calm herself.

Curly kept as quiet as a church mouse. He sat in the chair with his hands laced together in his lap. How could he tell Kay there was one more little sin she didn't yet know about?

There was Rose.

At last Kay stopped pacing.

She stood in front of Curly and suddenly smiled at him. "I love you so very much, you know that, don't you?"

"I know." Curly nodded. "I'm sorry for what I've done."

"It isn't totally your fault. The Barbary Coast is undoubtedly the most evil place either of us has ever been." Kay took a shallow breath and admitted honestly, "It is wicked in an . . . an alluring . . . glamorous way."

Curly's blue eyes widened with wonder and hope. "You see it too? You can see why I—"

"I'm human, just as you are. Curly. I'd be completely blind not to see that places like the Golden Carousel are not without appeal, an excitement, a powerful degree of attraction."

Kay thought of the dark, dangerous Nick McCabe and a tiny little shiver skipped up her spine. She shrugged and her smile became more encouraging, forgiving. She laid a gentle hand atop her brother's shoulder.

"If sin were not appealing," she said softly, "would there be so many sinners?"

Curly shook his head. "No, there wouldn't. I didn't think . . . I was afraid you'd never understand."

"But I do. And so does our Heavenly Father. He knows the dangers. Knows the incredible power of the Devil. That's why the Bible tells us, 'Be not be overcome with evil, but overcome evil with good.' "

Curly again nodded and smiled for the first time since leaving the Golden Carousel. "That's it. I was just overcome with evil."

"I guess so." She touched his face affectionately. "But now you'll put all that behind you and—"

"Kay, I can't," Curly interrupted.

Kay snatched her hand away as if his skin had burned her. "What? You can't? Have you totally lost your faith?"

"No, but I've lost my heart."

Kay started to speak, but Curly stopped her. He jumped up, took Kay by both shoulders, spun her about, and sat her down in the chair.

In a great rush of words Curly Montgomery told his sister that he had fallen helplessly, hopelessly in love. He was in love with the sweetest, kindest, most beautiful girl in the world. He worshipped her, adored her, couldn't go on living without her.

Why, there was no reason why he should, Kay quickly told him. Tremendously relieved that despite his short flirtation with life on the wild side, her dear baby brother had met and fallen in love with a pure, innocent young girl, Kay rose and happily hugged him.

"Curly, I think it's wonderful. When will I meet her? Where does she live? What's her name?"

"Rose Reilly," Curly said, ready then and there to get everything off his chest and out in the open. "Rose is . . . Kay, my sweetheart Rose —she's the featured act at the Carousel Club."

Kay felt her knees turn to water. "The Wild Irish Rose?"

"You know her?"

Curly Montgomery did his best to lay aside his deep abiding passion for the beautiful Rose Reilly. And Rose made a valiant attempt to forget her big, red-haired Curly.

Both tried.

It didn't work.

The painful separation lasted for a week.

In that long, lonely week a redeemed Major Curly Montgomery marched with the Salvation Army, preached the gospel, raised money, cared for the homeless, tended the sick, and clung tenuously to his restored faith.

But oh, how he missed his sweet darling Rose. The never-ending desire to be with her—to hold her again his arms—reached the intensity of physical pain.

It was the same for Rose.

In those anguished days—and nights—they were apart, the pale, wan Rose continued to thrill crowds at the Pacific Street saloon. She sang beautifully. She danced divinely. She stripped seductively. She laughed at jokes of paying customers. She sipped champagne at tables of the rich. She charmed and conquered with her warmth and youthful beauty.

And she ached for the one man in all the world whose arms she longed to have hold her.

Rose finished her last performance of the evening. Her bright but false smile vanished the second the heavy black velvet curtain rang down. She sighed, turned, and rushed off the stage. Not bothering to change out of costume, Rose threw on a yellow rain slicker, ducked out of the club, and walked wearily home.

A light rain was falling, had been throughout the long dismal late September day. Rose carried no umbrella. The rain peppered her sad face, mingling with the hot tears that streaked down her cold cheeks.

Chilled, miserable, Rose Reilly reached the dark, silent home she had shared with Curly. Inside the once-cozy sitting room, she lit every lamp in an attempt to brighten both the room and her spirits.

To no avail.

Shadows lingered in the room's corners. Gloom shrouded her heart.

Rose Reilly could stand it no longer. So she did the only thing she could do. She drew her yellow rain slicker back on, hurried to the door, and left the Vallejo Street house, going back out into the cold, rainy night.

Walking as rapidly as her high-heeled dancing slippers would allow, the hopeful Rose Reilly headed anxiously back to Pacific Street. There she turned and hurried down toward the bay to a long-abandoned waterfront warehouse on Drumm Street.

Rose's heart was pounding and she was short of breath when she ducked inside the dank, shadowy ramshackle building. She slipped through the darkness unnoticed and onto a makeshift pew behind a post at the very back. A wooden table nearby held a huge coffee urn, several loaves of bread, pots of butter, and sliced ham.

Lanterns cast diffused light over a pitifully sparse crowd. A handful of men and a couple of women were scattered about on the temporary seats, some sound asleep and snoring loudly. Others stared and listened with open-mouthed interest to the soft-spoken man in the pulpit.

Rose's wide-eyed gaze was drawn to the tall, commanding preacher.

There on the rostrum stood her lanky, lovable, red-haired Curly. He looked different. Older. Serious. But handsome, so very handsome.

Curly now wore the distinctive Army blue. His trousers and jacket were well fitted to his tall, spare frame. A band of scarlet decorated the stand-up collar of his military-style uniform jacket. Pinned to his broad chest a gleaming silver S caught and reflected the lantern light. He was hatless and those flaming tousled curls fell over his forehead in the same appealingly, boyish way she remembered.

In Curly's raised right hand was a Holy Bible.

Entranced, the girl who loved him listened reverently as Major Curly Montgomery spoke in a calm, sure voice. With quiet authority he brought to the assembly a message of hope and solace. He assured each and every single soul in the shadowy waterfront warehouse on that chill rainy night that the Almighty was willing and ready to forgive them for their sins.

Rose waited until the stirring sermon was over, the small flock fed, and the warehouse almost empty. Then she walked shyly, uncertainly down the center aisle toward the front.

Curly gathered up his notes, put them inside his breast pocket. He extinguished the lamp atop the rostrum and stepped down from the raised board platform.

He looked up and saw her. A glorious apparition moving toward him from out of the darkness. He squinted. His heart kicked against his ribs. His youthful face broke into a wide grin and his blue eyes sparkled with joy. He hurried down to meet her, took both her hands in his.

"Rose," he said, his voice cracking with emotion, "you've come. Thank God."

Trembling now, Rose asked with childlike sincerity, "Curly—Major Montgomery—can even my kind of wickedness be forgiven?"

"Forgiven and forgotten," Captain Kay softly assured, stepping out of the shadows to join the pair. "Completely wiped out. As if it had never happened. Rose, I'm Captain Kay Montgomery. Curly's sister." Kay smiled at the pretty chestnut-haired woman, gripped her hand warmly, and added, "I hope soon I'll be your sister too."

"What's wrong with tonight?" asked Curly, slipping his long arms around Rose's waist and pulling her back against his tall frame. His lips just above her ear, he said, "Marry me, Rose Reilly. Right now. Tonight."

As Rose joyfully shook her head, Captain Kay beamed with happiness and pride.

Another triumph for the Army of God.

But the Devil had his own faithful troops.

Nick McCabe was Adam naked.

Nick lay lazily stretched out on a soft, silk-sheeted bed in a large, well-appointed, high-ceilinged bedroom.

A fine collection of Charles X furniture—table, benches, and chairs —filled the opulent master suite. Across from the bed a Venetian gilt mirror hung over a Regency marble console. A mercury-glass chandelier suspended from the ceiling cast prisms of subdued light over the elegant room, the custom bed, the naked man.

Sumptuous draperies that framed a spectacular view of the city and the bay ruffled gently in the chill autumn breeze of the late September night. Honey-colored walls and lots of gold and silver in the form of tables, chairs, sconces, and picture frames gave the spacious bedchamber a look of pure glamour.

The smooth dark skin, the perfectly toned muscles, and beautifully contoured lines of the man's naked body made him appear to be a work of art. His bare masculine presence there on the shimmering white bed made the exquisite room look complete.

A silver bucket with a bottle of French champagne chilling in its icy depths rested on one gold gilt night table beside the bed. On the other a bust of Athena, Goddess of Wisdom, was turned so that she could survey the bed's occupant.

Or occupants.

The wise Athena could clearly see that the dark, naked Adonis lying alone on the bed was distracted, preoccupied, even as his beautiful blond companion padded barefoot toward him across the deep Ispahan rug.

Nick McCabe lay naked in Adele Packard's big white bed at her Sacramento Street mansion high atop Nob Hill. Adele was not naked, not totally. But as she moved toward Nick, the incredibly provocative nightgown she wore left little or nothing to the imagination.

Fashioned of shimmering Chinese silk as white as her unbound hair, the flimsy garment plunged in front to where a sash was tied around Adele's small waist. The lovely gown reached the floor, but was slit on each side all the way up her voluptuous body, held in place by the sash at her waist.

When she walked the teasingly provocative gown exposed her long slender legs, her flaring hips, her ribs, the sides of her breasts. And more.

Adele had purposely paraded around the large room, discharging her nighttime duties. She had brushed her long white-blond hair before the Venetian mirror. She'd slowly, carefully rubbed skin-softening lotion on her slender arms and legs, stretching and stroking seductively.

And all the while she'd talked to the unresponsive man in the bed. She mentioned the opening of the opera season. Told of a new restaurant. Joked about her stuffy, straitlaced brother Patrick.

"Aren't you glad, darling," Adele said, finally joining Nick, "that one member of the Packard family enjoys a bit of adventure?"

She climbed atop the bed, knelt there, and sat back on her bare heels. The front panel of the white silk gown was caught and held tightly between her ivory thighs. Adele smiled down at the naked Nick, moved her head about so that the long white tresses would swing around over her left shoulder. She laid a hand on his taut, ridged stomach.

"Nick," she murmured in a smoky voice. "Darling, have I made you wait? I'm sorry."

She bent her head, leaned down, and began sprinkling wet, open-mouthed kisses on his chest and belly, using her tongue to arouse him. She lifted and lowered a shoulder. The white nightgown slid off and down her bare arm. Just as she'd intended. A soft coral-nippled breast escaped its white silk covering. It pressed against Nick's ribs.

Nick's tanned hand lifted from the mattress, went into the shiny white blond hair at Adele's crown. He urged her head up, drew her into his arms, and kissed her.

After only a couple of hot, open-mouthed kisses, Nick lifted Adele astride his supine body.

Adele laughed and rose up onto her knees to coyly withdraw the caught gown from between her parted thighs. She carefully spread out the shimmering silk panel on Nick's dark, hair-covered chest and belly, playfully concealing from him the thick triangle of white-gold curls and glistening feminine flesh they guarded.

Nick's dark head remained on the pillow. He slid one hand under the covering white silk, drew his middle finger down Adele's taut belly. She took in a quick breath. Nick smiled sexily. And then he caressed that which he could not see.

Adele arched her back and sighed aloud with pleasure. Loving his masterful touch, wanting him on this particular occasion to do it all—to guide himself up inside with no help from her—she eased her arm free of the gown's fallen bodice.

"Do everything, won't you, darling," she murmured breathlessly. "You do it so well, so right."

And she raised both arms, put her hands behind her head, and locked them there.

"Yes, oh yes, Nick," she breathed, looking straight into his silver eyes. "Ummmm, ahhh, make love to me."

Nick made love to her.

His skillful loving was extraordinarily pleasurable to the eager Adele. She enjoyed every delicious sensation of it, completely losing all track of time.

She kept her hands clasped behind her head throughout and her eyes open wide. It was extremely erotic to have Nick's hands touching, urging, guiding while neither she nor he could see those hands under the gown's white silk covering.

When he settled her comfortably, deeply on his hard, pulsing flesh and moved his hands to her waist, Adele still insisted on the gown remaining spread out on his chest.

And so with one creamy breast fully exposed and swaying with her frantic movements, Adele Packard ground her hips and moaned and rode her dark, naked lover's hard surging flesh to ecstasy.

Adele loved the fact that where their throbbing bodies were joined

—where Nick's crisp raven curls and sleek velvet hardness melded with her damp blond coils and wet burning softness—remained modestly covered right until the act's satisfying completion.

Even when she was in the beginning throes of sweet release and Nick exploded within her, sending her over the top, the white silk curtain of modesty remained in place.

Not until total gratification had been obtained by both did Adele strip off the nightgown, toss it aside, and fall tiredly over to stretch happily out beside Nick.

It wasn't long before Adele realized her handsome lover's thoughts were elsewhere on that cold, rainy September night.

Within minutes, she wanted him again. She lay on her side turned to him, her weight supported on an elbow. She purposely pressed her soft, naked curves to his hard, dark body. Her bare toes toying with a hair-dusted leg, she slowly slid her bent knee up his hard-muscled thigh. At the same time she reached for his groin, cupping him gently, stroking him skillfully. Without result. Frowning at the flaccid flesh enclosed in her hand, she sighed fretfully.

"What is it, darling?" Adele looked down into his face. "Is it another woman?"

"Yes," Nick said, reaching for a cigar. "But not in the way you think." He shoved a pillow against the bed's tall headboard and sat up.

"What other way is there?" Adele, pressing her slender body close, again laid a soft hand on him. She toyed with the line of black hair going down Nick's naked belly. "And who is she?"

Nick puffed his cigar to life and said, without taking it from his lips, "A red-haired, hot-tempered meddling little soul saver."

"Oh? The Salvation Army captain?" Nick had told Adele about losing his English bouncer to Captain Kay Montgomery.

Nick's sharp teeth almost cut his cigar in two. "She's the one." His silver eyes narrowed. "Last night I lost Rose Reilly to her and that damned Salvation Army."

Adele shrugged a bare ivory shoulder and said, "So you lost one of your dancing girls. You've plenty of others."

Nick's dark eyebrows turned darker. "Jesus, I'm not talking about just *any* girl. Rose Reilly is the biggest draw on the entire Barbary Coast."

Chapter 13

 What was she going to do about Nick McCabe?

Kay stared at the glistening waters of San Francisco Bay. Arms crossed over her chest, bottom lip caught between her teeth in concentration, she stood at a broken-paned window of the waterfront warehouse.

The autumn sun was high and bright, but it did little to lift Kay's drooping spirits. Nor did the deep blue bay, sparkling just beyond the oyster stands on the wharf. On this clear fall afternoon the bay's choppy waters glinted in the sunlight like moving mirrors, dazzling in its brilliance.

But Kay was not charmed. She had too much on her mind to enjoy the view.

Almost Thanksgiving already. Late November, she reflected worriedly, and so much to be done. So little time to do it.

Shaking her head despairingly, Kay turned from the window. She glanced at the neat stack of greenbacks carefully counted out atop a warped, splintery three-legged table. Exactly $100. The awesome amount paid weekly on the Corps' mortgaged property. No matter how short the Army's meager funds, Nicholas Daniel McCabe had to be paid each and every week, right on time.

Or else.

If payment was not made—if so much as one week passed without him receiving his $100—the spiteful saloon owner would foreclose on the valuable piece of waterfront property.

Kay's delicate jaw hardened and she gritted her teeth.

Beside the counted money lay a small blue ledger book. A record of each payment that had been made, along with the balance owing. A frightful sum was still unpaid.

Kay sighed, pulled out a chair from the table, and carefully sat down.

At the rate the debt was being reduced, it would take 155 weeks! Or 38 months and 3 weeks. Or 3 years, 2 months, and 3 weeks.

Kay groaned aloud. She put her elbows on the table and covered her face with her hands. And groaned again.

Of all the clubs on the Barbary Coast, why did Curly have walk into the Nick McCabe's place? Of all the saloons where he could have gambled, why did he have to buck the tables in the Golden Carousel? Of all the greedy, grasping hands into which the Army's land could have fallen, why did it have to be those tanned, tapered fingers of the heartless Nick McCabe!

Kay rubbed her eyes with her knuckles. Then spread her hands, cupped her cheeks, and stared into space. She frowned at the unpleasant prospect of seeing the tormenting Nick McCabe. In less than an hour, she would encounter the silver-eyed devil.

Kay bounded up out of the chair, her blue eyes flashing with a mixture of anger and anxiety. How typical of the mean-spirited saloon owner to demand that only *she* be the one to make the weekly payments. At the appointed hour each Wednesday afternoon, she was to personally deliver the money to his Golden Carousel Club.

Kay realized she was viciously grinding her teeth when her jaws began to ache. She stopped, relaxed her mouth. But she wondered if the beloved General William Booth or perhaps even the blessed Jesus himself mightn't have found it impossible to love their enemies if they'd had the misfortune to meet up with the diabolic Nick McCabe!

Eyes closing in frustration, Kay asked herself: How could her Army raise more money? They *badly* needed money. There wasn't enough money for uniforms or food and lodging. Much less enough to pay off Nick McCabe and begin construction of the Corps' permanent rescue mission.

Money was needed for a dormitory to house homeless men. A shelter for wayward women. To help feed the orphans at Battery Place. To nurse the sick back to health. For literally dozens of necessary causes.

Kay's eyes came open.

There was never enough money. Never. Kay got fierce headaches trying to sort it all out, attempting to come up with a solution. Where was the money to come from? What could she do to raise money?

"Money, money, money!" Kay muttered aloud, agonized by the weight of the problems resting squarely on her shoulders.

Captain Kay Montgomery kept her own counsel. She worried alone and in silence. She saw no purpose in unnecessarily burdening the others. She did her best to conceal the profundity of the problems. The eager recruits had no conception of the near-impossible mission before them. She didn't want them to know. They hadn't been told of the May deadline; wouldn't be told. Only she and Curly knew.

*　*　*

Kay snapped out of her fretting when she heard the sudden close eruption of laughter. A woman's high, musical laugh.

Kay began to smile.

She'd recognize that infectious girlish laughter anywhere. She left her post at the window, hurried to greet the sweet, uncomplaining young woman who was her sister-in-law.

Kay's smile changed to a nervous laugh when she caught sight of them. Curly was with Rose. They had come in out of the November sunshine, blinking and laughing. Rose was draped around Curly's lanky body, riding him piggyback. Her arms were locked tightly around his neck. Her long skirts pushed up, revealing bare shapely knees hooked over Curly's bent arms.

The happy bride was giggling and nibbling on her husband's right ear. Curly was growling and warning—or promising—his playful wife just what he intended to do with her once he got her inside.

Kay felt the blood rush to her face as she blushed with discomfort. Anxious to make her presence known, she called out loudly, "Afternoon, you two." And quickly stepped into a bright pool of sunlight.

Identical expressions came over the faces of the startled married lovers. Surprise, followed immediately by embarrassment. Curly's boyish face turned as red as Kay's, while Rose's grew pale as a sheet.

Hurriedly lowering Rose to her feet, Curly needlessly cleared his throat. "Hey, there, Kay. Ah . . . we . . . we didn't expect to find you here."

Curbing the urge to say that was more than obvious, Kay saved them and herself further mortification. "I know. I should have been gone a half hour ago. I'm leaving now."

"Oh?" Curly shuffled from one foot to the other while Rose smoothed down her wrinkled skirts and straightened her jacket. "We . . . Rose and I . . . we had a few spare minutes . . . uh . . ." Curly's eyes were focused on his carefully polished shoes.

By now the happy, sunny-dispositioned Rose was again laughing as her darling, boyish Curly stumbled over his words. The delightful sound of her laughter filled the big, raftered warehouse. Rose stepped in front of her tall uniformed husband, spread her arms wide, and hugged her sister-in-law.

She whispered in Kay's ear, "Forgive our frivolous behavior. Curly and I are *so* in love . . . we grabbed the opportunity to spend a few stolen minutes alone."

"I'm on my way out," Kay replied, nodding, embracing the smaller woman.

Eager to be gone, Kay quickly released Rose. She returned to the splintered table, snatched up her blue jacket, and pulled it on. Then she scooped up the counted greenbacks, stuffed them into a pocket, and drew on her black straw bonnet. Tying the streamers as she went, Kay made a beeline for the exit, keeping her eyes averted from Curly's.

Over her shoulder: "I'm going now. I—I don't know when . . . lock the door behind me."

Kay rushed out into the brilliant California sunshine. Her cheeks burned at the sound of more laughter erupting behind her just before the door was soundly slammed and bolted.

Air exploded from Kay's tight lungs. She drew a quick, deep breath and set out, walking at a brisk, determined pace. Anxious to get far away from the warehouse and the lovers who were engaged in foolish horseplay. As she swiftly headed north on Drumm Street, Kay felt a slight unfamiliar twinge of envy. Rose and Curly were so happy, had so much fun together, were so totally in love.

What, Kay wondered fleetingly, might it be like to love a man with all your heart? And to be cherished in return? To play nonsensical lovers' games? To tease and tickle and laugh and . . . and . . . to make love?

Kay swallowed hard.

She shook her bonneted head, raised her firm chin, and dismissed such thoughts. But it was only scant few minutes later that Captain Kay Montgomery again experienced a twinge of longing.

The law stopped her at the corner.

A policeman stood in the intersection of Battery and Pacific, directing traffic. His tailored blue uniform was smartly fitted to his angular frame. On his head was a tall black constabulary hat and on his hands were cotton gloves of snowy white. Brass buttons glittered on his chest as the officer raised a white-gloved hand to stop the carriage traffic.

Snorting horses were abruptly pulled up and moving carriage wheels ground to a stop. The policeman then turned, smiled, and signaled the waiting assembly of Battery Place orphans to safely proceed across the street.

Smiling, Kay watched the children.

Their uniforms were neatly pressed, their hair was carefully combed. The girls wore white cotton blouses, pleated skirts of royal-blue wool, white cotton stockings, and well-polished black shoes. The boys were equally spiffy in white starched shirts with navy four-in-hand ties, short blue trousers, white knee stockings, and shiny black shoes.

Each child in the chattering group—escorted by two grown-ups—was clean, sharp, in step, and happy.

But at the very rear—lagging several steps behind—a boy trailed the procession. A somber little boy, tiny and painfully thin. The tail of his white shirt was half in, half out of his short blue pants. His navy tie was askew. One white stocking drooped down around his ankle. A large, unsightly scab decorated his left knee. His hair, a striking bright red, was badly mussed. A cowlick at his crown sent an unruly shock sticking straight up.

Kay couldn't take her eyes off the tiny boy.

Without warning, a strong mothering instinct seized her. She felt her heart squeeze in her chest as she stared at the adorable red-headed straggler. Her intense blue gaze stayed locked on the boy until the group had passed completely and had been swallowed up in the crowds of people clogging the busy streets.

Even then Kay squinted against the sun's harsh light searching for that tiny head of flaming red. At last she gave up, came back to her senses, sighed, and proceeded on her way.

But with her went the unforgettable image of a sad-faced, red-haired little boy.

At the Golden Carousel Club's back door, Kay impatiently rang the bell. Ling Tan, Nick's smiling Chinese servant, admitted her, bowing and directing her to the back staircase. Ling Tan escorted Kay up to Nick's private apartments.

"Boss be right out, Missy Captain," said the polite Chinese servant, ushering her into a spacious sitting room and leaving her there alone.

Frowning, refusing to sit, Kay stood stiffly near the closed door, ready to dash to safety should the need arise. Minutes passed and Nick McCabe didn't appear. Annoyed that he would keep her waiting, Kay cautioned herself not to let the inconsiderate saloon owner upset her.

She allowed her gaze to drift around the luxurious room. The long sofa and upholstered easy chairs looked sturdy, expensive, and very comfortable. And masculine. So did the solid, gleaming mahogany tables, the massive gray marble fireplace, the deep plush carpet, the heavy curtains.

Kay cautiously ventured forward toward the ceiling-to-mantel mirror mounted above the fireplace. Bordered in gleaming silver, the mirror's immense size was impressive. Kay moved closer, looked into the fine polished mirror. She frowned, leaned closer. A stray lock of red hair had come loose and was feathered across her left cheek. Kay was instantly reminded of the little orphan's uncombed red hair.

She looked about. Saw no one. She hastily took off her black Army bonnet, tossed it on a nearby chair. Standing directly before the mirror, she smoothed back her wayward red hair and carefully pinned it in place. Studying her reflection, Kay pinched her pale cheeks to give them color. She turned her head from side to side, harshly assessing her image. She bit her lips to plump them a little. And forgetting herself, Kay smiled with pride as she touched her appealingly high cheekbones with appraising fingertips.

"Ah, Captain, you'll have to say an extra prayer for that little display of vanity."

Kay's hands fell to her sides and she whirled about. Nick McCabe, clicking his tongue, stood in the doorway, a muscular shoulder leaning against the polished door frame.

"I have no idea what you're talking about," Kay replied, her cheeks again flushing with color.

"You were primping, Captain. And I saw you." Nick lazily pushed away from the door, came toward her. In his hand was a half-full glass of liquor and, from the look in his heavy-lidded silver-gray eyes, it was not his first drink of the day.

"I was doing nothing of the kind," Kay calmly said.

"You'd dare add the sin of lying to the transgression of being puffed up with pride?" Nick shook his dark head. "Well, now my faith *is* shaken."

"I am not a liar nor am I am vain," Kay said, trying to remain cool. The man was obviously three sheets to the wind. To argue with him would be futile and foolish. "I was merely tidying my disheveled hair as I'm concerned with maintaining a degree of dignity."

Knowing he could make her lose her dignity and her temper, Nick said, "By all means you must never lose your dignity."

"I won't," she said, "so save your concern."

For a moment Nick remained silent, studying her thoughtfully, making her feel uncomfortable.

"Well, so here we are, Captain Kay," Nick finally said with a wicked grin. "Alone in the private lair of Nick McCabe. You look right at home here."

Kay wisely ignored the taunting jest. She noted Nick's freshly laundered white shirt, his impeccably tailored dark trousers with the perfect break in the crease. The expensive handmade shoes of glove leather.

"I would say, Mr. McCabe," Kay announced with a smile, "that you are the one guilty of being shamelessly narcissistic."

"Captain, I resent that." Nick's deep voice was well modulated. "My thoughts are constantly filled with mankind's pressing problems."

Kay was not amused. "McCabe, it's easy to see that your interests are limited to your appearance, your women, and the wherewithal for both."

Nick replied in slightly slurring tones, "Is there really anything else?"

"For you? Apparently not." She made a face, indicating she found him disgustingly shallow. "Still, I shall continue to pray that you will one day want to lead a more meaningful life."

"And yours is more meaningful, I suppose?"

"Infinitely, I would hope. Do you ever do anything for anyone other than yourself? I think not. You do what you please when you please."

"Ever try it, Captain?" Nick lifted wide shoulders, causing the fine fabric of his white shirt to pull across the flat muscles of his chest.

Refusing to respond to his question, Kay said, "Besides that, you're spiteful and sarcastic and you're blatantly irreverent. Selfish and greedy and hedonistic. An infidel, a sinner."

"Amen. All those things," Nick agreed, toasting her with his glass. He tossed his drink back and smiled that ruthless, dangerous smile that made Kay's heart turn over. She noticed, for the first time, a small whiplash scar across one eye. It gave him a sinister look. "And you, Captain? A saint, I suppose?"

"A soldier for Christ," Kay stated.

"Ah, that's right. There she is—the hope of Heaven." Nick moved closer.

Flustered, Kay retreated. "You're drunk," she accused.

"Not yet, but I'm working on it," admitted Nick.

"You're bad, Nick McCabe."

"And bad for you, Captain." He drained his glass. His lips glistened with the liquor. "You don't trust me as far as you can throw me, do you?"

"No," Kay confessed, "I don't."

"Well," Nick said in a surprisingly soft voice, "you're right not to."

"But I intend to change you from the corrupt and wicked man you are, Nick McCabe."

Nick's grin was evil, his reply quick. "While you seem to know me well, I'm afraid you don't know yourself."

Again he moved closer. Stood so dangerously close Kay could feel heat emanating from his tall, lean body, caught his clean masculine scent, the smell of liquor on his breath. Lids low over flashing silver eyes, gaze fixed on her mouth, Nick said, "Captain, I could have you sinning along with me by sundown."

Kay didn't back away. Immediately angered by his arrogance, she stood her ground, her blue eyes snapping.

Shaking her head piteously, she told him, "You grossly overestimate your charm, McCabe."

"Do I?" His right hand lifted to her cheek. Tanned fingers traced the fragile, perfectly formed cheekbone he'd caught her admiring. "You might be surprised. Heaven alone knows."

"You're wrong. *I* know." She angrily brushed his hand away. "You're so conceited . . . so sure of yourself. It's laughable."

"You aren't laughing," he accused, moving closer still, filling the entire scope of her vision.

Kay involuntarily cringed, took a backward step, and glared at him. "I didn't come here to endure your insults. I will not tolerate your insufferable disrespect!"

"And I didn't ask you here to tell me how to run my life," Nick replied.

"Someone needs to."

Nick's silver eyes flashed with fire, then grew frighteningly cold. "Lady, you're going to wish to Christ you'd never met me."

"I already do."

"Money, Captain. That's all we have to talk about. If you've got my money, let's see it. If not . . ."

"I have it!" Kay took the folded bills from her pocket, slapped them down on the marble mantel, snatched up her black bonnet, and started to storm away.

"Hold on." Nick's hand shot out so swiftly Kay gasped. His long fingers encircled her arm and he pulled her back. "Sister, you're not leaving until I count it."

Incensed, Kay was forced to stand there while Nick slowly, methodically counted the money. Dramatically he placed the stack of bills atop his left palm, licked the tip of his right index finger, and unhurriedly rifled through them, counting aloud while Kay seethed.

Totally out of patience, feeling the uncontrollable urge to brain him,

Kay said, "That's it. I'm getting out of here!" She whirled away, stalked to the door.

"Sure. Run along." Nick looked up. "But remember next week, same time, same amount. And don't be late."

Kay gave no reply. Teeth gritted, she yanked the heavy door open wide and left him. She practically ran down the long open corridor and took the stairs two at a time. Outside, she sagged against the building, balled her fists, shut her eyes and counted to ten.

What was she going to do about Nick McCabe?

Chapter 14

What was he going to do about Captain Kay Montgomery? Scowling, Nick McCabe sat behind the mahogany desk in his silent office. Nick's left eye was varying shades of purple, blue, and black. It was swollen completely shut. His right was narrowed with fury. His full bottom lip was split; it hurt to talk, smile, or even scowl.

Nick's broad bare chest was bruised. A couple of ribs on the right side were cracked. A tight white bandage circled his trim middle. The flesh beneath was itching.

Clutched in Nick's battered right hand—no skin left on the knuckles—was a colored flyer he'd angrily ripped off the black leather door of his Golden Carousel. The crumpled handbill was one of hundreds that had been circulated up and down the Barbary Coast for the past two weeks.

The proclamation read:

> Come one, come all!
> The Grand Parade of the San Francisco Salvation
> Army Corps #1 will march up Pacific at 2 P.M.
> Friday, December 14, 1883.
> You are invited to join the procession.
> Follow Christ's Army to an open-air revival
> meeting at the corner of Pacific and Grant.
> And stay for a hot meal!

Nick gritted his even white teeth, winced with pain, and cursed loudly. He threw the wadded handbill across the room and reached for the half-full bottle of bourbon. Muttering to himself, Nick poured a leaded jigger glass to the brim, lifted it in his discolored right hand, and drank it down in one long swallow.

He wiped his glistening lips on a muscular forearm and shook his dark, aching head.

He should have known. Should have known from that first day when the flame-haired Captain Kay had awakened him with her damn bell-ringing that she was big trouble. When he'd watched her stride away from him, confident and full of courage, he should have known what was in store for him.

He hadn't. Not then.

Admittedly, in the beginning, he'd dealt with the problem in the typical Nick McCabe manner. He ignored it. Most problems soon went away.

But Captain Kay Montgomery hadn't gone away. Wasn't going away. He'd been foolish to convince himself that she would. He'd thought her an irritant, not a threat. He'd been wrong. Wrong about her leaving. Wrong about her being no threat.

Hell, she was lethal.

"Damn her and her entire brigade!" Nick swore aloud and slammed his throbbing fist down atop the desk. He yelped in pain as stars exploded behind his eyes and his flat belly lurched in rhythmic shudders of agony.

It wasn't the first such occasion that Nick had nursed his battle wounds. Since he'd lost Big Alfred to the Salvation Army, he'd been exposed, vulnerable. Unprotected. Word had quickly spread of the British bouncer's defection. Hoodlums and toughs who'd long been harboring hard feelings couldn't wait to throw a few well-aimed punches at Nick.

Troublemakers came out of the woodwork.

Add to their number the drinkers who became increasingly unruly as the evening wore on. The gamblers who turned nasty when the cards or the dice turned against them. The ogling, shouting spectators jeering Rose Reilly's latest replacement.

Rarely did a peaceful evening pass at the Golden Carousel.

Moaning softly with pain, Nick slid down onto his spine, leaned his head back, and closed his one good eye against the invasive December sunshine.

Nick was much less concerned with the pounding his face had taken than with the pounding his bank account was taking. More than a decade of hard work and savvy had gone into building the Golden Carousel into the most successful saloon on the Coast.

Captain Kay Montgomery had spent less than four months tearing it down. At the rate she was going, he'd wind up physically maimed and totally broke within a year!

The loss of Big Alfred had hurt. Badly. But the loss of beautiful, talented Rose Reilly had made his Carousel Club—the glittering jewel of the Barbary Coast—just another joint.

Nick's long dark lashes lifted and lowered restlessly.

The latest in a string of fancy girls he'd given the chance to take Rose's place was as big a bust as her predecessors. Dee Dee Diamond was a looker, and she'd bragged how she'd "set the place on its ear." Desperate, he'd hired the statuesque Dee Dee and hoped for the best.

But when Dee Dee Diamond had taken the stage last night, her voice was high and squeaky, her dancing awkward and clumsy. She never got the opportunity to finish the act. The sparse crowd of spectators had come to their feet to shout, hiss, and finally throw drinks at the stage.

The crying Dee Dee Diamond had fled to the safety of the dressing room while Nick was left to deal with the disappointed audience. Chairs, tables, and fists were thrown as total revolt erupted in the spacious grand salon.

Nick's good silver-gray eye opened. His dark head remained pressed to the swivel chair's tall tufted back. He grimaced at the prospect of another afternoon spent interviewing untalented talent. The grimace deepened when his thoughts went past the afternoon and on to the upcoming night.

Neither his face or his body could withstand any further pummeling. Yet he had no choice but to pull on a tux, take his place down in the club, and hope he was still in one piece come morning. And that . . . that . . .

Nick's eye narrowed. His dark head slowly, carefully lifted from the tall chair back.

He heard something. The sound of music. Music moving toward him.

Nick turned his head to the side, listened intently. The music grew steadily louder. Moved closer. So close he could make out the tune being played.

"Onward Christian Soldiers."

"Damn her." Nick let out a long painful sigh of defeat. "Damn the red-haired captain. And damn her parade up my street!"

Captain Kay Montgomery was smiling.

The day was well suited to the Grand Parade. The morning fog had moved out. The crisp December air was cold but invigorating. Army blue bunting blew in the soft western breeze. A faint, pleasing scent of the ocean carried on the wind off the bay. Afternoon sunshine reflected in the tall windows. Citizens lined the streets in anticipation.

Captain Kay and Big Alfred Duke led the much-heralded Salvation

Army parade up Pacific. They were mounted on Palomino ponies, courtesy of the Marlen Company Livery Stables.

Captain Kay Montgomery felt absolutely wonderful. The big man at her side was one of the kindest, gentlest human beings she'd ever known. A fearless giant, Alfred Duke also had impeccable manners, possessed the patience of Job, and was compassionate to a fault.

The quintessential opposite of his former employer.

Kay was still astounded that this gentle giant had thrown down the cause of evil, picked up the Army's banner, and committed to follow *Him* all the days of his life.

Directly behind Kay and Big Alfred were a handsome pair of youthful soldiers. The beaming Major Curly Montgomery and his blushing bride, Rose Reilly Montgomery, had rededicated their lives to the Corps. And to each other.

Kay glanced over her shoulder at the glowing newlyweds.

Curly had never looked happier, healthier; had never possessed more personal magnetism. The beautiful, chestnut-haired Rose Reilly Montgomery hardly resembled the near-naked, seductive dancer from the Carousel saloon. Covered from chin to ankle in Army blue, Rose was a vision of wifely modesty and Christian chastity.

And more beautiful than ever.

Following Curly and Rose came the Salvation Army band, their uniforms snappy, their instruments gleaming in the winter sunlight. The band had grown. Giles on his cornet, Bobby Newman on the big bass drum, and Matthew on accordion were now joined by a half-dozen new recruits playing tubas, banjos, and bells.

Pride and joy swelled Kay's heart.

Turning back to face ahead, she raised her hand high and waved to the crowds lining the streets. Her smile was as bright and sunny as the perfect December afternoon.

Then she saw him. And seeing him was enough to set her teeth on edge.

Nick McCabe, looking devilishly handsome and decidedly dangerous, and sporting a bad shiner, leaned indolently against a lamppost outside his Golden Carousel. Crisp white shirt stretching across his wide shoulders, dark trousers tailored to his slim hips and long legs, his arms were crossed over his chest. Lid low over his cynical silver-gray eye, idly he observed the passing parade.

Kay fixed Nick straight in his one good eye. Nick tossed her his killer grin. Kay swatted it away with a dismissive sweep of her hand. Nick laughed.

He heard the muttering going on around him. Building in intensity. The majority of spectators looked on the parading Salvation Army as a rowdy band of fanatics. So Nick was not particularly surprised, nor was he particularly sympathetic, when the crowds lining both sides of Pacific began shouting insults.

The protests didn't end with hoots and howls. Clumps of mud, rotten fruit, and eggs started flying through the air. His lazy silver gaze resting solely on Captain Kay, Nick saw an overripe tomato hit her squarely in the chest.

Nick's lean body reflexively jerked, as if the hurled fruit had struck his own bruised chest. Muscles tensing, he instinctively started to step into the street, but caught himself. He stayed just as he was. Unmoving.

The rotten tomato splattered all over the front of Kay's midnight-blue uniform. She gasped but held her head high. She struggled valiantly to maintain as much dignity as she could muster.

She continued to smile bravely.

A pelted egg hit the crown of her black straw hat, broke on impact, and slowly dripped down and off the bonnet's broad black brim.

Nick's arms never came uncrossed. His lid never lifted one iota over his cynical silver eye. His stance remained the same. He made no move to help the stubborn woman warrior.

She was getting no more than she deserved, no more than she'd asked for. The fiery redhead had disrupted other Barbary Coast lives as much as his, and he could easily understand why they'd want to throw things at her.

He'd like to throw *her*.

Captain Kay, Big Alfred, Curly, Rose, and the rest of the troop moved slowly up Pacific, dodging fruit, eggs, and mud. Big Alfred looked questioningly at Captain Kay. In his hazel eyes she read the unmistakable message: He'd love to take care of the unruly crowd! All she had to do was give him the nod.

Kay shook her head, but smiled to let him know she appreciated the unspoken offer. Kay was not afraid. Faith was her armor against fear and hostility. Her uniform badly soiled, the last remnants of a thrown egg dripping off her hat brim, Kay kept her back militarily straight, her face serenely composed.

Nick appeared bored. He yawned.

He wasn't extraordinarily impressed by Kay's bravery and mettle. That's what he told himself.

The jaded Nick McCabe didn't lift a finger to help her.
But someone else did.

Patrick Packard, one of San Francisco's most prominent and respected citizens, was down on Pacific Street that fine winter afternoon.
Not by choice.

Pat Packard was never comfortable on the wild, rollicking Barbary
Coast. Not on those rare occasions when he'd been roped into escort-
ing his headstrong sister on a round of the area's lively nightspots.
And not today as he waited impatiently for his attorney to conclude a
business engagement and drive him back uptown.

Pat Packard sighed.

Had he known that this would happen, he'd never have agreed to
luncheon with the always-busy lawyer Lavender. Dysard K. Lavender
had been on retainer with the Packard family for as long as Pat could
remember. And while Pat agreed with his sister Adele that the middle-aged attorney was a clever, aggressive man, he personally had
never liked Lavender.

Dysard K. Lavender had made his fortune in the slave trade. It was
Lavender who was responsible for supplying the cheap Chinese labor
that had built the vast Packard railroad empire. And made the Packard family extremely wealthy. But Pat didn't like the successful society
attorney.

Pat Packard sure didn't like being kept waiting in a parked carriage
on one of the Barbary Coast's most notorious streets. He cast another
anxious glance at the closed door of Three Fingers Jackson's Top Hat
Club. What could be keeping Lavender?

Pat Packard totally forgot about Dysard K. Lavender and Three
Fingers Jackson when he heard the martial music. He turned and
watched with interest as the parade made its way up the street. He was
shocked and appalled at the shabby way the Salvationists were
treated.

His attention was drawn to the slender, mounted young woman
leading the possession. He watched her exclusively. He saw her smile
and wave to the crowd. Heard her call to the spectators, inviting them
to fall in and follow. To come along to Grant Street and join the open-
air services.

And he watched, horrified, as a ripe tomato hit her squarely in the
chest. He found her reaction to the unprovoked attack nothing short
of amazing.

The young woman's dignity, composure, and fearlessness in the face

of adversity thoroughly impressed Pat Packard. Captured by her incredible poise, Packard swung down out of the carriage and rushed
into the street, to Kay's aid.

Nick McCabe's heavy lid finally lifted slightly over his one good
silver-gray eye. He watched the street drama unfold with quiet amusement. He immediately recognized the tall, blond aristocrat. His mouth
stretching into a half grin that hurt his punished lip, Nick wondered
what Adele's straitlaced baby brother was doing slumming down on
the Barbary Coast.

He wondered as well why Packard would rush to the aid of this
religious zealot. A woman who preached on street corners in the city's
skid row. Part and parcel of the vulgar throng Packard and his blue-
blooded friends held in contempt. Perhaps the pristine Packard, like
so many of the filthy rich, had chosen to help the Salvation Army
captain in order to feel good about himself.

The wealthy were like that. Nick knew.

Or, could it be that Packard was grandstanding so his upper-crust
pals could read about his feat of derring-do in the newspaper? Skeptical, Nick casually looked around. Sure enough, a young reporter from
the *San Francisco Call* was hurrying into the street with pad, pen, and
tripod flash camera.

Pat Packard acted purely out of instinct. He had no idea a reporter
was anywhere around. Packard commandingly grabbed the bridle of
Kay's nervous, big-eyed Palomino. He stepped up beside her, the expression on his smooth, handsome face one of respect and admiration.

With a flourish he withdrew a snowy white Irish linen handkerchief
from his inside vest pocket. Graciously he handed it up to Kay.

"God bless you, good sir," Kay said, taking the monogrammed
handkerchief and blotting at the soggy tomato stains saturating her
uniform jacket. "You're very kind."

"And you're very courageous, miss. It is miss, isn't it?"

"Actually, it's Captain Kay Montgomery." She presented her free
hand for him to shake. "And you?"

"Patrick Packard. Pat," he said, taking her hand gently in his.

"Hold it just like you are!" shouted the approaching *Call* reporter.
"Good. Perfect. Give us another shot of that."

Observing the entire exchange with interest was the cynical Nick
McCabe.

Nick watched as the eager newspaper reporter flashed several photographs of the heroic railroad scion and the grateful Salvation Army captain.

He saw the loud, unruly mob again surge forward in another barrage. It was then that Big Alfred Duke calmly dismounted. Looping the Palomino's reins around the saddle horn, the massive Englishman took off his soiled blue uniform jacket and tossed it over the saddle. He rolled up his sleeves to reveal swelling biceps.

That's all it took.

The hecklers and garbage throwers dispersed.

Pat Packard stood in the middle of Pacific Street and talked animatedly to the bravest, the most enchanting young woman he had ever had the privilege to meet. Pat smiled shyly and nodded when Kay invited him to come to the Army's prayer meeting. He promised he would. And could he call on her some afternoon?

Mounted above him, Captain Kay looked down into his eyes as she said, in a gentle voice, "Yes." She thrilled him with her smile and bid Pat Packard good day.

Big Alfred remounted and the procession again moved proudly on up Pacific Street. Although he reluctantly stayed behind, Pat's warm green eyes followed Captain Kay.

Smiling, he returned to the waiting carriage feeling buoyant. The Top Hat Club's front door flew open and Dysard K. Lavender stepped out into the bright December sunshine.

Dysard K. Lavender was smiling too.

The middle-aged, portly, balding attorney's one eye was flashing with self-satisfaction. The other was covered with a black eye patch.

Nick McCabe's narrowed gaze touched the expensively dressed, one-eyed attorney with fleeting interest, then dismissed him. His attention went back to the parade quickly moving up Pacific and out of sight.

The Army band was again playing.

Frowning, Nick pushed away from the lamppost and went back inside the Golden Carousel, wearily shaking his dark head.

What was he going to do about Captain Kay Montgomery?

Chapter 15

His name was Joey.

Kay had learned that and more about the tiny red-haired boy who'd unwittingly stepped on her heart as he'd straggled along behind the marching children of Battery Place.

On that November afternoon when Kay first laid eyes on Joey, she had hurried to the orphanage the minute she had concluded her business at the Golden Carousel. She'd cornered the unflappable head supervisor, Madge Simpson, and fired question after question at her.

The big, grandmotherly Madge told Kay what she knew—which wasn't much—of the red-haired boy who'd been so callously delivered to Battery Place well after midnight.

"I was up late tending a sick child," Madge began, shaking her gray head, "else I wouldn't have been awake. I wouldn't have seen a young woman coming up the walk in the middle of the night, dragging that poor child along behind her."

"His mother?"

"None other," Madge said with disgust. "A pretty young thing she was, but indecently dressed, face all painted and all. I spotted the pair through the open curtains. So I hurried to the front door and went out to meet them. The fancy young woman stopped short, startled.

"I looked from her to the child and asked, 'Do you need help, Miss? A place to spend a night? A hot meal? Come on inside? It's cold and damp out, the baby must be freezing.' "

Kay said nothing. She remained absolutely silent.

Madge Simpson made a sour face. "She just jerked that poor little fellow forward, shoved him at me, and said calmly, 'Take him off my hands. He's been in my way since the day he was born.' Then, quick as a wink, she turned on her heel and hurried away.

"And that little fellow went running after her, begging her not to go, not to leave him, saying 'Mommy, Mommy, no.' It was heartbreaking. Poor dirty-faced, skinny little thing in thin, ragged clothes chasing after that heartless hussy.

"I went chasing after them in my nightgown, but my arthritis has been so bad of late I couldn't keep up. A carriage waited just beyond the gates. A man was inside. He held the door open wide for the fancy girl.

"Little Joey had somehow managed to catch up with his mother. She climbed up into the carriage with that child clinging tenaciously to her skirts." Madge closed her eyes, grimaced, opened them. A pained expression was etched deeply on her fleshy face as she lived again last night's sad drama.

"Do you know what his own mother did then?"

"What?" Kay swallowed hard, barely unable to breathe.

"That cruel, painted Jezebel jerked her skirts free of his clutching little fingers and hissed, 'Get back, Joey! Stay away from me!' Then she lifted a slippered foot and kicked the child squarely in his tiny stomach. Knocked him flat on his back. Her gentleman friend slammed the carriage door shut, laid the whip to the horses' backs, and the pair rode off into the night!"

"Poor little boy," murmured Kay.

"I know," Madge replied with a long sigh. "I know, but then I suspect it's for the best. Battery Place will surely be a better home than what Joey's been used to."

Kay nodded, finally smiled. "Yes. Yes, it will. May I see Joey?"

Madge shrugged. "Yes. But don't expect much. He hasn't spoken a word since I picked him up last night and brought him inside. Won't talk to me. Won't play with the other children." Madge brightened, said, "He'll come around, though, so don't you worry, Captain Kay."

But Joey hadn't come around.

Three weeks had passed. The tiny red-haired boy hadn't spoken a word. Hadn't cried. Hadn't laughed. Hadn't shown any emotion.

Madge told Captain Kay that in those weeks investigation made into Joey's background had produced sparse but telling facts. Locals said the mother was a young dark-eyed, dark-haired prostitute known on the waterfront as Michelle. Michelle had split up with the father, a big handsome red-headed gambler called Yancy, when Joey was a year old. The mother didn't want her son, so Joey went to live with his gambler father.

But Yancy had been knifed to death in a crooked card game. That had been a few months back. After his death, Joey had been sent back to his mother.

She had neglected him, locked him outside in the cold frequently. Left him alone days at a time in one of those old board shanties down at Clark's Point. Then Michelle met a customer who asked her to go away with him. He wanted just her. He didn't want a four-year-old kid tagging along. Neither did Michelle.

So, in the middle of that cold November night, they had dropped Joey off at Battery Place like some unwanted cat or dog.

Kay was deeply touched. Her visits to Battery Place took on new meaning. She could hardly wait to get there each day. At three o'clock every afternoon she arrived hoping to find a changed Joey. A talking Joey. A laughing Joey. A happy Joey.

On this cold clear Monday afternoon of December 16, Captain Kay hurried anxiously through the gates of Battery Place.

Kay smiled as she rushed up the long stone walkway.

Each and every time she came to call Kay was struck anew by the eye-pleasing beauty. Most orphans' asylums were old, bleak, dark, and depressing.

Not Battery Place.

Battery Place was a big, bright, sunny residence where children lived, laughed, and learned to love again. A safe haven. An island of refuge located squarely in a neighborhood teeming with crime and danger.

High brick vine-covered walls enclosed the spacious grounds where healthy, growing children frolicked and played. The vast property boasted tall old trees that were perfect for climbing—their limbs now winter bare. A carpet of grass, browned by the season, was constantly trampled by the tireless feet of romping, laughing children.

At the center of these expansive grounds sat a spacious, sprawling two-story brick Victorian home. The bricks of the large imposing structure were not of the standard dark-red hue. Nor were they brown. Or even yellow.

The enormous house of solid brick was painted a gleaming snow white! Plate-glass windows in every single room gave the vast interior an open, airy feel.

The theme of cheery brightness was carried out through the big comfortable house. There were no dark colors. Walls of white dominated the common areas. Pastels had been chosen for sleeping rooms.

The boys' bedrooms were painted sky blue, mint green, aquamarine. The girls' quarters sported either shy pink, pale purple, or sunshine yellow. It was clearly evident that a great deal of love and careful planning had gone into the large, cheerful dwelling. Kay had wondered more than once who was responsible for this fine, comfortable home for orphans.

Kay experienced a jolting tingle of anticipation when she reached the big front door decorated with a Christmas wreath of holly.

Would this be the day Joey spoke? Laughed? Cried?

Inside the home's broad white-walled foyer Kay heard a piano being played at the back of the house. Children were singing. Shouting. Laughing. The aroma of freshly baked pastries drifted in from the large white kitchen.

Kay was hanging her bonnet on the coat tree when Madge Simpson appeared. Smiling, the big gray-haired woman wiped her hands on her apron.

"Captain Kay, good afternoon," Madge greeted her warmly. "Come in, come in."

"Hello, Madge." Kay sniffed the air, smiled. "Something smells mighty good."

"Doesn't it? The older girls are baking their Christmas cookies. You'll have to sample a taste."

"I'll do that," said Kay. Then anxiously, eyebrows lifted: "Madge?"

Madge shook her gray head. "No change."

Kay sighed. Then quickly smiled again. "Sounds like everyone else is having a good time."

"Lord, they can't keep still lately. All of them counting the days till old Santa comes." A loud piercing squeal, followed immediately by an eruption of childish laughter, almost drowned out her words. Madge's gray eyes twinkled and she added, "Go on back. See if you can't calm them down before I get a raging headache."

Madge returned to her kitchen. Kay made her way down the long hall to the huge open room they called the gymnasium. Here the children roughhoused when it was too cold or wet to play outdoors. And the smaller children took their afternoon naps each day after lunch.

"Kay, Kay! Captain Kay." A half dozen little girls squealed and jumped up and down when Kay stepped into the sunny gymnasium.

Kay laughed and threw her arms open wide. But her eager gaze moved swiftly around the room searching for that small head of bright copper hair. She didn't find it. Exuberant children—boys as well as girls—rushed her with such eagerness she was knocked off balance.

Kay went sprawling.

She wound up flat on her back on the polished hardwood floor. The little children thought it was funny. They fell down atop her, giggling and shrieking with joy. Kay laughed harder than anyone. She and the happy kids laughed and tumbled around on the floor until Kay had given every single one a big, warm, squeeze-the-life-out-of-them hug.

Finally, wiping tears of laughter from her eyes, Kay levered herself up into a sitting position.

And she saw Joey.

Across the sunny room the tiny, red-haired little boy sat all alone on the floor with his back pressed against the white wall. A pair of tanned knees were drawn up to his skinny chest, his short fingers laced tightly around them.

Helplessly drawn to the solitary Joey, Kay rose, dusted off her blue uniform skirt, and stepped carefully over a tangle of arms and legs of laughing children.

Approaching with caution, she reached the thin, solemn-faced Joey. But she might as well have not been there. Joey never looked up. Never acknowledged her presence.

"Wouldn't you like to come play with the rest of us?" Kay asked softly. "We're having an awful lot of fun."

No reply. No movement of his head. No indication he'd heard her speak.

Kay sank slowly to her knees before him. His hair, the dazzling color of a bright copper penny, blazed golden red in the afternoon sunlight. His eyes, those large, vivid blue eyes, were downcast, shaded by a row of incredibly long, thick red-gold lashes. Kay knew without being able to see them that in the depths of those beautiful blue eyes was a never-absent sadness.

Joey's complexion was miraculously not that of a redhead. Against the white of his little uniform shirt, his arms were brown as berries. So were the skinny legs poking out of his short blue wool pants. Not one single freckle marred the perfection of his little olive face.

But on his left cheek was a smudge of fresh dirt. Wondering with fond affection how this sad, silent little boy had managed to get dirty sitting quietly against a wall, Kay was tempted to take the handkerchief from her skirt pocket and clean his adorable face. She checked the urge.

"Joey, I'm Captain Kay. You must know me by now. I come every day." She spoke softly, slowly. "Can you say Kay? Hmmmm? Kay? Joey, won't you call my name? Say hello to me?"

Long golden-red lashes fluttered restlessly, then lifted minutely. Sorrowful blue eyes fixed on her face for one fleeting second, then looked away. Joey again stared wistfully into space.

Kay tried once more. But it was no use.

She sat there on her heels before the mute child attempting to befriend him, to draw him out. She'd tried before. Every day since Joey had come. She failed in all attempts. So did everyone else. It frightened Kay. Would she or anyone ever find the key to unlock Joey's heart?

Kay gave up. For now.

She went back to the frolicking, happy children. She quieted them down, drew up a chair, and read to them from the their favorite story books for the rest of the afternoon. As she read in a firm, clear voice, Kay kept stealing glances at the tiny, copper-haired little boy who sat alone and apart.

When the supper bell loudly rang, Kay closed her book. And looked again at the lonely little boy. How she longed to go to the unhappy child, pluck him up from the floor, and hold him comfortingly in her arms. To convince him that everything was going to be all right, that he'd never be hurt again.

But that was something she couldn't promise Joey. Nobody could.

The hungry children all raced out of the big gymnasium, ready for their evening meal. All, that is, but Joey. He didn't move. Just continued to sit there against the wall, hugging his knees. Madge blustered into the room, exchanged quick glances with Kay, and went to Joey.

Hands on hips she said, "Joey, honey, it's suppertime. Come on now. Go wash your hands and take your place at the dining table. Remember, you're between David and Keith. Joey, you hear me?"

Without looking up, the tiny red-haired boy rose to his feet. Slowly he crossed the large room where long shadows now announced the approach of night. Kay's eyes clung to Joey's skinny frame. Shoulder blades poked against the white fabric of his white shirt. One shoe lace was untied. That cowlicked tuft of flaming hair stuck straight up at the back of his head.

When Joey reached the wide arched double doorway, he stopped. The tiny boy half turned and looked straight at Kay. For one fleeting second his enormous sad blue eyes met hers.

Then he was gone.

Chapter 16

It was payday for the landlord.

Captain Kay ground her teeth.

Any man with one drop of human kindness in his heart would have excused payment until after the first of the year. It was, after all, the Christmas season. Goodwill among men. A time for generosity. A time to demonstrate some small degree of selfless charity. To extend kindness and compassion. To share with those less fortunate. To be a responsible, caring human being.

But then of course Nick McCabe was not generous, selfless, kind, or compassionate. He could not have cared less about the holiday season. Or its meaning.

Kay sighed and reached for her black bonnet. She could put off the disagreeable task no longer. It was again that day of the week. Wednesday. And that hour of the day. Three o'clock. She was due at the Golden Carousel with $100 in cash for the mean saloon owner.

Kay tied the streamers of her straw bonnet snugly beneath her chin, fastened the top button of her Army blue tunic, touched the silver S brooch pinned to the stiff military stand-up collar, and headed for the door.

She stepped out of the waterfront warehouse and was greeted with thickly swirling fog and damp frigid air. She shivered involuntarily and hugged herself, feeling the chill all the way to her bones. For a split second Kay wished whimsically that she was piled up in a soft, warm feather bed in a big comfortable, heated house with a good book and a box of brightly wrapped chocolates beside her.

Captain Kay immediately scolded herself. Distressed that such nonproductive thoughts so easily intruded of late, she warned herself against the danger of such daydreams. In this dank, cold weather, how easy it would be to become slothful. To neglect righteous, worthwhile duties and put her own welfare before that of others.

She'd have to closely guard against such temptation, even as the Apostle Paul had done in the New Testament. She certainly didn't want to become like the hedonistic Nick McCabe!

Kay had no time to waste. Her busy day had started at dawn and wouldn't end until close of evening prayer services. There was no time for idleness in her full schedule. Kay clicked off all the things she had yet to do.

She walked to her customary brisk pace, holding fast to the brim of her bonnet, anchoring it against a strong, biting bay wind. Eyes squinted, she reviewed the remainder of the day's schedule, recalling with pleasure that Patrick Packard was to meet her at the warehouse at six o'clock. It was Patrick's idea that they have a hot, tasty supper at the China Moon Cafe, after which he would stay for the night's services.

Kay's slight frown disappeared with the recollection. The blond, slender Patrick Packard was a good man. So kind, so helpful. So totally unselfish. Already he had made a generous cash contribution to the Corps' coffers.

Thrilled and grateful, Kay had immediately come up with a splendid idea. The Packard donation could be used to purchase gifts for the orphans of Battery Place. Curly, Rose, Big Alfred, and the others wholeheartedly concurred. All agreed that despite the many pressing needs of the Corps, this princely sum should definitely be used to provide each child of Battery Place with a gaily wrapped Christmas gift. If anyone deserved a joyous Christmas, surely it was these innocent children who had no families of their own.

Kay's smile broadened at the prospect of the tiny red-haired Joey opening his package. Maybe that would do the trick. Maybe if he found something inside he badly wanted, Joey would at last show emotion. She could hope. The image of a happy, smiling Joey made Kay again feel a deep gratitude to Pat Packard for his generosity.

In less than a week, the kind, handsome Patrick Packard had already become a friend. He had so gallantly come to her aid at Saturday's Grand Parade. And that very night, Patrick—scrubbed clean and impeccably dressed—had attended the open-air prayer meeting. And had stayed to ask Curly's permission to formally call on Kay. Flattered, and charmed with his fine manners, Kay had known instinctively that Patrick Packard was a good, trustworthy gentleman.

All thought of Patrick Packard fled—along with the last traces of her smile—when Kay reached the Golden Carousel.

Kay turned into the narrow alley and quickly made her way to the building's rear entrance. Dreading what had always proved to be an unpleasant encounter, eager to get it behind her, Kay rang the bell on the heavy back door.

Instantly the smiling Ling Tan stood before her, greeting her warmly.

"Chilly cold out today, Missy Captain," Ling Tan said, inviting her inside, pointing her toward the staircase. Bobbing his head, he said, "Big fire burn in boss's fireplace upstairs. Warm self while wait few quick minutes for boss."

Kay balked, stopping short. She bit out her words, "I'm expected to wait again today? Where is McCabe?" She exhaled in huff. "Still in bed?" Her eyebrows knitted and she pursed her lips.

Ling Tan's slanted eyes disappeared completely as he chuckled. "No, no. Not in bed. Been up long time. Rise and shine this morning! Early, early."

"Will wonders never cease," Kay said in flat tones of disinterest. "Where is he? I have things to do."

"Most apologetic, Missy Captain," offered Ling Tan, his smile now gone. "Boss go to fancy soirees. Big society luncheons and teas up 'on hill.'" He brightened as he added, "But due back any minute. Be here before you know it."

As Ling Tan spoke, shrill feminine laughter floated in from the club's grand salon. Kay glanced toward the wide corridor leading into the club. Her attention came back to Ling Tan.

"Tell your tardy boss—if and when he arrives—that I'm waiting in the club. If he wants his money, he can come to me." Inclining her bonneted head, Kay indicated the sound of the women's laughter. "I'll visit with the Carousel ladies while I wait."

A look of extreme discomfort came over the Chinese servant's face. "Oh, not wise, Missy Captain. You know. Not wise. Boss not like when speak too long with his ladies."

Kay did know.

Nick McCabe was highly annoyed any time he saw her talking with his dancing girls. The dark saloon owner was still angry over the loss of Big Alfred and Rose. And a couple of the girls whose job it was to ride nightly on the Golden Carousel had followed Rose into the ranks of the Corps. Nick McCabe was afraid still more girls might be persuaded to jump ship.

"I know he doesn't like it," said Kay. She smiled at the worried little man and added, "I'll accept full blame, Ling Tan."

Ling Tan clasped his hands before him, uneasy. But ever polite, he nodded and asked, "May I bring Missy Captain refreshment. Hot coffee? Cup of tea or—"

"A cup of tea sounds wonderful, Ling Tan. Thank you so much."

Kay took off her bonnet, smoothed down unruly locks of flaming red hair, and patted the neat bun at the back of her head.

In the arched, curtained doorway of the grand salon, Kay paused. Across the large, shadowy room, four female entertainers sat at the hexagonal mahogany bar. Talking and laughing. Kay recognized three of the women. Trixie, Babette, and Darlene. The fourth, a striking dark-haired woman in a blue wool wrapper, was a stranger to Kay.

Kay's eyes lifted from the women and the mahogany bar to the unmoving golden carousel above their heads. She was—and had been since her first shocked glimpse—absolutely fascinated with the magical, steam-driven merry-go-round. It was a beautifully crafted piece of work. A mechanical marvel. The meticulously carved wooden horses actually appeared to be alive.

Golden manes and tails streamed out as if windblown. Powerful, perfectly shaped golden bodies displayed the ply and pull of sleek firm muscle, like that of real-life, hard-breathing equestrians. Gleaming withers seemed to actually quiver. Eyes were wide and wild, nostrils flared.

Mesmerized, Kay stared unblinking at the exquisitely carved creatures. Blue eyes clinging to the carousel, she was seized with a ridiculous urge to ride one of the magnificent golden steeds. How would it feel to climb up into a gold-and-white gilt saddle and blithely ride as the merry-go-round began to turn until it spun faster and faster?

Kay felt her face flush hotly, as if she were considering engaging in some truly evil act. She guiltily lowered her eyes, composed herself, and moved forward toward the women.

"Captain Kay," the blond Trixie stopped in midsentence as she caught sight of Kay. "Girls, look who's here."

"Hello, everyone," Kay greeted the foursome. Smiling at each woman in turn, Kay was introduced to the striking brunette in the blue robe. Shaking hands with Angel Thompson, Kay noticed the young woman's arresting almond-shaped eyes, her unblemished milky white skin, and her long stockinged legs immodestly revealed by her carelessly parted robe.

"I hope we'll be friends, Angel." Kay laid her hat down on the polished mahogany and climbed on a bar stool beside the brunette dancer.

Eyeing Kay's uniform, Angel replied in a surprisingly low, smoky voice, "You're not some kind of female law come to take me in for indecent exposure, are you?"

"No, nothing like that," Kay assured. "I'm a captain in the Salvation Army." She looked from Angel to the others. "And I'd like to talk with you about the Almighty."

"Who?" Trixie asked with an impudent toss of her blond curls. "Oh, you mean Nick?"

The girls broke up with laughter. A good sport, Captain Kay laughed with them. They were still laughing when a deep masculine voice from out of the shadows lazily inquired, "Someone asking for me?"

All heads turned to see the tall, dark Nick standing in the arched doorway, backlit by the light from the corridor.

"Speak of the devil," Kay automatically quipped, and the girls laughed again.

"Good God above," said Nick, a look of genuine disbelief on his dark face, "if it isn't Kay Montgomery bellying up to the bar."

"That's Captain Montgomery to you, McCabe," Kay snapped.

"Hi, Nick. Hello, boss," the entertainers murmured in honeyed tones, their faces beginning to glow at the mere sight of him.

All but Kay's.

Her face went cold as stone, spotting, even across the room, the fact that he was inebriated.

Nick flashed Kay a wicked little smirk. Then favored the girls with one of his most appealing, slightly crooked grins. Kay didn't miss the swift, silent exchange take place between Nick and Angel Thompson. His silver gaze touched Angel's long legs, then lifted to her face. With a glance, the lift of a dark eyebrow, Nick McCabe conveyed something secret—something personal. Something just for Angel.

Kay caught the message pass between the pair and felt embarrassed. And irritated. Had Nick McCabe already added the beautiful Angel Thompson to his long list of lovers? The devil was no better than an alley tomcat!

Not realizing she was making a terrible face, Kay tensed as the drunken, darkly handsome Nick crossed the big salon, determinedly approaching the bar. He wore an impeccably tailored suit of fine gray flannel, but the stylish short-cut suit jacket and matching waistcoat were unbuttoned and carelessly pushed apart as he dug his hands deep into his pants pocket.

A burgundy silk bow tie was untied and hanging loose around his neck. The stiff collar of his white shirt was open at his tanned throat. With no waistcoat buttoned over his torso, the thick, black hair covering his broad chest showed through the soft cotton fabric of his white shirt.

Teeth and fists clenched, Kay realized her eyes were fixed and lingering on that dark evidence of his masculine virility. She quickly lifted her gaze to Nick's face, but not before he'd caught her looking. Nick winked at her. She blushed.

He said, "Captain, you're blushing."

"Well, stop it!" Kay said.

"Stop what?" he asked, as if puzzled.

He still had the black eye, but it had quickly lightened in color. He was able to fully open and use his eye. Oddly, that fading badge he'd won in an some violent fracas was strangely appealing. It added a touch of vulnerability to a man who had heretofore appeared impervious.

Kay could understand his appeal to women. What she couldn't understand was how any self-respecting female would put up with a man who had no morals. A man who would never commit to any one woman but loved them all with careless abandon.

Kay had been shocked to the roots of her flaming red hair when Patrick Packard had confided that his only sister, Adele, was seeing Nick McCabe socially. Was the refined Adele Packard totally ignorant of Nick's profession? His sinful way of life?

After warmly and personally greeting each woman present, Nick turned to Kay and said, "Captain, you look as if you'd just detected a foul odor."

He stepped up beside her, reached down, and turned her bar stool so that she was facing him. Continuing to hold to the stool, he shot a long arm out, gripped the mahogany bar with his hand, and leaned down close to her face.

"And so I do," said Kay. "The liquor on your breath, McCabe. You're drunk."

"Guilty as charged," Nick readily admitted. "I've been to number of charity functions where a degree of liquid hospitality was pressed on me." A lock of raven-black hair fell across his tanned forehead as he leaned even closer and added, "I accepted more foolishly than wisely."

Kay quickly lifted a flattened palm against his chest and gave him a backward push. "Fools generally behave foolishly."

"Fool? You call me a fool before my employees? Why, it's enough to take the heart out of man."

"What heart?" Kay rejoined.

Unruffled, Nick grinned and looked around, enlisting the support of the entertainers. "What about it, ladies? You going to let this Army captain insult me? Am I a mean, uncaring man?"

"Oh, no, boss. No, certainly not," all swiftly and emphatically agreed.

"He's really not, Captain Kay," Trixie said earnestly, "Nick's the best boss a girl could have. So protective and understanding. Right, girls?"

"Right, Trixie! Absolutely."

Kay sighed and rolled her eyes heavenward. Beaten by the devilishly grinning Nick McCabe, she slid down off the bar stool. Anxious to pay him and be gone, she was reaching into her pocket for the money when he plucked her bonnet off the bar and took hold of her elbow.

"If you'll excuse us, girls," he addressed the dancers, "the captain and I have private business which must be attended."

"Where do you think you're taking me?" Kay hung back. "We can handle the transaction right here." She withdrew the money, held it out to him.

Swiftly Nick covered her hand with his, enclosing it and the money. "I never conduct my affairs anywhere other than my office or up in my apartment," he stated.

Kay lifted an accusing eyebrow. Nick read her thoughts and corrected himself. "Business affairs, Captain." Propelling her across the shadowy, carpeted club, he lifted a hand and waved to the girls left behind at the bar. "Love affairs? Now that's something else entirely," Nick said softly, leaning down close to Kay's ear. "Why, I imagine that even a tumbledown waterfront warehouse being used as a mission would be suitable for a stolen hour of amour."

Eyes flashing, Kay hissed, "Don't you speak to me of such things, Nick McCabe!"

"I'm serious, Captain. I understand Patrick Packard is calling on you this evening. Is he?"

"What if he is!"

"Have him come early," Nick suggested. "Then lock old Patrick up inside that warehouse and see if I'm not right about anyplace being the right place for lovemaking. Be good for you both."

"I will not listen to any more of this filth. Kindly shut your mouth!"

His hand at the small of her back, Nick guided Kay out into the corridor. "Captain, I'm only thinking of you. You always look so . . . ummmm . . . lonely."

"You lout!" Kay shouted, then raised her hand and slapped him hard.

Rubbing his stinging face, Nick grinned and said, "Now I see why."

Chapter 17

Kay was immediately repentant.

In horror she stared up at Nick, shocked by her own rash act. The red imprint of her hand was clearly visible on his tanned cheek. And to make matters worse, she'd struck the right side of his face—further punishing his battered eye.

"McCabe, I'm sorry! I'm so sorry," Kay said miserably, her face screwed up into a frown of sympathy. She quickly lifted a hand to soothingly stroke his stinging cheek.

But Nick's long fingers firmly enclosed her wrist and drew her hand away. His full sculpted lips stretched into a Satanic grin and his hooded silver-gray eyes held a devilish gleam.

"Ah, Captain, Captain." The timbre of his voice was low, the words slightly slurred. "I can't tell you how disappointed I am in you."

Kay knew better. She knew he was tickled pink that he'd so easily caused her to lose control. She attempted to free her wrist from his tight grip. Nick wouldn't permit it.

"I know, McCabe. I know," Kay said. "If it'll make you feel any better, I'm disappointed in myself. I lost my temper. I shouldn't have. And I certainly shouldn't have slapped you. I apologize, McCabe."

"An apology?" said Nick, drawing her closer by her imprisoned wrist. "You? Is this the end of the world? Has old Gabriel finally blown his horn?"

"Look, I've said I'm sorry and I am. Please forgive me. I *do* genuinely apologize."

"Apology accepted," said Nick. With a grin, he quickly added, "However, you'll surely need to do penance for that violent show of temper." He chuckled softly when a new flash of fire sparked in Kay's blue eyes.

"You just never know when to quit, do you, McCabe?" she bit out her words and forcefully jerked her wrist free.

"Funny, I was thinking the same thing about you, Captain." The twinkling light abruptly vanished from Nick's eyes. The smile left his lips. "Shall we go upstairs to continue our little meeting?"

"No!" Kay was quick to answer. "Absolutely not. *We* will not go upstairs! This little meeting is adjourned." She thrust the folded bills at him. "Here, take your money! Take it and count it quickly." Nick's hands remained at his sides. He made no move to take the money.

Voice lifting, Kay said, "I want you to take this money. I want you to count it. I want to get out of here. I want—"

"I want, I want," Nick interrupted, mimicking her. "With you it's always 'I want this, I want that.' " His eyes narrowed. "Let me tell you what I want."

"I don't care what you want, McCabe."

"Now that's a mistake, Captain. A big mistake. I strongly suggest you learn to care. And quickly."

Kay tilted her head to the side. "Care what a drunken saloon owner does or does not want?" she asked incredulously. "You must be kidding."

"I do not kid," Nick said with a sudden hard edge to his voice. "Now get yourself up those stairs and make it snappy. That's what *I* want. And I always get my way."

Kay laughed in his face. "Not this time, Big Boy. Not with me you don't." She swiftly stuffed the money into the breast pocket of his gray suit jacket then backed cautiously away and taunted, "The only way you'd ever get me up those stairs would be to bodily . . ." Kay realized what she was saying and stopped in midsentence.

Nick reacted so swiftly it took her breath away. He snatched her right off her feet and swung her up into his arms in the blinking of an eye.

"Not a bad idea," he said drunkenly, and began climbing the stairs with her in his arms.

"You bully! You brute!" Kay loudly objected to his caveman tactics. "Put me down! I am *not* going upstairs with you!"

"You're wrong," Nick coolly informed her. "Upstairs is exactly where you're going. And upstairs is exactly where you'll remain until I allow you to leave."

"If you don't put me down, I'll scream bloody murder," warned Kay. Nick ignored the threat, continued to drunkenly ascend the carpeted stairs, slipping once, almost falling. "I will," Kay assured him. "I'll scream loudly enough for everyone to hear."

"Go right ahead," said Nick. "Yours won't be the first woman's scream ever heard under this roof."

"Oh!"

Squirming and scratching, Kay caught sight of Ling Tan over Nick's shoulder. The servant had stepped into the wide downstairs corridor, bearing a tray with china teapot and cups.

"Ling Tan," she called desperately to him, "help! Help me!"

The slender Chinese servant looked up, saw the pair, and almost dropped the tray. He worriedly hurried to the base of the stairs. "Boss, something wrong? Missy Captain fall and get hurt?"

Nick stopped, turned, blinked bleary-eyed at Ling Tan. Then he looked appraisingly at Kay while she frantically struggled in his arms. "No. No, she's just fine." He smiled down at Ling Tan. Then his glance shifted back the angry Kay. "Your halo still intact, Captain?"

Kay shrieked at him. "You ill-bred, contemptible, irreverent, disrespectful—"

"Yes, she's okay," Nick again assured the concerned servant, turned, and proceeded up the stairs. "Bring the captain's tea up to my quarters," he called down.

Furious, Kay hissed, "This is a crime, Nick McCabe, a heinous crime punishable by death! It's is nothing short of forced abduction!"

"That's what you call it. I call it 'explaining things in a manner even you can understand.' "

"You won't get away with this," she screeched when Nick stepped onto the second-floor landing.

"Wanna bet?" Nick answered breezily as he reached the door of his apartment and carried Kay through.

Once inside the comfortable sitting room, Nick didn't release Kay. He continued to hold her firmly in his arms. He carried the angry, struggling Kay across the deep lush carpet to the gray marble fireplace.

Again she vehemently protested, "I *am* upstairs. You can put me down now, you've made your point."

"Nope," said Nick. "Not yet. After Ling's come and gone. Then I'll put you down."

Weaving a little, Nick stood, feet apart, directly before the gray marble fireplace in which a bright, warming fire snapped and crackled. White-orange flames danced and leapt in the hearth, shooting high up to the wide marble mantel.

The mantel above which hung a huge silver-framed mirror reflecting the images of the pair. Kay fell silent as she caught sight of the two of them in the mirror.

Her face was bloodred, her eyes wild, her bonnet missing. A thick wedge of red hair had escaped the bun at her nape and was framing her left cheek, the curling ends fanned out on her throat. The silver S brooch was missing from her military collar, lost somewhere in the heated tussle. A couple of brass tunic buttons had come undone, wantonly exposing the rising swell of her pale bosom. One of her hands was behind Nick's back, frantically gripping the fine gray fabric of his suit jacket. The other was flattened on his chest.

Kay was grateful that no one could see the uncivilized woman reflected in the silver-framed mirror. She looked nothing like a smartly uniformed, capable, compassionate Salvation Army captain.

The man holding her offensively close in his long powerful arms was as disheveled as she. A lock of raven hair had fallen into Nick's bruised right eye. Her handprint was gone from his cheek, but a couple of scratches decorated his temple and chin. She knew her sharp nails were responsible. A fine sheen of perspiration shimmered on his dark face as if he were too warm, while his darkly lashed eyes appeared to be of silver ice.

Her fists hammering ferociously at Nick's chest had scattered gold studs in their wake. And left his white shirt immodestly open down his dark torso. Crisp dark hair covered the hard flat muscles of his chest and narrowed into a thick well-defined line going down his taut abdomen.

There was a piratical mien about him. He looked swarthy and dangerous. All he lacked was a gold ring in his ear.

Staring into those pale silver eyes in the mirror, Kay became alarmingly aware that her hand was resting squarely on his slow, rhythmically beating heart, her fingers threaded through damp, springy chest hair.

Kay involuntarily shuddered.

A mysterious sensation suddenly seized her, one she'd never before experienced. It was totally foreign and frightening. It was also strangely thrilling. She was uncomfortably warm, almost feverish. At the same time she shivered as if from the cold. She felt curiously giddy yet inexplicably troubled.

The puzzling emotion was totally new to Kay, so she didn't recognize it for what it was. She knew only that Nick McCabe was responsible.

Much too quickly Kay jerked her hand off his naked chest and released her hold on his jacket. Her body stiffened. She caught the almost imperceptible curling of Nick's upper lip and was mortified. He knew what had happened to her. Knew how strongly he had affected her.

"I want you to—" Kay began, but caught herself. "McCabe, won't you please put me down?"

"Promise to behave yourself? Not run for the door?"

"Yes. I mean no. I mean . . . oh, you know what I mean."

"In that case . . ." Nick lowered her feet to the floor with deliberate slowness, keeping an arm snug around her narrow waist. Kay felt her stomach, her hips, her legs slipping, sliding slowly, provocatively down against his tall, rock-hard frame. She clutched at his biceps with cold, clammy hands while her toes searched anxiously for the floor.

She felt so faint and dizzy, she continued to cling to Nick for support even after her feet were planted firmly on the carpet.

Anxiously Kay stepped back from Nick when Ling Tan bustled in with the tea tray. Eyes darting nervously from Nick to Kay, the servant placed the tray on a mahogany drum table and poured two cups of hot black tea.

"Be anything more, boss?" Ling Tan asked respectfully, noting Nick's scratched chin, his open shirt. As well as Kay's pinkened face and untidy hair.

"No. That'll be all." Nick promptly ushered Ling Tan to the door and locked it behind him.

Kay tensed.

"Relax," Nick said with his back still to her. "Sit down."

Kay remained standing.

Turning, Nick approached her. "Drink your tea." He shrugged out of his suit jacket and matching waistcoat, tossing both across a chair back. "I seem to have lost the studs from my shirt." He loosely gripped the sides of the open white shirt, adding, "If you'll excuse me for a minute I'll see to a fresh one. That is, unless you don't mind my bare chest."

"Please put on a shirt."

She picked up a cup of tea from the tray and sat down with the injured pride of the conquered. As soon as he was gone, she set the cup aside and anxiously buttoned her tunic up to her throat. She tucked her hair back in place, straightened her skirts, rose and looked about on the carpeted floor for her S brooch. She didn't find it.

She was again seated on the long sofa sipping her tea when Nick returned. His black hair was brushed back from his eyes. The scratches on his face had been sponged of blood. He wore a shirt of navy silk with the gray suit trousers.

In his hand was a glass of liquor. Kay glanced nervously at the locked door. This dark, drunken saloon owner had stirred a dangerous excitement in her. Kay fought it the only way she knew how. By insulting him.

"Drinking again?" she asked with a note of contempt in her voice. "You're already quite drunk, McCabe."

"I'm having a drink," he said. "That doesn't mean that I'm drunk."

"You look drunk. You walk drunk. You smell drunk."

Nick held up his liquor glass in mock salute, lifted it to his lips, and drained it in one long swallow. Then went to the drink trolley and poured himself a fresh one. Weaving slightly, he came to the sofa and dropped down beside Kay.

"Get this straight, Captain"—the words were slurred—"if I want to drink, I'll drink. If I want to get drunk, I'll get drunk." Kay shrugged, focused her attention on the black tea in her cup. "Look at me!" Nick said, and his tone of his voice made Kay's head snap around. "I do as I like in this town and anyone who gets in my way . . ." He shook his head and paused. "You're in my way, Captain, and it's beginning to annoy me."

"Obviously you're a man who's easily annoyed," said Kay, indicating his healing black eye. "Still enjoy barroom brawls? Isn't it about time you outgrew such foolishness?"

A vein pulsed on Nick's forehead. Every muscle in his lean body tensed. "Some day you're going to say something smart and I'll forget you're a woman."

"I was merely pointing out that—"

"I'll do all the pointing out around here, Captain," Nick interrupted, his eyebrows turned menacingly dark. "I've you to thank for this shiner. You persuaded Big Alfred to leave me and join your Band of Angels." Kay opened her mouth to speak. He silenced her with a look. "You think I like getting my brains beat out? I sure as hell don't, but I have no choice. I have to defend myself and my club."

"I'm sorry."

"No, you're not sorry. You took my bouncer, my star attraction, a couple of the Carousel girls. You'd be happy if you could put me out of business. But that's not going to happen. You'll never ruin the trade at the Golden Carousel."

"Probably not. You always were frightfully clever, I imagine."

"That's right, Captain, I'm smart. Damned smart."

"Really? Then I suppose we do have one thing in common."

"We have plenty in common," Nick said, took a drink, reached across Kay, and slammed the glass down on an end table. "I bring the lost in out of the darkness into the light and relieve them of their material burden. You do the same thing."

"Sacrilege! The hinges of Hell yawn for you, McCabe."

"No doubt, but Hell will have to wait. I like it right here. I like my life. I like my saloon most of all. This club means more to me than anything. Or anyone."

"Your saloon is the Devil's own workshop," retorted Kay. "And you, Nick McCabe, are a devil!"

"A devil, you say?" he said with a wicked grin, and leaned familiarly close. "Would you like to meet Satan's little helper?" His hands went to his belt buckle.

"Oh!" Kay gasped her outrage and shot up off the sofa as if she'd been fired from a cannon. "You vile, vulgar, disgusting . . ."

"Bastard?" Nick rose to face her. "That I am, Captain. And you're a psalm-singing pain in the—"

"Nick McCabe!" Kay's breath left her body in a loud *whoosh*. She whirled away and hurried for the door. Nick beat her to it. He slammed a muscular shoulder up against the heavy door, blocking her way.

"Don't come sniffing around my girls again, trying to steal them from me. Do and you'll find yourself in hot water."

Forcing herself to look unflinchingly into those liquor-brightened silver eyes, Kay said, "I'm not afraid of you!"

"But you're afraid of yourself," he said with an evil smirk. "Remember what happened earlier as I held you in front of the fireplace?"

Kay's face flushed with heat. "Nothing happened."

"Captain, you know it's a sin to tell a lie." Nick shook his head and in a thick, lowered voice added, "Tonight when you're lying there in your bed in the darkness, you'll catch yourself remembering the strange, exciting little 'nothing' that happened here today."

"Let me out of this room!"

"Go." Nick yanked the door open wide. "Get out of my sight." He took her hand in his and pressed into her palm the silver S brooch. "But first, Captain, take this pin and stick it right up—"

"Nick McCabe!"

"—there on your collar."

Chapter 18

"You're a big surprise to me."

"Selling children?"

"It isn't altogether legal. You might call it criminal." The sallow-complected man licked his thin upper lip. His beady black eyes gleamed as he added, "You've no objection?"

"Objection?" echoed the portly, one-eyed man seated behind an enormous desk of black walnut. "How do you think I became rich in the first place?"

The two men were speaking quietly in a huge, luxurious office. The corner office was located on the top floor of the tallest building in San Francisco's financial district. The north facing office afforded an unobstructed panorama of the bay.

Seated in his tall-backed swivel chair of burgundy leather, the man behind the desk had a bird's-eye view. He could amuse himself by simply looking out the tall plate-glass windows. If he chose to do so, he could effortlessly monitor all activity in the busy port. He could see the scrappy tugs plying the choppy waters of the harbor. Could watch the stately oceangoing vessels as they steamed grandly into port. Could even glimpse the tiny sailboats, bobbing up and down, circling the peninsula.

This same spectacular view was offered to any guest seated across from him in one of the matching easy chairs.

But on this cold, gray December morning, neither the tastefully dressed, one-eyed gentleman behind the walnut desk nor the flashily outfitted man whose index finger was missing from his right hand were interested in the expansive vista.

A meeting was under way. A meeting that had been called for by the portly one-eyed man.

Seemingly casual and of little consequence, the meeting was anything but.

Conducted in secrecy at the early hour of dawn, the two-man conference was of the utmost importance. Decisions made in that sky-high office would forever alter lives. Ruin lives. End lives.

This was a clandestine meeting between San Francisco's prominent society attorney, Dysart K. Lavender, and the Barbary Coast's lowest lowlife of all, Top Hat Saloon owner Three Fingers Jackson.

It would appear that two men of such diverse backgrounds and professions would have little or nothing in common. But appearances could be misleading.

Dysart K. Lavender, respected attorney, devoted husband, proud father, patron of the arts, generous philanthropist, and Three Fingers Jackson, disdained brothel owner, thrice divorced, childless, tight with a dollar, and incredibly greedy, were partners.

Partners in a highly profitable commercial venture that had made hundreds of thousands of dollars for the wealthy Dysart K. Lavender, tens of thousands for Three Fingers Jackson. The partnership was strictly secret. As was the nature of the enterprise.

Lavender was the undisputed first among equals. And at the partnership's inception, he had calmly promised Jackson if their secret was ever exposed, Jackson would be held solely responsible.

Three Fingers Jackson knew Lavender meant every word he said. He was deathly afraid of the corrupt, corpulent attorney; terrified the truth might leak out and he would be blamed. And punished.

He was ill at ease each time the well-bred attorney dropped in at his Top Hat Club. He'd warned Lavender that it was dangerous, that someone might see him there, put two and two together. But Lavender wouldn't listen. Considered a quiet family man by the city's bluebloods, Lavender occasionally showed up at the Top Hat club with a couple of elegant lady friends seeking an afternoon of drunken, bawdy fun.

Even now, at dawn in this empty office building, Three Fingers Jackson was edgy. He was eager to get the business at hand taken care of and be gone before anyone could catch him in Lavender's fancy office.

Three Fingers Jackson had witnessed firsthand how cruel the lawyer could be, so he never objected that Lavender took the lion's share of the money while he took all the risks.

Looking now at the heavy-jowled man with the black eye patch, Three Fingers licked his thin upper lip and impatiently awaited his instructions.

Dysart Lavender swiveled his chair away from the desk. He rose and moved aside a low Jacobean chest. He crouched down to the baseboard and slid open a secret panel. He reached into the hidden cabinet he'd had built into the wall and took out a silk-lined drawstring purse heavy with precious jewels.

He then withdrew a folded piece of cream parchment from the small silk-lined bag, brushing emeralds and diamonds from the paper as if they were an annoyance. He replaced the jewel-filled bag inside the secret compartment and stood up. He held the folded paper in his hand.

Lavender sat back down and swiveled to face Three Fingers Jackson. He leisurely unfolded the sheet of parchment upon which a list was written in his own distinctive scrawling hand. Opening his one eye wide, the attorney read to the sallow saloon owner seated across from him.

"A half-dozen boys between the ages of eight and twelve. Another half-dozen slightly older, but none older than sixteen. A dozen girls from six to fourteen." Lavender looked up. "Think you can fill the order by a January fifteenth deadline?"

Jackson nervously licked his upper lip. "I've got my scouts out on the streets now. We already have several kids marked for pickup." He exhaled and worriedly confided, "It's not as easy finding the kids these days. Those Salvation Army people get to them before we can; warn 'em to stay off the streets. Take the homeless kids to the orphanage."

"That bunch of religious fanatics still on the Coast? They'll surely give up one day soon. Meanwhile, you'll just have to outsmart them." Lavender paused. "Think you can?"

"Sure I can."

"Good. Good," said Lavender. "This barter's a big one. We're dealing with a new customer with deep pockets and continuing demands. We must prove we can be counted on to deliver the goods."

"I understand," said Jackson. Then, curious, he asked, "The new customer—who is it? What will he do with the children we sell him?"

Lavender stroked his chin. "You don't have know who the customer is. As for his plans for the kids, it's my understanding that most of the younger boys will be made house slaves to prominent families in China. The older ones will become unpaid sailors, manning cargo ships between here and the Far East. The strongest of the girls will be used for household slaves and cooks in China."

"And the others?"

"The rest of the boys and girls—the prettiest of the lot—will stay right here in San Francisco. They'll be sent into to opium dens to supply sexual pleasures to the deviates."

"Good enough," said Jackson. "I'll see if my spotters can locate some cute kids and—"

"Oh, that reminds me," Lavender interrupted. "The customer has requested we find a girl for him personally. He's very selective; has refined taste. He wants a young Chinese woman, small in statue but perfectly formed. A graceful creature with soft, well-cared-for hands. Her hair must reach at least to her waist. She must be intelligent, clean and disease free, and very beautiful."

Three Fingers Jackson frowned. "That's a mighty tall order."

Lavender nodded. "A China doll."

"Girls of that description don't usually go about on the city streets alone," said Jackson.

"I know. See what you can come up with. Down the road you may have to resort to grabbing somebody's pretty young wife or daughter out of the home. Whatever it takes."

"I'll handle it," said Jackson. "Now back to the regular order. When should I move? Tonight? Tomorrow night?"

Carefully folding the parchment back into its original shape, Dysart K. Lavender smiled. "No. No need to be in that big a hurry. Wait till after Christmas."

Three Fingers Jackson grinned, his beady black eyes glittering with malevolence. "You're all heart, Lavender."

"Yes, I am. The Yuletide season is a time when families should be together."

"God, you're one cold bastard," Three Fingers Jackson said, laughing.

The attorney touched the perfectly tied four-in-hand at his fleshy throat. "December thirty-first would be a splendid time to strike. Kick the New Year off right."

And a pleased smile lighted the fleshy face of the one-eyed Dysart K. Lavender, respected society attorney and cunning mastermind of the predatory, law-eluding peddlers of human flesh.

The Shadow Clan.

Chapter 19

 On Christmas morning in the city by the bay, a happy young girl threw her arms around the neck of a blinking, sleepy Nick McCabe.

"Mr. Nick, you are too good to me!" trilled a joyful Ming Ho, her face pressed against the soft lapel of Nick's dark robe. "Thank you! Thank you!"

"You're very welcome." Nick patted her slender back and kissed the top of her dark head. "Merry Christmas, sweetheart."

"Merry Christmas to you!" Ming Ho gave his neck one last squeeze and released him.

"Look, Father, look." She spun about to show a beaming Ling Tan the delicate locket of gold resting in her palm. The locket was but one of a half-dozen gifts Nick had given her.

"Very beautiful," said Ling Tan. And he too thanked Nick McCabe for his thoughtfulness and generosity.

Nick waved away their gratitude, shrugged wide, robe-clad shoulders, and said in a half-gruff voice, "Enough of this foolishness. Beat it, you two, I have to dress." But his silver-gray eyes shone warmly.

Back in their apartment, Ming Ho handed the gold locket to her father. She eagerly swept her heavy black hair off her fragile neck, turned her back to Ling Tan, and stood very still while he closed the tiny clasp.

"There," he said, giving her slender shoulders a squeeze. "Locket very beautiful. Wearer of locket even more beautiful."

"Now, Father," Ming Ho gently scolded, "you think me pretty because I'm your daughter." She skipped happily over to the mirror above the mantel to admire the locket.

Her father smiled and fondly admired her. Maybe he was a little prejudiced, but not much. Ming Ho *was* beautiful. She had been beautiful since birth. Now as she approached her seventeenth year, she was an exquisite little creature. Tiny but perfectly formed, with gentle womanly curves. Her hair was a long magnificent mane. Thick, glossy, and of a blue-black hue, the fragrant tresses reached to well below her narrow waist. Her feet were dainty. Her hands were small and meticulously cared for, soft and soothing to the touch.

Ling Tan abruptly clapped his hands together. "If most beautiful daughter not wish to go out in nightclothes, best start getting dressed. Chop chop."

"Yes," agreed Ming Ho, whirling from the mirror, "I must hurry. The morning has flown!" She flew then, right into her bedroom.

An hour passed before Ming Ho reappeared, looking unusually pretty in a stylish suit of soft crimson wool. Her head was bare, the raven hair parted in the middle and flowing down her back. The gold locket glittered on the bright red wool.

Cheeks flushed with excitement, Ming Ho—with her father's blessing—was to spend this Christmas day quite differently from in years past.

The Salvation Army was serving Christmas dinner to anyone and everyone who showed up at their waterfront warehouse mission. Ming Ho had volunteered to help out. Later, after everyone had been fed, she would go to the Battery Place orphanage with the Corps members for a big Christmas party.

Ever the protective father, Ling Tan immediately began warning his young daughter and issuing last-minute instructions. Ming Ho, with the typical that-could-never-happen-to-me arrogance of youth, sighed with impatience.

"Oh, Father," she said, "I've told you a dozen times Big Alfred is coming for me. After the party, he'll escort me back home, so stop being such a worrywart." She glanced at the clock on the mantel. "I'm late! Big Alfred's probably already downstairs."

Ming Ho gave her father's cheek a glancing kiss, dashed to the door, and hurried out into the wide upstairs corridor. Her father followed closely on her heels.

Nick, dressed to the teeth in a handsomely cut suit of the finest wool and a black Chesterfield coat, stepped out of his apartment, late for his holiday engagement at Adele Packard's Nob Hill mansion.

Nick looked up, saw a vision in red floating toward him, skirts daintily lifted. He grinned, crossed his arms over his chest, and watched her approach. Ming Ho stopped short when she reached him.

Smiling down at her, Nick said, "You look like . . . like a real china doll." She glowed. He offered her his bent arm. "May I see you downstairs to your escort?"

A half frown came over Ming Ho's expressive young face. "Nick, you know my escort is Big Alfred?"

"Sure I do. I'll wish the Englishman a Merry Christmas."

"Good! That will make him most happy!" Ming Ho exchanged smiles with her father. Then bade him a last good-bye and descended the wide staircase on Nick's arm. The couple crossed the shadowy grand salon and stepped out into the cold, brilliant sunshine.

"Little Ming Ho," Big Alfred warmly greeted her, then looked up in surprise. "Laddie!"

Nick grinned and firmly shook the big man's hand. "Happy holidays, Big Al."

"And the very same to you, my boy," said Big Alfred, his hazel eyes twinkling with relief and joy. "You're looking well."

"Aw, I don't know. I'm getting a little soft," said Nick, patting his flat belly. "Can't find a good sparring partner."

Big Alfred's bushy eyebrows bristled hopefully. "I could be persuaded to go a few rounds with you now and then. That is . . . if you'd like."

Nick said, "Really? Think the iron-petticoated captain would allow it?"

"Now, Nick, Captain Montgomery's nothing like you perceive her to be." Big Alfred wagged his head back and forth. "The captain's a very easygoing, understanding woman."

"She is, Nick. Honest." Ming Ho spoke up. "You don't know her. Not really."

"Perhaps not." Smile still bright, Nick warned Ming Ho, "Just make sure you come home wearing that same bright-red suit, not Army blue. Your father and I plan on having San Francisco's first lady doctor in this family."

Ming Ho smiled and nodded. Nick patted her shoulder and again shook Big Alfred's hand.

Alfred Duke said, "Laddie, let's get together at the Athletic Club after the holidays."

Nick grinned and cocked a finger at him. "You're on."

Nick walked to the waiting carriage and climbed inside while Ming Ho and Big Alfred set out down the street.

"Ho! Ho! Ho!"

Santa Claus walked into the Battery Place gymnasium that cold Christmas day at shortly after three, a large pack of presents on his back.

Old Santa was gigantic. The red fabric of his suit stretched across a broad, powerful back, massive shoulders, and muscular arms. With one huge gloved hand, Santa easily bore his heavy burden of toys and games and candy.

The flowing white beard, the ruddy cheeks, the belly that shook when he laughed immediately convinced the excited children of Battery Place that this awesome giant was surely the one and only Santa Claus. Their wide shining eyes riveted to the enormous Saint Nicholas, none noticed that the bass "ho, ho, hos" he bellowed had the distinctive hint of a British accent.

Captain Kay was in the sunny gymnasium, seated on a straight back chair between Ming Ho and her sister-in-law, Private Rose Reilly Montgomery. Kay inspected Santa Claus with eyes as wide as the children's. She watched as he laughed and took a turn about inside the large circle of children seated on the floor. She tensed when he completed the tour and moved directly toward the smallest child in the circle.

The tiny blue-eyed boy with hair of flaming copper.

Kay tingled with anticipation when old Santa reached into his heavy pack, brought out a brightly wrapped package, bent and handed it down to Joey. Her excitement escalated when Joey's short fingers reached for the offered present. She clasped her hands tightly together in her lap when the puzzled child looked up at the gigantic Santa towering above.

Old Santa swung his pack down from his shoulder, dropped it to the floor, and slowly, cautiously crouched down before the mystified Joey. So attuned was Kay to the pair, she was able to shut out all the noise and laughter going on around her in order to hear what Santa said to Joey.

With a touch of tenderness in his gravel-gruff voice, Big Alfred said, "Little laddie, don't you want to open the present old Santa Claus brought especially for you?"

Open-mouthed, Joey stared at Santa's twinkling hazel eyes, the broad ruddy face, his flowing white beard. He shook his copper head and lifted his narrow shoulders, a quizzical look on his little face.

"Who is Santa Claus?"

Kay quickly covered her mouth with her hand to stifle the sob of despair burning her tight throat. A four-year-old child who'd never heard of Santa Claus. What must his brief, tragic life have been?

Kay bit her lip as Big Alfred patiently explained that Santa was the spirit of Christmas. That Santa Claus loved all little boys and girls and he brought them presents each Christmas. The gentle giant then sat completely down, cross-legged, on the hard floor, and picked up Joey in his huge hands. He placed Joey on his lap. He helped the bewildered child unwrap the present.

Kay's heart sank when Joey touched the set of wooden, brightly uniformed toy soldiers but didn't pick any of them up. His big blue eyes didn't light up with happiness. He didn't shriek with joy, or laugh, or turn and hug old Santa's neck.

Big Alfred knew the other boys and girls were anxiously waiting. He gently sat Joey back on the floor, placed the open box of wooden soldiers on his little knees, and rose. Before Santa could hoist the heavy sack up onto his back, Joey had already laid the box aside.

Kay bit the inside of her lip until she tasted blood.

She had personally chosen the toy soldiers for Joey from a store full of toys. She'd spent hours trying to decide on exactly the right present. She'd lain awake nights considering what might delight the tiny four-year-old boy who never spoke or smiled. And now Joey had set the soldiers aside without a second look.

Santa Claus passed out the remainder of the gifts. Squeals of joy and shouts of happiness rang out as, one by one, the excited children unwrapped their presents. After the very last package had been ripped open, Christmas carols were sung. Candies and cookies were devoured. The children showed one another their new toys and games.

The party ended at five o'clock, and everyone agreed it had been a smashing success. Everyone but Kay.

While Big Alfred saw Ming Ho safely home, and Curly and Rose slipped away for Christmas supper alone, Kay dejectedly returned to the waterfront warehouse with Giles Lawton, Bobby Newman, Matthew, and a half dozen other soldiers.

Few people showed up for evening services that cold Christmas night, so Kay cut her sermon short. Afterward the tireless soldiers split up in pairs to hit the streets, carrying the metal kettles they had painted a bright Christmas red.

For once, Captain Kay begged off. She stayed behind while the others spilled out of the warehouse singing "Adeste Fidelis." When their voices had died away, Kay extinguished the lamps.

In the chill winter moonlight, she walked the three blocks to the large, cheery Sansome Street quarters of Big Alfred where she and several of the Corps—at Big Alfred's generous invitation—had recently moved.

A much nicer place than the old Kearney Street boardinghouse, the large, clean dwelling was dark and silent on this starry Christmas night. Inside Kay hopefully called out. Was anyone home? No answer.

As she walked down the wide shadowy upstairs hall, Kay saw no slice of light beneath Big Alfred's closed door. Nor beneath any other doors evenly spaced along the wide corridor.

In her own chilly room, Kay didn't bother to light a lamp. She undressed in the moonlight and anxiously climbed into the soft, clean bed, her teeth chattering. She yanked the covers up to her chin and shivered.

Her shivers soon stopped. She grew warm and comfortable. But sleep did not come.

A deep loneliness gripped Kay Montgomery.

Christmas was a season for families. She fondly recalled the wonderful times from years past when the Montgomery family had all been together. This year her dear mother and father were far, far away. Now Curly had a wife of his own and would soon have a family. Just this week Rose had confided she thought she was pregnant.

Kay felt unshed tears sting her eyes and was immediately ashamed of herself. She should be happy for Curly and Rose! And she was, of course, only . . . only . . . Dear Lord, was she—Captain Kay Montgomery—guilty of envy? Was there any uglier sin than that?

How dare she lie here feeling half sorry for herself simply because she was alone on Christmas night!

She couldn't help it. It was Christmas, she was alone, and she was lonely. Patrick Packard was at a fancy midnight Christmas supper at his sister's Nob Hill home. Kay made a face. Patrick Packard had mentioned that Nick McCabe was also to be at the gala Packard family gathering.

The thought of Nick McCabe caused an involuntary shiver to surge through Kay. She was again seized with that strange, breathless sensation she'd experienced when Nick had held her in his arms before his marble fireplace.

Kay's slender back arched and her bare toes curled.

She shut her eyes tightly, shook her head about on the pillow, and gritted her teeth. She drew a deep exasperated breath, sighed, flopped over onto her stomach, and punched her pillow viciously.

She knew what was really bothering her! It was neither the blond, trustworthy Patrick Packard nor the dark, dangerous Nick McCabe. It wasn't even that she missed her mother and father, though that was surely part of it.

It was that a four-year-old boy had never heard of Santa Claus.

Chapter 20

 Up before sunrise the next morning, Captain Kay Montgomery was again her optimistic self, ready to meet the new day's challenges. Refreshed from a good night's rest, she discharged her duties with the usual high degree of confidence and efficiency.

Kay's first stop was at the waterfront mission where the Corps served hot coffee and sourdough bread to Barbary Coast indigents every morning. Then, with the willing Rose at her side, it was on to the homes of the sick and downtrodden.

As Salvation Army soldiers, they didn't simply stop by and look in on the city's ill. They carried food and medicine to those in need. They went into the worst slum shanties, rolled up their sleeves, bathed sick mothers and diapered their babies, cleaned house, did laundry, and cooked nutritious meals.

Every Corps member had been taught a truth that should have been evident to anyone. If they were to reach those most in need of redemption, they had to carry the word and comfort of a loving, forgiving God to where the lost were most likely to be found. Could the sick, the naked, and the impoverished be expected to show up each Sunday morning at the great ostentatious edifices the city's religious leaders called "God's house"?

General William Booth, the Corps founder, didn't think so. Neither did Captain Kay Montgomery. She knew the hungry couldn't learn the lesson of salvation unless first they were fed. Nor could the sick be comforted by words of encouragement with no show of hands-on healing help.

The Army's soldiers practiced what they preached. And they did it with patience, understanding, and cheer.

Kay and Rose were kept so busy the morning fairly melted away. It was nearing noon when the two young women walked back to the mission. Curly, Bobby Newman, Giles Lawton, and Matthew were there serving a meal of hot soup, bread, and coffee to the destitute.

Kay caught the look of adoration and concern Curly bestowed on

Rose the minute he looked up and saw her. Rose smiled warmly at her tall, red-headed husband and nodded, reassuring him she was fine.

To Kay she softly said, "Already he treats me as if I might break. I've told him that I'm young and strong and healthy and he's not to worry." She laughed that warm, infectious laugh. "But isn't he just the cutest, sweetest man you've ever seen! So protective. So concerned about my 'delicate condition.' "

Kay laughed too, but then her brows knitted and she gave Rose a concerned frown. "Curly's right, Rose. I'm so thoughtless. I've asked far too much from you this morning and—"

"Nonsense," Rose exclaimed. "I've never felt better in my life. I'm going to have Curly's child! Isn't it wonderful? I'm the happiest woman alive!"

Smiling at the glowing young mother-to-be, Kay said, "I'm happy for you." She hugged Rose. "And I shall spoil my niece or nephew as befits the old spinster aunt." Kay swiftly released her sister-in-law.

"Why, Kay Montgomery! Who says you'll be a spinster?"

Kay didn't answer. Already she was hurrying to take off her bonnet, don an apron, and pitch in.

After lunch Kay and the soldiers divided up bundles of the Corps weekly bulletin, *The War Cry*. They then went out into the streets to distribute them.

Captain Kay presented her very last copy of *The War Cry* to a startled, toothless old man hugging a barber pole on lower California Street. She smiled at him, invited him to the mission, then went on her way.

She had purposely worked her way toward Battery Place. She was now less than a block away. It was nearing three o'clock. The young children would be up from their naps. Kay hurried toward the big white house.

She raced up the porch steps as if she too were a child and rushed in the door out of breath. Completely at home here, Kay didn't bother announcing her arrival to Madge or the staff. She tossed her bonnet on the coat tree, hurried through the big house, crossed the sunny gymnasium, and rushed outdoors into the huge back yard.

Children, dressed warmly against the cold, ran and screamed and shouted. And laughed.

Shading her eyes against the afternoon sunshine, Kay searched anxiously for a quiet, sad child off alone somewhere, away from the others. While her anxious gaze touched the far reaches of the yard, Kay became conscious of a child's happy laughter.

It was laughter she couldn't recall hearing before. She'd grown so close to the Battery Place children, she could tell who was laughing with her eyes closed.

Kay had never before heard this childish irresistible giggling. She momentarily deserted her search for little Joey. Her gaze followed the sound of that unique, heartwarming laughter to its source.

And her blue eyes widened in disbelief.

Across the big yard, some thirty yards away, a tiny boy giggled and tumbled about on the winter brown grass with a tiny, yelping puppy. The boy's hair and the puppy's coat were the exact same hue.

A brilliant golden red.

For a long moment Kay was too stunned to believe what she was hearing. What she was seeing. Joey rolling about on his back, wrestling with a puppy. Joey giggling and squealing while the frisky puppy barked and wagged his tail and licked the laughing Joey in the face. Joey with his short, sweater-clad arms hugging the frolicsome puppy and kissing it back.

Kay's hand went to her breast.

She stood there in the winter sunlight, smiling foolishly, her heart pounding. She could think of no single moment in her life when she'd been more touched than now. The sight of the tiny pair rolling around in the dry brown grass, the child giggling, the puppy yelping, was something she would remember all her days on earth.

Kay couldn't help herself. She couldn't stay away from the child and his puppy. She drew a much-needed breath and headed toward the pair. She reached them before the transported Joey realized she was there.

"Hi, Joey," she said softly, not wanting to frighten him, then dropped down on her knees beside him.

His face aglow, Joey looked up at her. He said nothing, but the smile remained on his face. He sat up, his arm around the puppy.

"Your puppy is sure pretty," Kay said.

The red-coated collie licked Joey's face and Joey again went into peals of heartwarming giggles. Kay giggled with him, as happy as he, if not more so.

"May I pet your new puppy?" She made the blunder of reaching out before permission was granted.

Joey frowned and clutched his puppy so tightly it whimpered. Hugging the struggling ball of fur possessively to his skinny chest, Joey glared at Kay and quickly turned his back on her. Kay knew she'd made a big mistake. How thoughtlessly she had behaved. Joey was obviously terrified she'd take the dog away from him.

"You don't want me to pet him. Okay. That's all right," she said in low, even tones. "It would likely scare him for a stranger to touch him. Don't you think it would scare him?"

Joey was facing away from her, squeezing the squirming pet. He said nothing. But the small red head with its telltale cowlick moved slowly up and down.

"Yes, you're right. It would scare him," Kay agreed. "I'll wait until you tell me it's okay for me to pet him." Again the small red head bobbed. "What's his name? Have you named him yet?" Kay asked.

Joey didn't reply. He got up onto his bare, skinned knees, shot to his feet, and ran away, carrying in his short arms the barking, struggling puppy that was almost as big as he.

Kay let Joey be for the remainder of the afternoon. She frolicked with the other children, played with their new Christmas toys, and read to them from their new books.

On her way out she casually asked Madge who had given the collie dog to Joey.

"Land sakes, Captain Kay, I can't keep up with who gives what to the kids! Why, yesterday all afternoon and evening long good-hearted city folks came by with presents."

"So you didn't notice who . . ."

"What does it matter? It's nothing short of a miracle, if you ask me," Madge said. "I went in to herd the young ones up bed last night around seven and there was Joey, big as you please, laughing and rolling around on the floor with that puppy!" She shook her graying head, "I couldn't believe it. And then he cried so hard when I tried to take the dog away from him, I just set them both in the tub, bathed them, and put them to bed." She laughed then and her eyes twinkled. "Do you know that dog was still in bed with that child when I woke Joey for breakfast this morning!"

"If I ever find out who gave the puppy to Joey, I'm going to give them a great big kiss!" Kay declared with a laugh and left. She hummed all the way to the mission.

Kay was back at Battery Place the next afternoon. And the next.

On the last day of 1883 Kay was there, sitting on the back steps while the orphan children played in the yard. The sun had disappeared. A chill wind had begun to kick up. Fog started rolling in off the bay.

Kay rose and went directly to where Joey laughed and wrestled with his collie puppy. She knelt on the brown grass, sat back on her heels, and smiled.

"Your dog certainly loves you, doesn't he?"

Joey sat up and looked at her, an arm tight around the collie. His big blue eyes fixed on hers, he studied Kay thoughtfully, skeptically.

Kay said, "Let's play a game. I'll see if I can guess his name. You think I can?"

Joey shook his head.

"I'll bet I can." Kay cocked her head to one side. "Hmmmm, let's see now, is it Rover? No? May I try again?" Joey nodded. "Is it . . . Red? Pal? Spot? Whiskers? No? None of those?" Kay shook her head and sighed. "Well, I give up!" She slapped her palms down flat on her thighs.

Joey's blue eyes gleamed. He laughed because it was funny that she couldn't guess. Joey cocked his head to one side, just as she had done.

Rubbing the puppy's throat, he said simply, "Mac."

Kay's lips fell open in astonishment. She could hardly hide her bursting excitement. But she was determined not to frighten or upset Joey. And so she casually nodded and in easy, conversational tones said, "Mac? Your puppy's name is Mac?"

"Mac," Joey confirmed, nodding.

Kay grinned at him. "I like it. Mac. Mac. Has a good ring to it. Mac's a very good name for him."

"Mac," said Joey, as if confirming.

Then he put both arms around the tolerant Mac and pulled the shaggy little bundle of energy up in front of him. He looked at Kay questioningly. But she didn't know what he wanted. He shoved the dog closer to her. Kay caught on. Joey was giving his permission for her to pet Mac.

"Hey, Mac. How you doing, boy?" she said, stroking the collie, crooning to it. "Yes, sir, you're a big, bad boy, Mac."

Mac growled low in his throat with pleasure.

Joey giggled.

Then his short fingers brushed Kay's hand as together they petted the contentedly growling Mac.

Chapter 21

"I like that."

He wasn't really doing anything. Just lightly caressing the graceful curve of her slender throat.

"I like that a lot. Promise you won't stop for a million years."

"I haven't done anything yet." His tanned, stroking fingers reached the hollow of her throat, slipped enticingly out along a fragile collarbone.

"You're driving me mad," said Adele Packard, tossing a mane of lustrous blond hair. "But delightfully so."

"Your body's a delight, my sweet." Nick's deep, masculine voice was seductive. "Perfection. A priceless work of art."

"Nick . . . darling," she murmured, eyes closing with building excitement. His long tapered fingers gently cupped a bare ivory shoulder, then glided slowly down her pale slim arm. She sighed. "Vow you'll not rush me."

"I vow it," Nick said, his sculpted lips stretching into a slow, sensual smile.

They were in the spacious, high-ceilinged drawing room of Adele Packard's Sacramento Street mansion. The servants had been sent to their quarters with the admonition to remain behind closed doors until their mistress rang for them.

It was the thirty-first day of December, 1883.

At early dusk on that cold, drizzly New Year's Eve, Nick had arrived wearing formal attire. He was surprised when Adele answered the door. He was further surprised that she was not dressed for the evening. She wore a white peignoir suitable only for the privacy of her bedchamber. She was barefoot. Her white-blond hair flowed loosely down her back.

Adele had instructed Nick to come early. She told him she was having an intimate gathering of her closest friends for precelebration drinks. Those invited were to stop by at five for a glass of chilled champagne, then be on their way to separate destinations.

It had been a ploy to get Nick to the mansion early. Adele had a plan, but it wasn't to have friends over for champagne toasts. It was to have time alone with Nick McCabe.

Adele wanted their long New Year's Eve celebration to begin and end in the same way. Making love.

Nick smiled indulgently when Adele confessed what she'd done. She was his kind of woman. She lived for the moment's pleasure, just as he did. He'd never had any hope or desire for leading a decent life. The road of adventure and excitement that he traveled surely led to ruin at the end. But he couldn't escape even if he had wanted to. He was born to it. It was all he'd ever known.

The beautiful blue-blooded, white-haired Adele Packard was greedy and decadent and frivolous. Like him. She radiated an appealing evil splendor that was well suited to his lustful, savage tastes. She was a vulgar, hot-blooded woman who denied herself nothing. Nor did she deny him.

On that first night they met, they had come together in a ruthless kind of primitive ecstasy that was so wild and profane it was as if they were engaged in some spectacular battle of sexual destruction. As if neither would be completely satisfied until their naked foe had been carnally conquered. Totally vanquished.

Yes, the lady who lived on the Hill was anything but a lady in bed. That suited him fine. The icily beautiful, fever-blooded blond aristocrat took erotic satisfaction as her due. Anything short of incredible ecstasy left Adele Packard feeling cheated and angry. The twice-divorced woman who had stubbornly kept her maiden name liked her sex often, varied, and dirty.

Their lovemaking had admittedly been less than explosive of late. While he'd taken Adele with the usual reckless, hungry aggression, he'd spent precious little time at it. He'd been hurried in his lust, restless in his desire to satiate her and himself.

He'd explained that it had nothing to do with diminishing desire. She was beautiful and sensual and he wanted her. But he'd had a lot on his mind. He was preoccupied with the problems at the club. Financial worries hounded him night and day.

But then, how could he expect a woman like Adele Packard to understand? She'd been pampered, protected, and wealthy from the moment of birth. What did she care if he was in danger of losing his beloved Carousel Club? What did it mean to her that everything for which he'd worked so hard was tied up in his club?

She didn't listen. She didn't understand. She didn't care.

For tonight, Nick decided he'd forget his troubles. He'd give the spoiled blond beauty what she wanted, needed. He'd begin making love to her immediately. And he wouldn't stop until it was time for them to go a round of society parties before ending the evening at his Carousel Club.

And so now, as the tall-cased clock in the marble-floored foyer struck the half hour, Nick and Adele sat on the thick beige Aubusson rug in front of the brightly burning fireplace. Nick was fully clothed: pleated white shirt, midnight black tuxedo, black tie, and bloodred blossom in his lapel.

Adele Packard was totally nude.

She tingled with excitement as Nick caressed her, his silver eyes holding her gaze, his voice low and compelling. "Let me touch you. Let me look at you. You're so beautiful like this, naked in the firelight."

"Nick, Nick."

His dark hand gently stroked down the curve of her narrow rib cage. "Tell me I can make love to you here in your drawing room. Say I can do all the things to you I've ever dreamed of doing."

"Oh, God, darling, yes, of course . . . take off your . . ." She half turned to him.

He gently turned her back. "We'll make love until we must leave. And in the carriage on our way to old Crocker's party I'll make love to you again."

"Why, Nick, I never . . . yes . . . yes . . ." She found the idea of making love in the carriage while en route electrifying. "Promise you'll really do it. I want you to make love to me in my new black velvet Paris gown on the plush backseat of my carriage."

"I will," he assured her. "And after the parties, when we reach the Carousel Club, we'll make love in my apartment."

"Oh, Nick." Her eyes glittered. "Let's make love in your office! In that big swivel chair behind your desk. We'll hear the music from the club while we—"

"My office it is," he said, his tanned fingers brushing lightly over a pale, swelling breast.

Adele squirmed with pleasure. "Nick, take off your clothes."

"Not yet, sweet. Not yet." He gently plucked at a taut, pointed nipple with his fingertips. "For a little while be my naked goddess. Let me simply adore you. Let me make love to you with my eyes. My hands. My mouth."

"I will. I will." She sighed breathlessly.

"Let me bring you to ecstasy in a dozen different ways." Nick's lips pressed the crown of her flowing white-blond hair. "Let me love you while I'm fully dressed and you're naked."

"Do, please do. Oh, Nick, this is so sexy, so thrilling. I like being naked with you. For you."

"I like it too," he said.

Nick remained fully clothed. He brought the naked, responsive Adele to total rapture half a dozen times in the next two hours. Once while she sat on her heels facing him, her bare backside to the fire. Knees spread, hands resting on her pale thighs, she looked directly into Nick's gleaming silver eyes while his left hand moved between her parted legs, his fingers stroking, coaxing, bringing her to bliss.

She cried out when the sweet explosion rocked her and then fell forward against him, a dazed, postorgasmic expression on her face. Nick held her until she'd calmed, then he took her by the arms, sat her up, and swiftly moved around to kneel directly behind her. He drew her flushed, naked body back against him.

They knelt there together, his spread trousered knees cradling hers, his arms around her, dark hands caressing her hard-nippled breasts, her quivering belly, the white-blond curls between her parted legs. Soon she was begging for release again.

Nick gave it to her.

With the perfectly positioned middle finger of his dark right hand, he made slow, erotic circles on, over, and around that slippery nubbin of female flesh throbbing between Adele's open legs. With one slender arm thrown up and hooked behind Nick's neck, Adele squirmed and sighed and pressed herself eagerly down against that skilled, pleasuring finger.

"Nick, that feels so good . . . so good . . . darling, don't ever stop what you're doing. Touch me this way forever and ever."

"I will. You know I will."

"Ohhh . . . never, ever stop . . . I couldn't stand it if you did."

"I won't, sweet. Never."

"Nick, Nick . . ." At last she erupted into spasms of deep, shuddering ecstasy. "Nickkkkk!"

She went limp against him. He kissed the side of her flushed face and said, "You're a goddess. A beautiful goddess."

"You make me feel like a goddess. Your goddess."

"Mmmmm," he murmured, pressing kisses to her white-blond hair. "You're a goddess of love."

"That's all I ever want to be. Your love goddess."

"You are. My goddess of love."

"Are you my slave?"

"If you wish, goddess. I'll be your slave."

"Oh, Lord, you excite me," she murmured, already becoming aroused again. "Nick, pretend I am really your love goddess," whispered Adele, her voice husky. "And you're my dark, beautiful slave and must obey my every command."

"Command me, mistress. I'll obey."

Adele threw off Nick's hugging arms and stood up. She turned to face him and snapped, "Undress, slave!"

Nick obeyed.

He did anything, everything she ordered him to do. Adele Packard was a highly aroused, dangerous love goddess, pushing her handsome slave to the limits of his sexual prowess. The pair played slave and goddess for the better part of the next hour. Adele gloried in it. She ordered Nick to do all manner of lovely, naughty things to her and he complied, sending her into paroxysms of incredible joy.

Adele was unusually bold and playfully wicked. She commanded that Nick allow her to tie his hands behind his back with his discarded black silk tie. He agreed. She then further commanded that he stand naked and perfectly still before the fireplace while she did what she pleased with him. To him.

Nick obeyed the first half of her order. He stood there naked in front of the fireplace. But he couldn't stand still. Not with a blond, naked love goddess provocatively rubbing her bare, voluptuous body on his. Not with her soft lips pressing kisses to his bare, clefted back. Not with her pink tongue licking at his hair-covered chest. Not with her sharp white teeth nibbling at his contracting belly.

And certainly not when the goddess fell to her knees before him and looked up at him with an evil, predatory smile. She then cupped him in her hands as if his flesh were a living offering on which she aimed to feast hungrily.

In half fear, half frenzy, the bound Nick watched as the beautiful blond goddess placed her warm, wet lips over the throbbing tip of his thrusting masculinity. Instant pleasure rippled through him.

"God . . . oh . . . my . . . God," Nick groaned, his legs weak, his wrists pulling against their silk restraints.

When the pleasure-giving goddess at last released him, Nick sagged weakly to his knees before her.

The goddess smiled at her dark, sated love slave, touched the tip of her finger to his sensuous lips, and said, "Game's over. Let's go upstairs, bathe, and get dressed. We're due at the Crockers' at seven-thirty."

The slave grew rebellious. "The hell with the Crockers. Let's ring in the New Year in your bed."

"I wish we could, darling. But one of the Packards simply must put in an appearance at the parties."

"What about Pat? Can't he go?" asked Nick, as Adele rose and stepped behind him to untie his wrists.

"No, he cannot! He has a dinner engagement with that dreadful Salvation Army captain!" Nick didn't see the sour face Adele made. "My stuffy, straitlaced brother's a bit of a fool, but he is well bred. He'd never subject our family to ridicule by taking a woman of her station into the homes of our friends."

"You take me to the homes of your friends," said Nick. "I'm no patrician."

"That's different, darling." Adele stepped around to face him, the tie in her hand. "You're an asset to any hostess. What could possibly add a more welcome dash of excitement than the presence of a handsome, dangerous saloon owner from the evil Barbary Coast?"

Chapter 22

"I like that."

She smiled dreamily, her eyes heavily lashed and shining with pleasure. "I like that a lot."

"I thought you might."

"Promise there's plenty more where this came from," Kay said teasingly.

"I promise," assured an enchanted Pat Packard. "As much as you could ever want."

The pair were at Patrick Packard's Mason Street home, a large, stately house two blocks from his sister's Nob Hill mansion. It was shortly after six P.M. New Year's Eve. They were in the formal dining room enjoying dessert after a lengthy, seven-course meal. Kay was enraptured with the charlotte russe, a delicious treat she'd never before tasted. She felt almost sinful enjoying the sweet delicacy so much.

Kay sat across the damask-draped table from Pat Packard. No one else was present. Just the two of them. Dining alone by romantic candlelight. Sharing the sumptuous meal prepared by Pat's able kitchen staff.

Outside the temperature was steadily dropping. A cold drizzling rain was falling. The sky was shrouded in dark, low clouds. All San Francisco was socked in with thick, enveloping fog.

But the dismal winter weather had no effect on the diners in the candlelit dining room. Captain Kay expressed an almost childish delight with the delicious meal. She saw no need for pretense. She was ravenously hungry. She readily admitted it. She was absolutely starving for rich, tasty foods. And rich, tasty foods were served to her in incredibly generous portions.

From the lobster salad to the charlotte russe, Kay praised each palate-tempting dish and rolled her blue eyes with satisfaction. In all his life, Pat Packard couldn't recall seeing anyone enjoy a simple meal quite so much. Especially the dessert.

Nor had he ever seen Captain Kay in higher spirits than she was on this cold, miserable New Year's Eve. The holiday feast was not solely responsible for the added sparkle in Kay's expressive blue eyes. While she ate the light fluffy sponge cake filled with whipped cream and custard, Kay spoke excitedly about Joey.

She told Pat how Joey's new puppy had totally changed the sad, silent little boy.

"It's a miracle," she said. "A true miracle."

"That's wonderful, Kay," Pat replied. "And you've no idea who gave the puppy to Joey?"

"None. But I know this much, whoever's responsible for giving Joey the playful collie apparently knows much more about children than I do."

Kay talked and talked about the change in the adorable red-haired child. Pat listened with genuine interest, nodding and asking all the right questions. So much talk about Joey having no family quite naturally directed the conversation to their own families.

As they lingered over their coffee, Kay spoke with great pride and affection of her heroic parents, of the happy childhood she'd known. She talked fondly of Curly and Rose. Said she thought a close-knit, loving family was so important, didn't he?

He sure did. He told her he still missed his parents, ten years after they'd been killed in a steamship explosion. Kay listened attentively while he talked about his prominent family, and of the railroad empire his father had built. Pat seemed almost apologetic about his inherited wealth.

Kay put him at his ease. She encouraged him to tell her more. The reserved Pat Packard responded to her warmth, her honest interest. He told her of his privileged youth.

The house where he now lived had been built by his father in the late fifties when Pat was four years old, his sister Adele seven.

"He had excellent taste," said Kay. "Your home is very beautiful."

"It's comfortable," Pat replied with the nonchalance of one used to the fine things in life. "Many others on the hill are far finer."

Pat told Kay about the fortunes of San Francisco's elite. Told how back in the 1860s and '70s ordinary men became as rich as kings in silver and railroading. They began to live accordingly, building fabulous marble palaces atop Nob Hill. MacKay, Flood, Crocker, Hopkins, and Huntington. Men who were wealthy beyond belief. They erected Spanish palaces, medieval castles, and Roman villas high atop Nob Hill, each trying to outspend the other.

"Is your sister's home as elegant as yours?" Kay couldn't believe she had asked the question, it just popped out.

"Oh, my, yes." Pat smiled. "Adele's home is much grander than this." Kay's eyes widened, but she said nothing. "My sister's home was designed by noted architect John P. Gaynor and built by her second husband, a man of untold riches."

"Your sister's been married twice?" Kay's eyebrows lifted. "Tell me about her."

"Adele's very outgoing and confident. She's a beautiful but extremely willful woman. She was pretty from the day she was born. My father spoiled her unmercifully, gave her anything she wished for. And so did her husbands."

Pat said that when his sister turned twenty, she married a close friend of their father's who was twenty-five years her senior. Ted Stallings was a widowed railroading magnate. Adele thought it great sport to marry a man old enough to be her father, one who would pamper and spoil her just as father always had. But she was bored with Stallings by the time the pair returned from a year-long honeymoon in Europe. She divorced him without ever having moved into their home.

"Adele was twenty-six when she married Clayton Durant, a handsome Nevada silver king. She insisted he build her a mansion at the top of Sacramento Street. He built her the mansion and gave her anything else she wanted: jewels, furs, expensive art, enameled carriages, liveried footman, a summer house." Pat shook his blond head.

"Did she divorce Mr. Durant?" Kay asked.

"She would have, had he lived long enough," Pat said flatly. "Durant was killed in a mine mishap three years after their marriage and barely six months after they had moved into Gaynor mansion. He left everything he had to Adele." Pat took a drink of coffee.

Kay toyed with a heavy sterling teaspoon. "I should think Adele would be terribly lonely living in that big mansion by herself."

Pat Packard's fair face colored visibly. "My sister has never been lonely in her life." He lowered his gaze to his half-empty coffee cup.

Kay said softly, "Then she won't be alone on this New Year's Eve? You're free to attend tonight's prayer meeting with me?"

"Yes, I am." Pat's eyes lifted, met Kay's, and instantly lighted. "Adele has plans for the New Year, and they most definitely don't include me."

"Oh?" said Kay, a perfectly arched brow slightly raised. "A gala party?"

"If she's in the mood," replied Pat. "If not, she'll spend the evening at home, entertaining her one and only invited guest. Nick McCabe."

* * *

Midnight had come and gone.

The old year had passed into history. The new one was in its infancy. The gentry of San Francisco had ushered in the brand-new year at extravagant dinners and parties and dances. Oceans of chilled champagne had been consumed. Mountains of food had been devoured. Laughter and music and kisses had been the order of the evening.

And now, throughout the city by the bay, thousands of tired, happy revelers slept soundly, safely in their darkened homes.

Down on the Barbary Coast, the lights shone as brightly as ever. Every saloon, dance hall, card parlor, and bawdy house was open and jammed with loud merrymakers. The sounds of laughter, shouts, screams, and gunshots were as constant in the early hours of the new year as they'd been in the waning minutes of 1883.

Captain Kay Montgomery was on the crowded Barbary Coast that early January morning. She and her hearty band of soldiers braved the cold and the rain and the dangers of the streets. The Devil never slept. So they couldn't sleep either.

In the never-ending war against sin, Captain Kay's nightly battle was to draw the lost away from the glittering allurements of the saloons and dives and low music halls. A sidewalk soldier for God, she felt no sacrifice was too great for winning souls.

The drizzling rain had finally stopped. The clouds had rolled away and a few cold, twinkling stars appeared as the troopers patrolled in pairs. Captain Kay and Bobby Newman walked along Grant Avenue. In the crowds milling about on the sidewalks, Bobby Newman spotted a young Chinese boy begging from passersby. He immediately pointed the child out to Kay.

"Let's go," said Kay, and they hurried toward the child.

The boy looked up, saw them coming, and started running. But Bobby Newman was too quick for the child. Bobby caught the thin, dirty-faced Chinese youth. Kay questioned the boy about being out on the streets. The child swore he had a home and he would go there at once. Skeptical, Bobby Newman volunteered to see the boy safely there.

Captain Kay went on her way alone. She turned at Pacific and was passing the busy Top Hat Club when the door opened and three men dressed in identical black watch caps, black sweaters, and black trousers stepped outside. One was a slightly built Oriental. Another a scarfaced man nearly as huge as Big Alfred. The third of the trio—flanked by the others—was Three Fingers Jackson.

Three Fingers Jackson turned to face Kay, did not smile, stared at her with an almost sinister glare. Kay trembled as he licked his thin upper lip in an obscene manner. He had without a doubt the most ominous, evil presence Captain Kay had ever felt. Kay averted her eyes and the dangerous-looking trio quickly boarded a carriage waiting at the curb.

A chill shot up Kay's spine. She hurried up Pacific, walking fast, inexplicably unnerved. When she was several safe steps away, she stopped and looked back. She watched as the carriage turned the corner and went out of sight.

Her brow knitted, Kay stood there on the sidewalk for a long moment, wondering where the darkly dressed trio were going. Wondering what evil mischief they were up to at this hour. She shivered inwardly, then shrugged, turned away just in time to see a sleek, crested, midnight-blue carriage roll up to a stop before the Golden Carousel. The carriage door opened and out onto the gaslit street stepped the rough and raffish Nick McCabe.

Kay stared at him and had to admit the truth. The tall, dark Nick was sinfully handsome in full evening dress with silk top hat and black Inverness coat—the cape of which swung back from his wide shoulders. In one hand he carried a gold-tipped cane, in the other a freshly lit cigar.

Nick slammed the carriage door shut, tapped on the roof with his cane, and spun around flashing a big grin at no one in particular.

He was drunk.

Kay knew it by the way he grinned foolishly and by his walk. His casual, animal grace was missing tonight. Nick swaggered tipsily forward, attempting to walk straight, failing miserably. And not even realizing he was failing.

Kay quickly sank back into the shadows before he could spot her, having no desire to tangle with the drunken saloon owner. Undetected, she watched as Nick staggered up to the black double doors of his club, yanked them open, stood there on the threshold and shouted, "Happy New Year!"

Laughing, he stepped inside.

There was a shout, a crash, and a curse. Nick McCabe's silk top hat and gold-tipped cane came flying back out the double doors. The airborne Nick came right behind them. Hat, cane, and man wound up flattened on the sidewalk. None moved.

For a long terrible moment, Kay was unable to react. Her legs wouldn't work. She couldn't make herself go to him. Could only stare in horror at the prostrate body lying unmoving on the sidewalk.

"Nick!" she screamed at last, clawing at the streamers of her bonnet, tearing off the hat and dropping it as she frantically raced to him. "Nick!"

Kay fell to her knees at his side, her heart hammering, her eyes round with fright. She leaned close, gently cupped his dark face in her hands, and gasped a tiny whimper of relief when those pale silver eyes opened and looked up at her.

"Nick, are you badly hurt?"

Nick squinted quizzically at the pale woman hovering over him. Her blue eyes were filled with concern. Her loosened hair, caught in the light from behind, was a halo of dancing flames. In his drunken state, she looked very appealing to Nick.

"I hurt, Captain," he said, attempting a pained expression.

"I knew it," Kay murmured worriedly, her breath short. "Is it your head?" Tenderly, carefully she ran searching fingers over Nick's dark head.

"It isn't my head," Nick said, closed his eyes, bit his lip, and moaned dramatically.

"No? Then where, Nick? Tell me."

Nick's silver eyes slitted open. His voice a muffled groan, he said, "I . . . I'll have to show you."

"Yes, yes, show me." Nick took Kay's wrist and brought her hand down to his shoulder. "Here? Do you think you've broken a collarbone?"

Kay pushed Nick's caped coat apart and quickly unbuttoned his tuxedo jacket. Pressing her fingertips gently to his right collarbone, she said, "Does that hurt?"

"No. Not there."

Kay's hand moved lower, touching the flat hard muscles of Nick's chest, asking kindly, "Does this hurt? This?"

Captain Kay was intent on discovering if Nick had suffered any broken ribs. She never caught the devilish gleam in his silver eyes. She didn't realize that he was actually unhurt.

Nick was still merrily drunk and having a bit of fun at her expense. Kay caught on when she kept asking "here" and Nick kept saying "No —a little lower." When her spread palm lay on his washboard stomach directly above the black satin cummerbund at his trim waist, it suddenly dawned on Kay.

"Oooh . . ." Nick groaned. "The pain's getting worse. Slide your hand on down inside my—"

"Of all the lowdown tricks!" Kay exploded with anger. Furious, she snatched her hand away, doubled up her fist, and socked him right in the belly. "There! Now you won't have any trouble locating the pain!

"Owww!" Nick's moan was genuine this time. But he immediately grinned as Kay shot to her feet. His hand snaked out, reached beneath her long blue uniform skirts, and grabbed a slender ankle. "No hard feelings, Captain. Help me up?"

"Never," she snapped, and kicked free of his encircling fingers. "You're right where you belong, Nick McCabe. Flat on your back in the gutter!"

She whirled and marched away, red hair flying, blue eyes flashing.

"Well, a Happy New Year to you too, Captain!" Nick called after her, lifting a hand to his forehead to snap off a military salute. Grinning, he then rolled into a sitting position, reached for his smashed top hat, placed it on his head, and began happily humming "Auld Lang Syne."

Chapter 23

San Francisco Chronicle   January 1, 1884

SHADOW CLAN STRIKES AGAIN!

The notorious gang of kidnappers that has terrorized this city for the past eighteen months has struck again!

While revelers toasted the New Year, the vile, elusive Shadow Clan made sweeping nighttime raids through Chinatown and the waterfront snatching unprotected children from streets, alleys, and doorways.

When the sun rose this morning on the New Year, worried parents and guardians had reported an unbelievable number of missing children. Five boys and six girls were caught up in the cruel net of these loathsome . . .

The Lady in Black read the shocking news story at the breakfast table at eight A.M. New Year's morning. When she completed the article, she calmly laid the paper aside, lifted a fragile cup of steaming black coffee to her lips, and took a sip. But the hot coffee failed to warm her.

The Lady in Black pulled the wide lapels of her black velvet robe more closely together around her throat, feeling a terrible coldness seep through her bones and into her heart.

boys and six girls were caught up in the cruel net of these loathsome . . .

Captain Kay Montgomery read the newspaper story in stunned disbelief. She was shocked and horrified that such a thing could happen; that a corrupt gang of evil men could roam the streets stealing innocent children. And she was sickened at the thought of the terrible fate those helpless little children would suffer.

Her stomach was tied in knots. The blood in her veins had chilled to ice. It was one of those times when she was disgusted with the whole human race. One of those rare occasions when her faith grew dim and almost deserted her. She questioned if there really was a God.

How could a loving, caring Almighty God allow such dreadful things to happen?

Kay let the newspaper drop from her cold, stiff fingers. Her heart was heavy. She was confused and upset. She felt weary, as if she couldn't possibly go on. What was the use? The wicked seemed to flourish while the pure in heart suffered.

Kay put her elbows on the splintery three-legged table, leaned forward, and buried her face in her hands.

"Why?" she asked aloud, her voice a soft wail of despair. "Why, Lord, why?"

"Lassie?"

Startled, Kay quickly raised her head. Big Alfred stood in the doorway, twisting his billed Army cap in his big hands. He came quickly inside, closing the door behind him.

"Lassie, what is it?" Big Alfred's brow wrinkled, the way it did when he was thinking hard or was worried.

Unable to speak, Kay simply shook her head and blinked back the tears from her eyes.

The big Englishman hurried forward, anxiously circled the three-legged desk, dropped his billed cap atop it, and crouched down on his heels beside Kay's chair. His florid face set in lines of deep concern, Big Alfred laid a huge, gentle hand on Kay's forearm.

"Tell your old Uncle Alfred all about it, lassie."

"Oh, Big Alfred." Kay choked, turned, and threw her arms around his powerful neck. "I—I—"

Big Alfred rose, drawing Kay up from the chair. "There, child, there." He patted her back as if she really were a child. "What's troubling my bonnie lass this fine New Year's morning?"

Against his massive chest, Kay sobbed. "I'm not fit to be soldier in God's Army. My faith is not strong enough."

"Sure it is. No one has more faith than you, Captain."

"Then why am I afraid and filled with doubts and wondering . . . ?"

"Because you're human just like all the rest of God's children." Big Alfred saw the newspaper lying on Kay's desk. He knew what was bothering her. "Lassie, when we hear about something as awful as these beastly kidnappings, we can't help but wonder why the dear Savior we serve would allow such to happen." He shook his big head for emphasis. "We have to remember that old Satan has great power.

This was the work of the Devil, not our Heavenly Father. That's why we can never give up, lass. We must fight Satan day and night. You've said so yourself many times."

For a moment longer, Kay said nothing. She stayed as she was, wrapped safely in the fatherly, comforting embrace of Big Alfred Duke. The second she stirred, his gargantuan arms loosened.

Kay lifted her head, smiled at the big, understanding man. "I'm sorry. And I'm ashamed."

"You needn't be either, child. There's no cause."

"Thank you." Kay stepped back, drew a deep breath, smiled, and said, "Grab your cap, Big Alfred. Let's get back out there and do battle with the Devil!"

boys and six girls were caught up in the cruel net of these loathsome . . .

Nick finished reading the newspaper article. His bloodshot silver eyes narrowed with revulsion and contempt, he muttered oaths, rose from his easy chair, and paced fitfully.

It was early afternoon.

Nick had slept the morning away. He'd awakened with a fierce headache, a bad taste in his mouth, and a sore, throbbing jaw. The strange thing was, he didn't remember being in a fight. Didn't remember being hit.

Ling Tan had brought the *Chronicle* and hot black coffee shortly after noontime and said, "How feel, boss?"

"How does it look like I feel?"

"Pretty bad, no? Look pretty bad. Club look worse." Elaborating, Ling Tan had informed him that numerous brawls had left tables overturned, chairs splintered, dishes and crystal broken.

"I don't want to hear it." Nick had waved him away.

Now Nick pieced together what he could of the festive evening that had left him feeling so rotten. It had started with the prolonged bout of shameless lovemaking in Adele Packard's drawing room. Then the endless round of boring society parties. Their return to the Nob Hill mansion and an argument—over what he couldn't recall.

He did remember the angry Adele throwing an expensive Ming vase at him. It had narrowly missed his left ear, struck the marble fireplace, and shattered.

"Now see what you've done!" In tears, she'd shouted, "Get out! Get out!"

"I came here . . ." Nick mused aloud now as he paced his sitting room. "I came back to the club and . . . and . . . hell, I don't know what happened then." He lifted a hand, tried gingerly working his sore jaw back and forth. He cursed when a sharp pain shot through the entire side of his face like a jolt of electricity.

Frowning and cursing, Nick walked into the bedroom. On the floor by the bed lay his wrinkled tuxedo, his soiled white shirt, and his smashed top hat. Nick looked at the ruined hat, made a face, and kicked it aside. He untied the sash of his black silk robe, shrugged it off his shoulders, and dropped it atop the discarded clothing.

Naked, he crawled back into the rumpled, unmade bed, pulled the covers up to his chest, and folded his hands behind his aching head.

Hell, he'd just stay in bed all day. Maybe forever. Maybe then he could stay out of trouble.

This was one hell of a way to start the New Year. His club was in shambles. His head was splitting. His jaw was throbbing. His stomach was queasy.

Nick sighed heavily.

He needed Alfred Duke. Badly. If he had Big Al back, everything would be fine again. Since Angel Thompson's name had been added to the bill, business at the club had picked up. Angel was a hit. The Pacific Bank and the Union Ice House were fighting to have her face on their calendars. She wasn't the draw Rose Reilly had been, but people were hearing about her and the crowds were returning to the Carousel. In time the nightly take would be as good as ever.

If he just had Alfred Duke, everything would be . . .

Out of the blue a fragment of last night's lost hours came back to Nick. He was lying on his back, looking up at Captain Kay Montgomery. That flaming hair was blazing all around her head and she was bent over him, looking very worried and very pretty at the same time. And she was calling his name, saying "Nick, Nick."

Nick raised up onto his elbows, trying his best to recall what had happened, why the straitlaced Army captain would be leaning over him, calling his name. She hadn't called him McCabe as she always did. She'd called him Nick.

For the life of him, Nick couldn't remember anything more. But the clear recollection of the redhead leaning close, touching his face, calling him by his first name put a notion in Nick's head.

Hazy at first, the idea took hold and grew. Nick grinned as he began to carefully plot his course of action. Minutes passed while he pondered and planned. And he came up with a strategy to get his big English bouncer back.

Nick felt a surge of energy. All his aches and pains were suddenly gone. He was as fit as a fiddle.

He immediately rang for Ling Tan. The servant appeared.

Grinning, Nick said, "Ling, get word to Big Al to meet me at the Athletic Club this afternoon at four P.M. for a little sparring." Nick reached for a cigar. "Do you remember what foods Big Al likes best?"

"Sure thing, boss. He like platter-size sirloin steak cooked rare."

"Stop at the market, get a couple of the thickest, best-looking sirloins you can find." Nick lit his cigar, puffed it to life. "Some fresh vegetables and bread and—"

"Ling Tan bake pie, boss? Big Alfred love hot apple pie with melted cheese on top."

"Yes, bake him an apple pie and anything else you can think of. We'll dine up here in my apartment around six."

"Good enough, boss. Steaks be sizzling when get back from Athletic Club."

"Fine. That's all, Ling."

Ling Tan left hastily.

Nick leaned back on the pillow and sighed with satisfaction, the cigar clamped between his teeth.

Ah, yes, he had a plan all right. A plan to get Big Alfred back in the old Carousel Club where he belonged.

A diabolical, foolproof plan.

A plan that involved the red-haired Salvation Army captain.

Chapter 24

"This calls for a real celebration."

Flashing that famous McCabe grin, Nick held up a chilled bottle of Dom Pérignon and two crystal glasses.

Big Alfred's own broad smile faded. Gesturing with a big hand, he said apologetically, "No, Nicholas. Thanks all the same, but I must decline. When I joined the Army, I took an oath to abstain." He shook his great head for emphasis. "I no longer drink liquor."

Nick's grin remained confident. Shrugging wide shoulders, he said, "You call having one glass of champagne drinking liquor?"

"Champagne's alcohol, laddie. I'll have to pass."

"Sure. Okay. I understand." Nick was determinedly gracious. He set the champagne and glasses aside. "You're still allowed to eat, aren't you, pal?"

Big Alfred's smile returned. "That I am, my boy. And I don't mind admitting I'm famished."

Nick laid a hand on Alfred's shoulder and guided him into the apartment's dining room. "So am I. That hour of shadow boxing left me with a healthy appetite." Motioning Big Alfred to sit, Nick added, "Thanks again."

"Ah, don't mention it. We'll do it again and soon," said Big Alfred. He sat down and pushed his chair up close to the table. Nick took the place across from him. "You know, just the other day I was telling . . ." Big Alfred's words trailed away as a smiling Ling Tan bustled in carrying a large serving tray.

The Englishman's hazel eyes widened expectantly. He inhaled deeply. His florid face became a study in ecstasy as Ling Tan set a large platter before him. A two-inch-thick, crisply browned sirloin—the size of the china platter—sizzled in its own aromatic juice.

"What think, Big Al?" Ling Tan asked. "Steak okay, no?"

Alfred Duke spread a white napkin over his lap, lifted his knife and fork, cut a bite of the sirloin, and popped it into his mouth.

He chewed, sighed, and rolled his eyes. "I haven't tasted steak since I left the Carousel," he said with childlike honesty. "I'd forgotten anything could be so delicious. Excellent, Ling Tan!"

Ling Tan chuckled happily.

Nick grinned. "*Bon appetit,* old friend."

Big Alfred beamed, nodded, and again cut into the thick, juicy steak. "Mmmmm," he murmured, bliss written on his face, in his eyes.

Ling Tan quickly added to that bliss. The Chinese servant brought in large, steaming bowls of Irish potatoes, snap beans, carrots, sweet corn, and asparagus. A basket of hot rolls and breads and a plate of new-churned butter were placed directly before Big Alfred. Cold, fresh milk was poured into his heavy goblet. Then Ling Tan disappeared, leaving the two old friends alone.

For the first few minutes of the meal, Nick didn't engage his dinner guest in conversation. Wisely he allowed the big, hungry Englishman to concentrate solely on consuming the perfectly prepared food.

Nick wasn't particularly hungry. He had something far more important than food on his mind. But he shook out his napkin, draped it over one knee, and joined Big Alfred.

Waiting for the ideal opportunity, Nick began by talking about his club. He told his old friend business was picking up. From there the subject turned to the infamous Shadow Clan and the shocking New Year's Eve kidnappings. Both men strongly felt that the authorities were dragging their feet. Not enough was being done to identify and apprehend the gang members.

Finally, after a brief pause, Nick asked how things were going down at the Army's waterfront mission. And listened politely to Big Alfred's thoughtful reply.

"So . . ." Nick said casually, "the red-headed Army captain is the real thing, is she? Practices what she preaches?"

Swallowing quickly, wiping his mouth with the white napkin, Big Alfred nodded. "Indeed she does, Nicholas. Captain Kay Montgomery is the most amazing woman. Why, the lassie's . . ."

And with no further prodding, Big Alfred commenced a lengthy monologue in praise of Captain Kay Montgomery. Indomitable and inspiring were words he chose to describe the slender Army captain.

"Captain Kay's an oratorical genius," Big Alfred stated. "She's a natural leader. She possesses a fearless and daring spirit."

"All that?" Nick replied in flat tones. "She must be quite a woman."

"One of a kind, I'm telling you," Big Alfred said with firm conviction. "Why, that tireless, uncomplaining little lassie spends long days making house-to-house visitations, doing anything and everything that needs to be done."

"Most admirable."

Big Alfred spooned the last of the whipped potatoes onto his plate. "The captain's not afraid to get her hands dirty. I've seen her march into some of the darkest, filthiest holes you could ever imagine, roll up her sleeves, and go to work." Big Alfred shook his head admiringly. "She scrubs floors on her hands and knees. She tends the sick, she bathes babies, she deals with drunken fathers, she counsels troubled boys and girls."

The Englishmen continued to sing Kay's praises right through a large wedge of hot apple pie topped with melted cheese followed by a generous serving of rich caramel custard swimming in a thick cinnamon syrup. At last he pushed back from the table, patted his full stomach, and accepted a second cup of freshly brewed coffee.

"Sounds like the captain is a commendable leader," said Nick.

"She's a pistol," Big Alfred said.

Nick smiled, produced a silver box filled with Monte Cristo cigars, and offered one to Big Alfred. "A cigar with your coffee?"

"Ah, no, my boy, no," Big Alfred declined, his hazel eyes lingering on the neat row of expensive cigars in the silver box. "I took an oath to—"

"—abstain from using tobacco in any form," Nick finished for him.

"Aye, laddie. But you go right ahead."

Nick withdrew a cigar from the box, placed it in his mouth, and lit it. Slowly puffing it to life, he blew out a cloud of blue smoke. He purposely kept his voice level when he said casually, "You've given up just about everything for the captain." He paused dramatically and sighed. "I hope she doesn't have you fooled, my friend."

Big Alfred made a face. "Fooled? Of course she doesn't have me fooled! She's as good as the blessed Virgin Mary, she is."

"Ah, come now, pal. For all that Holy Joe stuff, she's just a woman, like any other," Nick said. "Same strengths. Same weaknesses." He grinned and added casually, "I could get her into bed as easily as—"

"Nicholas Daniel McCabe!" Big Alfred roared his outrage as he rose to his feet in anger. "You could *never* get the captain to—"

"Wanna bet?" Nick interrupted, knowing the big Englishman's weakness for wagering. "Or is gambling a sin like everything else that's halfway enjoyable?"

"Gambling in and of itself is no sin," stated the red-faced Englishman, eyes still snapping with anger.

"Please . . . sit back down." Nick's heartbeat speeded. "So gambling's no sin?"

Frowning, Big Alfred eased back down into his chair. "No. No, it's not. Captain Kay says that nowhere does the Bible deem gambling a sin. Why, the Roman soldiers cast lots for Jesus' robe."

Nick knocked the ash from his Monte Cristo. "That being the case, I have a sporting proposition that might just interest you."

Big Alfred couldn't hide his interest. "A sporting proposition? And what might that be, Nicholas?"

"I'll bet I can seduce Captain Kay Montgomery."

Again Big face flushed bloodred. "Don't you be jesting about the—"

"I'm not jesting," Nick interrupted again. "I'm proposing a most interesting wager and one that—"

"Stop, laddie! I'll hear no more. This has gone far enough." Big Alfred again came to his feet, moved toward the door.

"Listen before you say no." Nick rushed his words. "If I can't seduce the captain within a hundred and twenty days—four months—I'll forgive the fifteen thousand dollars the Army owes on the mortgaged property."

"I'm not listening. I'm not," Big Alfred said, but Nick saw the flash of excitement leap into his hazel eyes.

"But if I am successful—if she lets me make love to her"—Nick pressed on—"you come back here to the Carousel Club where you belong."

"Do you really suppose I'd make such an outlandish, dangerous bet?"

"Where's the danger? Haven't you spent the evening extolling the virtues of your fine, upright captain? She's one of kind, remember? I could never get her into bed."

"And you couldn't." Big Alfred was vehement. "I know you couldn't!"

"Then take the bet, old friend." Big Alfred was shaking his head, a pained expression on his face. "You have the utmost faith in Captain Kay," Nick said. "Or do you?"

Big Alfred was troubled, but at the same time he was tempted. What Nick was suggesting was intolerable, outrageous, unforgivable. And yet just this morning Captain Kay had confided that she and Curly had only until May to prove themselves. They'd been sent to California to establish the San Francisco Corps #1. They had been given exactly one year. If the Army didn't have a permanent mission built, staffed, and operating by May 1, 1884, they would be called home. Sent back to serve under others. The Army's founder, General

William Booth himself, was coming to California in the spring to check on their progress—or the lack thereof.

"Can you pass up a sure thing?" Nick knew the Englishman was in a turmoil. Nick leaned way back in his chair, drew on his cigar, and watched Big Alfred closely.

"You'd excuse the entire five thousand?" Big Alfred was thinking aloud.

"Every last cent. Turn over the deed and, as an added kicker, toss in fifteen thousand dollars cash toward the mission's construction costs."

Big Alfred's massive shoulders lifted and lowered as he sighed heavily. "Such an ungodly proposal."

"Or a golden opportunity," countered Nick.

"The captain would never forgive me," said Big Alfred.

"The captain would never know."

"You've always been like catnip to women," worried Big Alfred.

"The captain's no ordinary woman. She'd never yield to temptation." Nick grinned and added, "She's a saint."

"Aye! That she is, no matter what you think, laddie!"

"Then put your money where your mouth is, my friend."

Big Alfred glowered at Nick. "No one would ever know?"

"I give you my word."

"The captain's an angel come down to earth," Big Alfred told him. "She has a pure heart, an unshakable faith, and a conscience as clear as an infant's."

"Who you trying to convince? Me or yourself?" Nick snubbed his cigar out in the crystal ashtray. He saw anger flare in the flashing hazel eyes fixed on him. But he knew the big Englishman was weakening fast. Nobody loved the thrill of making a bet more than Alfred Duke.

And a wager of this magnitude was the thrill of them all.

"You're a bad lad, Nick." Big Alfred accused.

"Sure I am. That's what this bet's all about. Good versus evil. I say evil wins every time." Nick's smile was demonic.

"Not this time, my boy." Big Alfred had complete confidence in Captain Kay Montgomery. "You've got yourself a bet!"

Chapter 25

Down at the waterfront mission, it was another busy day for those who deal with the things in life that don't turn out well. Captain Kay Montgomery hadn't had a breather since sunup. Nor had she had anything to eat. A cup of black coffee had been her breakfast.

The Army's coffers had been virtually cleaned out by the added demands of a long holiday season. In this first week of the new year, the Corps was nearly as destitute as those they served. Which meant starting over again—with only four short months until that looming May 1 deadline.

At the noon hour Captain Kay grabbed a minute to herself. She walked into the cluttered, dismal little room she used for an office. She sat wearily down behind the three-legged desk. She slumped forward, exhausted, a strand of flaming hair falling across one blue eye. She was weak from fatigue and hunger. She was worried about money. Or the lack thereof. How could the Army hope to raise enough money to pay off the mortgage and build the mission before General Booth's springtime inspection?

Kay shook her head and commanded herself to take a mental recess from all her troubles. To spend a few reviving minutes thinking only pleasant thoughts. She would forget for a while the insurmountable obstacles in her path and think only happy thoughts.

Number one on that list was little Joey.

Kay's fair face immediately broke into a smile. The adorable redheaded boy and his dog, Mac, were right there before her. She could see them as clearly as if they actually raced around the room: Joey laughing, Mac barking.

For a brief, lovely moment Kay took strength and joy from the treasured reverie. And she looked eagerly forward to three P.M. when she would see Joey and Mac in the flesh.

Kay then summoned up her friend and companion, Patrick Packard. She purposely focused on the blond, soft-spoken aristocrat. Kay held the greatest admiration for him. Patrick was a perfect gentleman, eager to please and always attentive. He listened intently when she spoke of Joey, genuinely interested in the child who'd won her heart.

Patrick was kind. He was generous. He could be counted on to contribute substantial sums of money to the Army's good cause. Too bad there weren't more concerned citizens like Patrick Packard.

Abruptly and without warning the image of an unconcerned citizen popped into Kay's mind. But that was the other list—the one she tried not to think about.

Kay could see Nick McCabe as clearly as she'd seen Joey. Her dreamy smile vanished at the sight of that dark, good-looking face.

Nick was there before her with all that vile vitality, that menacing masculine beauty, that abundance of animal attraction with which God had endowed him.

Lucifer.

Nick McCabe always put her in mind of Lucifer. Those silver, Satanic eyes. That blinding, devilish grin. His wild, dangerous disposition. No doubt Lucifer himself was just as handsome, just as vital, just as reckless as the impish Nick McCabe.

Nick's dark, Satanic face was not the only thing about the man that was devilishly appealing. His tall, lean body was the finest configuration of muscle, bone, and flesh Kay had ever seen. It was impossible to look at Nick without comparing the physical perfection of his body to that of a divinely inspired Greek sculpture.

There was a grace about Nick's movements that was animal, slow and flowing. The easy grace of a great cat. A big, dangerous tiger stalking through the jungle, beautiful to behold, dangerous to encounter.

Suddenly the fine wispy hair rose on Kay's nape. She felt a shadow fall across her soul and she shivered. Nick McCabe's presence in the room was so powerful it was if he was actually there. She could feel him.

Kay slowly turned her head.

And there stood Nick McCabe.

Framed in the doorway in a strikingly masculine stance, he wore a seaman's wool navy jacket, the collar turned up around his ears. A pale-blue pullover shirt stretched across his chest, and dark twill trousers hugged his long legs like a second skin. His raven hair was windblown and falling over his forehead. His handsome face was aglow with good health. His sensuous lips were turned up into an appealing devilish smile.

Kay rose stiffly, her whole body tensed, her blue eyes wide.

"At ease, Captain," said Nick, and pushed away from the door.

Caught off guard, it took Kay a moment to don the armor she needed against the sinful charmer. She pushed the lock of flaming hair back in place, placed her hands on her hips, and looked directly at Nick.

"Well, look who's here," she said, shaking her head incredulously. "What, no dancing girls? No bodyguards?"

"A Salvationist with a sense of humor," Nick replied with a laconic grin. "Now, that's enough to restore my faith." He crossed to her, bringing with him the pleasing scent of clean cold air.

"What is it you want, McCabe?" asked Kay, unsmiling, folding her arms over her chest. "Can't you see I'm busy here?"

"What are you doing?" Nick glanced at the stacks of ledger books lying on the desk.

"God's work. That's what I do." Kay lowered her arms and stepped out from behind the desk.

"I could sure do with a little spiritual comfort myself," Nick said.

He came slowly closer, moving with that stately grace of a cat. With his dark hair, dark skin, dark jacket, dark trousers, he was darkness itself. Hot darkness flowing toward her. Surrounding her. Enveloping her.

Kay flinched, feeling his power. But her voice was firm when she said, "I'm certain you get all the comfort you need, spiritual and otherwise. Now why are you here?"

"To help out." Nick was now a couple of feet away. He smiled down at Kay, his teeth very white against his tanned face.

Kay was struck by Nick's great height. She didn't remember him being so tall. Standing as he was—uncomfortably close to her—she had to tilt her head back to look at his face. Her empty stomach involuntarily contracted.

The man who reminded her of Lucifer had taken on yet another identity. He stood there looking down on her like a lean, handsome Goliath. She foolishly wished for a slingshot.

Nick took a step closer.

"Wh-what are you doing?" Kay asked nervously.

"What do you want done?" Nick replied, his silver-gray eyes gleaming with mischief. He watched a pink blush move up out of the military collar of Kay's navy-blue uniform and up on her throat.

Taking a defensive step backward, Kay said, "Nothing, thank you. Nothing you can do."

"Captain, you'd be amazed at what I can do."

"Yes, well, Mr. Modesty, I have no need of your help, so if you'll kindly—"

"Okay, I'll tell you why I'm here." Nick again advanced, maneuvering Kay toward the broken-paned window. "I thought you might have lunch with me."

"Lunch? I'm sure you haven't had breakfast yet," Kay said sarcastically. "It's not quite twelve noon."

"You know you're right. Let's make it breakfast since neither of us has had any."

"What makes you think I haven't had breakfast?" Kay said.

"Have you?" Nick's knowing look dared her to fib. "Come on. Let's go have some ham and eggs."

"I told you, I've work to do."

"It can wait."

"So can you."

"No, I can't," Nick said. "You see, I want to learn more about your Army. I really do. Why, I spent my morning reading a copy of the *War Cry*."

"Really? Your lips must be tired."

Nick ignored the barb. "Have breakfast with me, Captain." A sardonic smile shaping his mouth, he opened his seaman's jacket, laid a hand on his stomach, and said, "I'm undernourished. Look at me. I'm wasting away."

"You're not wasting away, McCabe," Kay scoffed. "You're just a waste."

"Know what I think, Captain?" Nick leaned close.

"Do I care?" Kay attempted further retreat, her back bumping into the windowsill. Trapped, she felt almost panicky. There was an aura of strength and energy about Nick McCabe that was electric. Much as she disapproved of him and all he stood for, she couldn't keep from responding to his raw, powerful masculinity.

"Don't you?" Nick asked. He raised a long arm and rested his hand on the window frame, inches from Kay's left shoulder. "You should if you're what you profess to be."

"I beg your pardon," said Kay, clinging with effort to her composure. It was hard to do, cornered as she was by Nick McCabe, but she was determined. Kay stood her ground with brazen assurance, looking him squarely in the eyes.

"Aren't you a seeker of the lost?" Nick asked, his silver eyes startlingly pale against the darkness of his skin.

"The Army does its best to—"

"I'm lost, Captain," Nick smoothly interrupted. "Help me. Help me claw my way out of the black depths of sin."

Kay was not fooled. "You're welcome to come to our nightly prayer meetings, McCabe."

"That's not enough. I need firm and discerning guidance from you personally."

"Fine," Kay said sweetly. "I'll be more than happy to give you personal guidance."

"You will?" Nick dark brows lifted. He reached out and touched the silver S brooch on Kay's collar. "I knew I could count on you, Captain."

Kay brushed his hand away. "That you can," she said, smiling confidently at him. "Here's my personal guidance and advice to you, Mr. McCabe. Denounce your lunatic love of vice and relinquish your incessant need to gather filthy lucre."

With that, Kay agilely ducked underneath Nick's outstretched arm, effectively freeing herself from the mesmerizing power of his beautiful silver eyes.

When she'd put several steps between them, she turned and added, "As a captain in God's Army I abhor worldliness, cruelty, and intoxicants. I love the truth, the downtrodden, and the troubled."

"Well, that includes me," Nick said, frowning slightly now. "I'm troubled."

"No, you're not. You're just plain trouble." Kay tilted her head, indicating the door. "So why don't you take your broad shoulders and your black wavy hair and get out of here."

Nick's frown immediately turned back into a grin. So underneath that stiff collar and stiffer reserve was a flesh-and-blood woman after all. The good captain had noticed his good looks. She wasn't immune to his charm. And charm was what he did best. Nick knew that.

"Captain," Nick said softly, flashing his most irresistible smile as he languidly approached her, "I don't want to go. Not without you."

"That's your misfortune, McCabe."

Nick shook his dark head accusingly. "If there really is such as thing as God and retribution, aren't you afraid you'll have to answer to him for turning away this poor seeker of the truth and the light?"

"I'm not certain what you've come here seeking, but I know it's not Truth and Light." Kay lifted a hand, pointed to the door.

"I'm going nowhere unless you come with me." Nick grinned and didn't move. "Or can you work miracles and simply wish me away?"

"I can't work miracles," Kay said angrily as she grabbed his arm, dragged him to the door, and shoved him through it. "But I *can* cast out devils."

Chapter 26

 Nick McCabe's unexpected appearance at the waterfront mission had unnerved Captain Kay more than she cared to admit. Even to herself. She puzzled over his reason for coming. What possible purpose could he have for visiting either her or the mission?

She knew Nick McCabe. He was up to no good. She'd have to watch him closely. Be constantly on her guard. This man was trouble, and she already had plenty of that.

Kay leaned back against the door she'd just shut after Nick. She closed her eyes and gritted her teeth against the unfairness of life. Why was it that an out-and-out scoundrel like Nick McCabe was so strikingly handsome it was impossible to ignore his dark good looks? Furthermore, Nick was undeniably charming. Charming as only the worthless can be.

Kay opened her eyes, shook her head to clear it, and soon was smiling sanguinely.

The sinful saloon owner posed no threat to her. She was no starry-eyed young girl who could be swept away easily by a forbidden attraction to the wrong kind of man. She knew Nick McCabe's sort and she knew how to handle them. God knows, she'd had plenty of practice.

No telling what new mischief McCabe was up to, but there was no real danger. He was far too restless and easily bored to expend any effort or time on a single goal. And whatever he was after, he wouldn't get it. Not from her. She'd see to that.

Confident she could thwart any nefarious scheme Nick McCabe might possibly have cooked up, Captain Kay got right back to work. He was just another minor nuisance, so she gave no further thought to the handsome saloon owner.

At least not for the remainder of that day.

However, the very next afternoon Captain Kay stopped by the wharf district on her way to Battery Place. When she walked in the mission, she was greeted with the sound of merry laughter. It was a good sound. It made her smile. She was pleased to know that her fellow soldiers, her comrades, were cheerful and happy in their work.

Kay took off her bonnet and followed the sound of the laughter. But well before she reached the back room where the Army stored its food supply, Kay's smile slipped. It disappeared completely when she heard a low, masculine voice and knew at once to whom it belonged.

None other than Nick McCabe.

Nick McCabe was in the scullery of the waterfront mission, telling a half-bawdy joke. The punchline was delivered as Kay stepped, unnoticed, into the doorway. The soldiers gathered around Nick burst into unrestrained laughter.

Kay found nothing funny about the story or its teller.

Her temper swiftly rose as she stared, disbelieving, at the grinning, pleased-with-himself Nick. She cocked her head to one side and inspected him irritably.

He stood at a long work table with the others. His shirtsleeves were rolled up over his dark forearms. A white dishtowel was tied around his trim waist. He was busily peeling potatoes, wielding the knife with expertise. And easily entertaining his companions. The charming scamp was capable of turning any gathering into an exciting event.

Kay had the strongest urge to strangle him.

Instead, she put a pleasant smile back on her face. Dealing with people required tact, a sense of humor, and powers of persuasion. Kay had been blessed with all three. She could deal with Nick McCabe. And would. Immediately.

"Hello, everyone." She stepped into the room, nodding, waving, smiling brilliantly.

She was warmly greeted by all. No one greeted her more warmly than the tall, dark intruder.

Despite all her best efforts, there was a touch of impatience in her voice when Captain Kay said, "Mr. McCabe, are you very busy?"

Nick tossed her a bright, cheery, predatory smile. Nodding his head, he said, "Busy, yes. Still, I've always time to do someone a favor."

"Could I speak with you for a moment?"

"Sure thing, Captain. What can I do for you?" Smiling broadly, Nick stayed right where he was.

"In private, if you please, Mr. McCabe."

"Ah. You mean alone? Just you and me?" His silver-gray eyes flashed with devilment.

"It won't take but a minute," she said as calmly as possible, silently wishing she could brain him.

Her fellow soldiers never suspected that their captain was the least bit upset. They went on about their chores, the mood light.

"Be right with you, Captain," Nick said. He laid the knife aside and wiped his hands on his white apron.

Kay spun away. Her mouth drawn tight, she hastily retreated to the outer room. Girded to do battle with the annoying twinkly-eyed hustler, she waited.

"Anything I can do for you, just name it." Nick's approach had been so quiet he startled Kay.

She whirled around. "What are you doing here?"

"Why, the Lord's work," Nick said, beaming. "Same as you, Captain."

Kay struggled to keep her control. Everything about the man rubbed her the wrong way. That killer smile. The confident posture. The way his muscles swelled against the material of his damp shirt.

"McCabe, you're fooling no one," she bit out the words.

Grinning, Nick shrugged. "Am I trying to fool someone?"

As if he hadn't spoken, Kay said, "Keep in mind you're not the first *malviviente* I've dealt with."

"I'll have to take your word on that, Captain," Nick said. "Since I've no idea what *malviviente* means."

"Lowlife, McCabe. It means lowlife."

"Well, now, that went right through me like a knife." Nick dramatically placed a spread hand over his heart.

"You'll get over it," snapped Kay. "Now, turn in your apron and go back where you belong."

"Anything you say." Nick was surprisingly congenial. "You'll tell the gang I had to go, won't you, and that I'll—"

"I'll tell them."

Nodding, Nick took off his apron. Suddenly curious, he asked, "Why do they join this Army? Surely the pay's not much."

"No. It's not."

"What are they in it for?"

"To help people," Kay said. "Can you understand that? Can you conceive of working hard for something other than your own personal gain?"

"Nope," Nick admitted. "Not really."

"I thought not." Kay shook her head in disgust. "Have you no conscience?"

"Can't afford one," said Nick.

He smiled.

She didn't.

"Tell me, McCabe, why would a man like you be spending his afternoon peeling potatoes at a Salvation Army Mission?"

"The truth?" Nick asked.

"The truth," Kay said.

"To be near you." With that he deftly whirled the white apron around Kay's back, caught it with both hands, and pulled her to him. His voice had a peculiar warm timbre when he told her, "I wanted to see you."

Her lips parting in surprise, Kay blinked up at the smooth, suntanned face with its sharply cut features. He appeared handsomer than ever, and his words, although totally untrue, sent a tiny shiver of alarm mixed with pleasure racing up her spine.

Kay quickly closed her lips and made her face impassive. But she was incapable of hiding the glow emanating from her blue eyes. An inner light illuminated them. Nick caught the look and knew exactly what it meant.

Wisely, Kay didn't struggle. She didn't push on Nick's chest. She didn't demand that he release her at once. She assumed an icy demeanor and asked, "Do you expect me to believe you?"

"Sure. Why not?"

Kay shook her head scornfully. "While I'm sure your technique works well with the Carousel girls, I find your behavior foolish and offensive."

Unruffled, Nick grinned as he tightened his hold on the apron, reeling Kay in a little closer. His silver-eyed gaze purposely focused on her mouth, he said, "Captain, I haven't begun to behave foolishly and offensively. Yet."

His eyes lifted to meet hers and he wound the apron another turn around his right hand, taking up the slack, drawing her closer. So close Kay felt her trembling knees brush against his hard, muscled legs. A sudden, new force showed on his handsome face.

Looking directly into her eyes, Nick said, "Let me warn you now that when I do behave foolishly—even offensively—you are going to like it." He smiled. "Won't you, Captain?"

"Does Hell freeze!" Kay hissed, and at last began the struggle to free herself.

In the blink of an eye Nick released one end of the apron. It happened so fast and unexpectedly that Kay was thrown off balance. She had no choice but to grab hold of Nick's hard biceps to keep from falling.

"There, you see," he teased. "Falling for me already."

Kay angrily righted herself, stepped back, and said, "Look, Mc-Cabe, I don't know what you're trying to pull, but—"

" 'Til we meet again, *Mon Commandant,*" said he, then saluted smartly, pivoted, and left.

Chapter 27

They met again the next day.

Not that Kay wanted to see Nick. She had no choice in the matter. It was Wednesday and time to pay Nick McCabe another $100 on the Army's mortgaged land.

The thing was, Captain Kay didn't have the full amount. For the first time, she had been unable to scrape together the $100. She was short $43. She could well imagine what Nick McCabe might say or do when she showed up with only $57 of his money.

Kay was a bundle of nerves as she walked toward the Golden Carousel. She was painfully aware of the conditions surrounding their bargain. If McCabe wanted to be really nasty, he could claim the Army in default, keep the money paid thus far, and retain the property. Foreclosure could be the end of her San Francisco Corps #1.

Much as she hated the thought of pleading her case, Kay was prepared to do just that. If she could convince the black-hearted saloon owner to give her a few days' grace, it would be worth the humiliation. She could *not* allow the Corps to lose that land. It was up to her to somehow, some way keep that catastrophe from happening.

Kay reached the club.

Feeling a little like one of the early Christians must have felt when forced to enter the arena where a hungry lion awaited, Captain Kay Montgomery rang the back bell of the Golden Carousel.

A smiling, bowing Ling Tan answered immediately. The friendly servant welcomed Kay in from the cold and inquired after her health. Kay responded in kind, asking about his lovely daughter, Ming Ho.

The pleasantries exchanged, Kay gave Ling Tan her black straw bonnet, glanced up the stairway, and said, "Is the Beelzebub of the Barbary Coast in?"

Ling Tan chuckled good-naturedly. Nodding, he said, "If Missy mean Boss Nick, he here. Say he wait for Missy Captain downstairs in club."

"Why? So he can be closer to his liquor?" Kay smoothed at her wild red hair.

"No," Ling Tan defended. "Boss, he not drinking. Boss say Missy Captain not like it when he drink, so not drink today."

Kay's brow wrinkled. It was true she didn't like McCabe drinking when she came here, but he'd never let that stop him before. Odd that he'd suddenly care.

With a gentle hand to her elbow, the servant guided Kay to the arched, curtained doorway leading into the shuttered club. He left her there, bowing and backing away.

Kay jerked the tails of her military jacket down, took a deep breath, and prepared herself for the unpleasant task before her. She hoped several of the Carousel girls would be at the bar with Nick. Especially Angel Thompson. She would ask, in front of the girls, for more time to get his money. Surely he wouldn't want to appear mean and unreasonable in their eyes. Especially Angel's.

Kay reached out, swept the curtains aside, and stepped into the cavernous club. She blinked in the deep shadows. Only one portion of the large room was lighted—the hexagonal mahogany bar and golden carousel above it. The bar was empty. The girls were not there. Neither was Nick.

Uneasy, Kay moved forward, looking cautiously around. She walked straight toward the stilled golden carousel. She reached the mahogany bar, put out a hand, and gripped its edge. She automatically tipped her head back to look up at the beautiful gilded steeds.

And jumped half out of her skin when a deep, low voice from somewhere out of the shadows said softly, "Captain, would you like to take a ride?"

Kay wheeled like a child caught in some forbidden act. Eyes wide, she turned round and round, vainly searching for Nick. Blinking anxiously, she saw only darkness. She stood very still then, waiting, listening, every muscle in her slender body tensed.

Nick stepped silently out of the darkness, appearing before her like a mysterious apparition from out of a magical mist. Immaculately groomed and breathtakingly handsome, he wore a long-sleeved shirt of pure black silk open at the collar, a pair of black flannel trousers, and shoes of soft black leather. His raven hair was as black as his clothes, and it gleamed under the light from above, a gaslit chandelier suspended in the exact center of the golden carousel.

Kay was again reminded of warm, flowing darkness as Nick gracefully approached. Her pulse beat heavily and she was not sure if it was from fear or attraction. He neared her, their eyes met for a long moment, and then Kay heard that low-pitched voice that made her flesh tingle.

"I asked if you'd like to ride on the carousel, Captain?" Nick said, his pale eyes glowing like hot silver ice in his dark face.

For a second Kay couldn't speak. The confusion of her emotions had left her speechless. She felt she was in imminent danger. She realized with dismay that this dark, handsome man was capable of making her feel things she'd never felt before.

Icy fear clutched her rapidly beating heart and she wondered: Was he capable as well of making her do things she'd never done before? Could he persuade her to romp and play uninhibitedly in this gilded, evil fairyland? If he encouraged her in that deep, compelling voice, would she climb up on one of those golden horses for him?

Nick took another step toward her. Kay swallowed hard and said, "No! I do *not* want to ride on this—this vulgar monstrosity." Her loud voice reverberated in the empty grand salon.

"I didn't mean to upset you," Nick said softly.

"You didn't," Kay snapped. "You couldn't if you wanted to."

"But you're trembling." Nick lifted his hand. His long fingers caressed Kay's upper arm in a message of reassurance. "Relax, Captain. I'm not going to hurt you."

Kay shrugged and attempted to laugh. But it sounded hollow even to her. She realized she was powerless to change the tone of this strange meeting. That further frightened her. She felt helpless. As if she was in Nick McCabe's hands. That he controlled her and their shared mood of . . . what? She wasn't sure. She realized Nick was guiding her away from the hexagonal bar, his hand at her back.

She balked. "Where are we going?"

Nick smiled down at her and directed her attention across the shadowy room to the lofty mezzanine. A match flared in the darkness and candles sprang to life on an unseen table above. She wanted to say no. She should have said no. But a curious nature had always been hers, and she wondered what Nick McCabe intended. The allure, the mystery was all too appealing.

So she allowed him to usher her across the room, up the marble steps, and to the black velvet banquette where the white candles in their silver candlesticks lighted the damask-spread table. Nick remained fully in charge, handing her into the plush banquette and sliding in beside her. He leaned back and allowed his knees to spread wide apart so that one of them came in contact with Kay's. She inwardly cringed, but made no attempt to move away. If she did, he'd think she was affected by his touch. She preferred to let him believe she hadn't noticed that his leg was pressed against hers.

"There's something I have to tell you, McCabe, and I may just as well get it over with," Kay said, turning to look at him.

"You can tell me anything," he said, the glow of the candles reflected in his silver eyes.

"I don't have it," Kay said flatly. "I don't your money today. Not the full amount. I could only come up with fifty-seven dollars, but I'll do my—"

"It's all right. I understand."

Kay couldn't believe her ears. She started to speak, but a white-jacketed waiter rolled a cart up to the banquette. While he placed a white china saucer, coffee cup, and plate before her, Kay stared at the array of pastries atop the cart. Her mouth began to water.

The waiter disappeared after pouring their coffee from a gleaming silver urn. Nick smiled at Kay and picked up her plate. She watched intently as he placed on the plate a piece of white coconut cake, a couple of sugar cookies, a small wedge of pecan pie, and a hot cinnamon roll.

"Oh, McCabe, may I have one of those too?" Kay, forgetting her manners, pointed to the stacks of cream-filled ladyfingers.

Nick laughed aloud. He continued to laugh when he set the plate before her and watched her blue, expressive eyes light with pleasure. Far too hungry to pretend nonchalance, Kay picked up her sterling fork, took a bite of the coconut cake, and nodded, murmuring "Mmmmm."

Nick was charmed by her childlike enjoyment of the rich desserts. It was delightful to be with a woman who found genuine pleasure in something as simple as a piece of cake.

Kay ate with relish. At Nick's insistence, she sampled everything on the cart. After swallowing the last bite of a strawberry tart, she said, rolling her eyes with bliss, "Oh, McCabe, you don't think me a terrible pig, do you?"

Nick smiled, lifted his white linen napkin, and dabbed a tiny blob of meringue from the left corner of her mouth. "I think you are utterly charming."

But Kay never heard him. She was pointing excitedly to a silver platter where perfectly cut pieces of chocolate fudge rested on white paper doilies. "Nick, look! Candy. Fudge with pecans. Oh, I didn't see that before. May I?"

"You're going to be ill, Captain," Nick said, noticing that she'd called him Nick.

"I don't care. I want a piece of that fudge. Please."

Kay ate the candy while Nick smiled like an indulgent parent. At last Kay licked her fingers, sighed, and leaned back against the high black velvet seat. The afternoon wore on and Kay made no move to leave. Nick joked, laughed, flashed his dazzling smile, and finally reached out and took her hand in his.

Kay's eyes widened when Nick lifted her hand to his mouth and blew his breath on her fingers. She felt its warmth all the way down to her toes.

Suddenly aware she'd been there too long, that she'd allowed him to become far too familiar, Kay said nervously, "I must leave. Let me go! Please, let me go."

Nick immediately released her. "You were always free to go, Captain. I'd never hold you against your will."

Chapter 28

"First warm day, we'll have a picnic."

"No. I really can't."

"Other plans?"

"I just don't want to."

In the next few weeks this same conversation took place between Captain Kay and Nick McCabe almost every day. Nick was determined he'd persuade Kay to picnic with him. He knew each time he asked that she would say no. He knew as well that sooner or later he'd convince her to say yes.

His arguments were sound. What could be safer than Seal Beach for lunch? Middle of the day. Bright sunshine everywhere. Plenty of people around. Get back to the waterfront mission well before dark.

Still Kay continued to turn him down. She refused, as well, to repeat the afternoon they'd shared in Nick's banquette at the darkened Carousel Club. She'd have said yes to a harmless outdoors picnic long before she'd have spent another moment with him at the club feasting on tempting desserts in the shadowy, seductive privacy.

She had no intention of doing either.

Nick had every intention of persuading her to do both.

And more. Much more.

Nick had shown up at the waterfront mission with such regularity for past few weeks, his presence was no longer a novelty. The troop all knew him, welcomed him, liked him, and wondered why Captain Kay was often downright rude to him.

Big Alfred was the only one who didn't wonder.

He kept a watchful eye on both Nick and Kay at all times. Pleased with what he saw, he was tempted more than once to say to Nick, "There, laddie, I told you so. One of a kind, our captain is."

He never said a word, but he beamed with satisfaction and shot looks at Nick that conveyed the clear message he was happy with his end of the bet. Alfred Duke was able to lie down and go to sleep each night untroubled. The feisty Army captain was in no danger. The lassie knew how to take care of herself. And scoundrels like Nick.

Big Alfred smiled to himself at the sweet irony of it. He'd spent seven years with Nick McCabe. He'd seen women of every size and description fall madly in love with the handsome saloon owner. Wives had left their husbands for him. Heiresses had risked their inheritance for him. Good girls had turned bad for Nick, and bad girls had turned good. Young and old, beautiful and not so beautiful, women were wild about the handsome king of the Barbary Coast.

But the red-haired Salvation Army captain wouldn't give him the time of day!

Or so Alfred Duke thought.

Big Alfred was blissfully unaware that Captain Kay *did* find the Golden Carousel owner more than a little attractive. She wasn't blind to Nick's dark good looks. Her strong, unwavering faith didn't make her immune to his fierce masculine appeal. She wasn't totally repulsed by his puzzling pursuit.

In truth, Kay was dangerously drawn to Nick, despite her keen dislike for all he stood for. She constantly had to remind herself that Nick McCabe was an irreverent, profane man. She told herself that his insolent flirting was discourteous, outrageous. She reminded herself that Nick said things to her no gentleman ever would.

Still, the raw, rugged maleness he so effortlessly exuded had an unsettling effect. Untapped, unwelcome passions sleeping deep inside Kay were being awakened by the playful, rakish rascal.

On this surprisingly warm February afternoon, Captain Kay was once again turning down Nick's invitation to go on a Seal Beach picnic. The two were alone in Kay's office. Nick had followed her there, disregarding her request that he leave her alone.

Kay stood at the window, Nick across the room.

"You may as well leave, McCabe," Kay said in brittle tones. "The answer is still no. It was no yesterday and it will be no tomorrow. No, no, and again no."

"Well, I can take a hint," Nick said, smiling. He moved toward her. "No picnic today?"

"No picnic ever."

"Let me get this straight: You want me to leave? Is that it?"

"Good for you, McCabe." Kay was sarcastic. "I do believe you've finally caught on."

Nick shrugged wide shoulders, causing the pale-yellow fabric of his shirt to pull across the flat muscles of his chest. "In that case, I'll just grab my hat and go."

Grinning, Nick picked up Kay's black straw bonnet from atop the three-legged desk and set it on his head, pulling it low over his gleaming silver-gray eyes. The black streamers hung loose atop his shoulders.

"Take that off!" Kay ordered, but couldn't keep from smiling. She crossed her arms over her chest and shook her head. "McCabe, you look silly."

Nick tied the long streamers in a bow under his chin. "I won't be the only one people call silly when I walk down the street wearing Captain Kay Montgomery's Army bonnet."

Kay's arms came uncrossed. She no longer smiled. "You wouldn't do that. Would you?"

"Naw. You know I wouldn't," said Nick. But he tossed her that I'm-about-to-wink-at-you look.

"Nick McCabe . . . you give me that hat!"

"Come and get it, Captain," said Nick, backing away toward the open door.

Kay couldn't allow him to leave wearing her Army bonnet, so she went after him. Nick stood his ground, waiting. Kay met him in the center of the room.

Neither was ever quite sure why or how it started, but in the tussle for the straw bonnet, somebody accidentally tickled somebody. And that somebody swiftly retaliated by doing some tickling of his own.

In no time Nick had found Kay's most ticklish spots. He tickled her delicate ribs, her underarms, her tummy. She squealed and laughed and squirmed.

And she tickled his sides, his stomach. Nick howled with laughter and begged her to stop. The pair banged and battled around Kay's little office, behaving like loud, naughty children. Shrieks and shouts and name-calling mixed with groans and sighs and giggles. Defensive slaps and punches and elbowing were all in good clean fun. So were the bear hugs and reckless clenches and snug embraces necessary to thwart the other's spirited tickling assaults.

Caught up in the fun of foolish play, neither Kay or Nick heard Alfred Duke call out when he arrived at the mission. They had no idea he had walked through the front door and into the empty auditorium. They didn't hear his heavy footfalls as, alarmed, the big Englishman headed immediately for Kay's office to investigate.

At the office's open door, Big Alfred stopped. Captain Kay and Nick were inside. And the manner in which he found them left Big Alfred staring open-mouthed.

Kay's face was flushed beet red. Her hair was not in its neat, prim bun at the back of her neck. It was loose and flying around her head.

The tails of her white long-sleeved blouse were outside the waistband of her Army blue shirt. A couple of the blouse's buttons were undone. A sleeve was twisted and pushed up past her elbow.

Nick's black hair was badly disheveled. His eyes, at that moment, were closed. His tanned face was tinged with color. His yellow shirt was open down his chest. Kay's Army bonnet bounced on his shoulder blades, its taffeta streamers tied around his neck.

The rumpled, disorderly pair bumped and crashed around in a wild dance of idiocy. Kay's bent left knee was caught between Nick's long legs. Her right hand clutched his shoulder in a death grip. Her other hand was inside Nick's open shirt, her sharp nails playing over the bare brown flesh of his abdomen.

Nick's right arm was hooked around Kay's waist, his hand up under the loose tails of her white blouse. The left was clutching her skirt in front, his long fingers curled inside the skirt's tight waistband. His chin rested heavily against the side of Kay's head. Her loose red hair was in Nick's eyes. Kay's flushed face was pressed to the hollow of Nick's throat, her laughter muffled against his neck.

Big Alfred couldn't believe it. He'd never seen Nick McCabe behave so foolishly, much less Captain Kay Montgomery.

He loudly cleared his throat.

The startled pair immediately looked around, the laughter dying in Kay's throat, her eyes wide with surprise. For a second longer Kay continued to cling to Nick as she gasped for breath, her heart hammering against her ribs.

"Afternoon, Al." Nick spoke first, his voice completely level. He was unruffled by Big Alfred's intrusion. His arm remained possessively around Kay's waist. "Come on in. It's good to see you."

Horrified, Kay gaped at the big, frowning Englishman. She suddenly became all too aware that her spread hand was on Nick naked stomach. Guiltily she jerked it away and squirmed free of Nick's embrace, her red face growing redder.

"Big Alfred . . . I was . . . we were . . . this must look like . . . like . . ." She faltered, swallowed, and tried again. Furiously stuffing the tails of her blouse back into the waistband of her skirt, she said, "You see, it's such a warm, lovely day, McCabe came by to—"

"—ask Captain Kay if she'd like to go on a picnic," Nick interrupted, calmly buttoning his yellow shirt. He smiled at the scowling Englishman and added, "But she refused."

Big Alfred looked from Nick to Kay.

Kay again piped up, eager to defend herself. "That's true. I turned him down just like always. I asked him to leave, but then he took my bonnet. I had to get it back so I—"

"You're grown, the both of you," Big Alfred stated simply. "Responsible adults. Answerable to no one." He turned and left.

"Wait! Big Alfred, you don't understand, we were . . . nothing was happening . . . I mean . . ." Kay stopped speaking. The big, fatherly Englishman had gone.

Kay felt terrible, like a child who'd been chastened by a disappointed parent. Nick was totally unfazed. He managed to make Kay burst into nervous giggles again when he swelled out his chest, mimicked the fierce face Big Alfred had made, and in a gruff British accent repeated his words verbatim.

"Shhhh!" Kay warned, laughing and slapping at him.

Nick grinned, handed the straw bonnet to the laughing Kay, and said, "So, how about it, Captain? Wanna go on a picnic with me?"

"Will you get out of here!" she shrieked, but laughter still shone from her expressive blue eyes.

Nick was cunning.

It was time, he knew, to show Kay a different side of himself. Throw her off balance. Make her uncertain.

Nick didn't come around to see Kay the next day. He knew she would be expecting him, so he didn't come.

Kay did expect Nick. She was certain he'd drop by and invite her to go on a picnic. Just as he did every day. She lingered at the mission longer than usual, making excuses for not going out. Pretending she was too tied up to get away.

But still no Nick.

Each time the mission's front door opened, she tensed, listened, waited. And then exhaled loudly when Bobby Newman or Giles Lawton or Matthew or one of the dozens of other soldiers came in off the streets.

By seven that evening Kay told herself she was relieved. Nick hadn't come. He wasn't coming. She was glad. She hoped he never came again. The lout!

The nightly knee drill began. It was Curly's turn to preach. Kay made sure everyone was welcomed to the services and had found a place to sit. Then she quietly took a seat in the shadows at very back of the old warehouse. Midway through Curly's sermon, Kay felt a sudden rush of cold air as the mission door opened then closed. A latecomer slid silently onto the bench beside her. Kay turned to smile a polite welcome.

There sat Nick McCabe in the shadows.

Nick didn't grin. He didn't wink. He didn't acknowledge her in any way. He sat very still, his knees spread, a hand resting on the bench between them.

In the eerie mixture of light and shadow his chiseled features stood out in bold relief. His slanting cheekbones were more pronounced than ever. His silver-gray eyes glittered in the half-light. Those beautiful eyes were strangely cold, yet they held an intensity that took Kay's breath away. This was a very different Nick from the one she'd tickled and laughed with only yesterday.

The dark, silent man seated beside her was a stranger. Mysterious, but fiercely compelling. Kay was drawn by his dark power, his strange scary coldness. Her eyes lowered almost fearfully from his harsh, handsome face.

The midnight-black jacket he wore was open to reveal a shirt of shimmering white silk. Beneath the silky shirt, his broad chest rose and fell with his slow, even breathing. Looking at him now, Kay recalled with vivid clarity the warmth and smoothness of the flesh beneath that shirt.

Her palms began to perspire. She willed herself to look away. To direct her attention to Curly and the sermon. She couldn't do it. It was impossible. This dark, compelling man was silently commanding her to look at him.

And no one else.

The very air around her seemed charged with tension, and Kay could hardly get her breath. As in a trance, her gaze once more lifted to meet Nick's. She was riveted by the penetrating, near-hypnotic stare of those cold, silver eyes. Eyes that turned from ice to fire as he stared at her.

Kay knew there was answering fire in her own eyes. She wondered if the blood pounding in her ears was as loud to him as it was to her. She wasn't sure what was happening to her. She felt as if her entire body were as icy-hot as those exotic silver eyes fixed on her. She was uneasy, at the same time lulled by a wonderful sense of well-being. She felt as if she were in danger, yet safer than she'd ever been in her life.

Kay studied the hard, handsome face and saw the power there. Once again she was reminded of sensuous, flowing darkness. She could feel that warm, tantalizing darkness closing around her, swallowing her up.

His hot silver eyes holding hers, Nick finally moved. He put out his hand to Kay. Without hesitation, she laid her cold, stiff fingers atop his smooth, warm palm. Heat instantly flashed through her body when Nick's long, tanned fingers closed firmly around hers.

Gracefully Nick rose and drew her up. He ushered her from the building and out into the cool, foggy night. He said nothing. He held her hand tightly in his and guided her along the boardwalk, away from the wharf district mission.

When they'd gone a few hundred yards, Nick stopped, turned Kay about, and gently pressed her back against the wall of a vacant building. He stood before her, his tall, lean frame blocking out the misty light from the lamppost at his back. His silver eyes bored right into hers.

Nick unbuttoned one of the pearl buttons going down the front of his white silk shirt. He lifted Kay's hand to his chest and guided it inside the opened shirt. He pressed her spread fingers down directly to his heart.

Kay could feel the heavy, even cadence. The beating of Nick's heart surged through her fingertips and coursed through her entire body as if it were her own heartbeat.

At last Nick spoke. In a low, caressing voice, he said, "Do you feel my heart beating through your hand?"

"Yes." It was a whisper. "Yes, Nick, I do."

"My heart is beating with yours."

"I know, oh, I know."

"Let me, Kay." Nick said softly, enticingly. "Let me."

"Let you?" she murmured, her hand stroking the hard wall of his chest. "I . . . what . . . ?"

"Let me feel your heart beating through my fingers," Nick said, and slid a tanned hand up her slim midriff toward her breasts.

"No!" Kay said, the spell broken as she came to her senses. "I most certainly will not!"

Nick's hand continued moving up, slowly, seductively. "Don't forbid me, Captain. Let me feel your heartbeat."

Kay snatched her hand out of Nick's shirt and began shoving on his chest. "You get your hands off me, Nick McCabe! Stop it! Stop it right now!"

"Be still. Don't fight me."

Kay fought him. And her voice rose shrilly when she hissed, "I think your behavior is outrageous. You're . . . you're mad!"

"Is this man bothering you, miss?"

A uniformed constable, slapping his nightstick against his palm, appeared from out of the fog. Standing beside them, he looked directly at Kay, waiting for an answer. Kay looked from the policeman to Nick. She swallowed, shrugged, said nothing.

"Well," Nick said evenly, "tell the officer. Am I bothering you?" His eyes glittered.

Kay hesitated, then finally said, "No. No, sir. The gentleman isn't bothering me."

"Then a good night to you both." The constable touched the bill of his cap and started off down the boardwalk.

Kay looked up at Nick and saw the old sinister smile, the devilish gleam in his silver eyes.

"I should have let him haul you off to jail!" she snapped.

"But you didn't," Nick said. "Why is that, Captain?"

"Oh, don't be so smug!" Kay said. "I'm going back to the mission." She turned and flounced away.

Nick easily caught up with her. Taking her elbow, he said, "Why? Why leave me when you spent the entire day waiting for me to show up?"

"I did not!"

"You did. You waited for me and I came for you," he said, "just in the *Nick* of time."

"You are out of your mind, McCabe!"

"I have an idea," Nick replied. "If it's warm tomorrow, let's have a picnic tomorrow."

"No. I can't."

"Other plans?"

"No. I just don't want to. Can't you understand, McCabe. I will never go on a picnic with you!"

"Never?"

"Never!"

Chapter 29

"Can a black spider come to Jesus?"

"You mean," said Captain Kay, not unkindly, "can a backslider come to Jesus." Kay then smiled warmly at the little girl and added, "The answer is yes. A backslider can come to Jesus."

"What is a backslider?" asked the curious child as she twisted on a chestnut curl beside her ear.

Captain Kay patiently explained before continuing the lesson. Kay sat cross-legged in the sunny backyard at Battery Place. A gathering of children surrounded her. They listened while she read a Bible story to them, interrupting often to ask questions.

Joey was in the group. He never asked any questions. But he listened intently and placed his tiny index finger perpendicular to his lips when Mac—squirming on his lap—made too much noise.

Kay could hardly conceal her amusement when Joey made mean faces at Mac to get the puppy to keep quiet. Joey's big blue eyes would narrow menacingly, the sweet little mouth would thin into a stern line, and he'd cock his tiny finger at Mac as if it were a weapon. His attempts to look threatening were funny; he was *so* cute.

Kay wondered where he had learned to make such faces. He was surely parroting somebody. Some grown-up.

The lively Mac wasn't particularly frightened by his master's mean visage. The collie was as likely to bark or lick Joey in the face as he was to mind him. Still, considering he was a healthy, happy puppy, Mac behaved fairly well during Bible classes.

When the day's lesson ended, Kay took the opportunity to speak to the children again about the dangers of being on the city streets. Every child at Battery Place had been warned repeatedly about a wicked group of men who were very dangerous and could not be trusted.

The children were never to talk with strangers. They were never to accept a ride in a carriage with someone they didn't know well. They were never to go outside the gates of Battery Place unless accompanied by an adult.

The older children knew about the Shadow Clan. Many had read or heard about the New Year's Eve kidnappings. They were aware of the kind of heinous crimes the Shadow Clan committed. They were cautioned to be constantly on their guard and to help look out for the little ones when they were on an outing.

"Now, remember," Kay said, looking from one turned-up face to the next, "we never go outside the gates alone. What else?"

In unison the children repeated the things she and the staff had told them they were never to do.

"That's very good," Kay praised. "Very good indeed. I guess that's all for today."

Kay laid her Bible aside while the energetic children eagerly leapt up and immediately began running and playing. Kay stayed where she was for a while. She leaned back, resting her weight on stiff arms.

The February sun was warm on her face. She felt lazy and content. Soon she was smiling as she recalled Joey's attempt at looking mean.

Her eyes automatically followed the red-headed boy. She was overjoyed to see him laughing. Better still, he was talking. He and Mac were actually playing with the other children. Joey was graciously allowing his new friends to pet his best friend, the cuddly, imperturbable Mac.

It came time for her to leave. Kay didn't want to go. She wanted to stay there forever, just as she was, watching the tiny boy behaving like any normal happy child. She stayed as long as she possibly could, savoring the moment, etching the lovely interlude deeply on her brain. Storing a beautiful memory to be enjoyed again and again through the coming years.

Hating to leave, knowing she had to, Captain Kay said good-bye. Crouched on her heels, she gratefully accepted warm hugs and kisses from all the children. All but one.

Joey.

The adorable child she most longed to hold for one brief moment in her aching arms kept his distance.

"Good-bye, Joey," Kay called to him, hoping he'd come closer, knowing he wouldn't.

"Bye," he said, staring at her with those huge blue eyes.

"Bye, Mac," Kay shouted to the puppy.

Mac barked and dashed toward her, his tail wagging a mile a minute.

"Mac!" Joey scolded loudly, and raced after his wayward puppy.

When Joey caught up with Mac, the collie was barking loudly and jumping on Kay, his paws sprinkling dirt and dead grass on her blue skirts. The exasperated Joey squatted down beside the yelping dog, put on his sternest face, and shook his short finger in Mac's face.

"Bad dog!" he said, eyes narrowed menacingly. Without even looking at Kay he scooped up the collie in his arms and ran off.

Smiling wistfully, Kay watched the irresistible pair, wishing she could scoop them both up in her arms and run off.

Still, Kay was pleased with Joey's remarkable progress. The sad-eyed, withdrawn little boy who'd been callously dropped off at Battery Place in the middle of the night now talked, laughed, and played. Like any normal child.

Joey pleasantly surprised her one chilly afternoon a few days later. Kay was preparing to leave. She was in a hurry, running behind schedule. As usual a number of children lined up to give her their affectionate hugs and kisses. So she fell to her knees and spread her arms wide.

She pretended total nonchalance when Joey—with Mac nipping at his heels—stepped up to her, grinned shyly, then threw his short arms around her neck. He locked his wrists behind her head and pressed his cheek to hers. Kay hugged him tightly, inhaling deeply of the sweet, clean, little-boy scent of him.

Joey abruptly released her, reached down, scooped up Mac, and presented the yelping, squirming puppy to Kay to be hugged. Kay laughed with joy, cupped the collie's face in her hands, and laid her cheek to the top of its head. Mac barked and licked her face.

"Mac likes you," said Joey.

Kay smiled at Joey. "I'm glad. I like Mac. I like you, Joey."

"You do?" He tilted his head to the side, the red cowlick sticking straight up at his crown.

"Yes. I like you very much."

"I like you too," Joey said, giggled with sudden embarrassment, turned, and ran away with Mac chasing after him.

Joey's trust grew daily. He did like Captain Kay. He liked it when she ran and played games him and Mac. He liked it when she ruffled his hair affectionately. He liked it when she hugged him warmly.

He absolutely loved it when she snatched him from the ground, pushed up his white uniform shirt, and blew on his belly until he squealed with hysterical laughter and begged her to stop. Only to plead with her to do it again.

Quickly they became fast friends. One springlike day at the end of February the two were on their knees in the sunny backyard at Battery Place, planting a new flower bed. Joey had his small spade, digging in the soft earth. Kay had the flower seeds, ready to be dropped into the newly made holes. A pail of water sat nearby.

Kay and Joey talked as they worked, mainly about the other children at Battery Place. Joey proudly recited the names of his best friends. He told Kay about the ones who sometimes had company. And of the ones who didn't. He said his friend, Perry, had been visited just that week by a cousin. And that his other friend, Bert, had an Uncle Henry. Bert's Uncle Henry had come to visit and he had brought Bert candy and presents.

Joey fell silent for a moment, his attention directed fully to his work. Tongue caught between his small white baby teeth in concentration, he grunted and groaned as he turned over a stubborn spadeful of dirt. Kay dropped in a few petunia seeds. Joey immediately began shoving the dirt back in place. Then he carefully tamped it down as he'd been shown.

"There," he said proudly. He shoved Mac away when the collie tried to dig up the newly planted seeds. Pulling his mean face, Joey threatened his puppy, "You want me to run off and leave you!"

Kay stiffened at Joey's choice of words. Had those cruel words been spoken to him? Had that threat been made to him?

Mac whimpered and laid his head on Joey's knee. Joey smiled and petted him soothingly. His smile abruptly vanished.

He looked up at Kay with eyes suddenly gone cold and said, "My mother gave me away."

Chapter 30

 An aged flower girl pushed her cart slowly along Pacific Street on an unusually warm sunny morning in early March. The woman was small and pudgy and wore baggy black pants and a drab green silk jacket, faded and frayed at cuffs and collar.

Her shoulders were stooped and rounded. Her watery dark eyes blinked owlishly at passersby. Her cheeks sagged against the corners of her mouth, forming sad droopy creases.

Abruptly the old flower girl's drooping mouth lifted into a smile. She stopped pushing the flower-laden cart. She stood on the wooden sidewalk as a tall, lean man, having emerged from a white stucco building, approached.

Kou Jen watched Nick McCabe stride purposefully toward her. Dressed casually in a pale-blue chambray shirt and faded denim trousers, there was something unmistakably rugged in his walk and in his bearing.

And this morning—Kou Jen quickly noted—there was an added spring to his lithe step. Furthermore, a million-dollar grin illuminated his dark, friendly face.

Kou Jen immediately suspected that this dark young man who was well known along the Barbary Coast for his charm, recklessness, and hot temper was up to something. For one thing, he was wide awake and out at an unusually early hour. For another, there was a wicked pleased-with-himself twinkle in his silver-gray eyes.

The smiling Nick stepped up to Kou Jen's flower cart. He bowed grandly to her, the movement sending a shock of unruly raven hair tumbling forward over his forehead.

"The top of the morning to you, Kou Jen, my only love," Nick said, reaching out to touch her withered cheek. "How are you on this splendid March morning?"

Kou Jen studied him. His smoothly shaven face was filled with the light of good health and friendliness. It was a handsome face whose charm could doubtless warm and win any heart. It had easily warmed and won hers.

Beaming with pleasure, she squinted up at the tall, handsome man and said, "I am fine, Nichoras McCabe." She chuckled and added, "Not quite as fine as you, though. What going on?"

Nick grinned and winked at the old flower girl. "Would you say that this is a good day for a picnic?" Carefully he chose a single blossom from the profusion of flowers heaped high on the wooden cart. He lifted the flower up to his nose and inhaled deeply of its sweet fragrance.

"Picnic? You go on picnic?" Kou Jen's eyes narrowed skeptically. "Did not suppose rich Nob Hill lady friend enjoy picnics."

Nick threw back his dark head and laughed. Then he said, "You're probably right." He broke the stem from the pale-pink rose and tucked the fragile blossom through a breast pocket buttonhole. "But it's not Miss Packard I'm taking on a picnic."

Kou Jen pinned him with knowing dark eyes. She bobbed her double chin up and down and stated simply, "You take Salvation Army captain."

Nick's easy grin confirmed it. "Think the little soul saver can refrain from exhorting pagans to repent long enough to enjoy a simple picnic?" Nick gestured to the flower-filled cart. "I'll take them all, darlin'. Ling Tan will be along to collect them."

He drew in his breath, making the low-riding waistband of his denim trousers fall away from his flat belly. He reached down inside a pocket of the snug denims, withdrew a shiny twenty-dollar gold piece, and placed it in Kou Jen's hand.

Kou Jen's eyes twinkled like Nick's. She said, "Better not do this thing, Nichoras McCabe. Not wise to be alone with Captain Kay. Most dangerous, I think."

"Now, now, Kou Jen. A picnic lunch shared at a public beach in the middle of the day. Nothing more to it. I'll be the perfect gentleman. The good captain is no danger."

The wise old Chinese woman's smile broadened. "You misunderstand, Nichoras McCabe. *You* the one in danger."

Nick laughed good-naturedly, then said, "Not on your life. Let the well-intentioned, red-haired Salvationist preach all she likes, I'll never surrender my soul."

"No, but what about your heart?"

Nick spread a palm on the left side of his chest. "This heart stays right where it is," he said with brash masculine confidence, and bid Kou Jen a smiling farewell.

"Maybe," said Kou Jen. She quietly chuckled at the arrogance of youth. "Maybe not. Maybe when least expect it, lose heart."

But the arrogant young man didn't hear her. Nick was already gone.

In her small office at the waterfront mission, Captain Kay Montgomery was a little edgy. The brilliant March sunshine streaming in the broken-paned window did little to calm her jitters. She was childishly expectant; at the same time filled with dread. And she was somewhat disappointed in herself.

After repeatedly informing the brash, cocky Nick McCabe that she would *never* agree to a picnic, she was this very minute nervously awaiting his arrival at the mission. He was taking her on a picnic.

Kay shook her head, but quickly assured herself that it would be just this one time. All right, so she'd given in. She'd finally agreed to a picnic at the beach with him. So what? It meant nothing. She was simply sick and tired of him asking. Today would be the first and last time she went anywhere with McCabe, and if he thought differently he was sadly mistaken!

Kay suddenly looked up and smiled. Nick McCabe had entered the auditorium and was presently speaking with Curly. The sound of Nick's deep, pleasing voice made her pulse quicken.

She hurriedly opened the middle drawer of her three-legged desk, withdrew a smoky, cracked mirror, and held it up to examine herself. She made a face. The sprinkling of freckles across the bridge of her nose seemed more pronounced today than usual. She sighed with despair, then shoved the mirror back into the desk drawer and rose, scolding herself for her sinful vanity.

She was crossing to the coat rack when Nick appeared in the doorway. A mischievous light danced in his silver-gray eyes.

"Your carriage awaiteth without, my lady," he announced grandly. Then he smiled warmly at Kay and said in a low, soft voice, "Hello."

"Hello, yourself," Kay replied, smiling back at him.

She was struck by how youthful, how boyish Nick McCabe looked standing there leaning lazily against the door frame. His blue-black hair was appealingly tousled and his denim trousers were neatly pressed and creased. A pale-pink rose adorned his breast pocket. He looked scrubbed and healthy and friendly.

And totally harmless.

She'd been a fool to have ever been frightened of being alone with him. Not to mention vain. A man who looked like Nick McCabe couldn't possibly want anything other than friendship from a devout woman who looked like her. What else did she have he'd want? What else could she possibly offer him? Nothing. Not a thing. All the same, she'd see to it that this outing was a one-time-only occurrence.

"Ready, Captain?" Nick inquired politely, breaking into her thoughts.

"Yes, I am." Kay advanced to the coat rack. "Just let me get my bonnet and jacket . . ."

Nick swiftly pushed away from the door jamb. In a fraction of a second he was beside Kay. His hand encircled her wrist as she reached for her black straw hat.

"Not today," he said, his voice unusually gentle. "This is to be your afternoon free of duty. From now until I bring you back, you're not Captain Kay Montgomery of the Salvation Army San Francisco Corps #1."

Kay exerted only minor resistance against his firm grip. "No? Just who am I then, McCabe?"

Nick waited a heartbeat before speaking. "A carefree young woman enjoying a picnic at Seal Beach with a friend." His long thumb caressed the inside of Kay's wrist before releasing her.

"But the bright sunlight . . . I'll freckle."

Nick could hardly hide his amusement. Already she was acting like a woman instead of an Salvation Army captain and they weren't even out the door. He lifted her bonnet from the coat tree and set it squarely atop her head.

"All right. Wear the bonnet to keep the sun off your face. But leave the jacket behind. You won't need it. It's nice and warm."

Satisfied, Kay nodded. Then flushed when Nick leaned close and whispered in her ear, "Just for the record, Captain, I think your girlish freckles are cute."

Before she could speak, Nick took her arm and guided her into the auditorium. There they stopped and talked briefly with Rose, Curly, and Big Alfred. While Rose and Curly were their talkative, sunny-dispositioned selves, Kay noticed that the big Englishman seemed curiously reserved. He wore a smile, but it didn't quite reach his expressive hazel eyes. Something was troubling him.

Nick gave Kay no time to wonder about it. Promising Curly he'd have her back before sundown, Nick hurried Kay out of doors and into the brilliant March sunshine.

Parked at the wooden wharf was a fancy for-hire rig he'd leased from the Minna Street livery stable of J. Thompkinson especially for the occasion.

Nick watched Kay's face closely. He caught her childlike expression of pure delight when he ushered her straight to the grand carriage. Her large blue eyes aglow, Kay eagerly started to climb up inside.

Nick's touch on her arm stopped her. He turned her to face him and spanned her narrow waist with his hands.

"I'm not totally devoid of manners," he said, his voice low, the words spoken slowly. "I always assist ladies into carriages."

"Oh . . . well, yes . . . of course." Kay raised her hands to his wide shoulders, ready to be lifted up into the fancy rig.

But Nick didn't immediately sweep her off the ground. He came very close, however, to sweeping her off her feet. He stood holding her waist, looking into her eyes longer than necessary. Kay felt a premonitory twinge of alarm. He was too close. He was too threatening. Too ruggedly masculine.

Gone was the appealingly boyish-looking fellow who'd stepped into her office door moments ago. It was the darkly handsome saloon owner who was looking into her eyes with far too much fire and familiarity. It was his firm fingers that held possessively to her waist. Kay had the frightful sensation that any second he might press her against him and hold her frighteningly close in the arch of his tall, lean frame.

That concern had no more than fluttered through her mind when Nick easily swung her off her feet and up onto the supple leather carriage seat. When he stepped back and circled the pair of matched bays harnessed to the rig, Kay took the opportunity to get her breath back.

A large cloth-covered hamper rested squarely in the middle of the plush leather seat beside her. Kay was relieved. The picnic basket couldn't have been more strategically placed had she set it there herself. Its presence between them would keep Nick McCabe from any attempts at sitting too close on their journey. Thank goodness.

Nick swung up into the seat, unwrapped the long leather reins from around the brake, turned his dark head, and smiled at Kay.

"Anytime you've had enough of me or our picnic, just say the word and I'll bring you straight back here to the mission."

"Why, thank you, McCabe." Kay felt herself relax. "I really shouldn't stay too long. A couple of hours perhaps."

"Fair enough," said Nick. He flicked the long loose reins atop the horses' backs and guided the matched bays out onto the busy waterfront avenue.

Kay felt herself unwinding totally as they rode along the shoreline. She listened with interest as Nick pointed out landmarks on the hills high above them. She looked toward Telegraph Hill with its formidable wooden stairway to the summit. Then at the old adobe walled Mission Dolores. The Tivoli Opera House on Eddy. The San Francisco Mint.

They were soon near the end of the Embarcadero with its many piers and wharfs and cawing gulls swooping low. Nick pointed across the bay's choppy waters to Alcatraz Island, the rocky fortress shining brilliantly in the sun.

Nick told Kay of his favorite places in the Bay City. And Kay couldn't keep from laughing at the expression on his face when she admitted she'd seen almost nothing of San Francisco other than the Barbary Coast. Truth to tell, she hadn't even heard of many of the spots he was so familiar with.

He was an enthusiastic guide and Kay was an eager sightseer. The time flew and soon they were high on the costal cliffs above the Bay. They were driving past the guard gates of the Presidio with their big guns on either side when Nick said casually, "Next time we'll picnic at the Golden Gate Park. There are several lakes there and—"

"McCabe," Kay interrupted, "there isn't going to be a next time. I'm far too busy to waste my time this way."

"—and lots of gardens and walkways," Nick continued as if she hadn't spoken. "And just wait until you see the Victoria Regina. It's a giant lily pond they brought up from the tropics. Everyone in the city goes to the pond to marvel at the huge-petaled blossoms."

Kay opened her mouth, closed it. Why argue? She was quite certain that she wouldn't be going to Golden Gate Park with its giant lily pond—or anywhere else—with Nick McCabe. But it was a beautiful day, and she saw no point in spoiling this outing.

Kay smiled and said nothing. And listened as Nick told her of places only he could show her. Places he'd favored since childhood. Secret places he'd never shown anyone else.

It would never happen, of course, but Kay thought idly what fun it would be to see the entire windswept city with this knowledgeable native who unabashedly loved it.

Kay sighed and inhaled deeply of the ocean's scent. She looked at the rugged coastline below and asked, "McCabe, do we have far to go?"

Nick's dark head swung around. His low-lidded gaze fixed on her, he said in deep, resonant voice, "Depends on where we're going."

Kay needlessly cleared her throat and asked, "What . . . what do you mean?"

His dark face breaking into a wide boyish grin, Nick said, "Nothing, really." He reached over and gave the streamer of her bonnet a playful tug. "I was just flirting with you."

Chapter 31

Everything was perfect.

It was an undeniably enjoyable picnic.

Not a trace of the customary coastal fog rolled in off the ocean to obstruct the breathtaking views. A high, strong sun shone steadily down throughout the warm afternoon, bathing the peninsula with a brilliant light. The air was cool, crisp, and crystal clear. A gentle easterly breeze, smelling pleasantly of the sea, kissed faces, billowed clothing, and ruffled hair.

At two P.M. Nick and Kay reached their destination on the rugged northwestern coastal cliffs above the ocean. Nick whisked Kay out of the carriage. A smiling young groom appeared to tend the horses and carriage. Nick gave the lad money, grabbed up a blanket and the heavy picnic hamper, and inclined his head toward the bluff's edge.

"Shall we?" he said to Kay.

"After you," she replied, not at all certain how they were supposed to reach the beach below.

"Then let's go. Time's awasting," said Nick.

Kay anxiously followed him along a narrow path down the steep cliffs. Their descent was swift and both were out of breath when they reached the stretch of soft sugary sand below. When Nick's heartbeat slowed, he immediately went in search of just the right place for their picnic.

Awestruck by the wild beauty of her surroundings, Kay was drawn to the ocean's edge. Holding the broad brim of her bonnet, she stared wide-eyed at the whitecapped breakers crashing noisily off shore. It was the first time in all the months she'd been in San Francisco that Kay had really seen the open Pacific Ocean. She was enchanted. Totally mesmerized by the beauty, majesty, and power of the vast body of water stretching before her as far as the eye could see.

Nick chose a protected spot just yards above the crashing waves at shoreline. Partially guarded by a semicircle of rock spires, the cozy sunlit stretch of sand would remain high and dry even as the evening tide came in . . . just in case they lingered longer than expected.

He dropped the heavy hamper on the sand, spread out the large beige blanket, and called to Kay. At first she didn't answer. Nick started to call again. He didn't do it. She had heard. He knew she had. She was too fascinated by the ocean to turn away.

Nick watched her and was touched.

Kay stood at the water's edge, hand clutching the brim of her bonnet. The strong ocean breeze pressed her Army blue skirts against her slender body and billowed out the back of her white, long-sleeved blouse. With each rhythmic crash of the surf on the sand, she squealed with joy and jumped back. Only to venture forward again as the tide rolled back out.

Nick crossed his long arms over his chest and cocked his head to the side. He tried to envision the slender red-haired woman without her bonnet. He could almost picture her bare-headed, her hair loosened from its customary bun, and tossing around her laughing face.

He wanted to see her without the bonnet. He *would* see her without it before the afternoon ended. If other women could be persuaded to remove their clothes the first time they were alone with him, surely the sassy Army captain could be persuaded to remove her bonnet.

"Kay," he called to her again. "I'm getting lonely up here by myself."

Kay turned, waved to him, and nodded. She reluctantly tore herself away from the restless, churning ocean swirling near her feet. She smiled when she joined Nick and dropped to her knees on the spread blanket.

"McCabe," she said breathlessly, her upturned face aglow with excitement, "it's absolutely beautiful here!" She swept her hand around in a wide arc.

"So it is," he said. "That's why I chose it. Sit."

Kay sat flat down on the blanket, curling her feet to one side. Nick dropped down beside her, stretched his long legs out before him, crossed his ankles, and leaned back on stiffened arms. The pair sat in the warm afternoon sunshine and watched the seals and noisy sea lions frolic on the smooth slippery rocks jutting up just off shore.

Behind them sheer stony walls towered toward the sky. The flat surface above was dotted with gnarled cypresses, their trunks permanently bent by the strong coastal winds. Around a lofty bend of the soaring bluff, the Cliff House, a six-story gingerbread-trimmed Victorian mansion, perched precariously high above the shore. The seaside tavern was filled with jovial patrons. Laughter from inside the big roadhouse floated out the open doors and echoed down craggy rocks to the beach.

After several minutes of companionable silence, Nick, staring out at the ocean, asked, "Hungry yet?"

"Starved" was Kay's honest reply.

They turned, looked at each other, and laughed. And rose to their knees and began eagerly unpacking the lunch Ling Tan had prepared for them. Nick tossed a folded red-and-white checkered cloth to Kay. She caught it and went about spreading it out atop the blanket. She placed the matching napkins on either side, directly across from each other.

Then she sat back on her heels and watched, puzzled, as Nick withdrew from the basket and unwrapped a sparkling crystal bud vase. He placed the vase at the center of the checkered cloth, plucked the pale-pink rose from his shirt pocket, and stuck it in the vase. His eyes lifted to meet Kay's, one dark brow raised quizzically.

"Yes, oh yes," she said, nodding and clapping her hands.

It was a wonderful meal. A long, leisurely lunch that drew ooohs and aaahs of approval from Kay.

There was fried chicken and green salad and crusty baked bread served on fine china plates and chilled limeade in crystal goblets. Nick watched, smiling, as Kay eagerly sampled the Roquefort, Camembert, and blue cheeses with various sizes and shapes of hard biscuits and saltine crackers. She praised the tender bite-size squares of smoked ham and the succulent roast beef sliced wafer thin. She nibbled eagerly on nuts and grapes and pears. And she absolutely relished the rich pound cake and fresh strawberries and thick cream. So much that she didn't hesitate to accept a large, second serving.

Uncomfortably full at last, Kay handed Nick her empty plate, sighed deeply, and said, "Please tell Ling Tan how much I enjoyed the meal."

"Will do," said Nick.

He made quick work of clearing the food and dishes from the checkered cloth, repacking everything into the hamper. Everything, that is, but the crystal vase containing the lone pink rose. That he left in place between them.

Again Kay sighed with contentment and said, "I suppose we better be getting back, McCabe."

"Sure. Anything you say."

Neither moved.

"Mmmmmm," Kay murmured lazily. "Yes, I suppose we should go now."

"If that's what you want, Kay." Nick looked her.

Kay thrilled to the sound of her name on his lips. A tingle skipped up her spine. She knew they *should* go. And right now. It was far too beautiful here. Too romantic. Too secluded.

"No," Kay said honestly, her eyes focused on the birds that wheeled gracefully about the cliffs. "No, not really. It's so lovely and peaceful here." She tipped her head back and squinted up at the cloudless sky, which glowed a rich vivid blue. She lowered her eyes, glanced at Nick, and added, "I suppose we could stay for a while yet."

"I suppose," he agreed in low, resonant tones.

Nick smiled at Kay, relaxed and confident, one arm now propped loosely on a raised knee. Realizing that this straitlaced young lady beside him would have to be treated different from any of the other women in his life, Nick was cautiously charming. He took care not to frighten or upset her in any way. At the same time he reminded himself that time was short. He now had less than a full month to seduce her. His aim for today was to put her fully at her ease.

He did just that.

They talked easily, comfortably, like two old friends. Kay wanted to hear more about the Bay City, and Nick was forthcoming.

"I've had a love affair with this city my entire life," he said, lids dropping low over silver-gray eyes.

"San Francisco is your home. You were born here?"

"Indeed," he said, but didn't elaborate. "And you? Where were you born, Kay?"

Again that foolish flood of joy at the sound of her name coming from him. Blood surged through her veins. "St. Louis, Missouri," she said.

"Tell me about yourself," Nick gently urged. "Start ten years ago."

"Ten years ago I was in school."

"Start five years ago."

She did. At Nick's encouragement, Kay talked of her work with the Army in St. Louis and Atlanta and how thrilled she'd been when she and Curly had been chosen to establish the San Francisco Corps #1. Her brow furrowed and she confided that she was terribly worried. She told Nick all about the looming May deadline. She didn't notice Nick's discomfort as she elaborated on the subject, fully explaining the dilemma.

Nor did she notice Nick's relief when finally she exhausted the subject. On a far happier note, she went backward in time, talking about her carefree childhood. She told Nick that the Montgomery family had never had much money, but there was always plenty of love and laughter in their home. She spoke with pride and affection of the two remarkable people who were her parents. The kindest, most loving two people on earth. From them she had learned the values and rules that governed her daily life.

Kay fell silent at last. Her gaze fixed on the restless ocean, she looked out past the surf line and into the swells. She smiled and, continuing to stare at the water, said, "My mother loved our father so, she beat us kids to the door when he came home."

"That's the way it should be." Nick's voice was low, soft.

Kay turned her head suddenly. And caught a fleeting glimpse of a strangely wistful expression on his dark, handsome face. It was gone the second he felt her eyes on him. He turned and smiled at her.

"Now it's your turn. Tell me about you," she said, thinking how appealing he was with the sun on his tanned face and the blue chambray shirt stretching across his wide shoulders and the wind tossing his dark hair about his head. She envisioned him at Joey's age. "You must have been a handsome little boy."

He favored her with a wide grin. "Do you doubt it?"

Kay laughed and shook her head. "Your mother spoiled you something awful."

"Naturally." Abruptly Nick scooped up the bud vase and rose and moved it to the blanket's edge. Kay gave him a puzzled look. He added, "Wouldn't you?"

Then before she could answer and with a swiftness that caught Kay totally off guard, Nick scooted around, stretched out on his back, and plopped his head squarely in Kay's lap. He hooked a bent arm around her back, gave her a gentle little squeeze, squinted up at her, and said again, "Wouldn't you?"

"Wouldn't I what?" Kay was so shocked and disconcerted at finding his head in her lap she'd forgotten what they were talking about.

Nick grinned and trailed a long index finger down the center of her back, making Kay involuntarily shiver and sit up straighter. "Spoil me? I asked, wouldn't you have spoiled me when I was an adorable little boy?"

"Get up, McCabe," Kay said, but with little conviction.

"Spoil me a little, Kay." He took her hand and placed it in atop dark wavy hair. "Rub my head. That's what I liked best when I was a kid."

Kay rolled her eyes to the heavens, but laughed softly. She accused him of *still* being spoiled. But she tentatively twined her fingers through the silky raven locks falling so appealingly over his tan forehead. She began to stroke Nick's head with a touch so tender and soothing he moaned aloud with pleasure.

As she massaged his temples, Kay attempted to learn more about Nick. She hoped to hear about his family, about his childhood. He skillfully sidestepped her questions, giving only teasing, noncommittal answers, and turned the conversation to other topics.

Which only made her more curious than ever. She got the strong impression that Nick didn't wish to talk about his parents or his youth. She wondered why. She'd taken it for granted that Nick had came from a good home despite the fact he was a saloon owner.

He had all the appearance of a life of privilege. There was a proud, noble bearing about him, and his manners were polished. He was intelligent, knowledgeable, always impeccably groomed.

How, she wondered, did his parents feel about the less-than-so-cially-acceptable occupation their son had chosen? Were they heart-sick over his blatant disregard for society's conventions? Had his choice of professions driven his family into ostracizing him? Or did they overlook his sinful existence? Surely his mother was disappointed as well as constantly worried because her handsome son had chosen a wild, dangerous life on the Barbary Coast.

"McCabe," Kay said casually, her slender fingers threading through the dark healthy locks, "your mother must worry herself sick about you."

"I'm a big boy, Kay" was Nick's cheerful, evasive reply. "And you're a big girl. How old are you?"

Kay looked down into those flashing silver-gray eyes. She said with a coy smile, "Can you keep a secret?"

"Sure can."

"Well, so can I."

Nick chuckled. He liked her answer. It was a good sign. She was acting like a woman. It was about time she looked like one. He non-chalantly reached up and tugged at a streamer of her bonnet. The bow beneath Kay's chin came undone.

"What are you doing?" Kay demanded, slapping at his hand.

"Taking your bonnet off," he said as he curled a finger over the loosened knot and untied the streamers. "Nothing sinister," he said softly, looking into her eyes.

"Now, McCabe I told you . . . I'll freckle."

As if she hadn't spoken, Nick plucked the bonnet off Kay's head and dropped it to the sand. Swiftly he drew the pins from the neat bun at her nape. A cloud of flaming red hair spilled down around her shoulders.

"There," he said, "now you look like a woman."

"McCabe! Give me back those hairpins!"

"A beautiful woman," he added, and watched as a sudden flush of color came into her pale cheeks.

He realized—almost with surprise—that what he said was true. Captain Kay was quite beautiful, although she did her best to hide it. Gentle feminine curves were always concealed beneath the Army blue uniform jacket and skirt. And the glorious hair was forever done up in a severe bun beneath her bonnet.

She was certainly beautiful as she was right now, with the wind pressing the soft cotton of her white blouse against her rounded breasts and tossing the ends of her glorious red hair around her face. Her neck looked almost too delicate to support her head, and the pale exposed throat was true perfection. Her lovely eyes were as blue as the skies overhead and her unrouged lips looked incredibly tempting.

"McCabe, did you hear me?" Kay's voice raised. "I said give me my hairpins."

"Sure," Nick said, but grinned and shoved the hairpins deep into the pocket of his snug denim pants. He closed his eyes then and said, "Later. I need a short nap."

"Oh, no you don't!" Kay gave his hair a forceful yank and laughed when he groaned and grabbed her hand. But she stiffened when he drew her hand to his mouth and pressed his warm lips to her open palm.

Nick's eyes remained closed as he murmured against her hand, "Don't be cruel, Kay." He kissed her palm one last time and drew her hand down to rest on his chest, beneath both of his own.

Nick was asleep at once. And much as she wanted to be angry with him, Kay couldn't quite manage it. She cradled his dark head tenderly and gently stroked his raven hair, studying the handsome features in repose. She sighed with contentment.

Relaxed, she daydreamed.

Half an hour passed and Kay was still looking intently at his face when Nick's eyes came sleepily open. He grinned boyishly at her, yawned, and rolled up into a sitting position.

"You look a little sleepy yourself," he said.

"Me?" she said, shaking her head. "Not really."

But she was. So she didn't put up much of a fuss when Nick urged her to rest for a few moments. She refused to lay her head on the denim-clad thighs he patted invitingly, but she lay down beside him. Lulled by the distant throb of the ocean, Kay fell into a comfortable doze.

Awakening just before sunset, she stretched lazily, and opened her eyes to see Nick's rugged profile framed against the pastel pink of the sky. He was, she thought idly, the most beautiful man she'd ever seen.

As if he'd felt Kay's eyes on him, Nick's head turned and he looked down at her with warm silver eyes.

Nick didn't speak. Neither did Kay.

Nick held out his hand. Kay took it.

Nick gently pulled Kay up into a sitting position. They looked at each other.

Nick rose to kneel on one knee. He urged Kay up to kneel facing him. They stared unblinkingly at each other.

Nick slowly pushed up to his feet. He looked down at the lovely red-haired woman kneeling before him. He drew Kay to her feet. His hands dropped away.

They stood there facing each other in the dying sun as the tide came in. Breakers crashed loudly down on the shore. Gentle sea breezes became chill night winds pressing their clothes to their bodies and whipping their hair around their heads.

"Can I kiss you, Captain?" Nick said, his voice lifting above the ocean's roar. "Is that against the rules?"

Chapter 32

Dense fog and drizzling rain covered the coast.

Captain Kay Montgomery shivered as she walked the sodden wooden sidewalks toward Battery Place. The umbrella she carried had seen better days. Small rips and tears in the worn black fabric allowed intermittent drops of rain to pepper her face and shoulders.

It was also cold—unseasonably cold for the time of year. Kay wore no warm coat over her Army blue jacket, and she was chilled to the bone. If she hadn't been dying to see Joey, she would have skipped her daily visit to Battery Place on this dark, miserable March afternoon.

Kay caught her bottom lip between chattering teeth. She shook her bonneted head worriedly. Admitting the truth—even to herself—was upsetting. And the truth was that while she loved all the sweet children of Battery Place, it was the red-headed, heart-tugging Joey for whom she gladly braved the rain and the cold.

Kay scolded herself. And not for the first time. She should be ashamed of herself. For her to care more for one needful child than another was unprofessional, selfish, and futile. She was guilty of having a favorite and that was not very admirable. Or Christian.

But even as she lectured herself, Captain Kay Montgomery quickened her pace. Eagerly she hurried toward the big white Battery Place mansion. And in her heart of hearts she knew it was to see the tiny red-haired Joey.

Envisioning the wide grin on Joey's face, Kay smiled. But her vision of Joey didn't stay with her long. His sweet little boy's face was nudged aside by the clearer, stronger vision of a grown man's face.

A darkly handsome face slowly descending to hers.

Kay made a misstep and her rain-wet cheeks flushed with sudden warmth as again—for at least the hundredth time—she relived the magical moment at sundown on Seal Beach when Nick McCabe kissed her.

Nick asked if he could kiss her. Before she could reply, his lips lowered to hers. Her gaze nervously following their slow, sure descent, she was vaguely aware of the sun setting behind Nick, a fiery ball sinking into the Pacific Ocean.

Then his mouth was on hers and her eyes slid closed in awed wonder. His lips were incredibly smooth and warm and tender. His kiss was amazingly gentle. Nothing at all as she had imagined it might be. There was nothing frightening about the softly seeking kiss or about the tall lean man kissing her.

Sighing, loving the way Nick so effortlessly molded her lips to his, she decided that a man who could kiss her this way couldn't be all bad. Underneath that brash charm was surely a caring, sensitive individual.

The recollection of that one sweet kiss sent warmth radiating through her despite the cold March rain. A foolish little smile on her face, Kay hurried on toward Battery Place.

Kay was still a block away when she squinted through the falling rain at a black-covered carriage coming up Battery Street toward her. She blinked away the droplets of water clinging to her eyelashes and looked squarely at the approaching carriage.

She recognized the gleaming black carriage. Atop the box the aging, solemn-faced driver was outfitted for the weather. A caped black oilskin slicker, worn over his tailored black livery, repelled the falling rain. The same oilskin covered the black visored cap on his graying head. On his hands were black kid gloves.

The old driver looked neither to the left or the right, but straight ahead. Ably he handled the spirited pair of blooded blacks pulling the shiny black carriage. The high-stepping creatures were tastefully embellished with expensive trappings of smooth black leather trimmed in touches of gleaming gold.

Watching from beneath her now thoroughly soaked umbrella, Captain Kay Montgomery knew that it could be only one special carriage. One special driver. One special passenger.

Her benefactress from her jailhouse days.

The Lady in Black.

Kay stopped walking. She stood there transfixed and stared openly as the funeral black carriage neared her. When the handsome brougham drew up even, Kay squinted anxiously and managed to get a glimpse of its mysterious occupant.

The face of the Lady in Black was not visible. The veil of her black hat touched her chin, concealing all but the outline of her features. A billowing cape of coal-black mink lay casually draped around her shoulders. Her high-throated dress was of rich midnight-black wool. There was not one touch of color on her person. Or in her carriage.

The Lady in Black sat with her back regally straight, not quite touching the black leather tufted seat. She too looked straight ahead, neither to the left or the right. Or so Kay thought.

Kay instinctively raised her hand and waved. To her surprise, a black gloved hand lifted, pushed back the black side curtains, and returned Kay's greeting.

Kay waved madly then, a wide smile coming to her face. She continued to wave until the carriage and the lady had passed.

Who was the Lady in Black?

What was her name?

Kay's curiosity over the mysterious lady was piqued anew. Who was she? And where was she bound on Battery Street on this cold, rainy March afternoon?

Kay shook her head and dashed toward the gates of Battery Place. She'd search out Madge before visiting with the children. See what Madge knew about the Lady in Black.

Kay let herself in. In the wide front corridor she collapsed her drenched umbrella. She was dusting the raindrops off her damp shoulders when a small head of fiery red popped around a corner and into sight.

A shriek, a laugh, and a bark followed.

And Captain Kay immediately forgot about everything and everyone except the irresistible little boy and his faithful puppy who were both running to meet her.

"No. It simply will not do."

"You're being unkind and there's no call for it."

Adele Packard released her hold on the gold-threaded brocade curtain. It fell back into place over the tall, rain-spattered window. She turned and crossed to her brother, who sat on one of the matching white sofas before the blazing fireplace.

"Unkind?" Adele repeated, choosing the sofa opposite Patrick. She sat down, swirled the long skirts of her peach velvet dressing gown over her crossed legs, and smiled at her frowning brother. "Darling Pat, how can you say that about me? I'm merely looking out for you . . . just as I've always done."

Carefully balancing a cup of black coffee on his knee, Patrick replied, "All I'm asking is that you meet Captain Kay. Give her a half a chance. You have the mistaken notion that Kay is a wild-eyed zealot who goes about shouting fire and brimstone warnings at everyone."

"And I'm wrong?" Adele said, incredulous. Her perfectly arched eyebrows lifted and she laughed gaily. Then she said, "A woman who marches in the streets ringing a bell? A female who wears drab uniforms and preaches to anyone unfortunate enough to happen hear her? Come now, Pat."

Patrick leaned up, placed the fragile blue enameled coffee cup and saucer on a marble-topped table. "You make her sound a fool and she's not. She's a strong, intelligent, unselfish woman, and all I am asking is that you allow me to bring her here this evening for dinner. Nothing more."

"Darling, darling brother. I'm having Nick here for an early dinner this evening."

"I know that. Couldn't the four of us dine together? Nick knows Kay and—"

"—and he can't stand the sight of her."

"You're mistaken again, Adele. As I understand it, they clashed when Kay first arrived on the coast, but since then they've made peace."

"Really?" she said, suddenly frowning.

It occurred to Adele that Nick hadn't mentioned the Army captain lately. Why? she wondered. He used to complain constantly about the meddlesome little do-gooder.

"I believe Nick has come to admire Kay, just as I have," said Pat.

"Mmmm. Pat, is Captain Kay at all attractive?"

"She's beautiful."

"You must be joking." Adele sat up straighter. "Surely a beautiful woman wouldn't be—"

"Good and kind and unselfish as well? Kay is. She's beautiful inside as well as out."

"How very sweet." Adele was snide. She smoothed her white-blond hair. "I may not be so sweet, but I'm very beautiful and I'm very smart. I can see that my dear baby brother is in danger of making a fool of himself over this scheming Salvationist." She smiled, rose, and went to sit beside him. Taking his hand in both of hers, she said, "Pat, you know that this . . . this . . . thing with Captain Kay cannot go on."

"Why not?" Patrick looked his sister straight in the eye.

"Because, darling, you're a Packard. The last of the male line. It's a waste of time for you to keep seeing the Army captain. You must choose a young woman suitable for your station in life. Someone who'll enhance our position socially and financially." She squeezed his hand affectionately. "A girl you can marry. One who'll fit in with our friends. I want some little nieces and nephews running around this house one of these days."

Patrick withdrew his hand. "Why not some children of your own, Adele? When are you going to marry again? Settle down and raise a family?"

Adele threw back her blond head and laughed. "If there's anything I don't wish to be, it's a mother." She wrinkled her patrician nose with distaste. "Nor," she added, "do I ever again want to be any man's wife. The truth is I enjoy Nick McCabe because I can't picture him as a husband, and certainly not as a father. Nick with children? Why, it's laughable." She did laugh, and then she said, "I'm completely satisfied with my life just as it is. Nick is the most exciting—"

She stopped speaking and looked up as the door opened and her uniformed butler stepped inside.

"Yes, Jamison? What is it?"

"Excuse me, Miss Packard. A message for you."

He came forward carrying a small silver tray in his white-gloved hand. A gray parchment envelope lay atop it. Rising from the sofa, Adele snatched the message from the tray and gestured for the servant to withdraw. She tore open the gray envelope, read the brief message inside, and reread it.

"That son of a bitch!" she hissed loudly.

"Who?"

"Nick McCabe, that's who! He's canceled this evening's dinner engagement!" She viciously tore up and envelope and allowed the pieces to flutter to the plush carpet. Turning, she said, "Pat, you're taking me out to dinner tonight!"

"But I'm going to evening services down at the—"

"No, you're not! You're my escort tonight. We'll go to the Palace. We're sure to run into some of our crowd there." She stormed across the room, jerked up a cut-crystal decanter, and poured herself a shot of straight gin. She drank it down, made a face, and cried, "Damn this miserable rain!"

"But, Father, I would be most careful. You would not have to worry."

Ling Tan shook his head so violently the long pigtail whipped back and forth across his shoulder blades. "Have told stubborn daughter many times cannot go out alone!"

"But it's only to the library, father," Ming Ho, hands on shapely hips, explained. "There are a couple of anatomy books I must study before I can complete my project for science class."

Ling Tan was as stubborn as his beautiful young daughter. "Cannot help that. Shadow Clan always a threat. Must wait till father free to go with you to library. This my evening to play *pai jow.* Have not missed game in six years. Will not miss tonight." He folded his arms over his chest.

"Of course, Honorable Father," Ming Ho said, knowing that the crossing of her father's arms meant the conversation was ended.

Sighing loudly, she went to window, pushed back the curtain, and looked out. Fog hung like thick gray spiderwebs and rain fell in a slow, steady drizzle. People hurried up and down the street, their heads ducked against the rain, coat collars turned up.

Nick stepped off the wooden sidewalk below. Watching him, Ming Ho said over her shoulder, "Father, have you any idea where Mr. Nick's going this afternoon?"

"Boss go to Athletic Club to meet Big Alfred. Why?"

Ming Ho whirled away from the window. "Then he'll be back by six. Do you suppose, Father, he could take me to the library?"

"No, cannot do! Boss have early dinner engagement with Miss Packard."

Ming Ho sighed with exasperation.

Big Alfred's right glove connected solidly with Nick's chin. Nick groaned. Nick threw a body punch into Big Alfred's midsection. The Englishman didn't make a sound.

Big Alfred slammed a mean left to Nick's jaw. Nick felt his teeth rattle. Nick tried a right cross. It kissed the air.

Regulars watching the fisticuffs looked at each other. The sparring between the two old friends was more violent than usual. It seemed to the spectators that the big Englishman was putting a trifle too much power into his punches.

It felt that way to Nick. Ducking and weaving as best he could, Nick was relieved when finally the grueling exercise rounds were over. Hooking a gloved hand around the big man's neck, he said, "Old pal, you planning on killing me in the ring?"

Big Alfred frowned and said nothing.

Nick, breathing hard, rubbed his sweat-drenched belly and said in a low voice, "Take it easy on me, will you." He grinned and added confidentially, "I haven't managed to so much as hold the good captain's hand."

Big Alfred's face brightened. He grinned down at Nick and said, "What did I tell you, laddie? She's one in a million. They don't come any finer than Captain Kay." Full of confidence again, the gigantic Englishman hitched up his baggy boxing trunks and happily declared, "My bet's as good as won. The captain'll have her rescue mission."

"Looks that way," said Nick. But he too grinned, every bit as confident as the big Englishman.

The two friends walked home together in the rain, Big Alfred bidding Nick good day at the Carousel Club.

Whistling, Nick climbed the stairs. Ling Tan was leaving for his weekly evening of *pai jow*. Ming Ho was following her father down the wide corridor, fussily turning up the collar of his overcoat and warning him not to leave his overshoes behind when he started home.

They looked up, saw Nick approaching, and smiled.

Ling Tan said, "Boss, I already lay out your evening clothes. Better hurry, chop chop, or be late to dinner with Miss Packard."

Nick shrugged wide shoulders. "I canceled the engagement."

"You did?" Ming Ho eagerly stepped in front of her father. "Oh, Mr. Nick, will you please escort me to the library? It wouldn't take more than an hour and I badly need to—"

"Get your coat," Nick said, snapping his fingers and grinning at her.

Ming Ho squealed with joy and flew back down the hall. Ling Tan's smiling eyes disappeared in folds of flesh and he said, "Should have refused her, boss. Spoil her, always letting her have her way."

Unruffled, Nick slid his hands deep in to his pants pockets. "Aw, go play your dominoes."

Nick, holding a large umbrella over their heads, escorted Ming Ho to the library six blocks away. The grateful young girl chattered excitedly as they walked. Clinging to Nick's arm, she told him about her science project, confided that she'd met a mannerly young man who'd invited her to an upcoming spring dance, and said she was going to have a special dress made for the special occasion.

Ming Ho talked. Nick listened. Neither noticed two men watching them from an alley. Two men who were dressed identically in black wool watch caps, black pullover sweaters, and black trousers. One was a slightly built Oriental. The other was a scar-faced man nearly as huge as Alfred Drake. The discerning eyes of both men rested solely on young Ming Ho, who looked like a tiny, exquisite china doll.

When Nick and Ming Ho got back from the library at shortly after seven, Ming Ho was content to spend the rest of the evening in bed with her library books. Nick bade her good night and went back out into the rain.

He headed straight for the waterfront mission.

Captain Kay took off her apron.

The evening meal had been served. The kitchen had been cleaned and everything was put away. It was half an hour before the evening services began. A quiet time at the mission when all the busy soldiers withdrew to take a short rest.

Finally the rain had stopped so some of the recruits went outdoors. Others sat around the clean kitchen, drinking coffee, relaxing.

Rolling down the sleeves of her white blouse, Kay ventured out into the dim, silent auditorium. No one was there. She rolled her aching shoulders, sighed with exhaustion, and was about to stretch out for a few minutes on one of the rickety pews when the mission's front door opened.

Nick McCabe stepped inside.

Kay looked up and her pulse quickened. She hadn't seen Nick since their Seal Beach picnic two days ago. At the end of that lovely day he'd invited her to have dinner with him the next evening. She'd told him the answer was no. He'd informed her that the answer was yes and she would meet him at Gorman's at six o'clock.

"McCabe," she said now, nodding to him and furiously attempting to tidy her hair.

He stood there in the half-light wearing his seaman's jacket with the collar turned up. Drops of rain clung to his shoulders and glistened in his black hair. He was smiling boyishly. He reached down inside his trousers pocket, withdrew a shiny gold coin, and began rhythmically flipping it into the air and catching it as he came slowly toward her.

He said, "I waited for you at Gorman's for an hour."

"Did you get angry?"

"No, I got hungry."

Kay laughed. "You're a little late for this evening's meal."

"I'm not hungry now."

"Then why have you come here, McCabe?"

Nick flipped the twenty-dollar gold piece in the air and caught it.

"We have to talk, Captain."

"Do we? I can't imagine what we really need to say to each other."

Nick tossed the coin. Caught it. Tossed it again. His gleaming silver eyes were riveted on Kay. He never once looked at the tossing coin. He moved steadily closer.

"I have things to do," she warned. "Will this take forever?"

"But before forever comes," Nick said, grinning, "there's one thing I have to know." He tossed the coin. Caught it. Kay waited, half tense, half expectant, as he advanced. When he stood directly before her, he said, "Are you free tomorrow? I am."

"I'm sure you are," Kay said with a note of contempt. Shaking her head, she added, *"Nihil agendo homines male agere discunt."*

"You know," Nick said, smiling, "that was right on the tip of my tongue."

Kay couldn't help smiling back at him. " 'The devil finds mischief for idle hands.' "

"Ah, yes, well then it's your Christian duty to keep mine from being idle. Come with me tomorrow afternoon. We'll ride on the cable cars."

"Not a chance," said Kay. "But why don't you come tomorrow afternoon to hear Big Alfred's first sermon?"

"Not a chance," said Nick.

"Are you staying for this evening's services, McCabe?"

"If I do, will you come tomorrow?" Nick flipped the coin in the air.

"I don't make bargains," Kay told him.

"Then I'm not staying," Nick told her. He tossed the coin.

Kay's hand shot out and plucked it from the air. "In that case, we'll accept this coin as your contribution. Thank you, McCabe. And good night."

"Night," Nick said, not moving.

"See you tomorrow," said Kay, smiling.

Chapter 33

"Now there's only one thing I want to know." Nick spoke in a low, soft whisper.

"What's that?" Kay whispered back.

"How can I kiss you with all these people around?"

"Shhh!" Kay scolded, glancing anxiously about. "Behave yourself, Nick McCabe. Someone will hear!"

Her blue eyes flashed an angry warning, but her fair face flushed with color and Nick knew she wasn't offended. He grinned, shrugged his wide shoulders, and then dutifully focused his attention straight ahead.

A large gathering had turned out for the Army's afternoon open-air meeting. Many were there out of curiosity. They had come to see— and hear—the bare-knuckle champion of the entire British Isles. Scattered among the fight fans were some Presidio soldiers and their girlfriends. A number of dark-suited businessmen from the financial district were present.

Nick spotted—right up front—a couple of toughs from Three Fingers Jackson's inner circle. Dressed in ruffled shirts and gaudy brocade vests, diamond stickpins flashing, they stood out like sore thumbs.

The site of the afternoon service was a vacant lot off Davis Street near the Embarcadero. The steadily growing crowd waited expectantly while the San Francisco Army Corps #1 band played their gleaming brass instruments. The strains of "Onward, Christian Soldiers" floated out over the assembled throng.

Abruptly the band stopped playing.

A giant of man, uniformed in Army blue, made his way to the portable wooden pulpit. He stepped up behind it and took off his billed cap. Big Alfred Duke wore a smile that outshone the sun. His brown hair was neatly combed. His ruddy face scrubbed. His midnight-blue uniform was neatly pressed, the brass buttons shining in the brilliant sunlight.

And on his left sleeve were the three newly sewn stripes denoting the rank of Salvation Army sergeant. Alfred Duke was very proud of his promotion. Those who knew and loved him were proud as well.

Captain Kay's blue eyes glistened with unshed tears of pride as the brand-new sergeant in God's mighty Army took his place in the pulpit, ready to preach his very first sermon. Curly and Rose Montgomery stood near Kay and Nick. Kay exchanged quick glances with her brother. Curly smiled, nodded, and swallowed hard. Then he gave his pregnant wife's thickened waist a gentle squeeze and waited for Big Alfred to begin.

"Ladies and gentleman, brothers and sisters, some of you have known me best as a fighter. I am still a fighter," said Alfred Duke.

"Sir, are you going to challenge the great John L. Sullivan?" called one of the soldiers.

"No, lad," Big Alfred said in a kind voice. "I've given up my campaigning"—he paused—"to fight a bigger battle."

"Like you gave up in the sixth round against Mike McCoole?" shouted the taller of the two Jackson toughs.

And he stepped up and spit on Big Alfred.

A collective gasp of horror rippled through the crowd. Nick started forward, his dark face a mask of fury. Kay anxiously caught his arm and stopped him.

"No, Nick!" she warned, her eyes pleading.

A muscle working furiously in his jaw, his body taut and straining, Nick looked at her. He nodded grudgingly and stayed where he was. She was right. This was Big Alfred's battle, not his.

Tension was almost palpable as the crowd waited. Curly's long arm closed more securely around his pregnant wife as Rose, afraid to look, buried her face on his chest. Kay's hand remained on Nick's arm, fingers encircling the biceps. She pressed so tightly, her nails dug into the hard flesh beneath the blue shirt sleeve.

Everyone knew that Big Alfred Duke was capable of putting away the tall tough, his grinning sidekick, and a half-dozen more men to boot with a few steel-fisted punches. Would he do it? Half the crowd hoped so, excited at the prospect of seeing the bare-knuckled champ back in action.

Chants of "Take him, Champ" went up from the electrified crowd along with whistles and applause.

Kay held her breath, clung to Nick's arm, and stared unblinking at Big Alfred Duke. Silently she prayed he would have the courage and the conviction to do the right thing. To refrain from violence. To behave as befitting a Salvation Army sergeant.

The Englishman raised a blue-sleeved forearm and wiped the spittle from his florid face. Then he clutched the sides of podium so firmly in his huge hands, the wood was in danger of splintering into a thousand pieces. Veins bulged in his powerful neck and his hazel eyes flashed.

And Big Alfred said in a clear, calm voice, "I have taken today's lesson from the New Testament book of Romans." He smiled then, opened his Bible, and placed it atop the wooden podium. "Chapter twelve, verse nine. " 'Be kindly affectioned one to the other . . .' "

Big Alfred plunged forcefully into the lesson, effectively gaining attention from the crowd.

"Rejoicing in hope . . ." Big Alfred spoke in loud, clear voice as if the disturbance hadn't occurred. "Patient in tribulation and . . ."

Big Alfred looked out over the crowd, an expression of inner peace in his eyes. "Recompense to no man evil for evil. If it be possible, as much as lieth in you, live peaceably with all men." He paused and looked directly at the tall Jackson tough who had spit on him.

"I always knew you were a coward, Duke," the man taunted, rolling a cigar from one side of thin mouth to the other. "You got lace on your underdrawers?"

He laughed then. So did his companion and a few others. The tall, muscular man dropped his cigar, stepped on it, and waited, expecting Big Alfred to come charging, his sermon forgotten, his dignity lost. His cause compromised.

A beatific smile then spread over Big Alfred's face and he continued with his sermon.

"Dearly beloved," Big Alfred's voice lifted, "avenge not yourselves." Knuckles turning white from gripping the podium, his booming bass voice silenced any lingering laughter when he quoted, "for it is written, 'Vengeance is mine; I will repay, saith the Lord.' "

The pair who razzed him were soundly scorned by the majority of the crowd. They lost heart and slunk away. Kay and Curly smiled at each other, relieved. Sister and brother exchanged a silent message, acknowledged a hoped-for certainty.

Sergeant Alfred Duke had passed a tough test with flying colors. The newly promoted Army officer had held his temper. He had turned the other cheek. He had manfully endured the ridicule of a heartless few before a witnessing crowd of hundreds.

Big Alfred had experienced the heady feeling of power that comes from vanquishing the enemy with the Word, not deeds. Thus uplifted, he finished a stirring, heartfelt sermon, having held his audience's undivided attention throughout.

"Let every soul be subject unto the higher powers," Big Alfred concluded, "for there is no power but of God; the powers that be ordained of God."

He smiled broadly, slammed his Bible shut, and stepped out from behind the podium as the San Francisco Army Corps #1 band took up their instruments and played. Cheering, congratulations, and laughter was the order of the day as the crowd swelled forward, eager to shake Sergeant Alfred Duke's big hand. Big Alfred was the center of attention.

But an expensively dressed lady in a gleaming dark-blue carriage parked across Davis Street never gave the uniformed Englishman a second look. Her eyes rested squarely on a man who wore no uniform of blue. A tall, lean man with coal-black hair who was dressed in impeccable gray flannels and pale-blue shirt.

"Pat, darling," said Adele Packard, her patrician nose wrinkling with distaste, her eyes narrowing, "surely you can see why you *must* end the relationship with your little Army captain." She turned to her brother and added, "Just look at that trash. We Packards simply cannot associate with their sort. Why, they're the laughingstock of the city." She shook her perfectly coiffured blond head.

"Look a little more closely, Adele," Patrick Packard said. "I do believe that's your lover standing beside Kay."

"I see him!" snapped Adele.

"Is it acceptable for Nick to associate with Captain Kay?"

Adele Packard's nostrils quivered with anger. "It is not. And I shall quickly set him straight about it, believe you me."

"Will you?" said Patrick. "When? Tonight?"

"Nick isn't coming tonight. He's busy again." Adele's gaze returned to Nick. "Tell William to get us out of here before we're seen."

The blue carriage drove away unnoticed. The crowds thinned and finally dispersed. Only Army members remained.

And Nick.

Nick stayed. And invited everyone in the small, happy group out to dinner.

"Tonight's dinner's on me. Let's go," Nick said, smiling. "We'll all walk up to Hurricane Gussie's and have thick steaks and fried potatoes."

"We really appreciate the offer," said Curly, a supportive arm around Rose, "but the little mother here needs to lie down."

"I'm sorry, Nick," said Rose. "My ankles are swelling again. But thank you just the same." She and Curly said their good-byes and walked away.

"Laddie, I can't go either," Big Alfred said with a frown. "I promised the warden at San Quentin I'd talk to the convicts this evening. I've a long ride." He hurried away.

"Afraid you'll have to count us out too," said Giles Lawton, speaking for himself, Bobby Newman, Matthew, and the rest of the Army band. "It's our night on kitchen detail. Time we get on back to the mission."

Bobby and Matthew both nodded and thanked Nick for the invitation. Taking their shining brass instruments and the big bass drum with them, the band trudged off.

Within minutes everyone was gone, leaving only Nick and Kay.

Turning to look at him, Kay said, "I suppose I should be going back myself."

"I suppose." Nick smiled boyishly and plucked at her sleeve. "Have dinner with me instead."

Kay brushed his hand away. She was tempted. She sighed, bit the inside of her bottom lip, and looked up at him. Nick read the indecision in the depths of her expressive blue eyes and his smile broadened.

"Yes, I suppose I should be getting back to the mission," Kay said again.

"You're repeating yourself."

"Am I?"

Nick nodded.

Kay shook her head. She looked away, said nothing.

Stepping closer, Nick again plucked playfully at her sleeve. "Your move, Captain."

Chapter 34

The name didn't fit.

Hurricane Gussie's sounded like just another hole-in-the-wall dive typical of the Barbary Coast. It wasn't.

It was a very fancy restaurant with marble pillars, tall potted palms, polished mahogany cabinets, and huge white tablecloths reaching to the floor.

At this early hour, the elegant eatery was totally empty of patrons. Kay assumed the supper crowd would soon start arriving and then every table would be filled.

A smiling, mustachioed man met Nick and Kay in the marbled foyer. Nick introduced Jess Hay, owner of the restaurant. Jess welcomed them warmly, took Kay's straw bonnet and carefully placed it on pegged rack, then ushered them into the vast, dimly lit restaurant. He led them to a large table near the room's center.

No sooner were they seated than an army of white-jacketed waiters silently appeared. One young slender waiter dexterously lit the tall red candles resting in gold-leaf candlesticks. Another shook out, then draped large white damask napkins over their knees. Still another poured tinkling ice water into gleaming crystal goblets. The head-waiter—Jess himself—placed gigantic gold-embossed red leather menus before them.

When Jess and the crew had disappeared, Kay leaned across the table and whispered, "Nick, this is grand. All these waiters tending us . . . makes me feel like I'm someone special."

Nick leaned back, making himself comfortable in the red leather chair as he looked at her. "You *are* someone special, Kay."

Kay blushed appealingly, lifted the red leather menu, and began studying it. She was reading of all the exotic-sounding foods listed when she heard the first sweet strains from violins wafting through the room. Eyes lifting, Kay looked around.

Her lips fell open in surprise when she saw a dozen musicians in white ties and tails slowly strolling toward the table.

"Nick," she whispered excitedly, "they're coming this way."

His gaze never leaving her, Nick grinned disarmingly. "I do believe they are."

"Serenading us. How lovely." She looked from Nick to the approaching violinists and back again. "Aren't you glad we got here early?" she confided with a wide smile. "We can pretend they're playing just for us."

Amused, Nick said tolerantly, as if to a child, "Sweetheart, they are."

Kay experienced a shiver of pleasure mixed with alarm. This romantic dinner, Nick's use of an endearment, the frankness of his silver-eyed gaze: All were warning signals. She was being tempted and she was in danger. Nick was going to make love to her. He was going to kiss her again the way he had at the Seal Beach picnic. Unable to stand his gaze, Kay looked away. Nick's eyes never left her.

But Kay was stirred by the sweet, romantic music of the violins, and within moments she had entirely forgotten that she might be in any danger.

She was enchanted with the elegance of the candlelit room. She was properly impressed with the impeccable service. She was tempted by the sumptuous meal served to them on fine Sevres china.

And she was woman enough to be thrilled to be dining alone with a handsome, fascinating man.

Animated, she talked and talked. Nick listened. His silver-gray gaze was focused solely on her. Charmed, he smiled as he watched her.

Kay was enjoying herself completely. Her arresting blue eyes flashed in the candlelight and she talked rapidly, like a child who was overly excited. She was so adorable. She exuded a rare kind of sensuous innocence that Nick found extremely appealing.

Kay stopped speaking in midsentence. She looked around at all the empty tables. Sincerely puzzled, she said, "Nick, I don't understand. We've been here for more than an hour and we're still alone. No other diners have come in. Where is everyone?"

Nick reached across the table and gently took her hand in his. Rubbing his thumb along her delicate knuckles, he said, "No one has come. No one will come." He squeezed her hand. "No one but you and I will be dining here this evening."

Kay raised a perfectly arched eyebrow. "No? And why not? How do you know there won't be—"

"I reserved the restaurant just for us. I asked Jess to close it to the public."

"You wanted to be alone with me?" Kay stated.

"I did, sweetheart. Yes."

Kay was flattered. "But you invited all the others, remember? Curly, Rose, Big Alfred . . ."

"And they all said no. God bless 'em."

"Yes, but you didn't know that they would."

Nick grinned. "I gambled and won."

Kay shook her head. She again looked around the large empty room. "You engaged this entire restaurant just for the two of us?"

"I did. Are you properly impressed?"

Kay's face broke into a girlish smile of pure delight, and she said, "Nick McCabe, are you courting me?"

Nick paused before answering. He grinned and said, "I'm afraid I am, sweetheart."

Kay sighed with undisguised pleasure. Nick winked with untamed deviltry. They lingered languidly over their dinner.

The violinists continued to softly play romantic ballads. Fresh-cut gardenias sweetly perfumed the air. Candles burned low in their golden holders. The potently romantic atmosphere took its toll on Kay's senses. She couldn't help but be tremendously flattered that the handsome Nick McCabe had gone to such lengths to woo her.

Dreamily listening as he talked, Kay realized that this was a special occasion, one she would never forget. For the rest of her days she'd remember this balmy night, this grand dinner, this handsome man who'd hired a restaurant and a dozen strolling violinists just for her.

When the pair left the restaurant, the sky was a bright flaming orange. The sun was setting and the warmth of the day was dying with it. A storm was brewing off to the south. There was an occasional flash of lightning, and thunder rumbled in the distance like an artillery barrage.

Nick and Kay stood beneath Hurricane Gussie's red canopy. Neither spoke. Nick held Kay's bonnet by its taffeta streamers. He tapped the black straw hat against his leg.

He turned, looked at her, and Kay caught her breath. She must get back to the mission. Nick's masculinity was too powerful. His extraordinary magnetism was drawing her helplessly to him, and if she didn't get away this minute . . .

Without a word, Nick commandingly put hand to the small of Kay's back and guided her across busy Montgomery Street and down the wooden sidewalks toward the Golden Carousel. When they stood before the club's black double doors, Kay finally balked.

"Nick, I can't . . . I need to get back to the mission."

Nick smiled, took her elbow in his hand, and drew her closer. His deep and vibrant voice bespeaking exciting promises of romance, he said, "Come inside, Kay. Have coffee with me."

Kay swallowed hard in an attempt to clear her addled senses. It was far from easy. Nick possessed an attraction of the most disturbing nature. She knew that to go inside with him on this enchanting night would be a mistake. But she wanted to go with him.

"No. No, Nick, I haven't time for coffee."

Thunder rumbled in the distance. A foghorn sounded out in the Bay. The old lamplighter coming up Pacific saw them talking together and left the nearest lamppost darkened.

"I have something that belongs to you," Nick said, his voice remaining low, level. He smiled appealingly. "A bell."

"That's right!" she said, recalling the hot summer day he had taken it away from her. "I want my bell. I've had that bell for a long—"

"Come with me."

They circled behind the white building and went in the back service entrance. Inside, Kay climbed the stairs with Nick. They met Ling Tan in wide upstairs corridor. The servant greeted her with a warm welcome.

Nick said, "Kay, you remember Ling Tan. He watches after me, keeps me out of trouble."

"And that's a full-time job, Missy Captain," said the Chinese servant.

"I can well imagine," Kay said, and smiled.

Ling Tan bowed, nodded, and repeated, "Full-time occupation keeping—"

"All right, all right," Nick broke in, "think you can spare a minute to bring us some coffee?"

"Sure thing, boss," Ling Tan replied and hurried away, chuckling and murmuring "full-time job."

Inside Nick's spacious sitting room a fire burned in the marble fireplace. A lone lamp resting on a round drum table burned low, casting shadows in the big room. Curtains were drawn completely open over the tall glass windows. Sporadic sprinkles of rain tapped against the panes.

Kay walked directly to the warming fire, stretched out her hands, and said over her shoulder, "My bell? Where is it?"

"In the bedroom," Nick told her, tossing her bonnet on the long sofa.

"Go get it." She turned to face him, putting her back to fire. "I want it. Give it me."

"I will," he said, and slowly, surely, approached. When he stood directly before her, he repeated, "I will, sweetheart."

His low caressing tone of voice hinted that he meant to give her more than just the bell. Kay felt heat flood her face. Nick's closeness made her a little dizzy. She closed her eyes. Her heart tried to beat its way out of her chest.

Nick very gently reached out and cupped her cheek in his hand. Kay's eyes came open. She brushed his hand away and trembled.

"You're nervous," he said.

"What makes you think I'm nervous?"

"You're shaking." His silver-eyed gaze held hers.

"Because you touched me," she said finally with complete honesty.

"Are you afraid—"

They fell silent as Ling Tan padded in with a fresh pot of coffee. They waited until he left, then Nick said as if there'd been no interruption, "Are you afraid of me, Kay?"

"Certainly not." Attempting to make light of the situation, Kay quipped, "But you're a bad boy and my mother told me to have nothing to do with bad boys."

She forced a smile and tried to maintain her composure. But Nick was so compelling, so darkly handsome. Kay lowered her eyes. It did no good. Above his gray trousers the blue shirt lay close against the hard flat muscles of his chest. The collar was open. His smooth olive throat was revealed. She had the almost overwhelming urge to lay her flattened palms on his chest and press her lips to the hollow of his tanned throat. Nick took Kay's face in his hands and lifted her head gently. He looked into her eyes and in a warm, soft voice said, "Kiss me, Kay."

His dark head descended. Kay kept her eyes open wide. When his mouth was an inch from hers, Nick murmured, "Kiss me like you've never kissed anyone else."

His warm, smooth lips settled gently on hers. His kiss was every bit as wonderful as when he'd kissed her that sunset at the Seal Beach picnic. Soon it became even better. While his mouth gently moved and molded her lips to his, Nick put an arm around Kay's narrow waist and drew her into his embrace. At first she stiffened.

She withdrew her lips from his and turned her head away. Nick immediately released her. His arms fell to his sides, but he didn't move back. He stayed where he was, his tall lean body almost touching hers. But not quite.

Her head bowed, Kay's forehead rested on Nick's chest, her face turned away. Her hands were balled into fists at her sides. Sensitive to her feelings, Nick took one of those tight fists in his hand, uncurled the stiff fingers, and raised them to his lips.

Gently he kissed the tip of each finger in turn and said, "Kiss me one more time and I'll keep my hands to myself."

Kay raised her head, looked at him. He lowered his lips and kissed her, with his hands clasped behind his back. Kay had no choice but to place hers on his chest to brace herself.

The kiss was sweetly stirring. Nick's mouth moved on Kay's with slow patient aggression. Kay's lips were pliant, responsive. When Nick cautiously ran the tip of his tongue along the seam of her lips, those lips tremulously parted to him.

Kay shuddered and sighed when his tongue touched hers, and her hands, of their own volition, went to the sides of Nick's trim waist. Nick deepened the kiss. His hands came unclasped and settled lightly on Kay's shoulders. He drew her a little closer, but was careful not to press her flush against his tall frame.

Kay sighed softly.

And then she was kissing him, as if she'd been waiting all her life to do just that. Finally she leaned in close, her breasts against his chest, pressing her slender body to his as she kissed him. She felt the cadence of his steady heartbeat against hers and it was thrilling. Two hearts beating wildly as one.

Kay kissed Nick McCabe like she never kissed anyone else. It had an immediate effect. Nick was stricken by a paroxysm of such terrible intensity that his knees buckled. Their lips finally separated. Trembling with emotion, they looked each other, smiled, and began kissing again. His kisses were masterful, adoring kisses that left Kay breathless. Hot, quick, wet kisses around her lips. In the hollow of her chin. Against the beating pulse at the side of her throat. And then fully on her lips once more, his tongue thrusting deeply into her mouth.

While he kissed her Nick eased the sides of Kay's blue jacket apart. His deft fingers went to the buttons at the high-throated collar of her white blouse. He flipped a couple open. Then another. His spread hand caressed her exposed, swanlike throat with infinite tenderness.

Melting in the heat of his enflamed kisses, Kay molded herself to him. She was astounded at the heat and hardness of his tall, lean body pressed so intimately to hers. Such leashed power. Such masculine strength. Such potent virility.

Awed, she let her hand slip into the sculpted small of his back. Her sensitive fingertips eagerly explored the fine configuration of muscle and bone. Glorying in the feel of the smooth hot flesh beneath his blue shirt, Kay sighed with bliss.

She had always wondered how his arms would be.

Now she knew.

The searing kisses continued as Nick began to slowly maneuver Kay away from the fire and toward the door of his bedroom. Kay never even realized that they were moving. Nick turned her about, took a small step here, another there, all the while holding her close in his embrace. If Kay felt movement she assumed she was simply dizzy from being in Nick's arms.

Nick's hot kisses, his body pressing against hers, drove all logical thought from her mind. Her head thrown back and resting on his strong supporting arm, Kay's eyes were closed in sweet rapture.

"Kay," Nick murmured at last as he tore his lips from hers.

"Nick," she whispered breathlessly, opened her eyes, and laid her cheek on his chest.

And saw a silver bell.

It was then she realized that they were no longer standing before the fireplace. They were no longer in the sitting room. There was a bed—a very large bed—directly beside the night table where the bell sat.

They were in Nick's bedroom!

Kay's head shot up. She looked into Nick's passion-heated eyes. She started vigorously shaking her head.

"Nick, no . . ." She anxiously freed herself from his embrace and quickly wheeled away.

Nick's hand shot out, clasped her wrist, and pulled her back. He wrapped his arms around her, drew her back against him, and kissed the back of her neck, high up on the nape below the neat red bun.

He raised his head, settled her more comfortably against him, and said, "I want you." Kay made a little keening sound in the back of her throat. "Do you want me, Kay?"

"Oh, Nick, Nick . . . this is outrageous. You shouldn't behave this way. *I* shouldn't behave this way. I shouldn't be in this room alone with you."

"Answer my question, sweetheart."

Eyes again tightly closed, head pressed back against his shoulder, Kay whispered in a half sob, "Nick, don't do this to me."

"Let me do this to you," Nick hoarsely whispered. His arms tightened possessively around her. "Come on, baby. Let me give you a night of heaven."

"No, Nick. I want more than just one night." She cast his arms off, turned to look at him. "I want a lifetime of heaven." Clutching her open collar together, she added in a choked voice, "An eternity."

Chapter 35

What am I going to do about Nicky?

Kay couldn't sleep.

Midnight had come and gone. One o'clock. Two. Still she lay there in her narrow bed wide-eyed and restless.

I kissed him, she thought dreamily, *and it was nice. It was much more than nice. It was . . . it was . . .*

Kay trembled in the darkness.

For twenty-five years she had led a safe, satisfying life of service to the Almighty. She had labored in the vineyards of the Lord and never once had evil threatened her. She had rubbed elbows with the wicked and remained clean. She had seen first hand sin at its most glamorous and never had she been tempted.

Then the Devil attacked.

And nobody had ever warned her that the devil would have black hair and silver-gray eyes!

Kay sighed again and turned on to her stomach.

She should never have gone to Nick's apartment. She should never have allowed him to kiss her way he had kissed her. Even now her bare toes curled from the vivid recollection and her breath grew short.

Kay suddenly smiled foolishly, hugged her pillow, and relived once more the romantic evening she had shared with Nick. Starting with the minute they walked into Hurricane Gussie's and ending with the moment she left him in his apartment.

It was without doubt the most exciting evening of her life.

Kay exhaled loudly.

She had to forget about Nick. She had to stay away from him! He was the kind of man no woman could ever really have. He loved all women and all women loved him. He was a sinner without conscience. He was hedonistic and selfish, living for today, uncaring of tomorrow. A charming scamp who could easily become a major problem.

She had plenty of problems without him.

Her biggest problem was that there was little hope the Corps could raise enough money to pay off the lien on the waterfront lot and begin construction on the permanent rescue shelter before the May deadline.

Mid-March already and the Army still owed more than fifteen thousand dollars on the land. The Corps was steadily growing but so were the needy they served. There was never an opportunity to save any of the money they collected. She and Curly were going to fail those who had entrusted them to carry the Army's banner forward. It would be a bitter disappointment to be sent back home, but without a miracle that's just what was going to happen.

The sobering prospect of leaving San Francisco made Kay immediately think of Joey. A sharp pain shot through her heart. The thought of leaving the Barbary Coast, of never seeing Joey again, was more than she could bear. She loved the redheaded little boy as if he were her own. Lately Joey was in her thoughts almost as much as Nick.

Kay groaned miserably.

The times she had mentioned Joey to Nick he had paid little attention, had shown no interest. That was Nick. Totally self-centered and far too childish himself to care about the welfare of a homeless little boy.

Why couldn't Nick be more like Patrick Packard? Pat was such a fine man. He had integrity. He was full of high ideals. He listened attentively whenever she spoke of little Joey. He seemed genuinely interested in the child. Furthermore, Pat was ever the perfect gentleman. He'd never dare kiss her the way Nick had kissed her . . . the way Nick had kissed her . . . the way . . . oh, who was she trying to fool!

Kay flopped back onto her back, folded her hands behind her head, heaved another loud sigh.

Despite her best efforts to think of something else—someone else —Nick McCabe filled her thoughts. She could see him in the darkness as clearly as if he were there in her room.

Nick, dark and handsome, smiling at her across the candlelit table at Hurricane Gussie's. Nick standing under the red canopy outside, tapping her bonnet against his leg. Nick taking her gently in his arms at his apartment. Nick kissing her. First with heartstopping tenderness. Finally with fierce passion. Kissing her again and again until all her senses were aroused, each sensation so exciting it was almost pain.

Kay turned her head to the side. Atop the night table a silver bell gleamed in the darkness. The bell Nick had taken away from her on that hot August day she'd first seen him. Tonight he had given it back to her.

Kay reached for the worn bell. It tinkled lightly when she lifted it. Staring at it as if seeing it for the first time, she wondered if in all those months it had sat atop Nick's night table, had he ever looked at it and thought of her? Had he ever picked it up? Held it his hands? Had those beautifully tapered tan fingers touched the bell?

Kay carefully cupped the bell in her palms and envisioned Nick cupping it in his hands in the very same way. Impulsively she pressed it to her breasts. Then she ground her teeth in frustration and thrust the bell away. It fell ringing loudly to the floor.

A longing as old as time overwhelmed Kay, and she drew her knees up to her aching chest and clutched her pillow. It was wrong—she knew it had to be wrong—but oh how she yearned to feel the warmth of his body in the cool night.

She ordered herself to stop thinking about Nick and go to sleep. But when sleep finally came, Nick's face dominated her dreams. And in those tortured dreams she was asking herself the same troubled question.

What was she going to do about Nicky?

Chapter 36

What am I going to do about Kay?

Nick lay in the dark, naked, the perspiration collecting on his lean frame despite the coolness of the room. Hands clasped beneath his head, covers kicked down the foot of the bed, he sprawled atop the silky sheets attempting to sleep.

And having no luck.

As soon as Kay left his apartment, Nick had bathed, dressed, and gone downstairs to the club. There he had stayed for the remainder of the night and on into the wee hours of morning, welcoming patrons, watching the show, and drinking. And doing his damnedest to forget about Captain Kay Montgomery.

The place was packed. The midnight show had gone off without a hitch. The crowd had cheered for Angel Thompson the way they used to do for Rose Reilly, and Angel had given them their money's worth. There'd been only one minor disturbance all evening, which he had easily quelled without so much as raising his voice.

Shortly after four A.M., Nick had climbed the stairs to his apartment, well satisfied with the evening's take and totally exhausted. And absolutely certain that he would fall asleep as soon as he fell into bed.

But he hadn't.

He'd been successful at pushing Kay from his mind while he was downstairs in the crowded club. But the minute he walked into the silent apartment, the spirited redhead began to torment him.

Nick's hands came out from under his head. He rolled over onto his bare stomach and viciously punched his pillow, exhaling loudly.

Suddenly he grinned foolishly.

Lord, she was cute with her freckled nose and big blue eyes and the flaming hair he'd unpinned that day at Seal Beach. She was a natural beauty with an amazing abundance of charm and fire. She wasn't stuffy, straitlaced, and judgmental as he had supposed. But she stood firmly for what she believed in and worked tirelessly for life's unfortunates. She wasn't afraid of anything or anybody, even when she should be.

And just as he'd always suspected, she was a warm-blooded woman. No, hot-blooded.

Nick groaned.

His bare belly tightened at the vivid recollection of the way she'd kissed him. Less than expertly, but with all her heart and soul. Therein lay the rub.

If he continued to court her, he'd soon succeed in seducing her. She was more than a little attracted to him, he knew that. In a strange way, he was just as attracted to her. He knew the reason. It was the vast chasm separating them that drew them together. They were fascinated with each other because each of them saw in the other something that each had given up.

He himself had given up any chance of leading a life of decency and respect. He would never know the peace and happiness that comes from having a home and a family. Long ago he'd made his deal with the devil. His future was the same as his past. His world was the world of the Barbary Coast: clubs, liquor, and loose ladies.

Kay had given up plenty too. She had renounced the kind of excitement that for him was commonplace. She had never sipped champagne from stemmed glasses, or placed a bet on the roulette wheel, or made love on silk sheets in a hotel bedroom. Her world was the world of the Salvation Army: missions, abstinence, and lost souls.

Nick exhaled and turned again onto his back.

Maybe he shouldn't have made the wager with Big Alfred. Maybe he didn't really need Big Alfred back at the club that badly. Maybe he could forget the whole thing.

Business was great again. Money was pouring in. He could spare the fifteen thousand, plus an extra five to start construction of a permanent mission. He might just do that very thing and let the other go. Leave the lovely Kay untouched.

Nick absently scratched his chest and chuckled at his change of heart. Was he getting soft in his old age? Since when had he ever been bothered by conscience?

Without turning his head on the pillow, Nick reached a long arm out to the night table. He felt around on the smooth surface, searching for the silver bell. Then he remembered. He'd given it back.

The smile left his dark face and he ground his even white teeth.

More than once during the last six months he had picked up that silver bell, cupped it in his hands, and smiled, recalling the day he'd met the fiery Salvation Army captain.

Nick's hand fell back to the mattress. He bunched up a portion of the white sheet with his longer fingers and twisted it tightly in his firm grip. A muscle danced in his jaw. His lids slid low over troubled silver eyes.

Dammit, what was he going to do about Kay?

Chapter 37

Kay had a raging headache.

Her temples throbbed and her eyes felt grainy and dry. Every step she took seemed to jar right up through her body to her aching head.

At the mission early that morning Big Alfred and Giles Lawton had asked if she was sick. She'd assured them that she was fine. Just fine. She didn't want them to know that her head was hurting and her eyes were stinging from the lack of sleep. And she wouldn't have dared let on that the lack of sleep had been caused by an irresistible silver-eyed, black-haired rascal whose burning lips and gentle hands had driven her half out of her mind.

And kept her awake all night.

Now as she walked toward Battery Place in the afternoon sunshine, Kay promised herself a much-needed nap. As soon as she visited briefly with Joey and the other children, she'd go straight to her room and lie down for a couple of hours. And this time she would sleep!

When she stepped into the corridor of Battery Place, Kay realized she was early. No loud shouts and laughter greeted her. No piercing squeals, no thunder of running feet. The quiet meant the children had not yet risen from their afternoon nap.

The big house was silent except for the ticking of the antique grandfather clock there in the hallway. Kay's eyes went to the tall-cased clock.

Just past two P.M. The children wouldn't be rising until almost three. She couldn't wait that long. She was out on her feet.

Much as she hated it, she'd have to leave without seeing Joey. Kay sighed, turned, and started back toward the front door. Almost there, she paused, glanced down the long hallway toward the gymnasium, and decided to at least look in on the sleeping children.

On Joey.

Smiling, Kay quietly tiptoed down the long hall and peered into the big darkened back room. On pallets spread on the floor lay small, sleeping children. Searching for that small head of flaming red, Kay blinked in stunned disbelief.

One of the sleeping children was not so small. One was not a child at all. One was a man. A fully grown man with ruffled raven hair and long sprawling limbs.

Kay blinked again.

Nick McCabe, sound asleep, his long outstretched arm pillowing the red head of a slumbering child, looked appealingly like an innocent little boy himself.

Kay felt the room around her spin. She gripped the solid door frame for support, closed her eyes, then opened them. She realized she was holding her breath, every muscle in her body growing more tense by the second.

It was a miracle.

It was the first time she had seen Nick McCabe acting out of regard for someone or something beyond his own selfish desires and needs.

Her eyes riveted to the big black-haired man and the tiny red-haired boy, Kay at last noticed the bundle of red fur snuggled cozily between the pair. Sleeping peacefully with his little master, Mac lay on his belly, his head held in the crook of Joey's curled arm, a hind paw pressing Nick's trousered thigh.

Mac! The dog's name was Mac!

Like a bolt out of the blue it dawned on Kay. Nick had given the puppy to Joey! That's why Joey called the dog Mac. Mac for McCabe! Nick had known Joey all along. He knew Joey as well as she did, if not better.

A hand at her tight throat, Kay stood there in the doorway and stared fondly at man, boy, and dog. A tenderness she hadn't known was possible welled up in her.

Abruptly she wheeled away and crept back down the hallway and out the front door. She had thought that she knew Nick McCabe. Knew him fairly well. Knew what made him tick. Knew him as a hard-drinking, womanizing, devil-may-care, saloon-keeping libertine. Or was that only the man he allowed the world to see?

Maybe she didn't really know him. There had to be *some* good in a human being who knew a houseful of orphans well enough to lie down and nap with them as if he were a regular visitor!

Kay's headache had disappeared. Her exhaustion was totally forgotten. She no longer needed a nap. What she needed—had to have—were some straight answers. She knew full well she'd never get them from Nick.

Kay's pace was brisk as she headed back to the mission. Praying Big

Alfred would still be there, she could hardly wait to question him. She would make him tell her all he knew about Nick McCabe.

Out of breath, Kay rushed through the mission's front door and waved away soldiers who immediately descended on her to ask what should be done about this, what about that? The troop was taken aback. They'd never seen Captain Kay behave as if she had no time for their problems.

Kay ignored their looks of hurt surprise and pressed on. She made her way to the back of the mission and the supply room. She gave a great sigh of relief when she stepped inside and saw Big Alfred unloading boxes through the open back door. A heavy wooden crate balanced on his broad shoulder, he looked up, saw her, and smiled.

Then he gave Kay a puzzled look when she said without preamble, "Put that down and come with me!"

Big Alfred swung the heavy box to the floor. Straightening and wiping his forehead on his shirt sleeve, he said, "Is something wrong?"

"No, something's right," said Kay. "Now come on. Hurry!"

Removing his work gloves, Big Alfred quickly followed Kay to the small room she used for an office. No sooner was he inside than she shut the door behind him, turned, leaned back against it, and said, "Tell me everything about Nick McCabe."

Big Alfred's hazel eyes squinted. He made a face. "What brought this on, lassie?"

"I just saw Nick at Battery Place. I want to know what kind of man he really is. I want to know everything about him that you know and I don't."

"I was just with Nick the last seven years." Big Alfred rubbed his jaw thoughtfully. "There's somebody else who's known him a lot longer; someone who knows just about everything there is to know about the lad."

"Who, Big Alfred?" Her widened blue eyes held his. "You must tell me. You *have* to tell me."

Big Alfred exhaled slowly, his massive chest swelling against his shirt. Then he nodded his great head. "Aye, lassie, aye. It's time you paid a visit to the Lady in Black."

Chapter 38

Below, the afternoon fog had begun to roll in off the bay as Kay approached the mansion on Russian Hill. The largest home on the hill, the huge white marble palace dwarfed its nearest neighbors.

Kay climbed the marble steps of the Greenwich Street dwelling, rang the bell, and waited. A uniformed butler opened the heavy door.

Kay smiled at the solemn-faced man and said quickly, "I'm Captain Kay Montgomery. I'm here to see the Lady in Black."

With an almost imperceptible nod of his graying head, the butler admitted her into a vast marble-floored vestibule. He took her bonnet and asked that she kindly follow him. Kay ascended one of the twin curving staircases with steps of marble and balustrades of intricately patterned gilded iron.

At the top of the stairs Kay was ushered down a long, wide hallway with upholstered benches and straight-back chairs, marble-topped tables, intricately carved consoles, and French armoires. Gold-framed paintings lined the walls.

The butler showed Kay into a large salon off the left side of the corridor.

"I will tell the Lady you are here," he said. "She will be with you shortly."

"Thank you."

He left her there. Kay looked around the luxurious room, which was decorated entirely in white and black. Sofas of shimmering black-and-white satin brocade faced each other before a white marble fireplace. There were heavy gilt consoles, straight-backed armchairs covered with white velvet, and monumental black marble-topped tables. The curtains and the carpet were of snow-white velvet. Handmade cabinets, marble statues, vases and candelabra of imposing proportions, and beautiful pictures gave the salon a stately appearance.

"Welcome to my home."

Kay jumped, startled, then whirled about to see the Lady in Black sweep into the salon. No black veil covered her face now so for the first time Kay got a good look at her. She was a handsome, dark-eyed woman with silver-streaked black hair done up in a severe bun. Her pale-skinned face was carefully painted, the cheeks and lips expertly rouged, the dark eyes outlined, the lashes curled. She was well preserved and strikingly attractive, but she was not young.

Kay's face broke into a wide smile. The dark-haired woman smiled back at her.

Dressed in a stylish gown of black merino wool, the Lady in Black lifted the flowing skirts of her dress and came forward to greet Kay. Extending a pale, bejeweled hand, she said, "I'm Camille Kelly. I'm delighted you've come to call on me."

Kay was surprised at the strength and firmness of the Lady's handshake. "Thank you, Miss Kelly. I'm Captain—"

"I know who you are, my dear," the Lady in Black interrupted, smiling warmly. "You're doing wonders for the poor, needy souls of the Barbary Coast."

"Thanks to your generosity," said Kay. "Allowing the Army the use of the waterfront warehouse has made all the difference."

The Lady in Black pretended dismay. "That Alfred Duke! I asked him not to say—"

"He didn't," Kay interrupted. "I put two and two together."

The Lady in Black nodded, smiling. Then she said, "But you didn't come here to talk of your good work or to thank me for the use the warehouse, did you?"

"No," said Kay. "I'm here to learn about Nick McCabe."

The Lady in Black showed no surprise. "Won't you sit down, Captain. I'll ring for tea."

Kay took a seat on one of the matching black-and-white striped sofas. The Lady in Black tugged on a bell cord beside the marble fireplace. Then she came and sat down beside Kay. She settled her long black skirts around her slippered feet. A pale hand, bedecked with diamonds, absently touched a worn gold watch pinned to her shirtwaist. The fingers handled the watch almost affectionately, as if it had great value. Then she folded her hands in her lap and turned fully to Kay.

"Now then, we'll have a nice, long talk."

"You're sure I'm not intruding?"

"Not at all," said Camille Kelly. "Captain, I seldom get visitors."

The hot tea arrived on a gleaming silver serving tray along with a small pitcher of cream, a bowl of sliced lemons, and a huge plate of tempting pastries. Kay accepted only a cup of tea.

The Lady in Black said, "Tell me, Captain, what has happened that you've come here today to ask about Nick?"

"I saw Nick at Battery Place this afternoon. I asked Big Alfred about it and he said you know more about Nick McCabe than anyone. Please, Miss Kelly, tell me about him. I must know."

Without preamble, the Lady in Black nodded and began to tell Kay a surprising and fascinating story.

"Long ago a pretty young girl with coal-black hair and huge smoky eyes worked as a servant in the San Francisco home of a rich mining magnate and his spoiled wife. The man took advantage of the beautiful young servant girl. She became pregnant by him and was immediately cast out of his home with no money and nowhere to go.

"The madam of a Barbary Coast brothel found the girl on the streets, hungry and alone. The madam felt sorry for the poor girl, who was only a child herself. She took her in and cared for her. The girl gave birth to her baby in the brothel. When the child was only a few hours old, the young mother died of the birthing fever. The madam wanted to keep the baby, to raise him as her own. But the authorities heard about the child. They came and took him away from her. The infant was placed in an orphans' asylum." The Lady in Black paused and looked at Kay.

Kay said softly, "Nick was the baby." It was a statement, not a question.

"Yes."

"And you were . . ."

"The madam," the Lady in Black calmly confirmed. Then she smiled wistfully and added, "I was not the kind of woman you are, Captain. There was a time when I was."

"I'm not judging you."

The Lady in Black patted Kay's tightly clenched hands. "I know that, dear." She sighed, picked up her teacup, and took a sip.

"So Nick grew up in the orphanage?" Kay wanted to hear more.

The Lady in Black made a face. "The worst place you could ever imagine. An old rat-infested building, cold and damp in the winter, stifling hot in the summer. The children who lived there were shown no love or affection. They were punished severely for the slightest infraction and sent to bed many a night without a bite to eat."

Kay said nothing. She listened raptly while the Lady in Black told of a sweet, sad, dark-haired baby boy who grew into a tough, rebellious street youth.

"Nick was a little demon. Brash, older than his years, stubborn. He was a scamp, but so often boys do things out of high spirits, not viciousness. Those who ran the orphanage didn't see it like that. Nick ran away again and again. Each time he was caught, sent back, and punished. He ran away for the last time when he was just fourteen. When they came after him, he told them they'd have to kill him to take him back. And he meant it.

"Even at that young age Nick was cocky and handsome, and it wasn't long until he was dealing faro at one of the Barbary Coast clubs."

The Lady in Black beamed with pride as she talked about Nick. It was easy to see that in her eyes, there was no wrong he could do.

"Nick grew up hard and alone. He learned to depend on no one but himself. A ragtag youth who found his place with the fancy girls and sporting clubs. He's a devil-may-care saloon owner who was reared in the gutters in poverty, seasoned on the streets of the Barbary Coast. With his charm, his poise, his looks, women don't stand a chance." She smiled and added fondly, "Yet there was a little boy—always—in everything he did. In everything he does."

The Lady in Black laughed suddenly, a warm, musical sound coming from deep down in her throat. "From the time he was seventeen or eighteen Nick was known as the bad boy of the Barbary Coast, successful in spite of his obstinate ways."

The Lady in Black paused and Kay mused aloud, "He can certainly be very stubborn."

Again the Lady laughed. "My dear, he tells me the same thing about you."

"Nick talks to you about me?"

"Now, don't look so troubled. Nick admires you; if he didn't, he wouldn't speak so highly of you. He wouldn't speak of you at all. Underneath that tough exterior, Nick is a kind, caring man. He's a very soft-hearted person, but he tries to hide it."

This time it was Kay who laughed. "And very successfully, I might add." Then: "The children at Battery Place?"

"Ah, yes. Little Joey. He gave the boy a puppy and . . . and . . . if I reveal even more about Nick, you must promise to keep it to yourself."

"I promise."

"As I've told you, Nick was put in that miserable old orphans' asylum." Kay nodded. "Well, when Nick grew up and became a prosperous man with his own club, he came to see me one day. He was all excited—like a little boy. He had a big roll of blueprints under his arm, which he promptly spread out on the floor." Her dark eyes flashed with the recollection. "He laid right down on his stomach and motioned me to do the same. Now, who could resist Nick? I stretched out beside him in the floor and listened while he pointed out all the planned rooms of the fine orphanage he was going to build. Just as soon, he said, as he'd saved another fifty thousand."

"Battery Place," Kay said.

"Battery Place," the Lady in Black confirmed. "His excitement rubbed off. I told him I'd be happy to donate fifty thousand toward the project." She laughed and said, "You know what that scamp's reply was? His exact words?"

"Tell me," Kay was smiling.

"He nudged me with one of those muscular shoulders, winked, and said, 'You're in for fifty, darlin', but you must agree to my terms. No one is ever to know I had anything to do with building the orphanage.'"

Kay shook her head. "So Nick McCabe built Battery Place and he doesn't want anyone to know?"

"Nick is as ashamed of his good deeds as you'd be of your sins. Besides, he's wise to the ways of the Coast, and it is a wisdom learned harshly. He has to stay tough and hard to survive. And always maintain the appearance of being tough and hard."

The fascinating tale was told.

The mystery of the hard, handsome Nick McCabe was solved.

The two women talked the afternoon away. Mostly about Nick. But Camille Kelly also revealed that her great wealth had come from wise and highly profitable investments. It had been twenty-two years ago that she'd left the Barbary Coast for this Russian Hill mansion. She laughed and said that perhaps in another twenty-two years—if she lived that long—she might finally be accepted by society.

She looked Kay in the eye and said, "I suppose if you had known what I once was you wouldn't have called."

Kay didn't hesitate to answer. "I'm not the least bit concerned with what you once were, Miss Kelly. You're a kind-hearted person who helped provide a good home for unfortunate children. I hope you'll allow me to visit again."

The Lady in Black smiled, genuinely pleased. "No wonder Nick finds you so enchanting."

Kay perfectly arched eyebrows shot up. "Nick said that?"

The smile left Camille's face. "Captain, I've said far too much already. Nick would have my head if he knew. It's not for me to open up his heart to you. He'll have to do that himself."

"Do you think"—Kay lowered her eyes—"is there any chance of Nick ever opening his heart to anyone?"

"His is a fragile heart, Kay. A fragile heart with a hard protective shell around it. But a little red-headed boy seems to have found the key to unlock that heart. Who knows? Maybe a pretty red-headed Salvation Army captain could be equally successful."

"Yes," Kay said, lifting her gaze to meet the older woman's. "He cares for Joey, maybe he . . ." She left the rest unsaid. "I must go."

She rose from the sofa. Camille Kelly stood up.

Fingering the worn gold watch pinned to her bosom, she said, "Nick gave me this watch. He bought it with the first money he ever earned on his own. He was fourteen, bless his heart. The watch is twenty-one years old. I have safes filled with diamonds, emeralds, and rubies. I'd let them all go before I'd part with this watch."

"You must love Nick very much."

"As if he were my flesh and blood," said Camille Kelly. "Can you understand that?"

Kay thought instantly of Joey. "Yes, I can. To you Nick will always be *your* own sweet, adorable little boy."

Camille Kelly took Kay's hand in hers. "Captain, not only are you charming, you're wise beyond your years. Promise you'll come back to see me."

"Count on it." They started toward the salon door. "Oh, yes, and by the way, belated thanks for bailing me out of jail."

Smiling warmly, the Lady in Black said, "My pleasure, Captain. My pleasure."

Chapter 39

 "Lay out one of my ruffled white shirts. Brush up my evening cape. Set out my gold studs. Tell Jake I'll be down for a haircut."

"Sure thing, boss," said Ling Tan, nodding. "Special occasion, yes?"

"Special occasion, no." Nick's tone of voice was sharp. Without looking up, he gestured the servant away.

Ling Tan made a face and hurried into the bedroom to prepare Nick's clothes for the evening.

Shirtless, his hair disheveled, Nick sprawled in his black leather easy chair. He'd been there since returning from Battery Place earlier in the afternoon.

His long legs were stretched out fully, his stockinged feet resting on the ottoman. He needed a shave, and the darkly whiskered jaws and chin made him look mean and disagreeable. His mood matched his appearance.

Nick leaned forward and picked up a brandy snifter. He took a deep swallow, then held the glass tightly against his naked chest. Lids low over cold gray eyes, he stared unseeing out the window at the gloomy fog blanketing the bay.

"What bothering you, boss?" Ling Tan pattered back into the sitting room, busily brushing Nick's black silk top hat.

Nick didn't look up. "Nothing."

Ling Tan lifted his thin shoulders. "Not true. Don't believe it. Sit two hours, drink, look grim. Something wrong. Something bad wrong."

Nick's cold silver-gray eyes finally lifted. "Can't a man relax in his own home and have one brandy before dinner?"

Ling Tan clicked his tongue against the roof of his mouth. "Supposed have brandy *after* dinner. Not supposed—"

"Finished laying out my clothes?" Nick interrupted, his dark face reflecting his less-than-agreeable disposition. He set the brandy down, reached into the pocket of his faded denim trousers. He took out a solid gold money clip in the shape of a dollar sign, peeled off a fifty, thrust it at Ling Tan. "Have a hired rig pick me up promptly at seven P.M."

"Now I remember. You take Miss Packard to theater this evening," said Ling Tan, stuffing the bill into the pocket of his loose silk kimono-jacket. "But no really want to. Is that it?"

"Go!" Nick bellowed, and pointed to the door.

"I going. Chop chop."

Alone, Nick poured another brandy, swirled it around in the balloon snifter, and stared into its amber depths.

He *didn't* want to go. He didn't want to take Adele Packard to the theater. He didn't want to take Adele Packard anywhere. He didn't want to spend the evening at Adele Packard's place. He didn't want to see Adele Packard.

Nick exhaled loudly.

He wanted to see Captain Kay Montgomery.

He wanted Kay here, in his apartment again, in his arms again. Just like last night.

Nick shook his head, disgusted with himself. He had lain awake half of last night thinking about Kay Montgomery. He'd sat around all morning thinking about Kay Montgomery. Well, he sure as hell wouldn't hang around here all night thinking about Kay Montgomery.

There was one sure way to get a woman out of your mind.

Get another woman.

Nick tossed off the last of his brandy and set the empty glass aside. He lowered his stockinged feet to the floor, ran a hand through his disheveled hair, and rose. He stretched up onto his toes, came back down, and absently scratched his bare belly.

What he needed was a haircut, a bath, and a shave. Then an evening spent hobnobbing with the city's swells before taking the lovely Adele Packard to her mansion for a night of enjoyable lovemaking.

On leaving the Lady in Black's Russian Hill palace, Kay flew down the hill. She could hardly wait to get the Golden Carousel.

To get to Nick.

With any luck she'd reach the club around seven P.M., well before it opened for the evening. Nick would be upstairs in his apartment. Alone.

Kay smiled and charged faster down the steep steps leading to the foot of Russian Hill. The heels of her sensible black shoes tapping on the wooden steps, she descended breathlessly, her thoughts on the darkly handsome Nick.

Knowing what she now knew, it was so much easier to forgive him for past sins. What chance had he had to be anything other than what he was? Wouldn't she herself have turned out differently if not for the kind, loving parents who'd guided her? Just look at Curly's slip. And he'd had all the advantages. Yes, it was now easy to understand and to forgive, to excuse his endearingly naughty behavior.

Nick was lovable and funny even when he was a louse. When he was charming, as he'd been last night at Hurricane Gussie's, he was without equal.

And when he was passionate . . . when his beautiful silver eyes filled with warmth and his smooth, perfectly sculpted lips . . .

Kay shivered, then giggled aloud.

Scolding herself immediately, she vowed there'd be no repeat of last night's lovemaking. A Salvation Army captain should never have allowed a Barbary Coast saloon owner to hold her in his arms and kiss her the way Nick had kissed her. It had been imprudent for her to listen to him boldly murmur "I want you" without rebuking him soundly.

It wouldn't happen again. She wouldn't let it. But she didn't distrust Nick. Not now. Not when she could so clearly see the little lost boy who was the young Nick. Alone and afraid; surviving as best he could, learning to guard his heart from hurt, when all he had ever needed or wanted was to be loved.

The late-afternoon fog was very dense as Kay approached the Carousel Club. It swirled thick and heavy around her so that she had to carefully pick her way down the street. When she reached the intersection of Pacific and Grant, she stepped down from the sidewalk, took a couple of steps, then jumped back in alarm.

Kay barely escaped being run down by an approaching carriage. Her heart in her throat, she clung to the cold steel of a lamppost as a fancy rig came around the corner. The driver never spotted her through the fog. She got only a fleeting glimpse of carriage's top-hatted passenger.

Kay never suspected that the passenger was Nick.

Nick sat back in the carriage, knees wide apart, eyes staring straight ahead. He didn't see the uniformed woman clinging to the lamppost.

Nick never knew that Kay stood on the fog-shrouded street corner.

The carriage passed.

Kay flew across Pacific Street.

She tried the black leather front doors of the Golden Carousel. Both were bolted. She scurried to the side of the white stucco building and slipped down the alley to the back service entrance. She rang the bell and waited.

Angel Thompson, wearing her skimpy sequined show costume, threw open the door. The statuesque brunette nodded to the slender redhead.

"Well, hello, Captain. Come on in. What can we do for you?" the dancer said to the soldier.

"Hello, Miss Thompson." Kay stepped inside. "Where's Ling Tan?"

"He took his daughter to the library to study," said Angel Thompson. "He feels there's always the threat of the Shadow Clan."

"Yes, of course. Nick? Is he here?"

Angel Thompson shrugged bare shoulders. "How would I know? Go on up and find out for yourself."

"Thank you. I believe I will."

Kay rushed up the stairs and banged on Nick's apartment door, her heart drumming in her ears, her breath short. No answer. She knocked repeatedly before giving up. Disappointed, she went back down the stairs. Determined not to leave without seeing him, she decided to wait.

Kay put a placid smile on her face and stepped through the curtained door into the dim club. Several of the Carousel girls sat around the bar, sipping punch, gossiping, laughing.

"Captain Kay," they warmly greeted her, "come join us!"

"How's the soul-saving business these days?" asked one.

"Have a drink," teased another.

Kay joined the girls. Out of breath from her long, fast trek, her throat dry, Kay said, "I am a little thirsty. I'd sure be grateful for some chilled juice." She glanced at the tall glass Angel Thompson held and said, "That grape juice you're drinking, Angel. It looks delicious."

Angel looked at her glass, looked at Kay, and began to smile naughtily. "Why, yes, Captain. Grape juice punch. That's exactly what it is. Shall I pour you one?"

The girls laughed gaily. Kay laughed with them and said, "Yes, please. Sounds very refreshing."

"Oh, Captain, it is," said the dimpled, heavily rouged Trixie Davis, and the girls laughed again.

Angel slid behind the bar to do the honor. Or the dishonorable. The grape juice she fixed for the unsuspecting Army captain was actually Pisco punch. A popular drink around San Francisco, its flavor—and its potency—made it the *crème de la crème* of beverages. The base was Pisco brandy, distilled from the grape known as *La Rosa del Perú*.

Perfectly colorless, fragrant, very seductive, terribly strong, it had a pleasing flavor with a fruity taste. The Carousel girls liked to sip it mixed with fruit juice.

Angel Thompson, turning her back to Kay, splashed a very generous portion of the Pisco punch into a tall glass, then filled the glass to the brim with chilled grape juice. Carefully composing her face, she turned and slid the glass across the bar to Kay.

"Thank you so much." Kay climbed onto a bar stool, picked up the glass, and took a long thirsty sip. "Mmmmm. Delicious," she said, licking her lips.

The girls broke up with laughter. Kay shrugged, took off her bonnet, slapped it down on the bar, and took another invigorating drink of the potent Pisco punch.

The elegantly gowned Adele Packard leaned over to Nick in the darkness of the ornate theater box and softly scolded him.

"Darling, can't you at least pretend interest in Miss Bernhardt's brilliant performance as *Joan of Arc*? Opera glasses all over the auditorium are trained on this box. On the two of us. I won't have people saying that my handsome escort is bored with the great actress. Or with me. After all, this is her farewell performance."

"Thank God," Nick said, forcing a smile and focusing on the stage far below. But the production couldn't hold his interest. Neither could Adele. He was restless. He was bored. He was thinking about Kay.

The curtain finally rang down on the interminably long presentation and Nick gave an inaudible sigh of relief. He stood up, helped Adele to her feet, and endured the obligatory after-the-show visiting with the gentry in the theater lobby. The endless gossip. The false enthusiasm. The supposed humor. The empty flattery. He hated it.

At last the chattering first nighters spilled out onto the sidewalks, Nick and Adele with them. Nick drew a deep breath of the fresh night air into his lungs. The hired carriage rolled up and he practically shoved Adele inside, eager to be gone.

She took it as a sign that he could hardly wait to be alone with her. She was overjoyed. Waving one last time to her friends outside Baldwins Theater, she turned, smiled seductively at Nick, and said, "Darling, you're as anxious as I. Just you wait until I get you alone. I've a deliciously naughty surprise for you."

Nick could only imagine what her surprise might be, but was certain it had to do with pleasingly unconventional lovemaking. Good! That's just what he needed. A night of wild eroticism with a woman who was more than willing do anything and everything to excite and satisfy both him and herself.

Eager to put himself in the mood for the upcoming carnal escapades, Nick drew Adele close and kissed her soundly on the lips.

Adele was thrilled. Her handsome lover couldn't wait to kiss her. She was doubly delighted that his impatient show of desire had been witnessed by the glittering theater crowd, waiting for their carriages. It electrified her to know that her envious friends saw Nick McCabe hungrily kissing her. She hoped they were sick with jealousy knowing she was going home to lie naked in Nick's arms.

When Nick ended the half-brutal kiss, Adele threw back her blond head and laughed happily. She quickly turned to wave one last good-bye to her friends, then shrugged her snow-white ermine cape off her bare shoulders.

As the carriage drew away from the curb and into the street, Adele dropped the coach's curtains and drew the shimmering skirts of her white evening gown up over her knees to her creamy thighs. Her daring French underwear was nothing more than sheer stockings, white satin garters, and wispy white lace that concealed none of her feminine charms. Laughing, she bunched the exquisite gown up around her waist and agilely climbed astride Nick's lap.

Wrapping her white-gloved hands around his neck, Adele urged his dark head back against the claret velvet seat, kissed him wetly, and whispered, "Darling, I'm going to get you so hot on the way home, you'll tear my evening gown off as soon as we get inside."

"I hope so," Nick said truthfully.

"I guarantee it," Adele murmured, and with total confidence went to work on him.

Chapter 40

 "Slim, I'll have another punch!" Kay slammed her empty glass down on the polished bar and motioned to the thin, sunken-cheeked bartender.

Slim was worried. His brow puckering, he said, "Captain, you'd be wise to exercise a bit of caution with that punch." He wrapped thin fingers around her empty glass. "How about a cup of black coffee?"

Kay's blue eyes twinkled. She smiled at the barkeep who had just come on duty. She reached out and playfully snapped the black garter encircling his white shirt sleeve. Then, shaking her head, she ordered in a loud voice, "Another punch, if you please, and make it snappy!" Kay giggled then, feeling inexplicably giddy and light-headed.

"You heard the captain," Angel Thompson, sitting on the stool next to Kay, said to the nervous Slim. "The lady's still thirsty."

"She may well be," said Slim, "but I'm not serving a Salvation Army captain another—"

"All right." Angel cut him off in midsentence. She shoved her own glass across the bar and said, "I'm thirsty myself. Give me a tall, refreshing Pisco punch."

Slim made a face, but served the brunette dancer. Angel Thompson smiled prettily at Slim, waited until he turned away to fill another drink order, then slid her glass in front of Kay.

"You look like you need this more than I, Captain," she said. "Bottoms up."

"Why, thank you, Angel," Kay said with genuine gratitude. She eagerly wrapped her hand around the chilled glass and lifted it to her lips. She smiled foolishly, took a drink, set the glass back on the bar. She ran the tip of her forefinger around the glass's rim and sighed. "Slim seems adamant about my not—"

"Pay no attention to Slim," said the dimpling Trixie, seated on Kay's other side. "He's such a tightwad. Why, you'd think he paid for the punch!" Trixie winked at Angel.

Kay nodded and took another swallow. Quite suddenly she became aware of conversations extraordinary to the one in which she was involved. She swiveled about on her bar stool and blinked in surprise to see that the spacious club was filling with people.

She was beginning to have a little difficulty focusing. She wondered why. And she wondered why people were pouring into the club at this early hour. Wasn't it just past seven P.M.? Didn't the Carousel Club always wait until straight up eight to open its black double doors?

Shrugging, Kay swiveled back to the bar.

She'd best drink down her punch and be on her way. For some unexplained reason customers were being admitted early. It wouldn't be wise to have club patrons see her sitting at the bar. They might get the wrong impression. They might even think that she was drinking alcoholic beverages.

Smiling at such an absurdity, Kay picked up her glass and took a long, thirsty pull.

"Mmmmm, mmmmm," she murmured, then set the glass down and wiped her lips on the sleeve of her blue uniform jacket. She tapped the brunette Angel Thompson on her bare shoulder and said, "Thanks again for giving me your punch."

"Glad to do it," said the smiling dancer.

"You're an angel, Angel," Kay said, slurring her words slightly, listing to one side atop her bar stool. She grinned and repeated, "Yessiree, you're an angel, Angel." She slammed her fist down on the bar for emphasis and went into peals of laughter.

Laughing gaily, she whipped her head around. To Trixie she said, "Did you know that Angel is an angel? And . . . an angel is Angel! Or is it . . . Angel is an—"

"Whatever," Trixie interrupted, laughing. "Tell you what, stay right where you are and we'll get you another punch in half an hour." With that, Dixie slid off the bar stool. So did Angel Thompson and a couple of the other entertainers.

"Wait! Why, where's everyone going?" Kay asked, puzzled.

Even as she spoke, music from the hidden pit band began to play, the melodic strains drifting across the big room. A smattering of applause and a few loud whistles went up from the growing crowd. Lights throughout the club began to dim.

Kay blinked, wondering at the sudden darkness. She heard a faint noise above. She leaned her head back and looked up. Squinting, she saw the darkened steam carousel above the hexagonal bar had begun to slowly drop down from the two-story-high ceiling.

When the golden merry-go-round stopped its descent, it was directly over the two bartenders' heads.

Seconds passed.

A low buzz went through the room. Then a collective gasp as all at once the Golden Carousel was flooded with light. On the back of each golden mount was a Carousel girl in glittering sequins. The exquisitely sculpted bodies of the carved wooden horses and the exquisitely formed bodies of the women astride were bathed in incandescence.

The golden creatures began to slowly move up and down. The sequined women began to spur and quirt. The shimmering horses moved slowly around the circle. The mounted ladies waved gaily to the crowds below.

Lips parted in wonder, Kay stared unblinking.

She watched the crowd-pleasing spectacle with unabashed fascination. She was enthralled. Mesmerized by the beautiful gleaming mounts going up and down and around the circle, prancing gracefully in gliding rhythm with the music. Never taking her eyes from the revolving golden carousel, Kay lifted her glass and drank. Then drank again.

She became uncomfortably warm.

Her gaze riveted to the magical carousel, she impatiently flipped open the brass buttons going down the center of her blue uniform jacket. She shrugged it off her shoulders, stretched her arms out full length at her sides, and allowed the hot, cumbersome jacket to slide to the floor.

Kay was barely aware of the noise and loud talk around her. Eight o'clock had come and gone and so had nine, but she was unaware. The prospect of customers spotting her seated at the bar strangely no longer troubled her.

Nothing troubled her.

This was not a Barbary Coast saloon. This was a lovely fairyland filled with beautiful music and silvery light and golden horses. The music, the light, the moving merry-go-round cast a powerful spell. Her head seemed to spin with the carousel, but pleasantly so. It was if she were looking into a giant kaleidoscope that exhibited ever changing symmetrical patterns of color, light, and beauty.

Kay was completely snared, caught up in a web of wonder.

Entranced, she began to feel that it wasn't enough to remain just a spectator to the dazzling sights and sounds.

She wanted to become a part of it.

It didn't work.

Despite all Adele Packard's best efforts to arouse Nick so fully he'd tear her gown off and take her before they reached her mansion, she wasn't successful.

The fact he could so easily resist her worried Adele. And when Adele was worried, she became annoyed. And when she was annoyed, she lashed out the person or persons responsible for her displeasure.

But Adele was a very wise woman. Sensing that some underlying problem was bothering Nick, she held her tongue. But her worry remained. So did her irritation.

There had been a time not so long ago when Nick McCabe would have responded to her attempts at seduction quite differently. Well, he'd respond that way again before the night ended. She had a few tricks left up her sleeve. She wasn't about to let the best lover she'd ever had slip away.

When the hired carriage rolled up before the Nob Hill mansion, Adele hugged Nick's arm and whispered, "Dismiss your driver, darling. Spend the night."

"Not this time," Nick said. He stepped across her and out of the carriage, then turned to assist her. "I need to get back to the club."

His refusal to stay the night further worried Adele Packard. Further irritated her.

But she smiled, certain she could change his mind. "Very well. A nightcap then?"

"All right," Nick said.

Inside the lighted mansion, Adele led Nick into the smaller of two downstairs drawing rooms. Lamps were turned low. The fireplace glowed with dying embers. Shadows dominated the room. A long beige sofa faced the fireplace.

"Darling, pour yourself a drink while I freshen up," Adele said.

"Adele, I'm not staying—"

"Be back in ten minutes."

She hurried from the room. Nick exhaled wearily. He splashed some cognac into a couple of snifters and carried them to the fireplace. He set one glass atop the marble mantel and held the other in his palm. Drinking the brandy, he stood staring into the low-burning fire. He picked up a poker and stabbed at the ashen logs.

A burst of flame leapt to new life and Nick, looking at the sudden colorful blaze, was instantly reminded of a brilliant head of flaming red hair whipping in the strong sea breezes on Seal Beach.

Nick ground his teeth.

He returned the poker to its stand, took a drink of the brandy, and turned his back to the fire. It was there he stood when Adele swept back into the shadowy room. She wore a long nightgown of midnight-blue satin. The slithery fabric hugged her curves like a second skin. Her hair had been unbound and brushed, it fell in silvery-white glory around her face and down her back.

She swayed directly to Nick, invitation explicit in every movement of her supple body. She was immediately disappointed. She saw no fire leap into his eyes, heard no sharp intake of air. He didn't reach for her, crush her to him. She felt almost panicky.

"Sweetheart," she cooed, stepping up before him, "are you ready for your surprise?" She wet her lips with the pink tip of her tongue. "Don't you remember, I promised you a surprise?"

"Look, I'm a little tired and—"

"You did forget, you naughty boy. But I forgive you," she said, shaking her long platinum hair back off her face. "Now, undress, darling, and stretch out on the sofa."

"You're not listening," Nick said, shaking his head.

"When you're naked, know what I'm going to do to you?" She laughed low in her throat. "I'm going to show you the surprise. It's going to be *sweet* fun, darling. I'll get some whipped cream from the—"

"No, Adele." There was a finality in Nick's tone of voice.

"No? Just like that, no? Have you suddenly become a prude?"

"No."

"Then what is it?" She stepped back and glared at him. "You no longer desire me?"

"I didn't say that."

"Have you any idea how many men want me? Do you?" Her voice had lifted.

"Dozens, I'm sure," said Nick, his tone flat.

"Can you imagine how many of those gentlemen would give up everything they own for me!" Her hands went to her satin-clad hips. "And you stand there and tell you're not interested?" She was almost shouting now, her voice shrill.

"That's not exactly what I said, but I suppose you're right. I'm not particularly interested in playing foolish games tonight." He shrugged wide shoulders.

Adele's eyes snapped with anger. "It's not the games! It's me, isn't it! You've been distant all evening, damn you. What's the matter? What's on your mind?"

"Nothing. Nothing at all."

"Oh, really? Well, there's something on my mind, come to think of it." She folded her arms across her heaving chest. "I saw you yesterday with that skinny, red-haired Salvation Army soldier. I've told Pat, now I'll tell you, I won't have it."

"Excuse me?" said Nick, glints of light suddenly appearing in his silver-gray eyes.

"You're to have nothing more to do with Kay Montgomery!" Adele's nostrils quivered with rage. "I simply won't allow my brother or my lover to be seen with that woman! What were you doing with her anyway, answer me that!"

Nick didn't answer. He just smiled coldly, turned, and set his brandy glass on the mantel.

"You look at me, Nick McCabe," Adele spat. "Yesterday afternoon Pat and I went for a drive. We happened down by the Barbary Coast and I saw you at some sort of open-air meeting with those heathen zealots. You stood there with Kay Montgomery! Or do you deny it?"

"Nope."

Adele's face flushed with new anger. "So? You *were* with her! What were you doing there? Why were you with her? How long were the two of you together? Were you ever alone with her?"

Very calmly Nick said, "I was there listening to Alfred Duke's first sermon. I was with Captain Kay because I wanted to be with her. How long were we together? Let's see, the rest of the afternoon. Then I took her out to dinner. Alone. And afterward we went back to my—"

"Stop! Don't tell me! I don't want to hear it! Never let it happen again, you hear me, Nick McCabe?" Adele was shouting now. "You're not to see her again."

For a long moment Nick looked at the raging woman, incredulous. Then he smiled and for the first time that evening the smile was completely genuine. For weeks he'd been considering ways to graciously end the relationship with Adele Packard. Now she was giving him the golden opportunity.

"Is that an order?" he said, his voice low and level.

"It most certainly is and you will obey!"

Nick's smile stayed in place when he said, "My dear, while you may well be within your rights to strongly request that your baby brother not see Kay again, you've got the wrong boy here. I never did take to being bossed about, much less by a woman. Not even one as beautiful as you." He touched her bloodred cheek, bid her good night, and stepped past her.

"Wait! Nick—" Adele caught his arm. "You're not leaving!"

"You're wrong, Adele." Nick disengaged her clutching fingers from his tuxedo sleeve. "That's exactly what I'm doing." He walked away.

"You bastard!" Adele Packard screeched. "You vile bastard! Come back here right now!"

Nick continued to walk unhurriedly toward the door. Panicky, Adele was tempted to fly after him. Her pride wouldn't allow it. She was a Packard. She couldn't quite bring herself to grovel at the feet of a low-life saloon keeper. "Go then and don't ever come back! You don't belong here in my home. You're trash, McCabe! Barbary Coast riffraff! That's all you ever were, all you'll ever be! Get out of my sight!"

Nick made no reply.

He left the drawing room with Adele screaming curses at him. At the door he calmly collected his cape and top hat and exited the mansion. Driving away, Nick didn't bother to look back. He felt no loss. He felt nothing but a sense of relief.

Unwinding, Nick lounged back in the carriage and considered how he'd spend the rest of his evening. He lit a cigar, puffed it slowly to life, and decided a good night's rest might be his best bet. Tuesday nights were generally quiet at the Carousel. No need for him to hang around downstairs.

Nick flicked his smoked-down cigar away when the carriage rolled up before the Golden Carousel. He draped his cape over his arm, plunked his top hat down on his head, and stepped out into the night.

On the sidewalk in front of the club, he heard shouts and whistles coming from inside. Nick reached the heavy black leather doors, pulled one open, and walked in. A crush of people stood on the marble apron entrance. Puzzled, Nick squeezed through the crowd and saw immediately why they were standing. All the tables were taken.

The club was jammed. Filled to overflowing. Standing room only and very little of that. The crowd was loud and boisterous. They were cheering and whistling and clapping. The air was charged with uncommon excitement.

The band was playing, but the bartenders were not serving. The singers were not singing. The waiters were waiting. And watching something.

Every eye was turned heavenward.

Nick's narrowed gaze lifted to the Golden Carousel and its riders. The flash of gold, the sparkle of sequins, the flaunting of flesh; nothing was out of the ordinary.

And then *she* rode into view.

Chapter 41

Mounted astride a glittering gilt horse, Captain Kay Montgomery clung to the reins with one hand, waved madly to the crowd with the other. Unbound, her flaming red hair streamed down her back and around her shoulders, the fiery tresses gleaming in the light as if burnished. Her full, moist lips were parted in a brilliant smile, and her luminous blue eyes flashed with unveiled excitement.

Gone was her uniform jacket. Her starched white blouse was open at the throat and the sleeves were rolled up to her elbows. Her long blue skirts were pushed carelessly up past her knees. Unconcerned, she flaunted a pair of long, shapely legs encased in white cotton stockings. She wore no shoes. Her stockinged feet were thrust deep into the gold-and-white stirrups, toes curled, knees hugging the golden steed's body.

It was easy to see that Captain Kay Montgomery was inebriated.

At once stunned and infatuated, Nick stared at the laughing, red-tressed beauty. His gaze resting solely on her, he momentarily forgot there was anyone else around. For a long moment no one existed but him and the incredibly appealing woman astride the golden pony.

Bathed in the light, her white flesh gleamed gold and her wild hair blazed like silken fire. Her slender, lissome body in all its feline beauty aroused an instant passion in Nick. To see her up there with her legs parted and hugging the wooden horse made him wonder how it would feel to have those long, lovely legs wrapped around him.

Nick slowly became aware that everyone in the crowded club was watching Kay ride on the carousel just as he was. Hot-eyed men eagerly ogled her, leering smiles on their flushed faces. Whistles and shouts and lewd gestures were directed at her.

Nick's face hardened.

He charged through the throng, pushing people out of his way, crossing the crowded club with long, determined strides.

Above on the spinning merry-go-round, Kay's blue skirts rose provocatively higher. A flash of creamy thigh above the gartered top of a white stocking brought a roar of approval from beaming male spectators. Unbothered, Kay laughed merrily and began to sing along with the music. In a sweet, clear voice she sang with great gusto the rousing words to "There Is a Tavern in the Town."

Stone-faced, Nick swiftly cut through the crowd, agilely mounted the hexagonal bar, reached out, and commandingly plucked Kay from the horse's back. Kay blinked at Nick in happy surprise and wrapped her arms around his neck.

"Nicky, Nicky!" she squealed. "You've come home at last! I waited for you."

Nick said nothing. Dexterously he swirled his evening cape over Kay, covering her completely, while she went back to singing, slurring the lyric, "And there my true love sits him down . . . sits him downnn . . ."

With her in his arms, Nick leapt down off the bar. He stalked purposefully across the club, the look on his face scattering patrons from his path. The disappointed crowd loudly voiced their displeasure. Shouts of "Don't take her away" and "McCabe, you're spoiling all the fun" followed the pair.

But nobody tried to stop Nick McCabe.

Nick headed straight for the wide marble staircase. Taking the stairs two at a time, he carried Kay straight up to his apartment as she continued to laugh and sing merrily. She fought a hand free of the covering cape. Reaching up, she playfully plucked Nick's top hat from his head and set it on her own.

At the door of Nick's apartment she reached out and helpfully turned the knob, willing and eager to go inside with him. Nick walked through, nudged the door shut with his shoulder, turned and leaned back against it holding Kay in his arms.

Having a little trouble focusing, Kay looked at Nick and smiled. She raised a hand and touched his bottom lip with her forefinger.

"Nicky, do you have any of that delicious punch up here?" she said. "I'm terribly thirsty."

"You've had enough punch."

"Have I?" She made a face, then impetuously ripped the top hat from her head and sailed it across the room, laughing when it came to rest squarely atop a darkened lamp's glass globe.

"Sweetheart, you're soused," Nick said, slowly lowering her to her feet.

"No! Why, all I drank was punch. But who cares anyway?" She flung her arms out wide, shrugging his long evening cape off her shoulders. It fell forgotten to the carpet. "Do you care, Nicky?" She threw her arms around his neck and teasingly ran a white-stockinged toe up his shin beneath his trouser leg.

"No." Nick's hands spanned her narrow waist. A muscle danced in his lean jaw. "No, baby, I don't care."

Slowly his hands slid up Kay's rib cage to her underarms. He drew her up on tiptoe and waited to see if she'd protest. Try to wiggle free. She didn't. Kay lingered in that position, poised perfectly in place, gazing into Nick's eyes with unmistakable invitation. When she heard his sharp intake of breath, she tipped her head back and laughed.

Nick bent and kissed her laughing mouth.

Kay stopped laughing.

She kissed him back and in her kiss was such bold recklessness it instantly put ideas in Nick's head, ideas that excited him but at the same time bothered him. He envisioned the two of them naked in the firelight, making uninhibited love all night. But along with the pleasing vision was nagging concern.

Kay sighed softly and tightened her arms around Nick's neck. She leaned forward and her breasts swelled against the fabric of her blouse. Nick deepened the kiss. Turning his head to the side, he slanted his mouth across hers, molding her lips to his, coaxing her, teaching her how to kiss. Eagerly Kay responded, offering herself to him with sweet blind trust.

Nick sagged back against the solid door, moved his feet apart, and drew Kay closer. His hands caressing her back, her waist, her hips, he pressed her soft pliant body to the hard ungiving contours of his own.

His blood ran hot. His need for her grew with every thundering heartbeat. The feel of her—beneath his lips, under his hands, against his body—was quickly turning pleasant yearning into dangerous desire.

If Nick was becoming helplessly aroused, Kay was equally carried away. She kissed him with urgent, almost violent intensity, her wet, willing mouth open wide, her tongue seeking his. She thrilled to the hot lips moving so masterfully on hers. She delighted in the gentle hands so expertly caressing her. She marveled at the power, the hardness, and the heat of the tall male frame against which she was so intimately crushed.

At last Nick tore his flaming lips from hers. He laid his head back against the door and closed his eyes. He felt Kay's breath, warm and stirring, against his skin. She pressed her lips to the hollow at the base of his throat and whispered his name.

Nick shuddered.

His heart thudded and his belly tightened.

He wanted her.

Forget the bet, he wanted Kay with a powerful longing. He wanted her with an intensity he hadn't felt for a woman in years. She intoxicated him. She challenged him. She frightened him. She awakened in him something he'd thought had left him and was forever dead. That bashful, boyish longing to be her beau, to court her.

That sweet, hot burning of youth.

Nick trembled.

He cursed himself for what he was about to do. What he wanted to do so badly he could taste it. He wanted to make love to Kay. He was going to make love to Kay. The time was now. Tonight he'd have her. To hell with tomorrow.

She filled him with an indescribable excitement. He meant to explore all the sensual mysteries and delights awaiting them. He was determined to forget her virtue, to disregard decency.

Opening his eyes, he wrapped a hand around the back of Kay's head and began kissing her again. And while he kissed her, Nick unfastened the buttons going down the front of her blouse. Kay followed his lead. With Nick kissing her eyes, her ears, her chin, she managed to open his white shirt and push it apart. She raked her nails down from a flat brown nipple to the waistband of his trousers.

Again Nick shuddered. And holding her close by her long, silken hair, he shrugged off his tuxedo jacket and white dress shirt, rolling his shoulders away from the door so the discarded clothing could fall to the floor. Then pressing worshipful kisses to Kay's flushed face, he peeled Kay's open blouse down her arms and off.

Her chemise was of plain unbleached cotton, but she couldn't have looked more beautiful had she been wearing satin and lace. Her pale shoulders and bare slender arms were as exquisite as her elegant throat. And the firm, high breasts that rose and fell rapidly beneath the bodice of cotton chemise were perfectly formed, the nipples outlined and erect.

Nick swallowed hard, smiled at Kay, cupped her glowing face in both his hands and said, "Sweetheart, you're so beautiful. I want you more than you can possibly imagine."

He drew her close again. Kay sighed, wrapped her arms around his bare back, and laid her cheek on his naked chest.

"I've always thought you're the most beautiful man I've ever seen," she said. "Now I know you're a gentle, caring one as well."

His fingertips playing across her delicate shoulder blades, his lips in her hair, Nick murmured, "I don't know about that, baby, but I'll take good care of you."

"I know you will," she said. "I know . . . I found out about Joey and Battery Place—and all the rest." She squeezed him more tightly. "Oh, Nicky, show me how to make you happy."

"Honey, I don't know what you think you've learned about me, but I'm the same man you've known all along."

"Really?"

"Really."

"Baby, I don't care," Kay said, smiling teasingly, mimicking him. "All I know is that you want me and I want you." She turned her face inward, rose again on tiptoe, and pressed a kiss to curve of his neck and shoulder. "Teach me, Nicky. I don't know how to love you but I want to learn."

Nick sighed wearily.

His bare shoulders slumped back against the door.

He couldn't do it. He couldn't take this sweet trusting woman to bed. She was undeniably tipsy. More than just tipsy. Face it, she was so drunk she didn't know what she was doing. If she wasn't she wouldn't be there in his arms. Nick could be domineering, even brutal with the women in his life, but this one for some mysterious reason called forth all his better instincts.

To make love to Kay now would be like taking candy from a baby.

And even he wasn't that big a heel. Was he?

Nick gently cupped Kay's bare shoulders, set her back, and looked into her beautiful eyes. "Sweetheart, we can't do this."

"You don't want me." She looked hurt. She leaned toward him and began frantically kissing his chest. "Nicky, I'll make you want me. I will. I will."

"Oh, baby, I do want you." Nick tipped her chin up. "It's not that. I do want you, but . . ." He wrapped his arms tightly around her and rocked her back and forth as if she were a child. "Honey, you're not yourself tonight."

"Yes, I am, I—"

"Shhhh, sweetheart. You don't know what you're saying. Let me take care of you. Relax here in my arms," he said, his voice low, gentle. "Kay, we've a lifetime to make love."

Nick held Kay protectively in his arms and talked to her, soothing her, explaining what had happened. Gently telling her that the punch she'd found so delicious was more than just fruit juice. After a couple of attempts at interrupting, Kay fell silent. She listened but was more interested in the sound of his deep resonant voice than in what he was saying. Charmed by warmth of his chest beneath her cheek and the strong arms that enclosed her, she felt herself becoming totally relaxed. Soon she was yawning sleepily.

Nick kissed her temple and asked if she'd like to lie down. She nodded. He picked Kay up and carried her into his bedroom. The bed had been turned down for the night. A lone lamp burned low on the night table beside it.

Nick sat Kay on her feet, took her arms, and draped them over his shoulders. He reached behind her and unfastened her skirt. He found the tape of her petticoat and swept both blue Army skirt and white petticoat down past her hips. He put his hands to her waist, lifted her free of the garments, kicked them aside, and sat her down on the edge of the bed.

Her lids slipping shut over her sleepy eyes, Kay reeled dizzily. Unable to keep her balance, she fell over backward and was instantly asleep. Nick smiled, picked up her discarded clothes, and tossed them over a chair. Then he knelt beside the bed. Patiently he peeled the white cotton stockings down her legs and off her feet. Her bare toes wiggled, she sighed deeply, but she remained fast asleep.

When he rose and stood looking down at her, Nick felt his heart kick painfully against his ribs.

She lay there asleep in his bed wearing nothing but her plain cotton chemise. Her long slender legs were bare and slightly parted. Her tousled red hair was fanned out around her head. Her eyes closed in slumber, the long dark lashes made spiky crescents on her pale cheeks. Her small perfect nose had that cute, impudent tilt. Her full soft lips were slightly parted.

Saved by her own innocence, she slept like a baby.

Nick shook his head and smiled. Gently he lifted her and placed her the right way in the bed so that her head rested on the pillows. He pulled a covering sheet up to her shoulders, turned out the lamp, and whispered in the darkness, "Sweet dreams, baby."

Chapter 42

Kay slept peacefully all night. The sleep of angels.

Nick didn't. He was deviled.

His long body sprawled uncomfortably on the too-short sitting-room sofa, he got very little rest. His hands laced beneath his head, elbows pointed out to the sides, he lay awake in the darkness tortured by the knowledge that Kay was in his bed.

Nick vacillated back and forth through the long, silent hours of sleeplessness.

One minute he'd feel really good about himself. It had been a gallant, sensible decision he'd made to leave the pure, trusting Kay untouched. It was the right thing to do, the only thing to do.

The next minute he'd be questioning his own sanity. He'd have to be nuts to pass up such an opportunity. What did he care if she was Salvation Army captain? She was a woman first, and a warm, willing one. He should just get up, go in the bedroom, strip, crawl into bed, and kiss her awake. And keep on kissing her until . . .

No! Lord, no! He couldn't do that!

And so it went as the long quiet hours ticked away toward morning. Dawn was nearing when finally Nick fell tiredly to sleep. He felt as if he'd slept only a few minutes when bright sunlight streaming through the open curtains awakened him.

Nick's eyes opened. He lifted his head and looked around, momentarily puzzled. Then he remembered. He levered himself up, swung his cramped legs around, and put his feet on the floor.

He was dead tired, yet he tingled with excitement. Kay was in his bedroom. Kay was in his bed. Was she awake? Would she remember last night? Would she be ready to pick up where they'd left off?

Grinning, Nick stood up. Wishing he had a shirt, he rubbed his naked chest and padded toward the bedroom. He paused in the open doorway and looked across at the bed.

He had to grab the door frame for support.

Kay was still sound asleep. Her breathing was slow and even. She'd kicked off the covers during the night. She lay on her back at the bed's center, a hand flung up beside her face, one bare leg slightly raised, knee bent, the other stretched out full length. A strap of the cotton chemise had fallen down her pale shoulder.

She looked like a innocent young girl.

She looked like a dangerously seductive woman.

Nick lifted a hand to his face. A dark stubble of beard covered his jaws and chin. If he had any hopes of spending the morning in bed with her, he'd better clean up before she awakened.

Nick moved catlike across the carpeted bedroom toward the bath. He took a hurried dunk in the tub, washed his hair, and slipped on a pair of clean faded denim trousers. He lathered his face and drew a sharp straight-edge razor over cheeks and chin with quick, gliding strokes.

It was while Nick stood at the bathroom mirror shaving that Kay began to rouse. She awakened with a pounding headache, a queasy stomach, and a dust-dry mouth. And a terrible memory lapse.

She looked anxiously around in an attempt to learn where she was as the lost evening came flashing back to her in bits and pieces. Her face screwing up in a frown of pain and despair, Kay sat up. She was in the middle of a huge white bed in a large dim bedroom. The room was far too big to be her own and the bed was three times the size of hers. And where was her nightgown? Good grief, she was nearly naked!

Holding her throbbing temples, Kay furiously pieced together what she could remember of last night and of the events leading up to it. Eyes squinched shut in concentration, she could recall with vivid clarity the informative afternoon visit with the kind Camille Kelly, the Lady in Black. Then she remembered going straight from the Russian Hill mansion to the Golden Carousel to hunt for Nick. She recalled sitting at the bar with the girls drinking punch and . . . and . . . ohhh, nooooo . . . no . . .

On a dare she had climbed astride one of golden carousel horses! She had ridden on the merry-go-round like . . . like . . . And then . . . then . . . Nick had come. Yes . . . Nick had come and he'd yanked her down off the horse and . . . and . . . he'd carried her upstairs.

Kay's eyes popped wide open and her face drained of color. Now she remembered everything! Heated kisses and caressing hands and shamelessly undressing and . . . and . . .

"Good morning, sweetheart. Feeling a little better?"

Kay's head snapped around. Nick McCabe was coming toward her, smiling, buttoning a fresh shirt. His hair was damp and falling over his forehead and his brown feet were bare. It was obvious. He'd just gotten up and was getting dressed. His appearance confirmed her worst fears.

She had slept with Nick McCabe!

Kay felt she was going to be violently sick.

Her eyes wild, her brain spinning, she frantically grabbed a sheet and covered herself.

"Can I bring you a cup of coffee?" Nick softly inquired. "Maybe something for your head?" He reached the bed.

"Don't come any closer!" Kay warned. Heartsick and ashamed, she behaved the way most human beings do in a similar situation. She lashed out at Nick. "Oh, I can't believe this, I can't. How could I have . . . have . . . and with you . . . you of all . . ."

The easy smile left Nick's face. "Now just calm down and let me—"

"Calm down!" she shrieked. She knee walked across the big bed and leapt up, anxiously clutching the covering sheet to her. "You tell me to calm after what we've . . . after we . . . you and I . . ." She paused for a second and gave him a half-hopeful look, praying he would tell her she was wrong, that nothing had happened. "We did, didn't we?"

"Did what?" Nick cocked his head and looked at her as if puzzled. "What are you asking me?"

It infuriated Kay. "You know exactly what I mean, Nick McCabe! How could you! You knew I was in no condition to . . . you ought to be ashamed of yourself. No gentleman would have—"

"But then you've always known I'm no gentleman," said Nick. "Isn't that the truth?"

"Yes it is! But I had no idea you'd stoop so low as to . . . to . . ." She rolled her eyes heavenward and shook her aching head. "I'll never forgive you for this, McCabe!"

It was a big mistake on Kay's part to say that to a man who had spent a sleepless night of torture because he couldn't bring himself to take advantage of her. It rankled Nick. Made him mad as hell. For once in his life he'd tried to do the right thing and this was his reward. Well, fine. She thought they'd made love. She could just go right on thinking it.

Nick began to smile again.

"Why, honey," he said, his tone one of familiarity, "how can you behave this way after what we've been to each other? After the night we just shared?"

Kay's pale face grew paler still. "Then it's really true? We did . . . you and I actually . . ."

Smiling, Nick had only to nod his head and say nothing more.

Kay's knees buckled at the silent affirmation. She would have sagged to the floor if Nick hadn't reached out to steady her.

"No!" she shouted, and pulled free of his grasp. "Go away. Leave me alone." Distraught, on the verge of hysterics, she cried, "Get out! Get out! Get out!"

Nick got out.

Shrugging his shoulders, he went back into the sitting room to wait. Five minutes later Kay came out to find Nick standing with his back to the cold fireplace holding her shoes and black bonnet in one hand, her uniform jacket in the other.

"May I have my things, please?" she asked.

"Sure." He didn't move. He made her come to him.

Kay stormed across the room, snatched jacket, shoes, and bonnet from him, and didn't linger to put them on. In stockinged feet she hurried out the door as if fleeing Satan himself.

Nick stood there where she'd left him for a long moment silently cursing her. Angry, frustrated, he waited until he was certain she was gone, then he stalked to the open door, stuck his head out, and shouted, "Ling Tan! Ling Tan, where the hell are you?"

"Right here, boss." The Chinese servant came rushing down the hall. "Want breakfast now?"

"No! What I want is a little peace around here!" Nick said.

"Oh, yes. Peace and quiet, no?"

"I'm tired. I'm going to bed." Nick shook his finger at the servant. "If I'm disturbed for anything less than the place burning down around my ears, heads will roll!"

Nodding, Ling Tan made a slicing gesture across his throat with his index finger. "Head roll if—"

"Right," Nick said, and shut the door in Ling Tan's face.

Unbuttoning his shirt as he went, Nick headed for the bedroom. Naked, he crawled into bed, reached for the covering sheet, and found it missing. He frowned, pulled the heavy counterpane up to his waist, turned onto his stomach, closed his eyes, and buried his face in a pillow. And caught the familiar pleasingly unique scent of the castile soap Kay used to wash her hair.

Nick inhaled deeply, smiled foolishly, and fell asleep.

Upset, Kay went first to the Sansome Street boardinghouse. The big old house was silent. None of the tenants was home. She was glad. She made it to the privacy of her room without seeing anyone.

Once inside, she let go. She dissolved into tears of misery. She threw herself down on narrow bed and wept bitterly over what she had done. She was no longer fit to be a captain in the Salvation Army. She had no choice but to resign.

The imbibing of alcohol could have been forgiven because she had consumed the punch not knowing it contained any liquor. Something like that could happen to anyone. It was not cause to leave the Corps.

What had happened between her and Nick McCabe was. She had voluntarily gone with him to his apartment. She had stood in shadowy sitting room and eagerly kissed him. Of her own free will she had gone into his bedroom and . . . and . . .

She would resign from the Army this very day.

The painful decision made, Kay dried her tears, took a long soaking bath, washed her hair, and put on a fresh uniform, the blue jacket sporting the distinctive red stripe denoting her rank.

Upon arriving at the mission in the early afternoon, Kay spotted the navy-blue carriage and the well-dressed man beside it. She stopped short and her hand flew to her mouth.

She'd entirely forgotten that she was to meet Pat Packard for a late lunch. She *couldn't* go to lunch or anywhere else with Pat. Not now. Not ever.

Kay drew a deep breath and started toward him.

Smiling warmly, his golden hair gleaming in the sunlight, Pat hurried forward to meet her.

A look of relief on his face, he reached Kay, took both her hands in his, and said, "My dear, where have you been? We've all been so worried."

Kay swallowed hard.

"Pat, I must talk to you," she said, looking him squarely in the eyes.

"Certainly, certainly. Whatever it is, we'll discuss it over a good meal."

Kay shook her head. "No. No, Pat. Let's sit in your carriage where we can talk."

Seated in the carriage, Kay told Pat Packard that she couldn't have lunch with him. She could no longer see him. Hurt, he asked why. Honest to a fault, she told him. Everything.

Stunned, he sat there silent for a minute staring at her. The expression on his face changed from disbelief to shock to hurt to anger. Finally, to disgust.

"You're actually telling me that you have known Nick McCabe in the biblical sense?" Kay nodded miserably. "You, a Salvation Army captain, have behaved in such an unseemly manner? And with an unprincipled rascal notorious for his conquests? A low-class Barbary Coast saloon owner? I don't believe it."

"I'm sorry, Pat."

"So my sister was right all along," Pat said, his expression one of contempt. He looked at Kay as if she were unclean, as if there were an offensive odor emanating from her. "Adele warned me about seeing a woman of your station. She said you are not *our* kind. That you wouldn't be the proper wife for me."

Kay smiled bitterly. "It seems your sister and I agree on at least one thing." She put out her hand. "Good-bye, Pat."

Pat Packard didn't shake Kay's hand. He turned and stared straight ahead. "Good-bye."

Kay climbed, unaided, down out of the fine blue carriage. Pat Packard immediately took up the reins and drove away. Back up the hill where he belonged.

Kay sighed and walked the few steps to the mission. She paused at the front door, inhaled, and went inside. Big Alfred was there. He came rushing toward her, a worried expression on his face.

"Lassie, lassie, where have you been? All morning I've been looking for you and—"

"Where's Curly?" Kay interrupted. "Is he here?"

"No. No, he's not. He and Rose went to—"

"Then I'll resign to you," Kay said. "You're an officer now. You can accept my resignation."

"Resign?" Big Alfred said. "What are you talking about?"

Kay unhooked the silver S pin from her stand-up military collar and handed it to the astonished Alfred Duke. Then she ripped off her red captain's stripes.

In a voice barely above a whisper, she stated, "I am resigning— effective immediately—my post in the Salvation Army." She withdrew an envelope from inside her uniform jacket, thrust it out to him. "Please forward my written resignation to General Booth immediately. I am unfit to serve in the Almighty's troops. I have dragged the crimson banner in the mire. I have let down all my fellow soldiers as well as my Savior. I have betrayed a sacred trust. I'm unworthy of wearing this uniform. I resign."

"But, lassie, surely . . ."

Kay forcefully shook her head, silencing him. Then with tears in her eyes she raised her trembling hand, saluted the towering giant of a man one last time, turned on her heel, and left.

Tears streaming down his florid cheeks, Big Alfred Duke stood there unmoving. He didn't need wonder what terrible sin had prompted Kay to resign from the Army.

He knew.

Nick McCabe had won the bet.

Chapter 43

Young Ming Ho raced up the back stairs, her arms loaded with heavy textbooks.

"Father, Father!" she called. "Where are you?"

Ling Tan immediately appeared in the wide upstairs corridor. Frowning fiercely, he laid a finger perpendicular to his lips.

He whispered, "Boss asleep. Say if anyone disturb him . . . off with head!"

Ming Ho started to speak again. Ling Tan pointed to door of their apartment. She nodded and quietly hurried inside, her father following. After carefully closing the door behind them, Ling Tan spoke, but in a soft voice.

"What daughter doing home this hour?" He glanced at the clock on the mantel. "Not even two o'clock."

Ming Ho laid her books down. "We were dismissed early; the spring faculty meeting. Isn't it wonderful!"

She suddenly noticed that her father was not dressed in his usual loose-fitting trousers and jacket. He wore an elegant sky-blue silk-satin kimono-jacket upon which a black dragon snorting red fire was meticulously appliquéd. His tailored trousers were of black flannel. She made a face.

"Most honorable father, are you going out?"

"You forget already?" Ling Tan said, incredulous. His thin chest swelled and he fingered the embroidered black frog at the throat of his mandarin collar. "Today the day of *pai gow* tournament. Best players in city invited to participate." He beamed. "Am honored to be considered one of best."

"I'm proud of you, Father," said Ming Ho. "And I'm most happy for you." Her head bowed.

"Do not look most happy," said Ling Tan. He reached out and lifted her chin. "Something bothering only daughter?"

Ming Ho sighed. "My new party gown is ready at the dressmaker's. I wanted to pick it up this afternoon."

Ling Tan firmly shook his head. "Will pick up tomorrow. Plenty soon."

Ming Ho was disappointed. Dejectedly she nodded. "Yes, Father. But if Mr. Nick wakes up . . ."

"No! Must *not* disturb boss." He wagged his finger back in forth in her face for emphasis. "Now I go. Chop chop. Be late for passing of porcelain bowl to determine order of the deal." He kissed Ming Ho's smooth cheek and was gone.

Ming Ho again sighed loudly and flung herself bellydown on the sofa. She was up immediately, pacing in frustration. She wanted that new dress, wanted it now, this afternoon. She wanted to try it on in the privacy of her room. To spin and turn and practice dancing in it.

Ming Ho looked at the clock. Two-thirty. Surely Nick was awake. She stepped out into the silent hall and hurried toward his apartments. The door was locked. Ming Ho laid her ear against it. No sound of any kind.

She turned, sighed, and walked back down the hall. In her own quarters she went to a window and looked out wistfully. The sun was shining brightly. People strolled leisurely up and down the sidewalks. All the dance halls and dives lining the streets were closed. The Barbary Coast was in the midst of its slumberous afternoon tranquility.

What could possibly happen to her in broad daylight? Nothing. Not a thing. She could walk the short six blocks in ten minutes, pick up the new dress, and be back before anyone suspected she was gone.

A happy smile on her face, Ming Ho hurriedly brushed her long black hair, tied it back with blue ribbon, picked up her small reticule, and rushed down the back stairs. On the ground floor she very quietly tiptoed to the back door, making sure none of the Carousel girls or anyone else saw her leave.

No one did.

The packing had begun.

In her room at the boardinghouse, Kay had taken down the scarred leather valise and opened it atop her bed. There was no need for delay. If she got everything ready today, perhaps as early as tomorrow morning she could be on board an eastbound train.

Kay opened the top drawer of a chest, took out her carefully folded nightgowns and chemises. She placed them in the valise and turned back for more. But her skirts brushed against the edge of the night table, knocking over a bell. A worn silver bell.

It tinkled softly.

Kay winced as if the giant bell of St. Mary's had clanged deafeningly in her ears.

The packing forgotten, Kay reached out and picked up the bell. Her thoughts again flashed back to that hot August day, the day the un-shaven, bare-chested Nick had taken the bell away from her.

If anyone had tried to tell her then that this day would come, she would not have believed them.

Kay sadly shook her head. She had arrogantly vowed that day that she would change the sinful saloon owner. She hadn't. She hadn't changed Nick McCabe. He had changed her. Nick McCabe had won.

Kay placed the silver bell in the open valise. She glanced at the small clock on the night table. Half-past two. At this very moment Joey was taking his afternoon nap with his short arms wrapped tightly around the imperturbable Mac. At three o'clock he'd awaken, full of energy and expecting her to visit.

Kay closed her eyes. Had it been only twenty-four hours since she had arrived early at Battery Place and found Nick asleep in the floor with Joey and Mac?

It seemed a lifetime ago.

Kay opened her eyes. Recalling the utterly outlandish idea that had gone through her mind at the time, Kay now chided herself for her folly. To have pictured—even for a few fleeting seconds—the three of them together as a family was . . . an impossible dream.

Kay inhaled slowly.

Foolish or not, she simply couldn't leave San Francisco without seeing Joey one last time. She would make her regular daily visit to Battery Place as if nothing had happened. Wear her uniform just as always. Pretend it was a day like any other. There would be no tearful good-byes. It was selfish on her part, she supposed, but she wanted the memory she took with her back east to be of a laughing, happy Joey.

Nick awoke with a start.

His heart beating fast, perspiration soaking his lean, bare body, he threw off the heavy black counterpane and sat up. He tried to recall details of the disturbing dream that had awakened him, but couldn't. Within seconds everything about the strange nightmare had totally vanished. But an uneasy feeling remained, and Nick shivered in the warmth of the closed bedroom.

He rose and walked naked into the sitting room. He went straight to the drink trolley, poured himself two fingers of bourbon, and downed it in one swallow. He wiped his mouth on his forearm and set the glass down.

Kay flashed into his thoughts. He gritted his teeth, turned, and picked up the carved crystal liquor decanter. The decanter's neck snagged between two fingers, Nick headed for his bath and a relaxing soak.

He stayed in the deep, long tub for a good half hour, his dark head resting against the rim, eyes half closed, a thin black cigar in one hand, the whiskey decanter in the other. He was determined to drink Captain Montgomery right out of his head.

The whiskey tasted awful. The cigar didn't taste all that great either.

"Aw, hell," Nick cursed, set the decanter on the floor and snubbed out the cigar. "Dammit all to hell!"

He sprang up out the tub, carelessly splashing suds. Water sluicing down his tall brown body, he stepped out and reached for a thick towel, anxious to get dressed.

The truth of it was, Big Alfred had won their bet. He, Nicholas Daniel McCabe, sure as hell hadn't made love to Kay Montgomery. So he'd pay off the wager. Take care of it today. Write a bank draft this very afternoon.

Get it over with.

Ming Ho smiled sunnily as she hurried down Pacific. She looked younger than her years. Her jet hair streaming loose down her back, her face aglow with excitement, she happily skipped along in the warm sunshine.

She had gone five of the six blocks when two men, dressed identically in black, stepped out of an alley and directly into her path. Ming Ho stopped short. Cold fear closed around her heart and she tried to back away.

Rough hands seized her and, before she could scream, a black, smothering hood fell over her head. She was swung off the ground and tossed into a carriage. A powerful male body pinned her against the coach's seat and a huge hand, clamped over her mouth, pressed the hood's black fabric so tightly over her nose and mouth she felt she would suffocate.

Gagging, her heart racing with terror, Ming Ho felt the swaying of the coach as it descended a hill. The ride was a short one. In a few terrifying minutes it ended, and Ming Ho was lifted into a pair of strong arms and taken from the coach.

Crushed to a broad chest, blinded by the hood, Ming caught the scent of the bay and knew they were down at the docks. There was another scent. A sweet perfumed fragrance like that of fresh-cut flowers.

Her blood chilled. They were at the Embarcadero. She would be sold into slavery in the Orient!

At last Ming Ho was lowered to her feet and warned not to make a sound. The black, smothering hood was removed. Ming Ho blinked, looked around, and saw that she was inside a dim, musty warehouse with boarded windows. Coughing, fighting for breath, she winced when she spotted a half-dozen young children. Their hands and feet bound, the children sat zombielike in a circle on the dirty floor. All were totally silent. Drugged.

Horrified, Ming Ho heard a slender Oriental man say to the big man with an ugly scar on his face, "Stand guard on the door while I put this one in the box. We can't tie her up like the others. It might mar her flesh."

The scar-faced giant grinned, displaying a mouthful of teeth with the front four missing. "Let's take turns with her first. She sure is a pretty little thing."

The Oriental swiftly backhanded the big man across the face. Blood spurted from his split bottom lip. "You fool! At the price she's bringing, she must be delivered untouched."

Sickened, panicky, Ming Ho began to plead, but it did no good. The cold-eyed Oriental took her away, led her to the far back of the building and into narrow, shadowy hallway. He stopped before a door and drew Ming Ho directly in front of him. Sobbing, she trembled violently against him.

Her abductor said, "Relax. Your fate is far better than that of the other children. Lucky for you you are so pretty. Skin like porcelain." He trailed his knuckles down her tear-wet cheek. Ming Ho stiffened. "Your body is small and perfect." His hand touched her tiny waist, moved down the curve of her hip and thigh.

Fighting desperately against the hysterics threatening to overcome her, Ming Ho was relieved when his hand left her, went to the door's heavy bolt. But when he opened the door and she saw the tiny, windowless room, she begged him not to do it, not to lock her inside.

"Please, I won't make any trouble," she cried. "Don't lock me up! Please don't."

"It's only for a short time." The Oriental gave her a cold smile. "Within the hour you'll be on board the most luxurious vessel in the bay."

He pushed her inside, closed the door, and threw a heavy bolt into place. She heard his footsteps falling away, leaving her there, locked up in total darkness. Ming Ho could hear rats scurrying about the straw-strewn floor. One ran across her foot.

"Father," she cried miserably, a terrified child longing for the safety of a parent's arms. "Oh, honorable Father, help me, help me."

Chapter 44

 Kou Jen puffed and grunted as she pushed her flower cart up Pacific. As slowly as she moved, it was faster than her usual snail's pace. Her wrinkled forehead and sagging cheeks covered with a sheen of perspiration, the aged Chinese flower girl gave it everything she had.

She would have parked her wooden cart down at the waterfront flower market, save for the fact that she couldn't walk without using it for support. So the small pudgy Kou Jen in her black baggy pants and drab green silk jacket anxiously pushed her cart up the street.

Her weak old heart pounding from exertion, the tired, sweating Kou Jen labored along, babbling to herself, "Must get to Nichoras McCabe. Must tell Nichoras. Have to reach Nichoras."

Tapped out early on, Ling Tan left the *pai jow* tournament. He threaded his way through the passageways and alleys of Chinatown.

Ling Tan had no reason to feel apprehensive, but he did.

As he turned on Pacific, he became inexplicably anxious to get home. He quickened his pace.

It was after five o'clock when Nick, immaculate in a white silk shirt and tailored navy trousers, stepped behind the heavy desk in his downstairs office. Tugging at the creases in his pants, Nick sat down in the tall-backed swivel chair and opened the desk's middle drawer.

He took out a large blue bank check ledger, plucked a pen from its ebony marble stand, and started to write. But a knock on his open office door interrupted.

Nick looked up.

Alfred Duke filled the doorway. He was not dressed in his blue military uniform. A pullover shirt of gray cotton stretched across his massive chest and over the bulging muscles of his arms. His trousers were of dark gray, his shoes were brown. His wide, powerful shoulders were slumped. His hazel eyes were badly bloodshot and his florid face was as gray as the civilian shirt he wore. In his right hand was a brown valise.

The big man glumly stepped inside. "You won, Nick."

Nick was already up out of his chair and shaking his dark head. Circling the desk, he smiled fondly at his worried old friend.

"Aw, pal, pal," Nick said, anxious to relieve Alfred Duke's needless suffering, "I was just writing out a ch—"

"Boss! Boss!" Ling Tan's desperate call reverberated through the back corridor.

Nick and Big Alfred looked at each other, turned simultaneously, and rushed into the hall. Ling Tan, out of breath, his black eyes registering alarm, hurried up asking, "Ming Ho? Boss, have you seen daughter, Ming Ho?"

"No. Not today," Nick said. "You sure she's not—"

"Have looked everywhere. Asked everyone. Daughter gone!" Ling Tan declared. Trembling, the slender Chinese servant said, "Ming Ho not here! Something happen to baby girl!"

Concealing his own concern beneath a cool exterior, Nick said, "Now relax, Ling Tan. There may be a simple explanation. Exactly when did you leave? When did you get back? Where might Ming Ho have gone in your absence?"

The worried father was anxiously answering Nick's questions when Angel Thompson, the leggy Carousel showgirl, dashed up. "Nick, there's an old flower girl out front says she has to talk to you." Angel glanced at Ling Tan. "Says she saw a couple of Three Fingers Jackson's men carry a small struggling girl—"

Before Angel could finish the sentence, all three men had bolted, crossed the cavernous, darkened club, and reached Kou Jen where she sat at a table near the front entrance.

"Tell us everything you know, sweetheart." Nick motioned Big Alfred to bring her some water.

"At flower market filling cart," said the exhausted Kou Jen. "Closed coach pull up before vacant warehouse next door. Building on stilts. Mason Import/Export once there. Big man with scar on face carry struggling girl with black hood over head." Kou Jen turned sorrowful eyes on Ling Tan. "Was Ming Ho. Recognize clothes and slippers."

"I go," said Ling Tan, and turned away.

"No, wait." Nick stopped him. "Contact the authorities. Have them meet Big Alfred and me at the old Mason Import/Export warehouse. Do it!" Nick said. "Time's wasting!"

Ling Tan raced out of the club. Big Alfred followed as Nick hurried back his office. Inside Nick circled his desk, took a set of perfectly matched Navy Colt 44's from a bottom drawer, and handed one, butt first, to Big Alfred. The Englishman shoved the heavy weapon down into the waistband of his gray trousers. Nick followed suit. He looked at Big Alfred.

"Let's go after those bastards."

"Aye, laddie!"

Kay sat on the back steps of Battery Place, arms wrapped around her knees. She was smiling. Warmed by the bright March sunshine and the bubbling laughter of four-year-old Joey, she savored this precious interlude of deep contentment.

Following every movement of the energetic red-haired child and his frisky red-coated puppy, Kay sighed with wonder. It seemed that both boy and dog had grown before her very eyes. Joey was no longer the sad-eyed, thin-faced urchin with the painfully skinny arms and legs. Mac was no longer a small, scared puppy.

Joey's cheeks had filled out, his eyes had lost most of their sorrow. His arms and legs were sturdy and tanned and he was quickly outgrowing his uniforms and his shoes. Mac had doubled in size and was robust and playful. Unaware of his own strength, the affectionate collie sometimes jumped on his master in such exuberant greeting, he knocked Joey down.

Joey didn't mind. He thought it was funny. On occasion when Mac eagerly leapt and flattened him, Joey would play dead. He'd lie there with his eyes closed, arms and legs sprawled, while Mac climbed all over him, barking and anxiously licking his face. When the brokenhearted Mac would began to whimper and moan plaintively at his loss, Joey would spring to life, clasp Mac in his arms, and laugh with the joy of having fooled his best friend.

"Kay, watch!" Joey shouted to her now.

"I'm watching," she called back, lifting a hand to shade her eyes from the sun's glare.

Joey held a red rubber ball in his hand. Mac was trying to take it away from him. Joey shook a short finger in Mac's face, leaned over, and whispered in the collie's ear. Then Joey straightened, drew back his arm, and threw the red rubber ball toward the high back fence.

Mac took off after it, racing wildly across the lawn, barking loudly. With an incredible burst of speed, the nimble collie caught up with the tossed ball before it could fall to the earth. Mac leapt high up off the ground and plucked the red ball out of the air with his teeth.

At the same time he turned his limber body about so that when his four paws came back down he was pointed in the direction of the waiting Joey. Ball gripped in his teeth, Mac sprinted back to Joey, his tail wagging fiercely.

But when Joey reached out to take the ball from him, Mac refused to release it. Tenaciously the collie clung to the ball while Joey did his best to take it away from him.

Kay couldn't keep from laughing as she watched Joey's futile attempts at retrieving the ball. She knew him well enough to suspect that the red-headed Joey was on the verge of losing his temper. She knew he'd lost it when he narrowed his eyes, cocked his finger as if it were a weapon, and warned Mac in a short to-the-point statement that smacked of Nick's influence, "That's it for you, pal!"

Then, crossing his short arms over his chest, he turned and walked away from the bewildered Mac. Joey came to join Kay on the back steps. By the time he reached her, he was already grinning again. He stopped on the bottom step, crouched down on his heels, put his elbows on his knees, and cupped his face in his hands.

"Mac doesn't know he's supposed to give the ball back to me," he confided.

"Well, I wouldn't be too hard on him," Kay said. "What he has learned is really quite remarkable and in time he'll catch on fully."

Joey grinned. "Hope so." He looked down and saw a fire ant crawling across the step. He wrinkled his nose, wet the tip of his forefinger, reached down, and smashed the ant flat. Then explained, "It wanted to sting my ankle."

"Oh, well, then lucky you got it in time," said Kay.

Joey nodded. "Mac got stung yesterday. He barked and . . ." Joey talked and talked and Kay, enchanted, would have sat there listening forever. But the clanging of a bell interrupted Joey's oration. He sprang to his feet.

"Is that the supper bell already?" said Kay, rising up onto her knees. "I had no idea it was getting so late."

"I'm hungry," said Joey, Mac now back at his side.

Kay smiled, reached up patted the small bright head of flaming hair. "Sure you are. Scoot on in there and wash up."

Nodding, Joey leaned over, wrapped his tanned arms around Kay's neck, and hugged her so tightly she felt the squeezing in her heart. Without another word, he released her, hurried up the steps, and flew across the wide porch with Mac following.

At the back door Joey suddenly paused, turned, and flashed Kay a wide smile. "See you tomorrow, Kay!"

Nodding, Kay smiled and said nothing.

Chapter 45

Shadows were lengthening as they moved quickly among the wharves and piers and clapboard warehouses lining the water's edge.

Silently Nick pointed out the old abandoned warehouse built on pilings directly above the shoreline. The windows were boarded up and an outside staircase at the back of the building had rotted and fallen down. The two men looked at each other. How could they get inside without being seen?

Squinting in the fading sunlight, Big Alfred inclined his head to a splintery pillar at the water's edge. Nick nodded. Going first, Nick shinnied up the rough pole like a logger. He reached a narrow catwalk ledge and motioned Big Alfred up. While the Englishman climbed the supporting pillar, Nick went to work slowly, silently prying boards from a window.

The two men slipped into the warehouse unnoticed. They found themselves in narrow corridor that opened into a wide, open loft above the main floor.

Voices came from below.

Nick eased farther out onto the landing where wooden kegs and broken crates served as camouflage. Ducking down low, he motioned for Big Alfred to do the same. Guns drawn, the two men crawled forward quietly and crouched behind the scattered barrels.

At the center of the large shadowy room below were a half-dozen Chinese boys and girls, bound hand and foot. They were remarkably pretty children, the kind prized by the vile operators of the city's opium dens. Those secret, shadowy lairs of unspeakable evil frequented by deviants.

But Ming Ho was not among them.

A huge, scar-faced man and a slender Oriental stood guard over the children. A loud rap sounded on the front door at the far end of the building. The Oriental moved quickly to the locked door, spoke softly in Chinese, cocked his ear to the door, then threw the heavy bolt back, and the door swung outward.

A quartet of men stepped quickly inside.

One was an aging, overweight Oriental. One was a tall, slim, wealthy-looking Occidental. One was Three Fingers Jackson. And the last, a one-eyed, portly fellow with a black eye patch, was one of the bay city's most prominent society attorneys, the respected Dysart K. Lavender.

No time was wasted on pleasantries. Three Fingers Jackson eagerly led the obese Oriental directly to the bound children. Lavender and the tall, slim man stayed where they were. The puffing, grunting Oriental looked over each trussed child with great interest.

At last he beamed with pleasure and nodded his graying head. "I will take them all. Deliver them at midnight." He thoughtfully stroked his beard and added, "I lost two of my prettiest boys this week. One managed to get loose and run away. The other was found dead this morning in one of the cubicles." A great shout of laughter issued from his heavy lips and his big belly shook as he added, "An overardent customer loved him to death."

Dysart K. Lavender, the one-eyed attorney, turned to the slim, well-dressed gentleman and said, "We've finally found your beautiful young China doll. But it's going to cost you."

"I'm prepared to pay any price—if she's everything you say," the tall man calmly stated. "I sail to Singapore next week without my wife and family." He smiled, rubbed his crotch, and added, "I'll take the girl with me. Nothing I enjoy more than sexually tutoring a beautiful Oriental child."

He laughed heartily, as did Lavender.

Lavender said, "She's exquisite. We've been shadowing this one for months. We went to a lot of trouble to—"

"I'm not interested in your problems, Lavender. Where's the girl?"

"Right here. Locked in a small back room." Lavender snapped his fingers at Three Fingers Jackson. "Jackson, go get the girl."

Above, Big Alfred involuntarily let out a snort of disgust. Jackson heard it, looked up, and spotted the top of Big Alfred's head. Gun drawn, he immediately took aim. Nick lunged as Jackson fired, shoving Big Alfred to safety. The bullet hit Nick in the chest.

The front doors burst open before Jackson could get off another shot. A squad of well-armed police poured in.

"Drop your weapons and get your hands in the air!"

Uniformed lawmen swarmed over the building within seconds. Lavender and his accomplices were quickly cuffed while the trussed children were freed from their bonds.

Big Alfred, hands in the air, stood up and shouted, "The girl's locked in a back room. Hurry!" He dropped to his knees beside the fallen Nick. "Laddie, laddie, are you hurt bad?"

Nick tried to smile at his worried friend. "A nick, nothing more."

But Nick's silver eyes slid closed and the bright blossom of blood on his white silk shirt front was rapidly growing. With one quick motion Big Alfred lifted Nick up in his arms. By then, a couple of the policemen had reached them.

Alfred Duke shouted at them, "Get Dr. Ledette! Have him meet us at the Carousel! Go!"

Despondent, Kay was on her way back to the boardinghouse. The sidewalks were in deep shadow. The day was slowly dying. The sun was setting in the west and Kay hated to see it go down. She felt as if it might never shine brightly again.

She turned the corner at Pacific Avenue. She was one block away from the Golden Carousel. Hoping she wouldn't bump into Nick McCabe, Kay took a deep breath and started up the avenue. She was halfway up the block when she stopped short, blinked, and stared.

Big Alfred Duke came running headlong up the street, the powerful muscles in his huge thighs and legs straining and pulling against his dark trousers. In his muscular arms he carried a man whose body was totally limp and lifeless.

Unable to move, unable to speak, Kay saw the big Englishman race toward the Carousel Club, cradling the man to his massive chest as if he held a helpless infant. The man's eyes were closed. The front of his white shirt was crimson with blood.

"Nicky!" Kay screamed, yanked up her skirts, and started running.

Her heart pounding with fear, she flew toward the pair as fast as she could run. She reached the sidewalk outside the Carousel just as Big Alfred kicked the black leather doors open and carried Nick inside.

Kay anxiously followed Big Alfred up the marble staircase, stripping off her bonnet and dropping it as she went. Commanding herself to stay calm, to get a firm grip on her raw nerves, she breathlessly followed Big Alfred into Nick's apartment. Dancing in front of him, she hurried to the bedroom and peeled the covers back on the unmade bed. Big Alfred carefully laid Nick down.

A wave of dizziness hit Kay when she saw the white silk of Nick's shirt was saturated with blood. Recovering, she took Nick's limp wrist in her hand and felt for a pulse.

"He's . . . ?" Big Alfred choked, couldn't finish.

"He's alive."

"Doc Ledette's on the way."

"Good! Help me get him undressed."

Nodding, Big Alfred helped Kay cut away Nick's bloodied silk shirt and remove his shoes and stockings. Kay went for a basin of water and clean washcloths. Big Alfred stripped off Nick's trousers and linen underwear. He searched for the top sheet to cover him. He spotted it draped across the back of chair, hurriedly snatched it up, and spread it modestly over Nick's bare body just seconds before Kay returned.

In minutes Dr. Joseph Ledette had arrived.

The Carousel girls filled the grand salon downstairs. Outside the club a curious crowd was gathering. The news was spreading through the Barbary Coast and would soon be heard on the hills above.

"He's lost a great deal of blood," Dr. Ledette announced as he carefully examined Nick.

"Will he be all right?" Kay and Big Alfred asked in unison.

"Hard to say at this stage of the game." The doctor paused, then added, "If he regains consciousness within the next forty-eight hours, his chances are good."

"If he doesn't?" Big Alfred said.

The doctor shrugged. He rose, began rolling up his shirt sleeves, and said, "This bullet will have to come out immediately. I need more light. Turn up the gaslights. Lay out plenty of bandages. Boil some water." He looked around. "Show me where I can scrub up and I'll get to it."

When Dr. Ledette was ready to begin, he looked from Kay to Big Alfred and said, "If either of you are squeamish, I'd advise you to wait outside."

Looking sheepish, Big Alfred nodded his big head and backed away. Her worried eyes resting on the pale, dear face below on the pillow, Kay began rolling the sleeves of her white blouse higher.

She said calmly, "I'll assist, Doctor." She looked up at him. "What are you waiting for?"

Chapter 46

 A steady stream of callers came and went, but Kay never left Nick's bedside. She refused to budge no matter how many of the well-meaning told her she looked tired, she needed rest, she should go home.

Kay didn't argue. She simply remained where she was, where she was determined to stay until she saw Nick's silver-gray eyes open. When he looked at her and spoke her name in recognition, she would go. But not one second before. Of them all, only the Lady in Black fully understood her stubbornness.

Gently squeezing Kay's slender shoulder, she whispered, "Watch over my boy, Kay."

Never taking her eyes off Nick, Kay replied, "You know I will."

Kay did watch over Nick. Throughout the night she was there beside him, begging him to open his eyes, to speak to her.

"I will not let you die, Nicky, I won't. Please, wake up."

With loving tenderness she cared for him. She sponged his fevered, perspiring body and toweled his sweat-soaked raven hair and held his hand pressed against her aching heart through the long uncertain hours of darkness.

Big Alfred and Ling Tan were never far from Nick's bedside. Big Alfred tiptoed in around four A.M. He leaned over the bed, looked down at the ashen Nick, and shook his great head sadly.

Touched by the deep concern written on his face, Kay rose and put a comforting hand on his shoulder. "Nick will make it. We won't let him go, you and I. We'll pull him through."

Choking, Alfred Duke said, "It's my fault. I got Nick shot. Jackson was aiming for me and Nick shoved me out of the way, saved my life."

Kay patted his muscular shoulder. "And you saved Nick's life. You got him home before he could bleed to death, and I'll be eternally grateful to you. So will Nick." She smiled at him. "Go get some rest. I'll call you if there's any change."

Again alone with the unconscious Nick, it was Kay who heard the muttered ramblings of his fevered delirium.

"Kay, Kay, no. Nothing happened, Kay. I didn't mean it. Nothing happened. Nothing happened."

"Shhh, Nick, shhh," she soothed, pressing her cool hand to his hot face.

"Nothing happened," murmured Nick. "Nothing happened. I'm sorry, I'm sorry . . . nothing happened."

His dark head tossing on the pillow, Nick thrashed restlessly as he mumbled. Kay didn't hesitate. She got into bed with him and used the weight of her body to keep him from flailing about.

The sun finally rose on a new day and a sleepy, exhausted Kay was thankful to the Almighty that Nick had lived through the night. He was still unconscious, but she had high hopes that before darkness fell again, he would be awake.

He wasn't.

As the shadows lengthened at the end of the long, tiring day and the Barbary Coast came to life as it did each night, the dark, wounded owner of the Golden Carousel didn't. Dr. Ledette had looked in his patient a number of times during the day but had refused to offer much hope. Camille Kelly had been there three times. Her mask of serenity never slipped, but Kay knew she was distraught.

Ling Tan was in and out. Big Alfred spent most of the day with Kay at Nick's bedside. More than once the Englishman heard Nick's feverish murmurings, "Tell him nothing happened. Nothing happened. Tell Big Alfred. Tell him. Nothing happened."

Big Alfred exchanged looks with Kay.

"He's been murmuring those same words to me," said Kay.

Darkness descended and with it an aura of dread cloaked the funereal quiet quarters. Ling Tan and Big Alfred, hovering just outside the sickroom, said little to each other, but frequently exchanged worried glances. Both were fearful that Nick wouldn't make it through the night.

Kay couldn't surrender to fear. If she did, Nick might sense it. She would not allow her fears nor anyone else's to be present in his room. If a visitor's doubts and depression couldn't be checked at the door, he was not to be admitted inside.

Night wore on. Midnight. Two A.M. Three.

Kay rose from her chair. She stood for a while, then carefully climbed up onto Nick's bed. She sat facing him, one stockinged foot beneath her, the other dangling off the side of the bed. She stared at the smooth, handsome face on the pillow. She reached out suddenly and brushed raven hair away from his cheek.

She carefully put an arm across his body and spread her hand on the mattress to support her weight. She peeled the covering white sheet down to Nick's trim waist.

"Nicky, my dearest Nicky," Kay said in a voice so soft it was nearly inaudible.

And she leaned down and kissed Nick's heart where it beat beneath his beautiful chest. Her lips brushed his flesh again and again as she silently prayed for him to awaken.

Kay lifted her head. She sat very still, watching Nick, whispering his name over and over like a litany. And in the darkest hour before dawn, Nick's long dark lashes began to flutter. Finally they lifted over those pale silver eyes. His mouth opened. He was looking straight at her. His eyes narrowed, bringing the object above him into focus.

"Kay?"

"Yes, Nick."

Nick attempted to lift his hand to her hair, but he was too weak. It fell back to the mattress. Kay took his hand and raised it to her hair, held it there. Nick tried to smile.

"Lord, you're pretty," he said.

Kay drew his hand around to her lips, kissed the palm. "You were delirious for thirty-six hours," Kay whispered, lowering her eyes, "Maybe you still are."

"If I say I am, will you stay?"

Kay smiled at him, relief and happiness flashing in her tired blue eyes. "I'll stay, no matter what."

She started to move, to get off the bed. Nick's hand fell to her knee. "Wait, I—"

"I was only going to step outside and tell the others that—"

"First there's something I have to tell you."

"Can't it wait until—"

"No." Nick's voice was raspy, as if his throat was sore. "Kay, when you spent the night here in my—"

"Please, Nick." Kay bowed her head.

"Listen to me, sweetheart. Nothing happened. Not a thing."

Kay looked up, her eyes widening. "I didn't . . . we never . . ."

"I never touched you. You slept in my bed, I slept on the sofa."

Kay exhaled loudly. She shook her head. "You devil, you let me think we . . ."

"I apologize. You said 'you of all people' like I was some kind of monster."

"Nick, I didn't mean it that way."

"I know." Nick licked his dry lips. "Now there's just one thing I really want to know."

"What? Tell me."

The slightest hint of his old devilish smile appeared. "Can a sick, thirsty man get a drink of water around this joint?"

Kay laughed with joy. "Coming right up!"

She kissed his temple, slid off the bed, and hurried to tell the others that Nick was finally awake. Dr. Ledette arrived at sunup, examined his patient, and proclaimed that Nick was out of the woods.

"See that he gets plenty of rest and the proper nourishment" was the doctor's instructions. "It wouldn't surprise me if he was up and around in a couple of weeks."

The gloom that had hung over the Golden Carousel lifted. Nick insisted the club's doors be opened for business as usual, assuring one and all that a little music and laughter drifting up to his sickbed would only speed his recovery. He added that what would most speed his recovery would be the continuing presence of Kay at his bedside. She assured him she'd be there so often he'd grow tired of looking at her.

Eagerly picking up the Army's banner again, Kay pinned on the shining S, sewed the red stripes back on her uniform, and marched back into the unending war on hunger and poverty and disease. And still managed to visit Nick several times each day. When she visited, she didn't just look in on him, relax in a chair at his bedside for a few moments, then leave. Not Kay. Each time she came she took off her jacket and bonnet, rolled up her sleeves, and went to work pampering and babying the patient.

Nick loved it.

Kay fed him from a tray placed across his knees. She read to him. She rubbed his long legs and arms. She massaged soothing lotion into his chest and on his back. She combed and brushed his raven hair. She shaved him. She saw to it he took his naps, sometimes dozing in the chair at his bedside while he slept.

She read all the newspaper articles to him on the capture of the notorious Shadow Clan. When she'd finished reading one of the lengthier columns, Kay lowered the newspaper and said, "Shall I read anything else to you this morning?"

Nick sat propped on his pillows, eyes closed, a small muscle in his jaw working rhythmically. His eyes opened, he grinned at her, and said, "How about reading that part again where it says I'm a hero."

Kay pursed her lips, rolled up the newspaper, and playfully slapped him on the shoulder with it. "It's time you take a nap."

"I'm not sleepy. Get me a cigar from the—"

"No!" She rose, stood at his bedside, arms crossed over her chest. "I don't think you should be smoking cigars—your chest."

Nick grinned and plucked at her sleeve. "In every woman there is a mother: 'You must do this. You must not do that.' "

"Well, if you don't have enough sense to know what's good for you, then maybe you need one." She began straightening his tumbled sheets.

"How's Joey?" he said, and Kay's head snapped around.

She beamed. "You love Joey just as I do, don't you?"

Nick shrugged bare shoulders. "That kid got a raw deal in life. It happens."

That's all he said, but Kay knew how he felt. She assured him Joey was fine. She went on to tell about the new ball trick he'd taught Mac, and soon she and Nick were laughing and sharing their favorite stories about Joey.

Finally Nick, smiling, said, "You suppose it would be possible for an invalid to have a swallow of brandy?"

"Absolutely not!"

The smile left Nick's face. He put on his meanest look, narrowed his eyes, cocked his finger at Kay, and said, "Woman, bring me a brandy if you know what's good for you!"

Kay didn't budge. "You don't scare me one bit."

"No?"

"No. It's a kind and gentle person who does something like you've done, Nick McCabe."

"Me? What did I do?"

Kay smiled at him. "You used your own money to build a wonderful home for orphans."

Nick's dark eyebrows darkened. "Camille talks too much. Next time she comes I'll—"

"—treat her with the respect and affection she deserves," warned Kay. "Now, no more foolishness. Either you take a nap or I'm leaving."

Nick slept for a couple of hours. Kay left, but before he awakened, she was back. When he woke, he saw her standing at the foot of the bed. She had taken her hair down and was brushing it. She was looking at him intently.

Nick blinked his eyes and opened them wide. "You're still here so it isn't a dream."

Kay smiled. "You were talking in your sleep."

Nick sat up in bed. "Was I? What did I say?"

Kay flushed. "You said you think I'm pretty."

"Just pretty? You're more than pretty. You're beautiful."

"Thank you."

"Don't thank me." Nick winked at her. "Thank your mother and your father."

Kay laughed and came around the bed, sweeping her unbound hair back over her shoulders. "It's time I go."

"So soon?"

"You sound like spoiled little boy," said Kay, tapping him on the forearm with her hairbrush. "I'll be back late this evening. Anything I can get you before I leave?"

"Ask Ling Tan to come in for a minute."

Kay laid the brush aside, wound her long, shiny red hair into a thick rope, and secured it at the back of her head. "See you later, Nick."

She turned to leave. He caught her wrist. He touched his lips with a forefinger. "A kiss before you go?"

Kay acted exasperated, but she bent to kiss his tanned cheek. Nick quickly turned his head and managed to capture her lips for a fleeting second.

"You're getting well," she said, and left.

"Most grateful, boss," Ling Tan came in, repeating what he'd said time and again. "Most happy you feeling better." Shaking his head until the long braid down his back danced, he added, "Only daughter, Ming Ho, so sorry for all the trouble she cause. Worry about boss. Apologize for—"

Nick rolled his eyes. Interrupting, he said, "I'm fine. Ming Ho's safe. Stop worrying. And no more apologies."

Ling Tan smiled and bowed. Then said, "Missy Captain say boss want to see me."

Nick nodded. "I want you to do something for me."

"Be happy to. What need?"

"First go down to my office, get the checkbook and bring it up here. I'm going to make out a bank draft for twenty thousand dollars. I want you to hustle over to Wells Fargo and draw out the cash in big bills.

Come on back here and then tonight take the twenty thousand in cash and place it in the Salvation Army's big red kettle."

Ling Tan said, "Will take care of, boss. Anything else?"

"Yes. Do it the Chinese way, my friend. Don't let anyone see you."

Chapter 47

 Twenty thousand dollars cash in large denominations was discovered in the Salvation Army's coffers at dawn the next day. No one knew who was responsible. Nobody had seen the contribution being made. The elusive benefactor had dropped all that cash into the big red kettle just outside the waterfront mission without being observed by a single soldier.

The entire troop was ecstatic, none more so than Kay and Curly Montgomery. The prayed-for miracle had occurred. They wouldn't be going home in disgrace as feared. They could redeem the Army's waterfront property and begin immediate construction of a permanent rescue mission. There was still more than six weeks to go before General Booth's visit. The San Francisco Corps #1 had been saved.

Kay couldn't wait to tell Nick.

She hurried to the Carousel shortly after sunrise and eagerly rang the back doorbell. When Ling Tan answered she rushed right up the back stairs. The servant anxiously followed, whispering warnings not to bother Nick. Nick was still asleep. Nick was a sick man. Nick needed his rest.

Kay just smiled at the protective Ling Tan and breezed through the door of Nick's apartment, shutting it on Ling Tan's muttering and scolding. Excited and gloriously happy, Kay went unannounced into the dim bedroom. She looked across to big bed and smiled.

Nick was awake.

Yawning, he turned his dark head and saw her. He blinked, rubbed his eyes, and grinned. "Kay Montgomery, is that you?"

"The one and only," she said, laughing.

Kay went to him, put a hand in his tumbled black hair, and kissed him.

Nick was shocked. "Have you forgotten who you are? Where you are, Captain?"

"Call it a fit of abandon."

Nick grabbed her hand. "Stay close in case you feel another fit coming on."

Kay laced her slender fingers through his. "Nick, you'll never guess what has happened! An unknown donor has contributed twenty thousand dollars to the Army!"

"You're kidding me."

"I'm not. It's true, it's true! Isn't it wonderful?"

"Sure is. I know you . . ."

"I'm sending Big Alfred over here later this morning with your money. Can you have the deed to the property ready for him?"

Nick nodded. "It's downstairs in the safe. I'll have Ling Tan get it."

"Good, good," Kay said. "While Big Alfred is picking up the deed, Curly and I will be meeting with a contractor." She squeezed his hand. "Why, the rescue mission could be framed and under construction within days. Oh, Nick, I'm soooo excited!"

"Me too. Let's have fits of abandon." He flashed his famous grin.

"You're impossible," she said, freeing her hand, but her eyes sparkled and she laughed.

Kay's face screwed up in deep concentration, she thought over the events of the past few days. Working backward, she recounted the hours to the day Nick was shot. In her mind's eye she saw Big Alfred running, carrying the wounded Nick in his arms and . . . and . . . now she remembered something she hadn't thought about before. Big Alfred had been out of uniform! He was dressed in civilian clothes that afternoon. Why?

As soon as Kay reached the mission, she nabbed Big Alfred, dragged him into her office, and shut the door.

"Sit down," she instructed, pointing to a chair. Baffled, he sat down. "Why were you out of uniform on the afternoon Nick McCabe was shot?"

Blood immediately rushed to his face and he squirmed. "Why, lassie, I . . . I . . . was I?"

"Yes, you were and I want to know why."

"Aye. Aye . . . I . . . truth is, I was considering going back to work for Nick at the club."

Kay stared at him, trying to read what lay behind his troubled hazel eyes. "So you were leaving the Army? Going back to Nick? Is that correct?"

Miserably, "Yes."

"But you didn't. Why not?"

Big Alfred fidgeted, clearly feeling the pressure. Mindless of his discomfort, Kay continued to interrogate him mercilessly. Relentless, she pressed on, hurling question after question at him. Many were leading questions. She would come up with a scenario and force him to confirm or deny its validity.

The grueling session lasted for a full half hour. She hated to do it to him, but Kay knew if she kept after him she could break down this gentle giant who was such a sentimental softie his eyes teared at good-byes.

Kay had now begun to question Nick's sudden interest in her. She wondered why there had been such a complete one-eighty in Nick. She was putting two and two together, and she didn't like what she was coming up with. Quickly the pieces of the puzzle were falling into place with the reluctant help of an agonized Alfred Duke.

Finally she forced the awful truth out of him. The wager, the stakes, the twenty thousand dollars!

Big Alfred said, "Lassie, I wouldn't blame you if you never spoke to me again. This whole thing was my fault and I—"

"No, it wasn't," Kay interrupted. "The blame rests solely with Nick McCabe."

"Now, that's not so, Captain. I was fool enough to—"

"Nick knew you have a weakness for wagering. He used you. He used me." Her eyes turned to blue ice. "He'll use neither of us again."

"What about the money? You going to give it back?"

"Certainly not." Kay smiled then, but it was a cold smile. "After all, as they say here on the Barbary Coast, 'You won that money fair and square.' "

Each time he heard someone enter, Nick looked eagerly toward the door, hoping to see Kay. Three days had passed since last she visited him.

Where was she? Why didn't she come? Didn't she know he needed her? Didn't she care that he was hurting and miserable and might never get well without her to nurse him back to health? Next time she showed up he'd remind her that a badly wounded man could die of cold neglect and indifference!

The long, lonely days continued to pass. No Kay.

As soon as he was able—and sooner than Dr. Ledette advised—Nick got up and dressed. A tight, clean bandage around his torso beneath his shirt, Nick left the apartment over the loud objections of Ling Tan.

Nick found Kay down at the construction site. He waited until she finished a conversation with a couple of builders. Finally the two men walked away, leaving Kay standing there alone, looking over blue-prints spread out on a rough worktable.

Nick approached, smiled, and said, "I've missed you."

"You dirty rat!" Kay snapped, her eyes closing with anger. "Don't come any closer. Not one step! I know all about your wicked wager with Alfred Duke!"

"Kay, sweetheart, please let me—"

"I'll let you do nothing! You've done quite enough, McCabe. Now get out of here. This is private property and you're trespassing!"

She whirled away from him but not in time to hide the tears of hurt that were filling in her blue eyes.

Nick left, but he was as willful as she.

He had no intention of staying away from her. He showed up again the next day. And the next. He held still for Kay's stinging upbraidings. Then he made Kay hold still and listen to his heartfelt apology. He admitted the devilish bet, but reminded her that when he could have pressed his advantage, he hadn't done it. Wouldn't she take that into consideration? Couldn't she find it in her heart to forgive him?

Nick went to tremendous lengths to win her approval. He concocted wild excuses to visit her. He was Nick at his best. And he was far too charming and handsome for Kay to resist.

In no time their relationship was back as it had been before. Nick could tell by the way her lovely eyes lighted when he showed up that she was as glad to see him as he was to see her. So he showed up often and supposed that everything was fine. And it was.

Until a rainy afternoon in early April when he had been teasing Kay and she had been laughing and he suddenly took hold her elbow, pulled her into his arms, and bent to kiss her.

"Don't, Nick," Kay said, evading his lips. "Don't kiss me unless you mean it. Unless you're so mad about me you can't live without me."

Nick was totally taken aback.

Shaken, he looked deeply into her eyes without words. She looked back at him and he saw that she meant it.

"Kay, honey, a woman like you . . . why, that would mean . . ."

"Marriage, Nick. That's what it would mean. I love you. I wish I didn't love you so much. But I do. I love you. I will always love you."

Nick swallowed hard. "Sweetheart, you couldn't love me. You don't know what you're saying."

"Yes, I do. I'm saying that I love you and if you don't love me, don't kiss me. Not ever again."

Nick tried to smile, to make light of the situation. "Kay, you know me. I'm not the marrying kind."

Kay nodded sadly. "I know."

Nick gently cupped her face in his hands. "I'm not good enough for you. You were raised in a fine home with Christian parents and I don't even know who my father . . . Honey, the Army is where you belong. The Barbary Coast is where I belong. Don't you see that?"

"Then please, Nick, go. Go back to the Carousel Club where you belong and leave me in peace."

Chapter 48

There was music and the tinkle of dealer's bells calling for drinks and cigars. The rattle of the chuck-a-luck cage, the clink of Mexican dollars, and the quieter click of ivory chips and markers.

Laughter and squeals of delight from lucky faro players. Cheers and whistles for long-limbed entertainers in glittering sequins. Oohs and aahs over tempting foods served by efficient white-jacketed waiters.

Nighttime at the Golden Carousel.

The music, the laughter, the gaiety hadn't rubbed off on a solitary man watching boredly from the mezzanine.

Alone in his private black velvet banquette, the club's dark-visaged owner found little joy in the scene below. He found little joy in anything. The boredom showed on his handsome face.

Nick McCabe appeared thinner, darker, and more expensively dressed than ever. Each evening he shaved, bathed, put on an impeccably cut tuxedo, and came down to the club.

But he wasn't himself. He didn't greet patrons at the door or circulate through the crowd. He no longer stood at the bar buying rounds of drinks. He didn't joke with the men or compliment the women or invite anyone up to his private banquette for dinner.

Alone, he sat high up in the black velvet booth, half hidden in the shadows of the colored lights from the carousel whirling below him.

Those who knew him best were worried about Nick. The wry, cool look in his silver-gray eyes, his quick easy smile—they were both gone now. He was quiet, moody, uncommunicative. Easily irritated.

Now as another endless evening wore on, Nick again refused dinner. A worried Ling Tan had ordered the kitchen staff to serve up oysters and thick beefsteak and vegetables to his brooding boss. It did no good. Nick waved the waiter away with a flick of his wrist and a decisive shake of his head.

Nick wasn't hungry.

His restless gaze swept over the crowd below. A disturbance at one of the roulette wheels drew his attention. Squinting through the haze of blue cigar smoke, he caught sight of a sore loser taking out his frustration on the croupier.

Nick pushed the white-clothed table aside and rose. He descended the marble steps to the main floor. Advancing toward the bullying customer, his teeth were tightly clenched, as were his fists, and there was fire in his pale silver eyes.

"Nick!" A customer reached out and grabbed Nick's arm. "Haven't seen you in weeks. Where you been?"

"Minding my own business," Nick said, pulled free of the man's grip, and moved on.

"What's eating him?" said the puzzled man.

"Don't know, but he's like a powder keg," said his companion. "Ready to blow up about the least little thing."

Both men shook their heads.

Nick crossed the crowded club. He stepped up beside the cursing loser and silenced him with a glare.

Then he said, "Friend, put your money on number seventeen, black and odd."

Blinking meekly at the mean-looking Nick McCabe, the loser shoved what few chips he had left onto the felt layout. The croupier spun the wheel. The white marble fell into slot number seventeen. "Seventeen," called out the croupier. "Black, odd." The surprised player reached greedily for the chips. Nick tapped the back of his hand.

"Let it ride. Then take the money and get out of here and never gamble in the Golden Carousel again. You're barred."

"Getting soft in your old age?" said a smiling, drunken regular.

"Shut up, Louie."

Nick headed for hexagonal bar where a trio of rowdy sailors stood drinking. One of the three, a big tattooed tough called Panzer, swilled down a tall mug of beer, wiped his mouth, and shouted, "McCabe, when we gonna see that red-headed preacher gal ride the carousel again?"

"You're not." Nick nodded to the slim man behind the bar. The bartender set a bottle of bourbon and shot glass before Nick.

Grinning, Panzer elbowed his drinking buddies, looked at Nick, and declared, "That's a cryin' shame. You oughta put her back up there and let the customers bid on her. Why, I'd pay fifty dollars to have her take me to heaven." He guffawed loudly.

And Nick lost his temper. Hot and heavy.

He was on Panzer before the big boatswain knew what was happening. Nick grabbed Panzer by his collar, jerked him forward, and slammed a hard fist into his ugly, grinning face with such brute force the tattooed sailor crumpled to the floor, out cold.

To his stunned shipmates, Nick said, "Get him out of here. I don't like looking at him."

Eyes round, the nervous pair anxiously dragged the unconscious man away. Nick scooped up the bourbon bottle and glass and climbed the stairs to his apartment. He was smiling. Hitting Panzer had felt good. He'd been itching to hit somebody for weeks.

But once inside, the smile left Nick's face and he sighed wearily. He stripped off his tuxedo jacket and black silk tie. He unbuttoned the white pleated shirt. Hands in his trouser pockets, he moved to a tall front window, stood staring out at the glow of the dock lights below.

A crushing sensation seized him, squeezing his chest so painfully he could scarcely breathe. He had an unutterable feeling of having lost something worth having. Something he'd never had before, would never have again.

Nick shook his head to clear it. Commanding the haunting image of the laughing red-haired Kay to leave him, to let him be, he spun away from the window. He went for the bottle of bourbon. He poured himself a stiff drink, swallowed it straight down, and poured another.

But Kay refused to go.

Nick dropped tiredly down into his easy chair. He sat there in the gloom with his bottle of bourbon and his regrets.

He drank himself horizontal.

The constant sound of hammers banging. The pleasant smell of new lumber. The companionable shouts of busy laborers. The welcome sight of the walls going up.

Daytime at the Embarcadero rescue mission construction sight.

The sounds, the smells, the sights never failed to bring a smile to Captain Kay Montgomery's face. She was there any time she could find a free minute. Grateful to the soldiers who pitched in, Kay praised the tireless workers.

She was amazed at the speed with which the impressive building was taking shape. It was nothing short of a miracle, and she was the happiest woman on earth.

Or she should have been.

During the daylight hours she was. Her days were too filled to think of anything or anyone except the momentous task at hand. Time was growing short. In less than a month General William Booth would arrive expecting to find the Embarcadero rescue mission up and running.

Kay was determined that he would.

So she, along with every soldier in the Corps, worked from sunup until long past close of day. She was glad to do it. She wanted to work hard. She wanted to get so exhausted that at night she wouldn't be haunted by a pair of pale silver eyes flashing in a dark, handsome face.

Kay never managed to get that tired.

At a time in her life when she should have been content, Kay was anything but. She missed Nick. She wanted Nick McCabe with a deep, abiding yearning that was close to physical pain. She loved him. She had waited a long time and had never fallen in love before. And then when she had, it had to be with Nick.

The sun was just beginning to rise on a warm clear morning near the end of April. A proud, pleased Captain Kay Montgomery stepped into foyer of the brand-new Embarcadero rescue mission. She left the front door ajar. She moved slowly up the aisle of the mission's auditorium, admiring the smooth, polished wooden pews.

Kay was alone in the new building. She'd planned it that way. She wanted to be the first to arrive on this, the first day that the mission began full operation. If she was lucky, she had at least a half hour of solitude to quietly enjoy this special occasion.

Smiling, Kay sauntered forward. She was almost to the altar when suddenly she stopped short. She sensed someone's presence. Her hands began to tingle. There was a gentle brush against the back of her neck, like a kiss.

Kay whirled around.

And she began to smile.

Nick McCabe stood in the foyer, backlit by the rising sun. He wore a freshly laundered shirt of pale-blue cotton with a pair of neatly pressed dark trousers. His raven hair was carefully brushed and his dark face was smoothly shaven. In his hand was red satin box and on his lips was a disarming, boyish smile.

"Nick" was all Kay could say as he came toward her.

"You've got a big surprise coming," Nick said when he reached her, "so don't be surprised."

"All right," she murmured, dizzy from the welcome sight of him.

Nick handed her the red satin box. "Chocolates," he announced.

"Thank you very much," she said, "I've never been given—"

"I would have brought flowers but I couldn't find Kou Jen at this hour." He took the box of chocolates away from her, placed it on a pew. He reached for her hands. She felt the heat, the pressure of his fingers on her palms. "Now, get ready to laugh."

"Whatever it is, I'm sure I won't laugh."

Nick nervously cleared his throat. Then he said simply, "Kay Montgomery, I love you."

"Nicky," she said joyfully, "I love you too and I—"

"Listen," Nick interrupted. "I spent hours preparing for this, so let me say my piece."

"Please do," Kay said, smiling, thinking he had to be the most beautiful creature God had ever created. She pulled her hands free of his and placed them on his chest.

Again Nick cleared his throat. "Kay, I'm mad about you. So mad about you I can't live without you. I love you. I wish I didn't love you so much. But I do. I love you. I will always love you. I'm asking you to marry me." He drew a breath. "That's it. That's all I have to say."

"That's plenty, darling." Kay looked into his eyes. "You may kiss me."

Nick smiled at her, lifted a hand up to her flaming hair. He studied the lovely, trusting face turned up to his. Her innocence had kept her looking fifteen at twenty-five. Nick shuddered. He'd heard it said that to the lover, the loved one stayed forever young. To him, Kay would always stay exactly as she was now. And she was breathtakingly beautiful with her big blue eyes shining with happiness and her red hair ablaze in the rising sun.

"Sweetheart, I'll love and care for you as long as I live," Nick said in a gentle voice that Kay hadn't heard him use before.

Her fingers slipped over his shoulder, touched the back of his neck. Nick drew her close and their lips brushed. Nick moved his tongue slowly across her closed mouth. Kay's eyes closed and her mouth opened to him.

They stood there in the pink-tinged auditorium of the new Embarcadero rescue mission and kissed as lovers anxious to be man and wife. And when, breathless, their lips at last separated and Kay laid her cheek against Nick's rapidly beating heart, she said softly, "Nick, there's just one thing."

Nick stiffened. His hand caressing her back, he said, "You've changed your mind already?"

Kay laughed, pressed a kiss to his chest through the fabric of his shirt, and raised her head to look at him.

"No, I haven't changed my mind." Her fingertips played along his firm jaw line. "Nicky, you love Joey as much as I do."

"I love the kid, yes."

"Now that we're getting married, can't we adopt him?"

"Sure. All right," Nick said, wrapping his long arms tightly around her. "But just Joey. No more."

"No?"

"No." Nick flashed her a devilish grin and said, "There are some things a man likes to do for himself."

Chapter 49

 Moonlight tinted the foggy beaches a soft silvery white. Sleek vessels plied the calm mirrored water of the bay. The muted sound of a foghorn came from far out in the Golden Gate. Wisps of fog rolled in over the twinkling grid of San Francisco lights.

Dominating the city's skyline, the Palace Hotel soared seven stories high. Carriages rolled up beneath its stunning glass-roofed Grand Court where they were met by doormen dressed as admirals. Just beneath the glass skylight, the Crystal Roof Garden was alive with exotic flowers. In the elegant Palace Grill lavish meals were served on renowned Palace Gold service.

The grand hotel's finest suites were on the very top floor. The most splendid of all was a beautifully appointed corner suite with breathtaking views and walls covered in rich cream silk.

In the suite's spacious bedroom a gigantic mirror framed in twisted gold hung directly opposite the bed where sheets of shimmering cream silk were turned down for the night. A half-dozen silk-cased pillows were fluffed up against a tall black walnut headboard.

On a black walnut night table beside the bed, a fragile candelabra of Dresden china held a half-dozen tall white candles. A clock of matching Dresden china softly ticked toward the hour of midnight.

A tapestry screen shielded the fireplace. Heavy drapes of peach brocade satin were tied back, and the tall windows and French doors were thrown open to the balmy spring night. Delicate petals of two dozen long-stemmed cream-white roses trembled in their Dresden china vase.

In that luxurious Palace Hotel bedroom a tall, dark man was alone in the night.

Nick McCabe, in white dress shirt and dark trousers, paced before the cold fireplace. He was nervous. He'd never been nervous before, not as he was tonight. He wished he could have a drink. Knew it was out of the question.

He raked a hand through his hair. He rubbed his perspiring palms on the fabric of his trousers. He went to the open French doors and pulled long deep breaths of fresh air into his lungs. He turned away and began pacing once more.

He dropped down into a wing-backed brocade chair, laced and unlaced his fingers. He leaned over and pulled up his black socks, first the right, then the left. Then, drawing his trousers legs back down, he was up and pacing again.

Nick kept anxiously glancing across the bedroom to the closed white door leading to the suite's mirrored-and-marble bath.

Inside that mirrored-and-marble bathroom Kay reached for a frothy lace nightgown, glad that the long-awaited hour was here at last.

The simple wedding service had been lovely. Everyone was there. Curly and Rose. Big Alfred. Little Joey. The Lady in Black. Ling Tan and Ming Ho. Even her beloved parents. They had come all the way from Atlanta, Georgia, to meet Nick and to share this happy day with them. On her father's arm she had walked down the aisle while the Corps band played the wedding march.

Anxious to be alone, she and Nick had stayed only long enough afterward to cut the wedding cake and accept best wishes for their lasting happiness. Then as everyone laughed and tossed rice, they had dashed out into the night to catch a hansom cab to bring them straight to this hotel.

Fresh from her bath, Kay smiled and picked up the gown the Carousel girls had given her as a wedding present. She slipped it over her head and gently urged it down her bare, slender curves.

Kay looked at herself in the mirror.

The nightgown was exquisite. The low bodice was supported by narrow straps going over her shoulders. Directly beneath her breasts the lace gown fell away in soft folds to the floor.

She may as well have been naked for all the nightgown covered. Kay's face flushed. She reached for the satin-and-lace robe, shoved her arms down inside, and buttoned the three satin buttons at her throat.

Again she looked at herself. Satisfied with what she saw, Kay turned from the mirror. Tingling with excitement and anticipation, she crossed the carpeted bath and reached for the gold doorknob.

Nick saw the gold doorknob turning. He stopped pacing.

The door opened and Kay stepped into view. Nick stared, silently drinking in her beauty.

She wore a robe of white satin and lace with long sleeves that reached to her knuckles. On her small feet were matching lace-and-satin slippers. Her glorious red hair was unbound, the fiery tresses falling around her face and down her back. One silky lock lay directly atop her bosom, curling appealingly around her left breast.

Their eyes met across the room. With that one look Nick's nervousness vanished. He'd half expected to see a frightened, tremulous Kay. He should have known better. Kay had never been afraid of anything in her life.

The chemistry between them had always been intense. Now she loved him as well. She loved him without doubt and without reservation. She had taught him the meaning of love. They'd shared their innermost thoughts and secrets. They'd have no trouble communicating with their bodies. Not when the want and desire that was surely shining out of his eyes was mirrored in hers.

Without a word they came together. Kay moved toward Nick with an easy, upright posture and soundless motion. Nick came to her with that familiar blend of athletic power and grace. They met at the center of the candlelit room.

Nick's arms went around her, drawing her into his embrace. Kay spread her hands on his chest. Nick smiled at her. His eyes lowered to her lush lips and the smile left his face. He bent his head and brushed a kiss to the left corner of her mouth. Then his lips slid around to her ear.

"Let me hold you in my arms, Kay," he whispered softly. "Let me love you tenderly."

"There's nothing I want more," Kay murmured, as something new and wild stirred within her.

"Ah, baby, baby," he said, holding her close to his muscular length, "all the joys in life you never found before you'll find with me tonight." He kissed her temple. "You'll see that love is a magical thing."

"Show me," she said, thrilling to the feel of his hard lithe body pressed to hers. "Be my love. Be my lover."

Nick's mouth immediately took hers in a heated, passionate kiss. As he kissed her, he deftly unbuttoned the three tiny satin buttons of her satin-and-lace robe.

He pushed the opened robe over her shoulders. Her mouth continuing to cling to his, Kay took her arms from around him, held them straight down to her sides. And sighed when the slithery satin sleeves slid down and the robe fell away, pooling at her feet.

Nick tore his lips from hers and set her back a little. New fire leapt into his eyes as he looked at her, and Kay felt their heat burn through the lace gown. It thrilled her to have Nick look at her in the wispy nightgown that hid nothing. Her cheeks grew hot but it wasn't from embarrassment. It was from rapidly growing excitement.

"You're so beautiful," Nick praised, his burning gaze touching her swelling breasts, her flat stomach, her flaring hips. "You take my breath away."

He drew her close again. He kissed her, a deep, commanding kiss of fire. At last his lips left her mouth, moved across her flushed cheek, and settled on the sensitive spot below her ear. He kissed her and kept kissing her as his mouth, hot and moist, moved languidly down the side of her throat. With one hand at the small of her back, the other resting on her hip, Nick drew her up on tiptoe as his dark head continued its slow, arousing descent.

Kay felt the breath leave her tingling body when his heated mouth reached the bare swell of her breast above the gown's low lace bodice. A soft little cry of pleasure escaped her parted lips when Nick kissed her rapidly beating heart through the sheer bodice. The silky raven hair of his head tickled her bare flesh, and the heat of his tongue touching her aching nipple through the lace made her shiver with pleasure.

Nick lifted his head. His hand went into her hair and he shuddered when she impatiently swept his open white shirt apart, leaned to him, and kissed his naked chest where his own heart raced with desire. His tanned fingers tangling in her hair, Nick looked at the fiery head bent to him and felt his legs grow weak.

Her lips never leaving the crisp hair covering his smooth olive chest, Kay impatiently pushed Nick's white shirt off his broad shoulders. Nick's hands fell away from her and he stood there trembling while she peeled the shirt down his long, leanly muscled arms.

When the shirt lay on the floor with her discarded robe, Nick cupped her cheeks and urged her face up off his chest. The candlelight reflected in the depths of his humid silver eyes, he said, "Nobody— *nobody* has ever made me feel the way you make me feel."

Before she could answer he kissed her. He kissed her as he'd never kissed her before, and Kay felt herself slipping into a beautiful, unexplored world of sensuality. It was as if she were embarking on a wonderful journey to a new, exciting place she'd never been before. A place known only to lovers. Only for lovers.

She sighed when she felt herself being lifted into Nick's powerful arms. She wrapped her arms around his neck, and Nick never stopped kissing her as he crossed the spacious room and gently lowered her to the soft, silk-sheeted bed.

Kay sighed again as Nick stretched out beside her. For a time they lay there kissing hotly, she in her lace gown, Nick in his dark trousers. Soon it seemed to Kay that even the sheer lace gown was too much. Her body was hot, burning hot, and she longed to feel the coolness of the silken sheets against her skin.

As if Nick had read her thoughts, he swept the lace nightgown off. It was done with such swift deftness, it seemed to Kay the unwanted gown had melted away, leaving her gloriously naked in his arms. Nick continued to kiss her lips, her cheeks, her eyes, her throat, and at the same time he gently caressed her.

With an extraordinary, delicate touch, as if her pale, nude flesh were some priceless work of art, Nick's long, tapered fingers moved with infinite tenderness over her.

The touch of his hands on her bare flesh ignited a new fire within her, and Kay found herself straining against the stroking fingers touching her in places she'd never been touched before. She loved the slow, sure way he was coaxing her toward that even greater intimacy yet to come. Trusting him completely, excited in a way she'd never known she could be excited, Kay gloried in her newly awakened sensuality.

All inhibitions were being slowly, surely whisked away by the hot, sensuous-lipped mouth and the dark loving hands. Her eyes opening and closing with bliss, her hair spilling over the silk-cased pillow, Kay lay there naked in the candlelit room, learning the mysteries of love.

Carried away, stretching and arching with pleasure, Kay softly moaned when Nick rose to finish undressing. Clutching at the silken sheets, she looked up at his tall, lithe body, his powerful shoulders, the tendons of his muscled thighs straining the fabric of his trousers.

She softly said his name as through half-closed eyes she saw him removing the trousers from his magnificent body. He stood there naked for an instant, his dark skin gleaming like tan satin in the candlelight.

And then he was back beside her, taking her in his arms. Kay closed her eyes and her hands sought his hot, smooth back and shoulders. His face bending over hers, Kay trembled when he kissed the hollow of her throat.

Nick lifted his head. He stared at the pale, angel-skinned body before him. Tempted to bend his head and hungrily feast on every dewy inch of her, Nick restrained himself. Despite the urgency of his body, he cautioned himself to take time with her. But his racing heart pumped blood to his face and brought a vein out on his temple.

Kay opened her eyes and looked up at him. In their flashing blue depths Nick saw all the love, all the awakened desire, all the trust she felt for him. The breath left his taut body when her hand moved from his shoulder to his chest and down over his tight belly. He moaned when her fragile fingers innocently brushed the tip of his throbbing masculinity.

His eyes closing, Nick bent his dark head and kissed her left breast. Kay gasped with shocked pleasure and her hand flattened on his belly. Nick cupped a palm around the arch of her hip. He opened his mouth and took the pink, pebble-hard nipple inside the wet warmth.

"Nicky," she breathed as any lingering inhibitions were plucked away by his loving lips.

With his mouth at her breast, Nick moved his hand from her hip to underneath her slender shoulders. Gently he lifted her. When both were in a sitting position, his lips released her nipple and slid up over her throat and chin to her mouth.

He kissed her, his tongue meeting and mating with hers. As they kissed, Nick rose to a kneeling position and drew Kay up with him. Her head thrown back against his arm, her fiery unbound hair streaming over that muscular, supporting arm, Kay knelt with her lover on the silk-sheeted bed in the rose-scented room, feeling his hard masculine power throbbing against her belly.

Nick again changed their positions. Slightly. He placed a knee between hers and settled her firmly astride his muscled thigh. Kay anxiously pressed herself against that hard sinewy thigh. Her breath shallow, she began the involuntarily rhythmic grinding of her hips against him.

His lips sprinkling kisses to her shoulder, Nick made himself wait until he was certain she was ready for penetration. Driven by instinct, Kay clung to him and slid her yearning body up and down on the hard male thigh that offered a degree of comfort to the raging fire burning within her. But not enough.

"My love," Nick murmured, gently eased her back against the pillows and followed her down, parting her legs and lying between.

His tanned hands stroked her flesh, and he teased at her pink nipples with his lips and tongue and teeth. When his fingers were wet with the silkiness of her passion, Nick brushed a kiss to her flat belly.

Kay gave herself to him fully. Transported by his searing lips and stroking hands and virile body, she abandoned herself to the passion he awakened in her. She felt his heavy tumescence against her, gently probing as he made every attempt not to be too rough with her.

Nick groaned aloud when her hand came between them and her fingers closed around him.

"Yes, baby, yes," he encouraged.

Kay drew him to her. She gasped and stiffened as he thrust into her, but Nick's handsome face was above hers, his eyes filled with loving apology. Her pain was brief and bearable and her soft moans were muffled against Nick's smooth shoulder. Nick lay completely still within her, waiting until her tensed, invaded body began to relax beneath him.

Only then did he begin the slow, sensual movements of loving. And as he moved rhythmically, plunging a little more deeply, cautiously stretching her to accept him, Kay clung to his shoulders and felt the discomfort turn to pleasure.

Nick knew.

He could tell she was starting to enjoy it, starting to respond. But he continued to keep the pace slow, the thrusts easy. As he tenderly loved her, Nick spoke quietly to her, telling her he'd never loved another woman. Just her. She was the only one. He promised that in time she'd find just how magical love could be.

Kay was slipping deeper and deeper into that longed-for wonderland of love and passion and ecstasy. She was surprised at herself. She never dreamed she could behave this way and feel so good about it. She was consumed with unbridled lust. On fire from head to toe. She was behaving like a wanton and loving every minute of it.

Nothing mattered but this sweet hot joy she now knew. If she had her way, she would lie there like this forever. Nothing could be more natural, more satisfying. Nothing on earth could possibly be sweeter than Nick in all his wild naked beauty held possessively within her parted legs.

It was thrilling beyond belief to know that she had tamed all that fierce strength and male power and animal hunger. Nick was *her* lover and hers alone. It was to her that his beautiful male body was giving this exquisite pleasure. It was from her he took his own.

Wonderful new things were happening to Kay. Nick was moving more rapidly now and she was moving with him. The new exciting sensation of it was growing, and Kay was suddenly torn by wanting the sweet pleasure to last forever and the fierce desire to have the throbbing need end at once.

"Nick, Nick, please . . ." she murmured breathlessly, head tossing wildly on the pillow.

"Yes, love, yes," Nick whispered, and again changed the pace of his lovemaking.

In seconds he brought Kay to a deep and shuddering climax that frightened her in its intensity. As the explosions rocked her, Kay clung to Nick and her blue eyes widened with shock and wonder. Incredible heat swept through her and the ecstasy was so intense she cried out as she reached the peak.

Kay clasped Nick to her while wave after wave of rapture rippled through her. And when finally she opened her eyes to see his handsome face above her, she saw that it was flushed with heat and that beads of perspiration dotted his hairline. He was breathing heavily, his chest heaving as if he had experienced the same wild joy she had known.

With her in his arms, Nick rolled over onto his side.

The candles had burned down and sputtered to darkness. The moonlight had lengthened; it now fell across the silken bed. The peach brocade drapes fluttered in the strengthening night breezes. The scent of the roses still sweetened the air, and a few fallen cream white petals lay scattered across the bed.

Moonlight bathed their intertwined bodies as the lovers' hearts thundered and they fought for breath. Neither spoke, neither moved, they just lay there totally sated, holding each other.

When at last they had calmed, Kay squirmed a little. Nick loosened his embrace. She raised up on an elbow and, with her fingertips tracing the deep cleft in Nick's long, smooth back, Kay said, "Know something, Nick?"

"What's that, sweetheart?"

Her tousled red hair tumbling half over her face and across her left eye, she smiled like the cat who'd just swallowed the cream. "Love certainly *is* a magical thing."

Nick laughed heartily. Kay laughed with him.

His long body shaking with delighted laughter, Nick swept the wild red tresses off his bride's beautiful flushed face and said, "Baby, I love you. Kiss me. Kiss me, Mrs. McCabe."

Kay kissed him.

And Nick McCabe heard bells.